世界经典文学名

查泰莱夫人的情人

Lady Chatterley's Lover

D.H.Lawrence

贺广贤　注释

世界图书出版公司

西安　北京　上海　广州

图书在版编目(CIP)数据

查泰莱夫人的情人：英文/(英)劳伦斯(Lawrence,D. H.)著；贺广贤注释. —西安：世界图书出版西安公司,2010.5
(世界经典文学名著文库)
ISBN 978-7-5062-9052-4

Ⅰ. 查… Ⅱ. ①劳…②贺… Ⅲ. ①英语—语言读物 ②长篇小说—英国—近代 Ⅳ. H319.4：I

中国版本图书馆 CIP 数据核字(2007)第 103168 号

查泰莱夫人的情人

著　　者　[英]戴·赫·劳伦斯
注　　释　贺广贤
责任编辑　陈康宁
内文插图　尚泽阔
封面设计　飞洋设计公司

出版发行　世界图书出版西安公司
地　　址　西安市北大街 85 号
邮　　编　710003
电　　话　029-87214941　87233647(市场营销部)
　　　　　029-87232980(总编室)
传　　真　029-87279675
经　　销　全国各地新华书店、外文书店
印　　刷　陕西新世纪印刷厂
开　　本　850×1168　1/32
印　　张　10.5
字　　数　300 千字

版　　次　2010 年 6 月第 1 版　2010 年 6 月第 1 次印刷
书　　号　ISBN 978-7-5062-9052-4
定　　价　14.80 元

[英] 戴·赫·劳伦斯

出版前言

学习英语的读者朋友们都知道，英语除了基础的词汇学习以外，要想提高英语水平，平时的英语阅读是非常重要的。单纯的英语学习是相当枯燥的，将其融入英文故事的欣赏，就会大大增加学习的知识性、趣味性。而在英语阅读里面，世界经典文学名著是一生都不会过时的绝佳赏析材料，是值得大家一生中去读的作品。

世界名著是世界文学名家身处他们那个时代，用他们的心灵去感知社会和人物，呕心沥血著成的精品。英文原版故事虽说讲述的是上几个世纪的故事，但很多都是原著小说家们的亲身感受或有生活中的原型，因此能使读者产生共鸣，触发同感，启迪人生。

通过对世界经典文学名著的赏析，可以使自己徜徉于其中，了解欧美社会的时代背景，深刻理解西方文化。这样既能大大提高自己的英语水平，同时可以培养和提高自己的个人修养。因此推荐给喜爱文学的读者朋友们，请您不妨一读，相信定会受益匪浅。

由世界图书出版西安公司隆重推出的**最新版“世界经典文学名著文库”系列丛书**，是世图西安公司几代编辑不断探索和总结经验、并组织完成的。其间悉心听取广大读者朋友们的评价和建议，历经数十载的改进和更新，云集国内知名的英美文学教授，遴选世界名著中精华的精华，对于各经典原著文中的难点、疑点加以精心评注。其中包含难词的解析、背景人物和事件的延伸注解，古英语表达的转换等等，可谓详尽准确。这些名著可以使读者朋友们在品读原汁原味的英文原版故事的同时，通过评注提供及时、必要的阅读参考，助读者朋友们在学习英语之路上一臂之力。

世图西安公司经过精心的调研，本批推出的品种都是读者朋友们喜闻乐见的名著作品：包括**《远大前程》、《查泰莱夫人的情人》、《名利场》、《双城记》、《小妇人》、《儿子与情人》、《红字》、《汤姆大叔的小屋》、《茶花女》、《艰难时世》、《远离尘嚣》、《雾都孤儿》、《战地钟声》和《无名的裘德》**等，以后还会相继推出其他名家的名著品种。读者朋友们可以根据自己的喜好，选择适合自己的经典故事进行阅读。

本套丛书各册内容均为无删节英文原版经典故事，原汁原味，并辅以名家中文评注，**既适用于英语专业学生作为课外学习和赏析，同时适用于有一定英语水平的读者大众**。通过对名著的赏读，提高英语阅读、特别是对英文小说的阅读能力。

欧美文学鉴赏，传世佳作珍藏！

由于编者知识和水平有限，书中难免有不足之处，欢迎学界人士和读者朋友们提出宝贵意见，以便我们在以后的名著整理工作中加以改进和提升，你们的支持是对我们编者及编辑最大的鞭策和鼓励。读者朋友们也可以登录**www.eb88k.com**（世图英语学习网），了解最新出版的世图英语图书信息和网站内容。

世界图书出版西安公司

2010年5月

作者简介

戴·赫·劳伦斯是英国二十世纪的天才作家，1885年生于诺丁汉郡一个煤矿工人的家庭。父亲是位目不识丁的煤矿工人，母亲是位出身名门、心高气傲的小学教师。父母婚姻的不幸铸就了家庭的不和，劳伦斯等5个子女就在贫困和家庭不和中长大成人。

劳伦斯自小体弱多病，在一项奖学金的资助下在诺丁汉读完三年中学，后被迫在一家经营医疗用品的公司当职员，后又从事小学教员工作。1906年开始在诺丁汉大学学院就读，其时开始发表作品。1911年《白孔雀》问世，第二年五月《逾矩》出版，1913年《儿子与情人》杀青，这是一部自传性的伟大作品，一经问世就在文坛上引起了强烈反响，使他一举成名，从而奠定了他在英国文学史上的地位。

1912年劳伦斯结识了诺丁汉大学法文教授的妻子弗丽达·威克利(Frieda Weekley)，其时她已是三个孩子的母亲，长劳伦斯6岁，不久他们相爱并私奔德国，从此便开始了他们浸长而颠沛流离的生活。1922年到锡兰，随后到澳大利亚，并从那里辗转到达美国和墨西哥。身体虚弱，经济拮据，笔耕不辍，他先后发表了《恋爱中的女人》、《羽蛇》等10部长篇小说，7部中篇小说以及许多游记、评论和大量的散文诗歌等。在肺病已相当严重时，着手写《查泰莱夫人的情人》。在朋友的协助下，这部巨著于1928年秘密全文出版，但随即遭禁。后来其健康状况日益恶化，于1930年3月2日在法国南部病逝，终年44岁。

劳伦斯是个天才的伟大作家。他热爱自然，热爱生活，热爱人类。反对现代工业文明对人类固有文明的干扰和破坏。他历尽艰辛，不畏艰险，不屈不挠，探索寻觅他所理想的社会生活环境。他甚至试图建立自己理想的庄园，虽然失败但他的卓绝努力令人钦佩。

他恣意放肆，桀骜不驯，文笔飞扬，入木三分的风格展示了他高傲非凡的人格风范。他对社会问题和艺术问题等许多方面的思考也有超人的独到之处。

劳伦斯对性问题的认识超前绝后。他的书《虹》1915 年 9 月出版，10 月即遭查禁；《恋爱中的女人》也遭数家出版社拒绝；而文坛奇葩《查泰莱夫人的情人》在美国和英国遭禁长达 30 年之久。其原因就是因为他对性的前瞻认识和直白描写。性究竟是什么？这是个历久弥新，令无数人不敢涉足的问题。而在他看来，性是宇宙中阴阳两性间的平衡物：吸引、排斥、中和、新的吸引、新的排斥、永不相同，总有新意。性行为是神圣的，是伟大的创造过程。男女间的交流，“就像幼发拉底河和底格里斯河环绕着美索不达米亚平原那样，天堂或者说伊甸园就在这交流中，人在此获得了自己的起始。”他甚至大声疾呼，没有性的英格兰是没有希望的。他的这些观点无疑与传统文化格格不入。因此，被冠以“不洁”“黄色”“淫秽”等罪名。现在他那些被查禁的书籍早已被解禁，在世界广为传阅。对此我们是否可以说，这是人类经过漫长、深刻的思考后，对他的观点的认同或肯定，不妨说这也是人类自身认识的提高和社会的进步。

另外，劳伦斯对艺术的评判也有自己的看法。《儿子与情人》出版之时，弗洛伊德的“精神分析说”在英美的知识界已广为传播，人们普遍认为劳伦斯的这部新作是为弗洛伊德的“恋母情结”提供了有力的佐证，然而这种论点一经提出就遭到了劳伦斯本人的断然否认，在他看来，艺术就是艺术，对艺术的评价不能太理性化。他反对用科学来评价艺术，科学和艺术不可同日而语。“当凡·高绘向日葵时，他揭示的或获得的是一瞬间作为一个人的他与作为向日葵的向日葵之间的活的关系。他的绘画压根儿不是再现向日葵本身。”如果有人执意以真实与否来衡量这幅画，那照相机拍出的照片会更高一筹，但那是何等的离谱就不言而喻了。同样，评价劳伦斯及其作品也是个见仁见智的问题，社会问题之复杂仅用一些科学知识来衡量恐怕是难以奏效的。不过有一点可以肯定，迄今劳伦斯已对世界文坛有了地震般的影响，随着时间的推进，他对世界文坛的影响将会更大。希望劳伦斯在中国有更多的知音。

导 读

这个故事发生在英国中部 Terershall 矿区，女主人公查泰莱夫人（Lady Chatterley）名叫康妮。1917 年，22 岁的康妮与查泰莱男爵家的次子克利福德（Clifford）结婚。婚后一个月，克利福德上了前线；半年后，受重伤的克利福德返回祖国，虽然幸免一死，但从此下身瘫痪，丧失了性功能。1920 年，克利福德的父亲去世了，他继承了爵位，成了克利福德男爵，而康妮也成了查泰莱男爵夫人。他们回到了查泰莱家族世代居住的庄园（Wragby），开始了死气沉沉的传统的贵族生活。

康妮的父亲是有名的皇家艺术学会会员，母亲是费边社成员，开放自由的家庭气氛使康妮和她的姐姐从小就受到了不拘泥传统的教育和艺术的熏陶。拥有健康的肉体和野性的生命力的康妮，终日照料着残废、自私、守旧的男爵丈夫，枯燥空虚的生活对她来说无异于守活寡。在此期间，一位失意的爱尔兰青年作家密克里斯经常到克利福德家里做客，康妮和他发生了性关系，并从他的身上得到了暂时的性满足，但很快，两人的关系淡了下来。

日见憔悴的康妮开始独自去树林中散步，以寻求大自然的抚慰。一次，她无意中窥到了看林人，梅勒士(Mellors)，在院子里冲澡的情景，看到了梅勒士赤裸的、如大自然般富于生机的身体。这次偶然的偷窥激活了康妮体内被压抑的性渴望，于是她有意与梅勒士接触。她发现这个看林人虽出身卑微，但却具有刚直的个性，他聪明豁达且善解人意。康妮从他强健而又男性十足的身体上体味到了真正的男性的爱。

不久，康妮发现自己怀孕了。尽管克利福德从延续家族烟火的角度考虑同意妻子从别人那里“借种”，但此时的康妮已无法忍受那令人窒息的贵族生活，于是她决定与克利福德离婚。于是她远走意大利，梅勒士也被迫离开了林场。尽管此中经历了许多波折，康妮和梅勒士相会之后终于决定摆脱一切羁绊，到乡间买一个农场，开始新的生活。

《查泰莱夫人的情人》是劳伦斯最后的也是最具争议的一部长篇小说。1928 年 7 月在佛罗伦萨出版，由于这部小说有较多的性描写而受到英国文学界的攻击，英国当局以“有伤风化”的罪名予以查封，直到 1960 年经法庭裁判后才获准正式出版。尽管这部小说因其中的性描写而被查禁达 30 年之久，但劳伦斯在小说中采用了自然主义和象征主义相结合的手法，对性爱的描写毫无猥亵之感，反而颇具优美的抒情意味。他描写的是一种真正的两情相悦的男女之爱，自然、健康而美好，与动物的性交是完全不同的，因而作者用自然而磊落的语言把它们表达了出来。

我们应当注意的是，劳伦斯并不是为了哗众取宠才在书中进行了十几处的性爱描写，他真正的意图是旨在通过对男人与女人之间的性爱关系的描写，反映人与自然和人与人之间的关系，确切来说，就是表明一种以自然完美的两性关系来摆脱现代机械文明对人性的压抑主张。这部小说是以二十世纪初的工业化和机械文明为主要社会背景的，在劳伦斯的眼中，工业革命压抑和摧残了人的自然本性。小说中对新矿区是这样描写的：“……在恶魔般的隆隆机器声中。在那里，在充满着机械的贪婪、贪婪的机械和机械化了的贪婪世界里，闪烁着火焰，奔流着火热的金属……一切生命都必将灭亡。”作者认为，工业化社会给人们勾勒出了一个虚幻的理想，把人的精神和生命诱导到对物质的崇拜上，它不仅破坏了自然环境，而且扭曲了人的自然本性。小说中终日坐在电动轮椅中的克利福德男爵就象征性地体现了现代工业对人性的剥夺。他自私、冷漠、虚伪，就像一个半人半机械的怪物。书中描写他是“现代工业和金融世界中一只令人惊异的螃蟹或大螯虾……”，像他这样的资本家疯狂地竞争、对工人进行残酷的盘剥，加速了工业化机械的疯狂运转。不但使自然生机遭到破坏，也使人与人之间的关系堕落成了一种冷冰冰的机械关系。从这层意义上来看，克利福德生育能力的丧失，就象征着他所代表的阶级已经丧失了生命力，而康妮对他的背叛便获得了一个新的道德背景。

CHAPTER 1

Ours is essentially a tragic age, so we refuse to take it tragically. The **cataclysm**[1] has happened, we are among the ruins, we start to build up new little habitats, to have new little hopes. It is rather hard work: there is now no smooth road into the future: but we go round, or scramble over the obstacles. We've got to live, no matter how many skies have fallen.

This was more or less Constance Chatterley's position. **The war had brought the roof down over her head**[2]. And she had realized that one must live and learn.

She married Clifford Chatterley in 1917, when he was home for a month on leave. They had a month's honeymoon. Then he went back to Flanders: to be shipped over to England again six months later, **more or less in bits**[3]. Constance, his wife, was then twenty-three years old, and he was twenty-nine.

His hold on life[4] was marvellous. He didn't die, and the bits seemed to grow together again. For two years he remained in the doctor's hands. Then he was pronounced a cure, and could return to life again, with the lower half of his body, from the hips down, paralysed for ever.

This was in 1920. They returned, Clifford and Constance, to his home, Wragby Hall, **the family 'seat**[5]'. His father had died, Clifford was now a baronet, Sir Clifford, and Constance was Lady Chatterley. They came to start housekeeping and married life in the rather forlorn home of the Chatterleys on a rather inadequate income. Clifford had a sister, but she had departed. Otherwise there were no near relatives. The elder brother was dead in the war. Crippled for ever, knowing he could never have any children, Clifford came home to the smoky Midlands to keep the Chatterley name alive while he could.

He was not really downcast. He could wheel himself about in a wheeled chair, and he had **a bath-chair**[6] with a small motor attachment,

---

①指第一次世界大战。②战争已使头上的屋顶毁于一旦。③伤痕累累。④生命力之顽强持久。⑤家族的根基所在。⑥巴思椅车(美国巴思温泉用的一种有篷轮椅),供残疾者用。

so he could drive himself slowly round the garden and into the line melancholy park, of which he was really so proud, though he pretended to be flippant about it.

Having suffered so much, the capacity for suffering had to some extent left him. He remained strange and bright and cheerful, almost, one might say, chirpy, with his ruddy, healthy-looking face, and his pale-blue, challenging bright eyes. His shoulders were broad and strong, his hands were very strong. He was expensively dressed, and wore handsome neckties from Bond Street. Yet still in his face one saw the watchful look, **the slight vacancy of a cripple**[1].

He had so very nearly lost his life, that what remained was wonderfully precious to him. It was obvious in the anxious brightness of his eyes, how proud he was, after the great shock, of being alive. But he had been so much hurt that something inside him had perished, some of his feelings had gone. There was a blank of insentience.

Constance, his wife, was a ruddy, country-looking girl with soft brown hair and sturdy body, and slow movements, full of unusual energy. She had big, wondering eyes, and a soft mild voice, and seemed just to have come from her native village. It was not so at all. Her father was the once well-known **R. A.** [2], old Sir Malcolm Reid. Her mother had been one of the cultivated **Fabians**[3] in the palmy, rather **pre-Raphaelite**[4] days. Between artists and cultured socialists, Constance and her sister Hilda had had what might be called an aesthetically unconventional upbringing. They had been taken to Paris and Florence and Rome to breathe in art, and they had been taken also in the other direction, to the Hague and Berlin, to great Socialist conventions, where the speakers spoke in every civilized tongue, and no one was abashed.

The two girls, therefore, were from an early age not the least daunted by either art or ideal politics. It was their natural atmosphere. **They were at once cosmopolitan and provincial, with the cosmopolitan provincialism of art that goes with pure social ideals**[5].

---

①残疾人若有所思的茫然。 ②英国皇家艺术学会会员，即Royal Academician的缩写。 ③费边社成员，费边社（Fabian Society）资产阶级的改良主义组织，成立于1884年。 ④拉斐尔兹派社成员。拉斐尔兹派社（Pre-Raphaelite Brotherhood）成立于1848年，由美术家和文人组成。 ⑤她们既是世界性的，又是乡土化的，艺术的世界性乡土主义与纯正的社会主义理想并行不悖，相得益彰。

They had been sent to Dresden at the age of fifteen, for music among other things. And they had had a good time there. They lived freely among the students, they argued with the men over philosophical, sociological and artistic matters, they were just as good as the men themselves: only better, since they were women. And they tramped off to the forests with sturdy youths bearing guitars, **twang-twang**①! They sang the **Wandervogel songs**②, and they were free. Free! That was the great word. Out in the open world, out in the forests of the morning, with lusty and splendid-throated young fellows, free to do as they liked, and — above all — to say what they liked. It was the talk that mattered supremely: the impassioned interchange of talk. Love was only a minor accompaniment.

Both Hilda and Constance had had their tentative love-affairs by the time they were eighteen. The young men with whom they talked so passionately and sang so lustily and camped under the trees in such freedom wanted, of course, the love connexion. The girls were doubtful, but then the thing was so much talked about, it was supposed to be so important. And the men were so humble and craving. Why couldn't a girl be queenly, and **give the gift of herself**③?

So they had given the gift of themselves, each to the youth with whom she had the most subtle and intimate arguments. The arguments, the discussions were the great thing: the **love-making and connexion were only a sort of primitive reversion and a bit of an anti-climax**④. One was less in love with the boy afterwards, and a little inclined to hate him, as if he had trespassed on one's privacy and inner freedom. For, of course, being a girl, one's whole dignity and meaning in life consisted in the achievement of an absolute, a perfect, a pure and noble freedom. What else did a girl's life mean? **To shake off the old and sordid connexions and subjections**⑤.

And however one might sentimentalize it, this sex business was one of the most ancient, sordid connexions and subjections. Poets who glorified it were mostly men. Women had always known there was something better, something higher. And now they knew it more definitely than ever. The beautiful pure freedom of a woman was

①叮咚叮咚的吉他声。 ②流浪之歌，该词由wander一词杜撰而来。 ③把自己当作礼物给对方。 ④做爱和爱不过是一种原始的本能，多少有点大煞风景。 ⑤摆脱古老而污秽的两性关系和主奴关系。

infinitely more wonderful than any sexual love. The only unfortunate thing was that men lagged so far behind women in the matter. They insisted on the sex thing like dogs.

And a woman had to yield. A man was like a child with his appetites. A woman had to yield him what he wanted, or like a child he would probably turn nasty and flounce away and spoil what was a very pleasant connexion. But a woman could yield to a man without yielding her inner, free self. That the poets and talkers about sex did not seem to have taken sufficiently into account. A woman could take a man without really giving herself away. Certainly she could take him without giving herself into his power. Rather she could use this sex thing to have power over him. For she only had to hold herself back in sexual intercourse, and let him finish and expend himself without herself **coming to the crisis**[1]: and then she could prolong the connexion and achieve her orgasm and her crisis while he was merely her tool.

Both sisters had had their love experience by the time the war came, and they were hurried home. Neither was ever in love with a young man unless he and she were verbally very near: that is unless they were profoundly interested, TALKING to one another. The amazing, the profound, the unbelievable thrill there was in passionately talking to some really clever young man by the hour, resuming day after day for months...this they had never realized till it happened! The paradisal promise: **Thou shalt have men to talk to**[2]! — had never been uttered. It was fulfilled before they knew what a promise it was.

And if after the roused intimacy of these vivid and soul-enlightened discussions the sex thing became more or less inevitable, then let it. It marked the end of a chapter. It had a thrill of its own too: **a queer vibrating thrill inside the body, a final spasm of self-assertion**[3], like the last word, exciting, and very like the row of asterisks that can be put to show the end of a paragraph, and a break in the theme.

When the girls came home for the summer holidays of 1913, when Hilda was twenty and Connie eighteen, their father could see plainly that they had had the love experience.

❶达到高潮。❷将有人与之交谈。❸一种身体之内的奇妙战栗，一种不由自主的最后痉挛。

L'amour avait possé par là [1], as somebody puts it. But he was a man of experience himself, and let life take its course. As for the mot a nervous invalid in the last few months of her life, she wanted her girls to be 'free', and to 'fulfil themselves'. She herself had never been able to be altogether herself: it had been denied her. Heaven knows why, for she was a woman who had her own income and her own way. She blamed her husband. But as a matter of fact, it was some old impression of authority on her own mind or soul that she could not get rid of. It had nothing to do with Sir Malcolm, who left his nervously hostile, high-spirited wife to **rule her own roost** [2], while he went his own way.

So the girls were 'free', and went back to Dresden, and their music, and the university and the young men. They loved their respective young men, and their respective young men loved them with all the passion of mental attraction. All the wonderful things the young men thought and expressed and wrote, they thought and expressed and wrote for the young women. Connie's young man was musical, Hilda's was technical. But they simply lived for their young women. In their minds and their mental excitements, that is. Somewhere else they were a little rebuffed, though they did not know it.

It was obvious in them too that love had gone through them: that is, the physical experience. It is curious what **a subtle but unmistakable transmutation it makes** [3], both in the body of men and women: the woman more blooming, more subtly rounded, her young angularities softened, and her expression either anxious or triumphant: the man much quieter, more inward, the very shapes of his shoulders and his buttocks less assertive, more hesitant.

In the actual sex-thrill within the body, the sisters nearly succumbed to the strange male power. But quickly they recovered themselves, took the sex-thrill as a sensation, and remained free. Whereas the men, in gratitude to the woman for the sex experience, let their souls go out to her. And afterwards looked rather as if they had lost a shilling and found sixpence. Connie's man could be a bit sulky, and Hilda's a bit jeering. But that is how men are! Ungrateful and never satisfied. When you don't have them they hate you because you won't; and when you do have

➊情爱已在此留下痕迹。➋自行其是，当家做主。➌留下了微小但却确凿无误的变化。

them they hate you again, for some other reason. Or for no reason at all, except that they are discontented children, and can't be satisfied whatever they get, let a woman do what she may.

However, came the war, Hilda and Connie were rushed home again after having been home already in May, to their mother's funeral. Before Christmas of 1914 both their German young men were dead: whereupon the sisters wept, and loved the young men passionately, but underneath forgot them. They didn't exist any more.

Both sisters lived in their father's, really their mother's, Kensington housemixed with the young Cambridge group, the group that stood for 'freedom' and flannel trousers, and flannel shirts open at the neck, and a well-bred sort of emotional anarchy, and a whispering, murmuring sort of voice, and an ultra-sensitive sort of manner. Hilda, however, suddenly married a man ten years older than herself, an elder member of the same Cambridge group, a man with a fair amount of money, and a comfortable family job in the government: he also wrote philosophical essays. She lived with him in a smallish house in **Westminster**[1], and moved in that good sort of society of people in the government who are not tip-toppers, but who are, or would be, the real intelligent power in the nation: people who know what they're talking about, or talk as if they did.

Connie did a mild form of war-work, and consorted with the flannel-trousers Cambridge intransigents, who gently mocked at everything, so far. Her 'friend' was a Clifford Chatterley, a young man of twenty-two, who had hurried home from **Bonn**[2], where he was studying the technicalities of coal-mining. He had previously spent two years at Cambridge. Now he had become a first lieutenant in a smart regiment, so he could mock at everything more becomingly in uniform.

Clifford Chatterley was more upper-class than Connie. Connie was well-to-do intelligentsia, but he was aristocracy. Not the big sort, but still it. His father was a baronet, and his mother had been a viscount's daughter.

But Clifford, while he was better bred than Connie, and more 'society', was in his own way more provincial and more timid. He was at his ease in the narrow 'great world', that is, landed aristocracy

❶威斯敏斯特，伦敦西部的贵族居住区。❷波恩，德国工业城市。

society, but he was shy and nervous of all that other big world which consists of the vast hordes of the middle and lower classes, and foreigners. If the truth must be told, he was just a little bit frightened of middle-and lower-class humanity, and of foreigners not of his own class. He was, in some paralysing way, conscious of his own defencelessness, though he had all the defence of privilege. Which is curious, but a phenomenon of our day.

Therefore the peculiar soft assurance of a girl like Constance Reid fascinated him. **She was so much more mistress of herself in that outer world of chaos than he was master of himself**[1].

Nevertheless he too was a rebel: rebelling even against his class. Or perhaps rebel is too strong a word; far too strong. He was only caught in the general, popular recoil of the young against convention and against any sort of real authority. Fathers were ridiculous: his own obstinate one supremely so. And governments were ridiculous: our own wait-and-see sort especially so. And armies were ridiculous, and old buffers of generals altogether, the red-faced **Kitchener**[2] supremely. Even the war was ridiculous, though it did kill rather a lot of people.

In fact everything was a little ridiculous, or very ridiculous: certainly everything connected with authority, whether it were in the army or the government or the universities, was ridiculous to a degree. And as far as the governing class made any pretensions to govern, they were ridiculous too. Sir Geoffrey, Clifford's father, was intensely ridiculous, chopping down his trees, and weeding men out of his colliery to shove them into the war; and himself being so safe and patriotic; but, also, spending more money on his country than he'd got.

When Miss Chatterley — Emma — came down to London from the Midlands to do some nursing work, she was very witty in a quiet way about Sir Geoffrey and his determined patriotism. Herbert, the elder brother and heir, laughed outright, though it was his trees that were falling for trench props. But Clifford only smiled a little uneasily. Everything was ridiculous, quite true. But when it came too close and oneself became ridiculous too...? At least people of a different class, like

❶与他这个能够自控的男人相比，她是位更善于驾驭纷攘的外部世界的女人。❷基钦纳（1850—1916），美国陆军元帅，第一次世界大战时任美陆军大臣。

Connie, were earnest about something. They believed in something.

They were rather earnest about **the Tommies**❶, and the threat of conscription, and the shortage of sugar and toffee for the children. In all these things, of course, the authorities were ridiculously at fault. But Clifford could not take it to heart. To him the authorities were ridiculous **ab ovo**❷, not because of toffee or Tommies.

And the authorities felt ridiculous, and behaved in a rather ridiculous fashion, and **it was all a mad hatter's tea-party for a while**❸. Till things developed over there, and **Lloyd George**❹ came to save the situation over here. And this surpassed even ridicule, the flippant young laughed no more.

In 1916 Herbert Chatterley was killed, so Clifford became heir. He was terrified even of this. His importance as son of Sir Geoffrey, and child of Wragby, was so ingrained in him, he could never escape it. And yet he knew that this too, in the eyes of the vast seething world, was ridiculous. Now he was heir and responsible for Wragby. Was that not terrible? and also splendid and at the same time, perhaps, purely absurd?

Sir Geoffrey would have none of the absurdity. He was pale and tense, withdrawn into himself, and obstinately determined to save his country and his own position, let it be Lloyd George or who it might. So cut off he was, so divorced from the England that was really England, so utterly incapable, that he even thought well of **Horatio Bottomley**❺. Sir Geoffrey stood for England and Lloyd George as his forebears had stood for England and **St George**❻: and he never knew there was a difference. So Sir Geoffrey felled timber and stood for Lloyd George and England, England and Lloyd George.

And he wanted Clifford to marry and produce an heir. Clifford felt his father was **a hopeless anachronism**❼. But wherein was he himself any further ahead, except in a wincing sense of the ridiculousness of everything, and the paramount ridiculousness of his own position? For **willy-nilly**❽ he took his baronetcy and Wragby with

❶(口)英国兵(=Tommy Atkins)。1815年开始在士兵登记表上填写的笼统的士兵名。 ❷(拉丁)=from the beginning。❸一时间好像是茶会上戴上了疯帽子,意指英当局信政局混乱不堪。mad hatter来自词组mad as a hatter,意为疯狂的。 ❹劳埃德·乔治(1863—1945),英国政治家,第一次世界大战后期在英国社会叱咤风云,曾任财政大臣,1916—1922年间任英国首相。 ❺霍拉肖·博顿利(1860—1933),英国政治家,曾创办《金融时报》,后因金融诈骗而入狱。 ❻圣乔治,公元三世纪基督教的殉教者,英格兰主要保护的圣人。 ❼不可救药的老古董。 ❽不管愿意与否。

the last seriousness.

The gay excitement had gone out of the war...dead. Too much death and horror. A man needed support arid comfort. A man needed to have an anchor in the safe world. A man needed a wife.

The Chatterleys, two brothers and a sister, had lived curiously isolated, shut in with one another at Wragby, in spite of all their connexions. A sense of isolation intensified the family tie, a sense of the weakness of their position, a sense of defencelessness, in spite of, or because of, the title and the land. They were cut off from those industrial Midlands in which they passed their lives. And they were cut off from their own class by the brooding, obstinate, shut-up nature of Sir Geoffrey, their father, **whom they ridiculed, but whom they were so sensitive about**[1].

The three had said they would all live together always. But now Herbert was dead, and Sir Geoffrey wanted Clifford to marry. Sir Geoffrey barely mentioned it: he spoke very little. But his silent, brooding insistence that it should be so was hard for Clifford to bear up against.

But Emma said No! She was ten years older than Clifford, and she felt his marrying would be a desertion and a betrayal of what the young ones of the family had stood for.

Clifford married Connie, nevertheless, and had his month's honeymoon with her. It was the terrible year 1917, and they were intimate as two people who stand together on a sinking ship. He had been virgin when he married: and the sex part did not mean much to him. They were so close, he and she, apart from that. And Connie exulted a little in this intimacy which was beyond sex, and beyond a man's 'satisfaction'. Clifford anyhow was not just keen on his 'satisfaction', as so many men seemed to be. No, the intimacy was deeper, more personal than that. And sex was merely an accident, or an adjunct, one of the curious obsolete, organic processes which persisted in its own clumsiness, but was not really necessary. Though Connie did want children: if only to fortify her against her sister-in-law Emma.

But early in 1918 Clifford was shipped home smashed, and there was no child. And Sir Geoffrey died of chagrin.

[1] 虽然他们嘲笑自己的老爸，但却不顾他人的嘲笑。

CHAPTER 2

Connie and Clifford came home to Wragby in the autumn of 1920. Miss Chatterley, still disgusted at her brother's defection, had departed and was living in a little flat in London.

Wragby was a long low old house in brown stone, begun about the middle of the eighteenth century, and added on to, till it was a warren of a place without much distinction. It stood on an eminence in a rather line old park of oak trees, but alas, one could see in the near distance the chimney of Tevershall pit, with its clouds of steam and smoke, **and on the damp, hazy distance of the hill the raw straggle of Tevershall village**[1], a village which began almost at the park gates, and trailed in utter hopeless ugliness for a long and gruesome mile: houses, rows of wretched, small, begrimed, brick houses, with black slate roofs for lids, sharp angles and wilful, blank dreariness.

Connie was accustomed to Kensington or the Scotch hills or the Sussex downs: that was her England. With the stoicism of the young she took in the utter, soulless ugliness of the coal-and-iron Midlands at a glance, and left it at what it was: unbelievable and not to be thought about. From the rather dismal rooms at Wragby she heard the rattle-rattle of the screens at the pit, the puff of the winding-engine, the clink-clink of shunting trucks, and the hoarse little whistle of the colliery locomotives. Tevershall pit-bank was burning, had been burning for years, and it would cost thousands to put it out. So it had to burn. And when the wind was that way, which was often, **the house was full of the stench of this sulphurous combustion of the earth's excrement**[2]. But even on windless days the air always smelt of something under-earth: sulphur, iron, coal, or acid. And even on the Christmas roses the smuts settled persistently, incredible, like black manna from the skies of doom.

Well, there it was: fated like the rest of things! It was rather awful, but why kick? You couldn't kick it away. It just went on. Life,

①特弗沙尔村天然地散落在潮湿朦胧的小山坡上。 ②房间里充满了野外秽物燃烧后散发的硫磺的恶臭味。

like all the rest! On the low dark ceiling of cloud at night red blotches burned and quavered, dappling and swelling and contracting, like burns that give pain. It was the furnaces. At first they fascinated Connie with a sort of horror; she felt she was living underground. Then she got used to them. And in the morning it rained.

Clifford professed to like Wragby better than London. This country had a grim will of its own, and **the people had guts**[1]. Connie wondered what else they had: **certainly neither eyes nor minds**[2]. The people were as haggard, shapeless, and dreary as the countryside, and as unfriendly. Only there was something in their deep-mouthed slurring of the dialect, and the thresh — **thresh of their hob-nailed pit-boots**[3] as they trailed home in gangs on the asphalt from work, that was terrible and a bit mysterious.

There had been no welcome home for the young squire, no festivities, no deputation, not even a single flower. Only a dank ride in a motor-car up a dark, damp drive, burrowing through gloomy trees, out to the slope of the park where grey damp sheep were feeding, to the knoll where the house spread its dark brown facade, and the housekeeper and her husband were hovering, like unsure tenants on the face of the earth, ready to stammer a welcome.

There was no communication between Wragby Hall and Tevershall village, none. **No caps were touched, no curtseys bobbed**[4]. The colliers merely stared; the tradesmen lifted their caps to Connie as to an acquaintance, and nodded awkwardly to Clifford; that was all. Gulf impassable, and a quiet sort of resentment on either side. At first Connie suffered from the steady drizzle of resentment that came from the village. Then she hardened herself to it, and it became a sort of tonic, something to live up to. It was not that she and Clifford were unpopular, they merely belonged to another species altogether from the colliers. Gulf impassable, breach indescribable, such as is perhaps nonexistent south of the Trent. But in the Midlands and the industrial North gulf impassable, across which no communication could take place. You stick to your side, I'll stick to mine! A strange denial of the common pulse of humanity.

Yet the village sympathized with Clifford and Connie **in the abstract**[5]. In the flesh it was — You leave me alone! — on either side.

❶当地人生性强悍。❷既没有头脑也没有眼光。❸平头钉矿工鞋发出的踢踏声。❹人们既不脱帽，也不鞠躬。❺在无形中。

The rector was a nice man of about sixty, full of his duty, **and reduced, personally, almost to a nonentity by the silent — You leave me alone! — of the village**[1]. The miners' wives were nearly all **Methodists. The miners were nothing**[2]. But even so much official uniform as the clergyman wore was enough to obscure entirely the fact that he was a man like any other man. No, he was **Mester Ashby**[3], a sort of automatic preaching and praying concern.

This stubborn, instinctive — We think ourselves as good as you, if you are Lady Chatterley! — puzzled and baffled Connie at first extremely. The curious, suspicious, false amiability with which the miners' wives met her overtures; the curiously offensive tinge of — Oh dear me! I am somebody now, with Lady Chatterley talking to me! But she needn't think I'm not as good as her for all that! — which she always heard twanging in the women's half-fawning voices, was impossible. **There was no getting past it**[4]. It was hopelessly and offensively nonconformist.

Clifford left them alone, and she learnt to do the same: she just went by without looking at them, and they stared as if she were a **walking wax**[5] figure. When he had to deal with them, Clifford was rather haughty and contemptuous; one could no longer afford to be friendly. In fact he was altogether rather supercilious and contemptuous of anyone not in his own class. He stood his ground, without any attempt at conciliation. And he was neither liked nor disliked by the people: he was just part of things, like the pit-bank and Wragby itself.

But Clifford was really extremely shy and self-conscious now he was lamed. He hated seeing anyone except just the personal servants. For he had to sit in a wheeled chair or a sort of bath-chair. Nevertheless he was just as carefully dressed as ever, by his expensive tailors, and he wore the careful **Bond Street**[6] neckties just as before, and from the top he looked just as smart and impressive as ever. He had never been one of the modern ladylike young men: rather bucolic even, with his ruddy face and broad shoulders. But his very quiet, hesitating voice, and his eyes, at the same time bold and frightened, assured and uncertain, revealed his

❶村里那种无言的“少管闲事”却使得他变得无足轻重。 ❷(基督教)卫理公会教徒。矿工们全都不信教。 ❸杜撰的人名。 ❹沟通简直不可能,鸿沟无法逾越。 ❺活蜡像。 ❻专卖高档商品的街区。

nature. His manner was often offensively supercilious, and then again modest and self-effacing, almost tremulous.

Connie and he were attached to one another, **in the aloof modern way**❶. He was much too hurt in himself, the great shock of his maiming, to be easy and flippant. He was a hurt thing. And as such Connie stuck to him passionately.

But she could not help feeling how little connexion he really had with people. The miners were, in a sense, his own men; but he saw them as objects rather than men, parts of the pit rather than parts of life, crude raw phenomena rather than human beings along with him. He was in some way afraid of them, he could not bear to have them look at him now he was lame. And their queer, crude life seemed as unnatural as that of hedgehogs.

He was remotely interested; but like a man looking down a microscope, or up a telescope. He was not in touch. He was not in actual touch with anybody, save, traditionally, with Wragby, and, through the close bond of family defence, with Emma. Beyond this nothing really touched him. Connie felt that she herself didn't really, not really touch him; perhaps there was nothing to get at ultimately; just a negation of human contact.

Yet he was absolutely dependent on her, he needed her every moment. Big and strong as he was, he was helpless. He could wheel himself about in a wheeled chair, and he had a sort of bath-chair with a motor attachment, in which he could puff slowly round the park. But alone he was like a lost thing. He needed Connie to be there, to assure him he existed at all.

Still he was ambitious. He had taken to writing stories; curious, very personal stories about people he had known. Clever, rather spiteful, and yet, in some mysterious way, meaningless. The observation was extraordinary and peculiar. But there was no touch, no actual contact. It was as if the whole thing took place in a vacuum. And since the field of life is largely an artificially-lighted stage today, the stories were curiously true to modern life, to the modern psychology, that is.

Clifford was almost morbidly sensitive about these stories. He wanted everyone to think them good, of the best, **ne plus ultra**❷.

❶以若即若离的现代方式。❷(拉丁)至高无上,完美无缺的佳作。

They appeared in the most modern magazines, and were praised and blamed as usual. But to Clifford the blame was torture, like knives goading him. It was as if the whole of his being were in his stories.

Connie helped him as much as she could. At first she was thrilled. He talked everything over with her monotonously, insistently, persistently, and she had to respond with all her might. It was as if her whole soul and body and sex had to rouse up and pass into these stories of his. This thrilled her and absorbed her.

Of physical life they lived very little[1]. She had to superintend the house. But the housekeeper had served Sir Geoffrey for many years, arid the dried-up, elderly, superlatively correct female you could hardly call her a parlour-maid, or even a woman...who waited at table, had been in the house for forty years. Even the very housemaids were no longer young. It was awful! What could you do with such a place, but leave it alone! All these endless rooms that nobody used, all the Midlands routine, the mechanical cleanliness and the mechanical order! Clifford had insisted on a new cook, an experienced woman who had served him in his rooms in London. For the rest the place seemed run by mechanical anarchy. Everything went on in pretty good order, strict cleanliness, and strict punctuality; even pretty strict honesty. And yet, to Connie, it was a methodical anarchy. No warmth of feeling united it organically. The house seemed as dreary as a disused street.

What could she do but leave it alone...? So she left it alone. Miss Chatterley came sometimes, with her aristocratic thin face, and triumphed, finding nothing altered. She would never forgive Connie **for ousting her from her union in consciousness with her brother**[2]. It was she, Emma, who should be bringing forth the stories, these books, with him; the Chatterley stories, something new in the world, that they, the Chatterleys, had put there. There was no other standard. There was no organic connexion with the thought and expression that had gone before. Only something new in the world: the Chatterley books, entirely personal.

Connie's father, where he paid a flying visit to Wragby, and in private to his daughter: As for Clifford's writing, it's smart, but there's

❶至于日常的实际生活，他们没有什么可享的。❷由于康妮破坏了她与弟弟的心灵沟通。

nothing in it. It won't last! Connie looked at **the burly Scottish knight who had done himself well all his life**❶, and her eyes, her big, still-wondering blue eyes became vague. Nothing in it! What did he mean by nothing in it? If the critics praised it, and Clifford's name was almost famous, and it even brought in money...what did her father mean by saying there was nothing in Clifford's writing? What else could there be?

For Connie had adopted the standard of the young: **what there was in the moment was everything**❷. And moments followed one another without necessarily belonging to one another.

It was in her second winter at Wragby her father said to her: 'I hope, Connie, you **won't let circumstances force you into being a demi-vierge**❸.'

'A demi-vierge!' replied Connie vaguely. 'Why? Why not?'

'Unless you like it, of course!' said her father hastily. To Clifford he said the same, when the two men were alone: 'I'm afraid it doesn't quite suit Connie to be a demi-vierge.'

'A half-virgin!' replied Clifford, translating the phrase to be sure of it.

He thought for a moment, then flushed very red. He was angry and offended.

'In what way doesn't it suit her?' he asked stiffly.

'She's getting thin...angular. It's not her style. She's not **the pilchard sort of little slip of a girl, she's a bonny Scotch trout**❹.'

'Without the spots, of course!' said Clifford.

He wanted to say something later to Connie about the demi-vierge business...the half-virgin state of her affairs. But he could not bring himself to do it. He was at once too intimate with her and not intimate enough. He was so very much at one with her, in his mind and hers, but bodily they were non-existent to one another, **and neither could bear to drag in the corpus delicti**❺. They were so intimate, and utterly out of touch.

Connie guessed, however, that her father had said something, and

---

❶身体健壮、养尊处优的苏格兰骑士。❷此时此刻的东西就是一切。❸切勿让环境迫使你守活寡。donil-vierge(法)半处女(=half virgin)。❹她决非那种干瘦的沙丁鱼,她是美丽的苏格兰红斑鳟。❺两人谁都没有勇气把话题扯到有关肉体的事情上去。corpus delicti(拉丁)罪证;犯罪事实。

that something was in Clifford's mind. She knew that he didn't mind whether she were demi-vierge or **demi-monde**[1], so long as he didn't absolutely know, and wasn't made to see. What the eye doesn't see and the mind doesn't know, doesn't exist.

Connie and Clifford had now been nearly two years at Wragby, living their vague life of absorption in Clifford and his work. Their interests had never ceased to flow together over his work. They talked and wrestled **in the throes of composition**[2], and felt as if something were happening, really happening, really in the void.

And thus far it was a life: in the void. For the rest it was non-existence. Wragby was there, the servants...but spectral, not really existing. Connie went for walks in the park, and in the woods that joined the park, and enjoyed the solitude and the mystery, kicking the brown leaves of autumn, and picking the primroses of spring. But it was all a dream; or rather it was like **the simulacrum of reality**[3]. The oak-leaves were to her like oak-leaves seen ruffling in a mirror, she herself was a figure somebody had read about, picking primroses that were only shadows or memories, or words. No substance to her or anything...no touch, no contact! Only this life with Clifford, this endless spinning of webs of yarn, of the minutiae of consciousness, these stories Sir Malcolm said there was nothing in, and they wouldn't last. Why should there be anything in them, why should they last? **Sufficient unto the day is the evil thereof. Sufficient unto the moment is the appearance of reality**[4].

Clifford had quite a number of friends, acquaintances really, and he invited them to Wragby. He invited all sorts of people, critics and writers, people who would help to praise his books. And they were flattered at being asked to Wragby, and they praised. Connie understood it all perfectly. But why not? This was one of the fleeting patterns in the mirror. What was wrong with it?

She was hostess to these people...mostly men. She was hostess also to Clifford's occasional aristocratic relations. Being a soft, ruddy, country-looking girl, inclined to freckles, with big blue eyes, and curling, brown hair, and a soft voice, and rather strong, female loins

❶(法)风流女人。❷行文的艰苦过程。❸现实的幻影。❹今朝有酒今朝罪,眼见为实。此两句是劳伦斯套用圣经的相关话语。

she was considered a little old-fashioned and 'womanly'. She was not a 'little pilchard sort of fish', like a boy, with a boy's flat breast and little buttocks. She was too feminine to be quite smart.

So the men, especially those no longer young, were very nice to her indeed. But, knowing what torture poor Clifford would feel at the slightest sign of flirting on her part, she gave them no encouragement at all. She was quiet and vague, she had no contact with them and intended to have none. Clifford was extraordinarily proud of himself.

His relatives treated her quite kindly. She knew that the kindliness indicated a lack of fear, and that these people had no respect for you unless you could frighten them a little. But again she had no contact. She let them be kindly and disdainful, she let them feel they **had no need to draw their steel in readiness**[1]. She had no real connexion with them.

Time went on. Whatever happened, nothing happened, because she was so beautifully out of contact. She and Clifford lived in their ideas and his books. She entertained...there were always people in the house. Time went on as the clock does, half past eight instead of half past seven.

CHAPTER 3

Connie was aware, however, of a growing restlessness. Out of her disconnexion, a restlessness was taking possession of her like madness. It twitched her limbs when she didn't want to twitch them, it jerked her spine when she didn't want to jerk upright but preferred to rest comfortably. It thrilled inside her body, in her womb, somewhere, till she felt she must jump into water and swim to get away from it; a mad restlessness. It made her heart beat violently for no reason. And she was getting thinner.

It was just restlessness. She would rush off across the park, abandon Clifford, and **lie prone in the bracken**[2]. To get away from the house...she must get away from the house and everybody. The work was her one refuge, her sanctuary.

[1]他们不必剑拔弩张。 [2]趴在蕨草丛中。

But it was not really a refuge, a sanctuary, because she had no connexion with it. It was only a place where she could get away from the rest. She never really touched the spirit of the wood itself...if it had any such nonsensical thing.

Vaguely she knew herself that she was going to pieces in some way. Vaguely she knew she was out of connexion: she had lost touch with the substantial and vital world. Only Clifford and his books, which did not exist...which had nothing in them! Void to void. Vaguely she knew. But it was like beating her head against a stone.

Her father warned her again: 'Why don't you get yourself **a beau**①, Connie? Do you all the good in the world.'

That winter Michaelis came for a few days. He was a young Irishman who had already made a large fortune by his plays in America. He had been taken up quite enthusiastically for a time by smart society in London, for he wrote smart society plays. Then gradually smart society realized that it had been made ridiculous at the hands of **a down-at-heel Dublin street-rat**②, and revulsion came. Michaelis was the last word in what was caddish and bounderish. He was discovered to be anti-English, and to the class that made this discovery this was worse than the dirtiest crime. **He was cut dead, and his corpse thrown into the refuse can**③.

Nevertheless Michaelis had his apartment in **Mayfair**④, and walked down Bond Street the image of a gentleman, for you cannot get even the best tailors to cut their low-down customers, when the customers pay.

Clifford was inviting the young man of thirty at an inauspicious moment in that young man's career. Yet Clifford did not hesitate. Michaelis had the ear of a few million people, probably; and, being a hopeless outsider, he would no doubt be grateful to be asked down to Wragby at this juncture, when the rest of the smart world was cutting him. Being grateful, he would no doubt do Clifford 'good' over there in America. **Kudos**⑤! A man gets a lot of kudos, whatever that may be, by being talked about in the right way, especially 'over there'. Clifford was **a coming man**⑥; and it was remarkable what a sound publicity

①(女子的)情人。②一个人所不齿的都柏林市井无赖。③他遭到口诛笔伐,他的臭名被扔进了垃圾箱(英文原句为比喻用法)。④梅费尔,伦敦西部高级住宅区。⑤(口)奖赏,荣誉。⑥有远大前程的人。

instinct he had. In the end **Michaelis did him most nobly in a play**[1], and Clifford was a sort of popular hero. Till the reaction, when he found he had been made ridiculous.

Connie wondered a little over Clifford's blind, imperious instinct to become known: known, that is, to the vast amorphous world he did not himself know, and of which he was uneasily afraid; known as a writer, as a first-class modern writer. Connie was aware from successful, old, hearty, bluffing Sir Malcolm, that artists did advertise themselves, and exert themselves to put their goods over. But her father used **channels ready-made**[2], used by all the other R. A.s who sold their pictures. Whereas Clifford discovered new channels of publicity, all kinds. He had all kinds of people at Wragby, without exactly lowering himself. But, determined to build himself a monument of a reputation quickly, he used any handy rubble in the making.

Michaelis arrived duly, in a very neat car, with a chauffeur and a manservant. He was absolutely Bond Street! But at right of him something in Clifford's county soul recoiled. He wasn't exactly... not exactly...in fact, he wasn't at all, well, what his appearance intended to imply. To Clifford **this was final and enough**[3]. Yet he was very polite to the man; to the amazing success in him. The bitch-goddess, as she is called, of Success, roamed, snarling and protective, round the half-humble, half-defiant Michaelis' heels, and intimidated Clifford completely: for he wanted to prostitute himself to the bitch-goddess, Success also, if only she would have him.

Michaelis obviously wasn't an Englishman, in spite of all the tailors, hatters, barbers, booters of the very best quarter of London. No, no, he obviously wasn't an Englishman: the wrong sort of flattish, pale face and bearing; and the wrong sort of grievance. He had a grudge and a grievance: that was obvious to any true-born English gentleman, who would scorn to let such a thing appear blatant in his own demeanour. Poor Michaelis had been much kicked, so that he had a slightly tail-between-the-legs look even now. He had pushed his way by sheer instinct and sheerer effrontery on to the stage and to the front of it, with his

❶米凯利斯把克利福德在戏里描写成一个高尚的人。❷陈旧的方式。❸这点是确定无疑的。

plays. **He had caught the public**[1]. And he had thought the kicking days were over. Alas, they weren't... They never would be. For he, in a sense, asked to be kicked. He pined to be where he didn't belong...among the English upper classes. And how they enjoyed the various kicks they got at him! And how he hated them!

Nevertheless he travelled with his manservant and his very neat car, this Dublin mongrel.

There was something about him that Connie liked. He didn't put on airs to himself, he had no illusions about himself. He talked to Clifford sensibly, briefly, practically, about all the things Clifford wanted to know. **He didn't expand or let himself go**[2]. He knew he had been asked down to Wragby to be made use of, and like an old, shrewd, almost indifferent business man, or big-business man, he let himself be asked questions, and he answered with as little waste of feeling as possible.

'Money!' he said. 'Money is a sort of instinct. **It's a sort of property of nature in a man to make money. It's nothing you do**[3]. It's no trick you play. It's a sort of permanent accident of your own nature; once you start, you make money, and you go on; up to a point, I suppose.'

'But you've got to begin,' said Clifford.

'Oh, quite! You've got to get in. You can do nothing if you are kept outside. You've got to beat your way in. Once you've done that, you can't help it.'

'But could you have made money except by plays?' asked Clifford.

'Oh, probably not! I may be a good writer or I may be a bad one, but a writer and a writer of plays is what I am, and I've got to be. There's no question of that.'

'And you think it's a writer of popular plays that you've got to be?' asked Connie.

'There, exactly!' he said, turning to her in a sudden flash. 'There's nothing in it! There's nothing in popularity. There's nothing in the public, if it comes to that. There's nothing really in my plays to make them popular. It's not that. They just are like the weather...the sort that will have to be...for the time being.'

He turned his slow, rather full eyes, that had been drowned in such

[1]他曾博得观众的喜爱。 [2]他不夸张，也不发挥。 [3]挣钱是人的一种天性，无钱万事皆空。

fathomless disillusion, on Connie, and she trembled a little. He seemed so old...endlessly old, built up of layers of disillusion, going down in him generation after generation, like geological strata; and at the same time he was forlorn like a child. An outcast, in a certain sense; but with the desperate bravery of his rat-like existence.

'At least it's wonderful what you've done at your time of life,' said Clifford contemplatively.

'I'm thirty...yes, I'm thirty!' said Michaelis, sharply and suddenly, with a curious laugh; hollow, triumphant, and bitter.

'And are you alone?' asked Connie.

'How do you mean? Do I live alone? I've got my servant. He's a Greek, so he says, and quite incompetent. But I keep him. And I'm going to marry. Oh, yes, I must marry.'

'It sounds like going to have your tonsils cut,' laughed Connie. 'Will it be an effort?'

He looked at her admiringly. 'Well, Lady Chatterley, somehow it will! I find... excuse me... I find I can't marry an Englishwoman, not even an Irishwoman...'

'Try an American,' said Clifford.

'Oh, American! ' He laughed a hollow laugh. 'No, I've asked my man if he will find me a Turk or something...something nearer to the Oriental.'

Connie really wondered at this queer, melancholy specimen of extraordinary success; it was said he had an income of fifty thousand dollars from America alone. Sometimes he was handsome: sometimes as he looked sideways, downwards, and the light fell on him, he had the silent, enduring beauty of a carved ivory Negro mask, with his rather full eyes, and the strong queerly-arched brows, the immobile, compressed mouth; that momentary but revealed immobility, an immobility, **a timelessness which the Buddha aims at**[1], and which Negroes express sometimes without ever aiming at it; something old, old, and acquiescent in the race! **Aeons of acquiescence in race destiny**[2], instead of our individual resistance. And then a swimming through, like rats in a dark river. Connie felt a sudden, strange leap of sympathy for him, a leap mingled with compassion, and tinged with repulsion, amounting almost to love. The outsider! The

❶佛祖想要达到的无始无终。❷自古至今,它就白种族的命运所默认。

outsider! And they called him a bounder! How much more bounderish and assertive Clifford looked! How much stupider!

Michaelis knew at once he had made an impression on her. He turned his full, hazel, slightly prominent eyes on her in a look of pure detachment. He was estimating her, and the extent of the impression he had made. With the English nothing could save him from being the eternal outsider, not even love. Yet women sometimes **fell for him**[1]... Englishwomen too.

He knew just where he was with Clifford[2]. They were two alien dogs which would have liked to snarl at one another, but which smiled instead, perforce. But with the woman he was not quite so sure.

Breakfast was served in the bedrooms; Clifford never appeared before lunch, and the dining-room was a little dreary. After coffee Michaelis, restless and ill-sitting soul, wondered what he should do. It was a fine November day... fine for Wragby. He looked over the melancholy park. My God! What a place!

He sent a servant to ask, could he be of any service to Lady Chatterley: he thought of driving into Sheffield. The answer came, would he care to go up to Lady Chatterley's sitting-room.

Connie had a sitting-room on the third floor, the top floor of the central portion of the house. Clifford's rooms were on the ground floor, of course. Michaelis was flattered by being asked up to Lady Chatterley's own parlour. He followed blindly after the servant...he never noticed things, or had contact with his surroundings. In her room he did glance vaguely round at the fine German reproductions of **Renoir and Cézanne**[3].

'It's very pleasant up here,' he said, with his queer smile, as if it hurt him to smile, showing his teeth. 'You are wise to get up to the top.'

'Yes, I think so,' she said.

Her room was the only gay, modern one in the house, the only spot in Wragby where her personality was at all revealed. Clifford had never seen it, and she asked very few people up.

Now she and Michaelis sit on opposite sides of the fire and talked. She asked him about himself, his mother and father, his brothers...other people were always something of a wonder to her, and when her

❶倾心于他。 ❷他非常清楚他和克利福德的关系。 ❸雷诺阿(1841—1921),法国画家,印象派先驱。塞尚(1839—1906),法国油画家,后印象派杰出画家之一。

sympathy was awakened she was quite devoid of class feeling. Michaelis talked frankly about himself, quite frankly, without affectation, simply revealing his bitter, indifferent, stray-dog's soul, then showing a gleam of revengeful pride in his success.

'But why are you such a lonely bird?' Connie asked him; and again he looked at her, with his full, searching, hazel look.

'Some birds are that way,' he replied. Then, with a touch of familiar irony: 'but, look here, what about yourself? Aren't you by way of being a lonely bird yourself?' Connie, a little startled, thought about it for a few moments, and then she said: 'Only in a way! Not altogether, like you!'

'Am I altogether a lonely bird?' he asked, with his queer grin of a smile, as if he had toothache; it was so wry, and his eyes were so perfectly unchangingly melancholy, or stoical, or disillusioned or afraid.

'Why?' she said, a little breathless, as she looked at him. 'You are, aren't you?'

She felt a terrible appeal coming to her from him[1], that made her almost lose her balance.

'Oh, you're quite right!' he said, turning his head away, and looking sideways, downwards, with that strange immobility of an old race that is hardly here in our present day. It was that that really made Connie lose her power to see him detached from herself.

He looked up at her with the full glance that saw everything, registered everything. At the same time, the infant crying in the night was crying out of his breast to her, in a way that affected her very womb.

'It's awfully nice of you to think of me,' he said laconically.

'Why shouldn't I think of you?' she exclaimed, with hardly breath to utter it.

He gave the wry, quick hiss of a laugh.

'Oh, in that way! ...May I hold your hand for a minute?' he asked suddenly, fixing his eyes on her with almost hypnotic power, and sending out an appeal that affected her direct in the womb.

She stared at him, dazed and transfixed[2], and he went over and kneeled beside her, and took her two feet close in his two hands, and buried his face in her lap, remaining motionless. She was

[1]她觉得他身上有种强烈的感染力。 [2]她看着他，不知所措，呆若木鸡。

perfectly dim and dazed, looking down in a sort of amazement at the rather tender nape of his neck, feeling his face pressing her thighs. In all her burning dismay, she could not help putting her hand, with tenderness and compassion, on the defenceless nape of his neck, and he trembled, with a deep shudder.

Then he looked up at her with that awful appeal in his full, glowing eyes. She was utterly incapable of resisting it. From her breast flowed the answering, immense yearning over him; she must give him anything, anything.

He was a curious and very gentle lover, very gentle with the woman, trembling uncontrollably, and yet at the same time detached, aware, aware of every sound outside.

To her it meant nothing except that she gave herself to him. And at length he ceased to quiver any more, and lay quite still, quite still. Then, with dim, compassionate fingers, she stroked his head, that lay on her breast.

When he rose, he kissed both her hands, then both her feet, in their suède slippers, and in silence went away to the end of the room, where he stood with his back to her. There was silence for some minutes. Then he turned and came to her again as she sat in her old place by the fire.

'And now, I suppose you'll hate me!' he said in a quiet, inevitable way. She looked up at him quickly.

'Why should I?' she asked.

'They mostly do,' he said; then **he caught himself up**[1]. 'I mean...a woman is supposed to.'

'This is the last moment when I ought to hate you,' she said resentfully.

'I know! I know! It should be so! You're frightfully good to me...' he cried miserably.

She wondered why he should be miserable. 'Won't you sit down again?' she said. He glanced at the door.

'Sir Clifford!' he said, 'won't he...won't he be...?' She paused a moment to consider. 'Perhaps!' she said. And she looked up at him. 'I don't want Clifford to know not even to suspect. It would hurt him so much. But I don't think it's wrong, do you?'

[1]他中断了自己的话。

'Wrong! Good God, no! You're only too infinitely good to me...I can hardly bear it.'

He turned aside, and she saw that in another moment he would be sobbing.

'But we needn't let Clifford know, need we?' she pleaded. 'It would hurt him so. And if he never knows, never suspects, it hurts nobody.'

'Me! ' he said, almost fiercely; 'he'll know nothing from me! You see if he does. **Me give myself away**[1] ! Ha! Ha! ' he laughed hollowly, cynically, at such an idea. She watched him in wonder. He said to her: 'May I kiss your hand arid go? I'll run into Sheffield I think, and lunch there, if I may, and be back to tea. May I do anything for you? May I be sure you don't hate me? — and that you won't?' — he ended with a desperate note of cynicism.

'No, I don't hate you,' she said. 'I think you're nice.'

'Ah! ' he said to her fiercely, 'I'd rather you said that to me than said you love me! It means such a lot more...Till afternoon then. I've plenty to think about till then.' He kissed her hands humbly and was gone.

'I don't think I can stand that young man,' said Clifford at lunch.

'Why?' asked Connie.

'He's such a bounder underneath his veneer...just waiting to bounce us.'

'I think people have been so unkind to him,' said Connie.

'Do you wonder? And do you think he employs his shining hours doing deeds of kindness?'

'I think he has a certain sort of generosity.'

'Towards whom?'

'I don't quite know.'

'Naturally you don't. I'm afraid you mistake unscrupulousness for generosity.'

Connie paused. Did she? It was just possible. Yet the unscrupulousness of Michaelis had a certain fascination for her. **He went whole lengths where Clifford only crept a few timid paces**[2]. In his way he had conquered the world, which was what Clifford wanted to do. Ways and means...? Were those of Michaelis

[1]我竟然会出卖自己。Me(口语)。[2]他已经跨越了整个历程，而克利福德则刚刚迈出了几小步。

more despicable than those of Clifford? Was the way the poor outsider had shoved and bounced himself forward in person, and by the back doors, any worse than Clifford's way of advertising himself into prominence? **The bitch-goddess, Success, was trailed by thousands of gasping, dogs with lolling tongues**❶. The one that got her first was the real dog among dogs, if you go by success! So Michaelis could keep his tail up.

The queer thing was, he didn't. He came back towards tea-time with a large handful of violets and lilies, and the same hang-dog expression. Connie wondered sometimes if it were a sort of mask to disarm opposition, because it was almost too fixed. Was he really such a sad dog?

His sad-dog sort of extinguished self persisted all the evening, though through it Clifford felt the inner effrontery. Connie didn't feel it, perhaps because it was not directed against women; only against men, and their presumptions and assumptions. That indestructible, inward effrontery in the meagre fellow was what made men so down on Michaelis. **His very presence was an affront to a man of society, cloak it as he might in an assumed good manner**❷.

Connie was in love with him, but she managed to sit with her embroidery and let the men talk, and not give herself away. As for Michaelis, he was perfect; exactly the same melancholic, attentive, aloof young fellow of the previous evening, millions of degrees remote from his hosts, but **laconically playing up to them to the required amount, and never coming forth to them for a moment**❸. Connie felt he must have forgotten the morning. He had not forgotten. But he knew where he was...in the same old place outside, where the born outsiders are. He didn't take the love-making altogether personally. He knew it would not change him from an ownerless dog, whom everybody begrudges its golden collar, into a comfortable society dog.

The final fact being that at the very bottom of his soul he was an outsider, and anti-social, and he accepted the fact inwardly, no matter

❶成功，这个婊子女神，有数不清的吐着舌头喘着气的狗在追逐她。❷只要他一出面，对上流社会的人都是一种侮辱，不管他伪装得多么斯文。❸在说话上对他们礼到为止，绝不大献殷勤。

how Bond-Streety he was on the outside. His isolation was a necessity to him; just as the appearance of conformity and mixing-in with the smart people was also a necessity.

But occasional love, as a comfort arid soothing, was also a good thing, and he was not ungrateful. On the contrary, he was burningly, poignantly grateful for a piece of natural, spontaneous kindness: almost to tears. Beneath his pale, immobile, disillusioned face, his child's soul was sobbing with gratitude to the woman, and burning to come to her again; just as his outcast soul was knowing he would **keep really clear of her**[1].

He found an opportunity to say to her, as they were lighting the candles in the hall:

'May I come?'

'I'll come to you,' she said.

'Oh, good!'

He waited for her a long time...but she came.

He was the trembling excited sort of lover, whose crisis soon came, and was finished. There was something curiously childlike and defenceless about his naked body: as children are naked. His defences were all in his wits and cunning, his very instincts of cunning, and when these were in abeyance he seemed doubly naked and like a child, of unfinished, tender flesh, and somehow struggling helplessly.

He roused in the woman a wild sort of compassion and yearning, and a wild, craving physical desire. The physical desire he did not satisfy in her; he was always come and finished so quickly, then shrinking down on her breast, and **recovering somewhat his effrontery while she lay dazed, disappointed, lost**[2].

But then she soon learnt to hold him, to keep him there inside her when his crisis was over. And there he was generous and curiously potent; he stayed firm inside her, giving to her, while she was active... wildly, passionately active, coming to her own crisis. And as he felt the frenzy of her achieving her own orgasmic satisfaction from his hard, erect passivity, he had a curious sense of pride and satisfaction.

'Ah, how good!' she whispered tremulously, and she became quite still, clinging to him. And he lay there in his own isolation, but

❶实在不应与她纠缠。 ❷恢复他的厚颜无耻，而她则茫然，失望，不知所措。

somehow proud.

He stayed that time only the three days, and to Clifford was exactly the same as on the first evening; to Connie also. **There was no breaking down his external man**[1].

He wrote to Connie with the same plaintive melancholy note as ever, sometimes witty, and touched with a queer, sexless affection. A kind of hopeless affection he seemed to feel for her, and the essential remoteness remained the same. He was hopeless at the very core of him, and he wanted to be hopeless. He rather hated hope. '**Une immense espérance a traversé la terre**[2]', he read somewhere, and his comment was: ' — and it's darned-well drowned everything worth having.'

Connie never really understood him, but, in her way, she loved him. And all the time she felt the reflection of his hopelessness in her. She couldn't quite, quite love in hopelessness. And he, being hopeless, couldn't ever quite love at all.

So they went on for quite a time, writing, and meeting occasionally in London. She still wanted the physical, sexual thrill she could get with him by her own activity, **his little orgasm being over**[3]. And he still wanted to give it her. Which was enough to keep them connected.

And enough to give her a subtle sort of self-assurance, something blind and a little arrogant[4]. It was an almost mechanical confidence in her own powers, and went with a great cheerfulness.

She was terrifically cheerful at Wragby. And she used all her aroused cheerfulness and satisfaction to stimulate Clifford, so that he wrote his best at this time, and was almost happy in his strange blind way. He really reaped the fruits of the sensual satisfaction she got out of Michaelis' male passivity erect inside her. But of course he never knew it, and if he had, he wouldn't have said thank you!

Yet when those days of her grand joyful cheerfulness and stimulus were gone, quite gone, and she was depressed and irritable, how Clifford longed for them again! Perhaps if he'd known he might even have wished to get her and Michaelis together again.

❶他在外表上丝毫没有任何暴露。 ❷(法)"一个巨大的希望越过了大地。" ❸短暂的快感过后。 ❹这足以使她产生一丝自信,产生某种盲目而稍有自大的心理。

CHAPTER 4

Connie always had a foreboding of the hopelessness of her affair with Mick, as people called him. Yet other men seemed to mean nothing to her. She was attached to Clifford. He wanted a good deal of her life and she gave it to him. But she wanted a good deal from the life of a man, and this Clifford did not give her; could not. **There were occasional spasms of Michaelis** ❶. But, as she knew by foreboding, that would come to an end. Mick couldn't keep anything up. It was part of his very being that he must break off any connexion, and be loose, isolated, absolutely lone dog again. It was his major necessity, even though he always said: She turned me down!

The world is supposed to be full of possibilities, but they narrow down to pretty few in most personal experience. There's lots of good fish in the sea...maybe...but the vast masses seem to be mackerel or herring, and if you're not mackerel or herring yourself you are likely to find very few good fish in the sea.

Clifford was making strides into fame, and even money. People came to see him. Connie nearly always had somebody at Wragby. But if they weren't mackerel they were herring, with an occasional cat-fish, or conger-eel.

There were a few regular men, constants; men who had been at Cambridge with Clifford. There was Tommy Dukes, who had remained in the army, and was a Brigadier-General. 'The army leaves me time to think, and saves me from having to face the battle of life,' he said.

There was Charles May, an Irishman, who wrote scientifically about stars. There was Hammond, another writer. All were about the same age as Clifford; the young intellectuals of the day. They all believed in the life of the mind. What you did apart from that was your private affair, and didn't much matter. No one thinks of inquiring of an other person at what hour **he retires to the privy**❷. It isn't interesting to anyone but the person concerned.

❶她偶尔与米凯利斯亲热一番。❷上厕所。

And so with most of the matters of ordinary life...how you make your money, or whether you love your wife, or **if you have 'affairs'** ❶. All these matters concern only the person concerned, and, like going to the privy, have no interest for anyone else.

'The whole point about the sexual problem,' said Hammond, who was a tall thin fellow with a wife and two children, but **much more closely connected with a typewriter**❷, 'is that there is no point to it. Strictly there is no problem. We don't want to follow a man into the W.C., so why should we want to follow him into bed with a woman? And therein lies the problem. If we took no more notice of the one thing than the other, there'd be no problem. It's all utterly senseless and pointless; a matter of misplaced curiosity.'

'Quite, Hammond, quite! But **if someone starts making love to Julia**❸, you begin to simmer; and if he goes on, you are soon at boiling point.'...Julia was Hammond's wife.

'Why, exactly! So I should be if he began to urinate in a corner of my drawing-room. There's a place for all these things.'

'You mean you wouldn't mind if he made love to Julia in some discreet alcove?'

Charlie May was slightly satirical, for he had flirted a very little with Julia, and Hammond had **cut up very roughly**❹.

'Of course I should mind. Sex is a private thing between me and Julia; and of course I should mind anyone else trying to mix in.'

'As a matter of fact,' said the lean and freckled Tommy Dukes, who looked much more Irish than May, who was pale and rather fat: 'As a matter of fact, Hammond, you have a strong property instinct, and a strong will to self-assertion, and you want success. Since I've been in the army definitely, I've got out of the way of the world, and now I see how inordinately strong the craving for self-assertion and success is in men. It is enormously overdeveloped. All our individuality has run that way. And of course men like you think you'll get through better with a woman's backing. That's why you're so jealous. That's what sex is to you...a vital little dynamo between you and Julia, to bring success. If you began to be unsuccessful you'd begin to flirt, like Charlie, who isn't

❶你是否有"外遇"。 ❷与一位打字员关系暧昧。 ❸make love to在当时指向某人求爱,如今则是"和……发生性行为"。 ❹粗暴地扼杀,阻止。

successful. Married people like you and Julia have labels on you, like travellers' trunks. Julia is labelled Mrs Arnold B. Hammond — just like a trunk on the railway that belongs to somebody. And you are labelled Arnold B. Hammond, **c/o**[1] Mrs Arnold B. Hammond. Oh, you're quite right, you're quite right! The life of the mind needs a comfortable house and decent cooking. You're quite right. It even needs posterity. But it all hinges on the instinct for success. That is the pivot on which all things turn.'

Hammond looked rather piqued. He was rather proud of the integrity of his mind, and of his not being a **time-server**[2]. None the less, he did want success.

'It's quite true, you can't live without cash,' said May. 'You've got to have a certain amount of it to be able to live and get along...even to be free to think you must have a certain amount of money, or your stomach stops you. But it seems to me you might leave the labels off sex. We're free to talk to anybody; so why shouldn't we be free to make love to any woman who inclines us that way?'

'There speaks the **lascivious Celt**[3],' said Clifford.

'Lascivious! well, why not — ? I can't see I do a woman any more harm by sleeping with her than by dancing with her...or even talking to her about the weather. It's just an interchange of sensations instead of ideas, so why not?'

'Be as promiscuous as the rabbits!' said Hammond.

'Why not? What's wrong with rabbits? Are they any worse than a neurotic, revolutionary humanity, full of nervous hate?'

'But we're not rabbits, even so,' said Hammond.

'Precisely! I have my mind: I have certain calculations to make in certain astronomical matters that concern me almost more than life or death. Sometimes indigestion interferes with me. Hunger would interfere with me disastrously. In the same way starved sex interferes with me. What then?'

'I should have thought sexual indigestion from surfeit would have interfered with you more seriously,' said Hammond satirically.

'Not it! I don't over-eat myself and I don't over-fuck myself. One has a choice about eating too much. But you would absolutely starve me.'

①是"care of"的缩写形式，意为"转交"。 ②随波逐流的人，趋炎附势者。 ③好色的凯尔特人。

'Not at all! You can marry.'

'How do you know I can? It may not suit the process of my mind. Marriage might...and would...stultify my mental processes. I'm not properly pivoted that way...and so must I be chained in a kennel like a monk? **All rot and funk**[1], my boy. I must live and do my calculations. I need women sometimes. **I refuse to make a mountain of it**[2], and I refuse anybody's moral condemnation or prohibition. I'd be ashamed to see a woman walking around with my name-label on her, address and railway station, like a wardrobe trunk.'

These two men had not forgiven each other about the Julia flirtation.

'It's an amusing idea, Charlie,' said Dukes, 'that sex is just another form of talk, where you act the words instead of saying them. I suppose it's quite true. I suppose we might exchange as many sensations and emotions with women as we do ideas about the weather, and so on. Sex might be a sort of normal physical conversation between a man and a woman. You don't talk to a woman unless you have ideas in common: that is you don't talk with any interest. And in the same way, unless you had some emotion or sympathy in common with a woman you wouldn't sleep with her. But if you had...'

'If you have the proper sort of emotion or sympathy with a woman, you ought to sleep with her,' said May. 'It's the only decent thing, to go to bed with her. Just as, when you are interested talking to someone, the only decent thing is to have the talk out. You don't prudishly put your tongue between your teeth and bite it. You just say out your say. And the same the other way.'

'No,' said Hammond. 'It's wrong. You, for example, May, you squander half your force with women. You'll never really do what you should do, with a fine mind such as yours. **Too much of it goes the other way**[3].'

'Maybe it does...and too little of you goes that way, Hammond, my boy, married or not. You can keep the purity and integrity of your mind, but it's going damned dry. Your pure mind is going as dry as fiddlesticks, from what I see of it. **You're simply talking it down**[4].'

Tommy Dukes burst into a laugh.

[1]一派胡言乱语。 [2]我没对小题大做。 [3]你在拈花惹草方面费得心思太多了。 [4]越说你的心灵越干涸。

'**Go it, you two minds**[1]!' he said. 'Look at me...I don't do any high and pure mental work, nothing but jot down a few ideas. And yet I neither marry nor run after women. I think Charlie's quite right; if he wants to run after the women, he's quite free not to run too often. But I wouldn't prohibit him from running. As for Hammond, he's got a property instinct, **so naturally the straight road and the narrow gate are right for him**[2]. You'll see he'll be **an English Man of Letters**[3] before he's done. A.B.C. from top to toe. Then there's me. I'm nothing. Just a squib. And what about you, Clifford? Do you think sex is a dynamo to help a man on to success in the world?'

Clifford rarely talked much at these times. He never held forth; his ideas were really not vital enough for it, he was too confused and emotional. Now he blushed and looked uncomfortable.

'Well!' he said, 'being myself **hors de combat**[4], I don't see I've anything to say on the matter.'

'Not at all,' said Dukes; 'the top of you's by no means hors de combat. You've got the life of the mind sound and intact. So let us hear your ideas.'

'Well,' stammered Clifford, 'even then I don't suppose I have much idea...I suppose **marry-and-have-done-with-it**[5] would pretty well stand for what I think. Though of course between a man and woman who care for one another, it is a great thing.'

'What sort of great thing?' said Tommy.

'Oh...it perfects the intimacy,' said Clifford, uneasy as a woman in such talk.

'Well, Charlie and I believe that sex is a sort of communication like speech. Let any woman start a sex conversation with me, and it's natural for me to go to bed with her to finish it, **all in due season**[6]. Unfortunately no woman makes any particular start with me, so I go to bed by myself; and am none the worse for it...I hope so, anyway, for how should I know? Anyhow I've no starry calculations to be interfered with, and no immortal works to write. I'm merely a fellow skulking in the army...'

---

①加油，你们这两个色鬼。 ②因此，循规蹈矩自然是对的，另参阅"Straight is the gate,and narrow is the way, which leadth unto life."《圣经·马太》。 ③一位美国文豪。 ④(法)伤残的，置身于论战之外。 ⑤结婚完事。 ⑥时机成熟时。

Silence fell. The four men smoked. And Connie sat there and put another stitch in her sewing...Yes, she sat there! She had to sit mum. She had to be quiet as a mouse, not to interfere with the immensely important speculations of these highly-mental gentlemen. But she had to be there. They didn't get on so well without her; their ideas didn't flow so freely. Clifford was much more hedgy and nervous, he got cold feet much quicker in Connie's absence, and the talk didn't run. **Tommy Dukes came off best**[1]; he was a little inspired by her presence. Hammond she didn't really like; he seemed so selfish in a mental way. And Charles May, though she liked something about him, seemed a little distasteful and messy, in spite of his stars.

How many evenings had Connie sat and listened to the manifestations of these four men! these, and one or two others. That they never seemed to get anywhere didn't trouble her deeply. She liked to hear what they had to say, especially when Tommy was there. It was fun. Instead of men kissing you, and touching you with their bodies, they revealed their minds to you. It was great fun! But what cold minds!

And also it was a little irritating. She had more respect for Michaelis, on whose name they all poured such withering contempt, as a little mongrel arriviste, and uneducated bounder of the worst sort. **Mongrel and bounder or not**[2], he jumped to his own conclusions. He didn't merely walk round them with millions of words, in the parade of the life of the mind.

Connie quite liked the life of the mind, and got a great thrill out of it. But she did think it overdid itself a little. She loved being there, amidst the tobacco smoke of those famous evenings of the cronies, as she called them privately to herself. She was infinitely amused, and proud too, that even their talking they could not do, without her silent presence. She had an immense respect for thought...and these men, at least, tried to think honestly. But somehow there was **a cat**[3], and it wouldn't jump. They all alike talked at something, though what it was, for the life of her she couldn't say. It was something that Mick didn't clear, either.

But then Mick wasn't trying to do anything, but just get through his

[1]汤米·杜克斯表现最出色。 [2]杂种也好，无赖也好。 [3]此处是“一个秘密”的含义，出自习语“let the cat out of the bag”(泄密)。

life, and **put as much across other people as they tried to put across him**[1]. He was really anti-social, which was what Clifford and his cronies had against him. Clifford and his cronies were not anti-social; they were more or less bent on saving mankind, or on instructing it, to say the least.

There was a gorgeous talk on Sunday evening, when the conversation drifted again to love.

'Blest be the tie that binds

Our hearts in kindred something-or-other' —

said Tommy Dukes. 'I'd like to know what the tie is...The tie that binds us just now is mental friction on one another. And, apart from that, there's damned little tie between us. We bust apart, and say spiteful things about one another, like all the other damned intellectuals in the world. Damned everybodies, as far as that goes, for they all do it. Else we bust apart, and cover up the spiteful things we feel against one another by saying false sugaries. It's a curious thing that the mental life seems to flourish with its roots in spite, ineffable and fathomless spite. Always has been so! Look at **Socrates**, **in Plato**[2], and his bunch round him! The sheer spite of it all, just sheer joy in pulling somebody else to bits...**Protagoras**[3], or whoever it was! And **Alcibiades**[4], and all the other little disciple dogs joining in the fray! I must say it makes one prefer Buddha, quietly sitting under **a bo-tree**[5], or Jesus, telling his disciples little Sunday stories, peacefully, and without any mental fireworks. No, there's something wrong with the mental life, radically. It's rooted in spite and envy, envy and spite. Ye shall know the tree by its fruit.'

'I don't think we're altogether so spiteful,' protested Clifford.

'My dear Clifford, think of the way we talk each other over, all of us. I'm rather worse than anybody else, myself. Because I infinitely prefer the spontaneous spite to the concocted sugaries; now they are poison; when I begin saying what a fine fellow Clifford is, etc., etc., then poor Clifford is to be pitied. For God's sake, all of you, say spiteful things about me, then I shall know I mean something to you. Don't say sugaries, or I'm done.'

---

[1]别人怎么愚弄他，他就怎么愚弄别人。 [2]苏格拉底(469—399BC)、柏拉图(427—347BC)均为古希腊哲学家。 [3]普罗泰哥拉 (490—420BC)，古希腊哲学家，教师和诡辩学家。 [4]亚西比德(450—404BC)，雅典政治家，伯罗奔尼撒战争中的将领。 [5]菩提树。

'Oh, but I do think we honestly like one another,' said Hammond. 'I tell you we must...we say such spiteful things to one another, about one another, behind our backs! I'm the worst.'

'And I do think you confuse the mental life with the critical activity. I agree with you, Socrates gave the critical activity a grand start, but he did more than that,' said Charlie May, rather magisterially. The cronies had such a curious pomposity under their assumed modesty. It was all so **ex cathedra**[1], and it all pretended to be so humble.

Dukes refused to be drawn about Socrates.

'That's quite true, criticism and knowledge are not the same thing,' said Hammond.

'They aren't, of course,' chimed in Berry, a brown, shy young man, who had called to see Dukes, and was staying the night.

They all looked at him as if **the ass had spoken**[2].

'I wasn't talking about knowledge...I was talking about the mental life,' laughed Dukes. 'Real knowledge comes out of the whole corpus of the consciousness; out of your belly and your penis as much as out of your brain and mind. The mind can only analyse and rationalize. **Set the mind and the reason to cock it over the rest, and all they can do is to criticize, and make a deadness**[3]. I say all they can do. It is vastly important. My God, the world needs criticizing today...criticizing to death. Therefore let's live the mental life, and glory in our spite, and strip the rotten old show. But, mind you, it's like this: while you live your life, you are in some way an organic whole with all life. But once you start the mental life you pluck the apple. You've severed the connexion between, the apple and the tree: the organic connexion. And if you've got nothing in your life but the mental life, then you yourself are a plucked apple...you've fallen off the tree. And then it is a logical necessity to be spiteful, just as it's a natural necessity for a plucked apple to go bad.'

Clifford made big eyes: it was all stuff to him. Connie secretly laughed to herself.

'Well then we're all plucked apples,' said Hammond, rather acidly

---

❶(拉丁)有权威的,权威性的。 ❷语出《旧约·民权记》中的(巴兰的驴子),巴兰骑驴途中看见天使拉在路上,便停下来,驴子开口非人语,责怪主人打它。 ❸让心灵和理智高于其他一切的话,它们能做的一切仅仅是批评,致命的批评。

and petulantly.

'So let's make cider of ourselves,' said Charlie.

'But what do you think of **Bolshevism**[1]?' put in the brown Berry, as if everything had led up to it.

'Bravo!' roared Charlie. 'What do you think of Bolshevism?'

'Come on! **Let's make hay of Bolshevism**[2]!' said Dukes.

'I'm afraid Bolshevism is a large question,' said Hammond, shaking his head seriously.

'Bolshevism, it seems to me,' said Charlie, 'is just a superlative hatred of the thing they call the bourgeois; and what the bourgeois is, isn't quite defined. It is Capitalism, among other things. Feelings and emotions are also so decidedly bourgeois that you have to invent a man without them.

'Then the individual, especially the personal man, is bourgeois: so he must be suppressed. You must submerge yourselves in the greater thing, the Soviet-social thing. Even an organism is bourgeois: so the ideal must be mechanical. The only thing that is a unit, non-organic, composed of many different, yet equally essential parts, is the machine. Each man a machine-part, and the driving power of the machine, hate... hate of the bourgeois. That, to me, is Bolshevism.'

'Absolutely!' said Tommy. 'But also, it seems to me a perfect description of the whole of the industrial ideal. It's the factory-owner's ideal **in a nut-shell**[3]; except that he would deny that the driving power was hate. Hate it is, all the same; hate of life itself. Just look at these Midlands, if it isn't plainly written up...but it's all part of the life of the mind, it's a logical development.'

'I deny that Bolshevism is logical, it rejects the major part of the premisses,' said Hammond.

'My dear man, it allows the material premiss; so does the pure mind...exclusively.'

'**At least Bolshevism has got down to rock bottom**[4],' said Charlie.

'Rock bottom! The bottom that has no bottom! The Bolshevists will have the finest army in the world in a very short time, with the finest mechanical equipment.

'But this thing can't go on...this hate business. There must be a

[1]布尔什维克主义。[2]让布尔什维克主义见鬼去吧！[3]简单地说。[4]至少布尔什维克已经做到极限。

reaction...' said Hammond.

'Well, we've been waiting for years...we wait longer. Hate's a growing thing like anything else. It's the inevitable outcome of forcing ideas on to life, of forcing one's deepest instincts; our deepest feelings we force according to certain ideas. We drive ourselves with a formula, like a machine. **The logical mind pretends to rule the roost, and the roost turns into pure hate**[1]. We're all Bolshevists, only we are hypocrites. The Russians are Bolshevists without hypocrisy.'

'But there are many other ways,' said Hammond, 'than the Soviet way. The Bolshevists aren't really intelligent.'

'Of course not. But sometimes it's intelligent to be half-witted: if you want to make your end. Personally, I consider Bolshevism half-witted; but so do I consider our social life in the west half-witted. So I even consider our far-famed mental life half-witted. We're all as cold as cretins, we're all as passionless as idiots. We're all of us Bolshevists, only we give it another name. We think we're gods...men like gods! It's just the same as Bolshevism. One has to be human, and have a heart and a penis if one is going to escape being either a god or a Bolshevist...for they are the same thing: they're both too good to be true.'

Out of the disapproving silence came Berry's anxious question:

'You do believe in love then, Tommy, don't you?'

'You lovely lad!' said Tommy. 'No, my cherub, nine times out of ten, no! Love's another of those half-witted performances today. Fellows with swaying waists fucking little jazz girls with small boy buttocks, like two collar studs! Do you mean that sort of love? Or the joint-property, make-a-success-of-it, My-husband-my-wife sort of love? No, my fine fellow, I don't believe in it at all!'

'But you do believe in something?'

'Me? Oh, intellectually I believe in having a good heart, a chirpy penis, a lively intelligence, and the courage to say "shit!" in front of a lady.'

'Well, you've got them all,' said Berry.

Tommy Dukes roared with laughter. 'You angel boy! If only I had! If only I had! No; my heart's as numb as a potato, my penis

[1] 有逻辑思维的人以为自己可以领导一切，可领导的结果却导致全然的仇恨。

droops and never lifts its head up, I dare rather cut him clean off than say "shit!" in front of my mother or my aunt...they are real ladies, mind you; and I'm not really intelligent, I'm only **a "mental-lifer"**[1]. It would be wonderful to be intelligent: then one would be alive in all the parts mentioned and unmentionable. The penis rouses his head and says: How do you do? — to any really intelligent person. **Renoir**[2] said he painted his pictures with his penis...he did too, lovely pictures! I wish I did something with mine. God! when one can only talk! Another torture added to **Hades**[3]! And Socrates started it.'

'There are nice women in the world,' said Connie, lifting her head up and speaking at last.

The men resented it...she should have pretended to hear nothing. They hated her admitting she had attended so closely to such talk.

'My God! "If they be not nice to me **What care I how nice they be**[4]?"

'No, it's hopeless! I just simply can't vibrate in unison with a woman. There's no woman I can really want when I'm faced with her, and I'm not going to start forcing myself to it...My God, no! I'll remain as I am, and lead the mental life. It's the only honest thing I can do. I can be quite happy talking to women; but it's all pure, hopelessly pure. Hopelessly pure! What do you say, **Hildebrand**[5], my **chicken**[6]?'

'It's much less complicated if one stays pure,' said Berry.

'Yes, life is all too simple!'

CHAPTER 5

On a frosty morning with a little February sun, Clifford and Connie went for a walk across the park to the wood. That is, Clifford chuffed in his motor-chair, and Connie walked beside him.

The hard air was still sulphurous, but they were both used to it. Round the near horizon went the haze, **opalescent with frost and**

①精神生活者。 ②雷诺阿(1894—1979),法国电影导演。 ③(希神)阴间,冥府。 ④天啊!如果她们对我不好,我何必在意她们是否够好。 ⑤希尔德布兰德,即是意大利籍教皇圣·格列高利七世(St.Gregory, 1020—1085)。 ⑥此处是"年轻人"的意思。

smoke[1], and on the top lay the small blue sky; so that it was like being inside an enclosure, always inside. Life always a dream or a frenzy, inside an enclosure.

The sheep coughed in the rough, sere grass of the park, where frost lay bluish in the sockets of the tufts. Across the park ran a path to the wood-gate, a fine ribbon of pink. Clifford had had it newly gravelled with sifted gravel from the pit-bank. When the rock and refuse of the underworld had burned and given off its sulphur, it turned bright pink, shrimp-coloured on dry days, darker, crab-coloured on wet. Now it was pale shrimp-colour, with a bluish-white hoar of frost. It always pleased Connie, this underfoot of sifted, bright pink. **It's an ill wind that brings nobody good**[2].

Clifford steered cautiously down the slope of the knoll from the hall, and Connie kept her hand on the chair. In front lay the wood, the hazel thicket nearest, the purplish density of oaks beyond. From the wood's edge rabbits bobbed and nibbled. Rooks suddenly rose in a black train, and went trailing off over the little sky.

Connie opened the wood-gate, and Clifford puffed slowly through into the broad riding that ran up an incline between the clean-whipped thickets of the hazel. The wood was a remnant of the great forest where **Robin Hood**[3] hunted, and this riding was an old, old thoroughfare coming across country. But now, of course, it was only a riding through the private wood. The road from Mansfield swerved round to the north.

In the wood everything was motionless, the old leaves on the ground keeping the frost on their underside. A jay called harshly, many little birds fluttered. But there was no game; no pheasants. They had been killed off during the war, and the wood had been left unprotected, till now Clifford had got his game-keeper again.

Clifford loved the wood; he loved the old oak-trees. He felt they were his own through generations. He wanted to protect them. He wanted this place inviolate, shut off from the world.

The chair chuffed slowly up the incline, rocking and jolting on the frozen clods. And suddenly, on the left, came a clearing where there was nothing but **a ravel of dead bracken**[4], a thin and spindly sapling leaning here and there, big sawn stumps, showing their tops and their

❶由霜和烟混合而成的乳白色浓雾。❷(谚)没有对所有人都有害的坏事,害于此者利于彼。❸罗宾汉,民间传说中劫富济贫的绿林好汉。❹一丛散乱的枯蕨草。

grasping roots, lifeless. And patches of blackness where the woodmen had burned the brushwood and rubbish.

This was one of the places that Sir Geoffrey had cut during the war for trench timber. The whole knoll, which rose softly on the right of the riding, was denuded and strangely forlorn. On the crown of the knoll where the oaks had stood, now was bareness; and from there you could look out over the trees to the colliery railway, and the new works at Stacks Gate. Connie had stood and looked, it was a breach in the pure seclusion of the wood. It let in the world. But she didn't tell Clifford.

This denuded place always made Clifford curiously angry. He had been through the war, had seen what it meant. But he didn't get really angry till he saw this bare hill. He was having it replanted. But it made him hate Sir Geoffrey.

Clifford sat with a fixed face as the chair slowly mounted. When they came to the top of the rise he stopped; he would not risk the long and very jolty down-slope. He sat looking at the greenish sweep of the riding downwards, a clear way through the bracken and oaks. It swerved at the bottom of the hill and disappeared; but it had such a lovely easy curve, **of knights riding and ladies on palfreys**[1].

'I consider this is really the heart of England,' said Clifford to Connie, as he sat there in the dim February sunshine.

'Do you?' she said, seating herself in her blue knitted dress, on a stump by the path.

'I do! this is the old England, the heart of it; and I intend to keep it intact.'

'Oh yes!' said Connie. But, as she said it she heard the eleven-o'clock hooters at Stacks Gate colliery. Clifford was too used to the sound to notice.

'I want this wood perfect...untouched. I want nobody to trespass in it,' said Clifford.

There was a certain pathos. The wood still had some of the mystery of wild, old England; but Sir Geoffrey's cuttings during the war had given it a blow. How still the trees were, with their crinkly, innumerable twigs against the sky, and their grey, obstinate trunks rising from the brown bracken! How safely the birds flitted among them! And once there had been deer, and archers, and monks padding along on asses.

[1]骑士和贵妇们骑马奔驰的情景。

The place remembered, still remembered.

Clifford sat in the pale sun, with the light on his smooth, rather blond hair, his reddish full face inscrutable.

'I mind more, not having a son, when I come here, than any other time,' he said.

'But the wood is older than your family,' said Connie gently.

'Quite!' said Clifford. 'But we've preserved it. Except for us it would go...it would be gone already, like the rest of the forest. One must preserve some of the old England!'

'Must one?' said Connie. 'If it has to be preserved, and preserved against the new England? It's sad, I know.'

'If some of the old England isn't preserved, there'll be no England at all,' said Clifford. 'And we who have this kind of property, and the feeling for it, must preserve it.'

There was a sad pause. 'Yes, for a little while,' said Connie.

'For a little while! It's all we can do. We can only do our bit. I feel every man of my family has done his bit here, since we've had the place. One may go against convention, but one must keep up tradition.' Again there was a pause.

'What tradition?' asked Connie.

'The tradition of England! of this!'

'Yes,' she said slowly.

'That's why having a son helps; one is only a link in a chain,' he said.

Connie was not keen on chains, but she said nothing. She was thinking of the curious impersonality of his desire for a son.

'I'm sorry we can't have a son,' she said.

He looked at her steadily, with his full, pale-blue eyes.

'It would almost be a good thing if you had a child by another man, he said. 'If we brought it up at Wragby, it would belong to us and to the place. I don't believe very intensely in fatherhood. If we had the child to rear, it would be our own, and it would carry on. Don't you think it's worth considering?'

Connie looked up at him at last. The child, her child, was just an 'it' to him. It...it...it!

'But what about the other man?' she asked.

'Does it matter very much? Do these things really affect us very deeply?...You had that lover in Germany...what is it now? Nothing almost. It seems to me that it isn't these little acts and little connexions we make in our lives that matter so very much. They pass away, and where are they? Where...Where are the snows of yesteryear?...It's what endures through one's life that matters; my own life matters to me, in its long continuance and development. But what do the occasional connexions matter? And the occasional sexual connexions especially! If people don't exaggerate them ridiculously, they pass like the mating of birds. And so they should. What does it matter? It's the life-long companionship that matters. It's the living together from day to day, not the sleeping together once or twice. You and I are married, no matter what happens to us. We have the habit of each other. And habit, to my thinking, is more vital than any occasional excitement. The long, slow, enduring thing...that's what we live by...not the occasional spasm of any sort. Little by little, living together, two people fall into a sort of unison, they vibrate so intricately to one another. That's the real secret of marriage, not sex; at least not the simple function of sex. You and I are interwoven in a marriage. If we stick to that we ought to be able to arrange this sex thing, as we arrange going to the dentist; **since fate has given us a checkmate physically there**①.'

Connie sat and listened in a sort of wonder, and a sort of fear. She did not know if he was right or not. There was Michaelis, whom she loved; so she said to herself. But her love was somehow **only an excursion from her marriage with Clifford**②; the long, slow habit of intimacy, formed through years of suffering and patience. Perhaps the human soul needs excursions, and must not be denied them. But the point of an excursion is that you come home again.

'And wouldn't you mind what man's child I had?' she asked.

'Why, Connie, I should trust your natural instinct of decency and selection. You just wouldn't let the wrong sort of fellow touch you.'

She thought of Michaelis! He was absolutely Clifford's idea of the wrong sort of fellow.

'But men and women may have different feelings about the wrong sort of fellow,' she said.

'No,' he replied. 'You care for me. **I don't believe you**

①由于命运已经破坏了我俩之间肉体上的结合。②仅仅是她与克利福德婚姻中的一段红杏出墙。

would ever care for a man who was purely antipathetic to me[1]. Your rhythm wouldn't let you.'

She was silent. Logic might be unanswerable because it was so absolutely wrong.

'**And should you expect me to tell you**[2]?' she asked, glancing up at him almost furtively.

'Not at all, I'd better not know...But you do agree with me, don't you, that the casual sex thing is nothing, compared to the long life lived together? Don't you think one can just subordinate the sex thing to the necessities of a long life? Just use it, **since that's what we're driven to**[3]? After all, do these temporary excitements matter? Isn't the whole problem of life the slow building up of an integral personality, through the years? living an integrated life? There's no point in a disintegrated life. If lack of sex is going to disintegrate you, then go out and have a love-affair. If lack of a child is going to disintegrate you, then have a child if you possibly can. But only do these things so that you have an integrated life, that makes a long harmonious thing. And you and I can do that together...don't you think?...if we adapt ourselves to the necessities, and at the same time weave the adaptation together into a piece with our steadily-lived life. Don't you agree?'

Connie was a little overwhelmed by his words. She knew he was right theoretically. But when she actually touched her steadily-lived life with him she...hesitated. Was it actually her destiny to go on weaving herself into his life all the rest of her life? Nothing else?

Was it just that? She was to be content to weave a steady life with him, all one fabric, **but perhaps brocaded with the occasional flower of an adventure**[4]. But how could she know what she would feel next year? How could one ever know? How could one say Yes? for years and years? The little yes, gone on a breath! Why should one be pinned down by that butterfly word? Of course it had to flutter away and be gone, to be followed by other yes's and no's! Like the straying of butterflies.

'I think you're right, Clifford. And as far as I can see I agree with you. Only life may turn quite a new face on it all.'

'But until life turns a new face on it all, you do agree?'

---

❶我相信你不会喜欢上一个我十分反感的人。 ❷倘若有了男人，你希望我告诉你吗？ ❸因为那是我们不得已而为之的。 ❹偶尔织出点冒险的花朵。

'Oh yes! I think I do, really.'

She was watching a brown spaniel that had run out of a side-path, and was looking towards them with lifted nose, making a soft, fluffy bark. A man with a gun strode swiftly, softly out after the dog, facing their way as if about to attack them; then stopped instead, saluted, and was turning downhill. It was only the new game-keeper, but he had frightened Connie, he seemed to emerge with such a swift menace. That was how she had seen him, like the sudden rush of a threat out of nowhere.

He was a man in dark green velveteens and gaiters...the old style, with a red face and red moustache and distant eyes. He was going quickly downhill.

'Mellors!' called Clifford.

The man faced lightly round, and saluted with a quick little gesture, a soldier!

'Will you turn the chair round and get it started? That makes it easier,' said Clifford.

The man at once slung his gun over his shoulder, and came forward with the same curious swift, yet soft movements, as if keeping invisible. He was moderately tall and lean, and was silent. He did not look at Connie at all, only at the chair.

'Connie, this is the new game-keeper, Mellors. You haven't spoken to her ladyship yet, Mellors?'

'No, Sir!' came the ready, neutral words.

The man lifted his hat as he stood, showing his thick, almost fair hair. He stared straight into Connie's eyes, with a perfect, fearless, impersonal look, as if he wanted to see what she was like. He made her feel shy. She bent her head to him shyly, and he changed his hat to his left hand and made her a slight bow, like a gentleman; but he said nothing at all. He remained for a moment still, with his hat in his hand.

'But you've been here some time, haven't you?' Connie said to him.

'Eight months, Madam...your Ladyship!' he corrected himself calmly.

'And do you like it?'

She looked him in the eyes. His eyes narrowed a little, with irony, perhaps with impudence.

'Why, yes, thank you, your Ladyship! I was reared here...'

He gave another slight bow, turned, put his hat on, and strode to take hold of the chair. His voice on the last words had fallen into the heavy broad drag of the dialect...perhaps also in mockery, because there had been no trace of dialect before. He might almost be a gentleman. Anyhow, he was a curious, quick, separate fellow, alone, but sure of himself.

Clifford started the little engine, the man carefully turned the chair, and set it nose-forwards to the incline that curved gently to the dark hazel thicket.

'Is that all then, Sir Clifford?' asked the man.

'No, you'd better come along **in case she sticks**[1]. The engine isn't really strong enough for the uphill work.' The man glanced round for his dog...a thoughtful glance. The spaniel looked at him and faintly moved its tail. A little smile, mocking or teasing her, yet gentle, came into his eyes for a moment, then faded away, and his face was expressionless. They went fairly quickly down the slope, the man with his hand on the rail of the chair, steadying it. He looked like a free soldier rather than a servant. And something about him reminded Connie of Tommy Dukes.

When they came to the hazel grove, Connie suddenly ran forward, and opened the gate into the park. As she stood holding it, the two men looked at her in passing, Clifford critically, the other man with a curious, cool wonder; impersonally wanting to see what she looked like. And she saw in his blue, impersonal eyes a look of suffering and detachment, yet a certain warmth. But why was he so aloof, apart?

Clifford stopped the chair, once through the gate, and the man came quickly, courteously, to close it.

'Why did you run to open?' asked Clifford in his quiet, calm voice, that showed he was displeased. 'Mellors would have done it.'

'I thought you would go straight ahead,' said Connie. 'And leave you to run after us?' said Clifford.

'Oh, well, I like to run sometimes!'

Mellors took the chair again, looking perfectly unheeding, yet Connie felt he noted everything. As he pushed the chair up the steepish rise of the knoll in the park, he breathed rather quickly, through parted lips. He was rather frail really. Curiously full of vitality, but a little frail

[1] 万一这辆车给卡住，(she指代the chair)。

and quenched. Her woman's instinct sensed it.

Connie fell back, let the chair go on. The day had greyed over; the small blue sky that had poised low on its circular rims of haze was closed in again, the lid was down, there was a raw coldness. It was going to snow. All grey, all grey! the world looked worn out.

The chair waited at the top of the pink path. Clifford looked round for Connie.

'Not tired, are you?' he said.

'Oh, no! ' she said.

But she was. A strange, weary yearning, a dissatisfaction had started in her. Clifford did not notice: those were not things he was aware of. But the stranger knew. To Connie, everything in her world and life seemed worn out, and her dissatisfaction was older than the hills.

They came to the house, and around to the back, where there were no steps. Clifford managed to swing himself over on to the low, wheeled house-chair; he was very strong and agile with his arms. Then Connie lifted the burden of his dead legs after him.

The keeper, waiting at attention to be dismissed, watched everything narrowly, missing nothing. He went pale, with a sort of fear, when he saw Connie lifting the inert legs of the man in her arms, into the other chair, Clifford pivoting round as she did so. He was frightened.

'Thanks, then, for the help, Mellors,' said Clifford casually, as he began to wheel down the passage to the servants' quarters.

'Nothing else, Sir?' came the neutral voice, like one in a dream.

'Nothing, good morning! '

'Good morning, Sir.'

'Good morning! it was kind of you to push the chair up that hill...I hope it wasn't heavy for you,' said Connie, looking back at the keeper outside the door.

His eyes came to hers in an instant, as if wakened up. He was aware of her.

'Oh no, not heavy! ' he said quickly. Then his voice dropped again into the broad sound of the vernacular: 'Good mornin' to your Ladyship! '

'Who is your game-keeper?' Connie asked at lunch.

'Mellors! You saw him,' said Clifford.

'Yes, but where did he come from?'

'Nowhere! He was a Tevershall boy...son of a collier, I believe.'

'And was he a collier himself?'

'Blacksmith on the pit-bank, I believe: overhead smith. But he was keeper here for two years before the war...before he joined up. My father always had a good opinion of him, so when he came back, and went to the pit for a blacksmith's job, I just took him back here as keeper. I was really very glad to get him...its almost impossible to find a good man round here for a gamekeeper...and it needs a man who knows the people.'

'And isn't he married?'

'He was. But his wife went off with...with various men...but finally with a collier at Stacks Gate, and I believe she's living there still.'

'So this man is alone?'

'More or less! He has a mother in the village...and a child, I believe.'

Clifford looked at Connie, with his pale, slightly prominent blue eyes, in which a certain vagueness was coming. He seemed alert in the foreground, but the background was like the Midlands atmosphere, haze, smoky mist. And the haze seemed to be creeping forward. So when he stared at Connie in his peculiar way, giving her his peculiar, precise information, she felt all the background of his mind filling up with mist, with nothingness. And it frightened her. It made him seem impersonal, almost to idiocy.

And dimly she realized one of the great laws of the human soul: **that when the emotional soul receives a wounding shock, which does not kill the body, the soul seems to recover as the body recovers**[1]. But this is only appearance. It is really only the mechanism of the re-assumed habit. Slowly, slowly the wound to the soul begins to make itself felt, like a bruise, which only slowly deepens its terrible ache, till it fills all the psyche. And when we think we have recovered and forgotten, it is then that the terrible after-effects have to be encountered at their worst.

So it was with Clifford. Once he was 'well', once he was back at Wragby, and writing his stories, and feeling sure of life, in spite of all, he seemed to forget, and to have recovered all his equanimity. But now,

[1] 当充满情感的灵魂受到伤害性打击时，若肉体未为打击所毁，随着肉体的康复，灵魂亦会痊愈。

as the years went by, slowly, slowly, Connie felt the bruise of fear and horror coming up, and spreading in him. For a time it had been so deep as to be numb, as it were non-existent. Now slowly it began to assert itself in a spread of fear, almost paralysis. Mentally he still was alert. But the paralysis, the bruise of the too-great shock, was gradually spreading in his affective self.

And as it spread in him, Connie felt it spread in her. An inward dread, an emptiness, an indifference to everything gradually spread in her soul. When Clifford was roused, he could still talk brilliantly and, as it were, command the future: as when, in the wood, he talked about her having a child, and giving an heir to Wragby. But the day after, all the brilliant words seemed like dead leaves, crumpling up and turning to powder, meaning really nothing, blown away on any gust of wind. They were not the leafy words of an effective life, young with energy and belonging to the tree. They were the hosts of fallen leaves of a life that is ineffectual.

So it seemed to her everywhere. The colliers at Tevershall were talking again of a strike, and it seemed to Connie there again it was not a manifestation of energy, it was the bruise of the war that had been in abeyance, slowly rising to the surface and creating the great ache of unrest, and stupor of discontent. The bruise was deep, deep, deep...the bruise of the false inhuman war. It would take many years for the living blood of the generations to dissolve the vast black clot of bruised blood, deep inside their souls and bodies. And it would need a new hope.

Poor Connie! As the years drew on it was the fear of nothingness in her life that affected her. Clifford's mental life and hers gradually began to feel like nothingness. Their marriage, their integrated life based on a habit of intimacy, that he talked about: there were days when it all became utterly blank and nothing. It was words, just so many words. The only reality was nothingness, and over it a hypocrisy of words.

There was Clifford's success: the bitch-goddess! It was true he was almost famous, and his books brought him in a thousand pounds. His photograph appeared everywhere. There was a bust of him in one of the galleries, and a portrait of him in two galleries. He seemed the most modern of modern voices. With his uncanny lame instinct for publicity, he had become in four or five years one of the best known of the young 'intellectuals'. Where the intellect came in, Connie did not quite see.

Clifford was really clever at that slightly humorous analysis of people and motives which leaves everything in bits at the end. But it was rather like puppies tearing the sofa cushions to bits; except that it was not young and playful, but curiously old, and rather obstinately conceited. It was weird and it was nothing. This was the feeling that echoed and re-echoed at the bottom of Connie's soul: it was all flag, a wonderful display of nothingness; At the same time a display. A display! a display! a display!

Michaelis had seized upon Clifford as the central figure for a play; already he had sketched in the plot, and written the first act. For Michaelis was even better than Clifford at making a display of nothingness. It was the last bit of passion left in these men: the passion for making a display. Sexually they were passionless, even dead. And now it was not money that Michaelis was after. Clifford had never been primarily out for money, though he made it where he could, for money is the seal and stamp of success. And success was what they wanted. They wanted, both of them, to make a real display...a man's own very display of himself that should capture for a time the vast populace.

It was strange...the prostitution to the bitch-goddess. To Connie, since she was really outside of it, and since she had grown numb to the thrill of it, it was again nothingness. Even the prostitution to the bitch-goddess was nothingness, though the men prostituted themselves innumerable times. Nothingness even that.

Michaelis wrote to Clifford about the play. Of course she knew about it long ago. And Clifford was again thrilled. He was going to be displayed again this time, somebody was going to display him, and to advantage. He invited Michaelis down to Wragby with Act I.

Michaelis came: in summer, in a pale-coloured suit and white suede gloves, with mauve orchids for Connie, very lovely, and Act I was a great success. Even Connie was thrilled... **thrilled to what bit of marrow she had left**[1]. And Michaelis, thrilled by his power to thrill, was really wonderful...and quite beautiful, in Connie's eyes. She saw in him that ancient motionlessness of a race that can't be disillusioned any more, an extreme, perhaps, of impurity that is pure. On the far side of his supreme prostitution to the bitch-goddess he seemed

❶那未泯的一点点灵魂被感动了。

pure, pure as an African ivory mask that dreams impurity into purity, in its ivory curves and planes.

His moment of sheer thrill with the two Chatterleys, when **he simply carried Connie and Clifford away**❶, was one of the supreme moments of Michaelis' life. He had succeeded: he had carried them away. Even Clifford was temporarily in love with him...if that is the way one can put it.

So next morning Mick was more uneasy than ever; restless, devoured, with his hands restless in his trousers pockets. Connie had not visited him in the night...and he had not known where to find her. **Coquetry**❷ ! ...at his moment of triumph.

He went up to her sitting-room in the morning. She knew he would come. And his restlessness was evident. He asked her about his play...did she think it good? He had to hear it praised: that affected him **with the last thin thrill of passion beyond any sexual orgasm**❸. And she praised it rapturously. Yet all the while, at the bottom of her soul, she knew it was nothing.

'Look here! ' he said suddenly at last. 'Why don't you and I make a clean thing of it? Why don't we marry?'

'But I am married,' she said, amazed, and yet feeling nothing.

'Oh that! ...he'll divorce you all right...Why don't you and I marry? I want to marry. I know it would be the best thing for me...marry and lead a regular life. **I lead the deuce of a life**❹, simply tearing myself to pieces. Look here, you and I, we're made for one another... hand and glove. Why don't we marry? Do you see any reason why we shouldn't?'

Connie looked at him amazed: and yet she felt nothing. These men, they were all alike, they left everything out. They just went off from the top of their heads as if they were squibs, and expected you to be carried heavenwards along with their own thin sticks.

'But I am married already,' she said. 'I can't leave Clifford, you know.'

'Why not? but why not?' he cried. 'He'll hardly know you've gone, after six months. He doesn't know that anybody exists, except himself. Why the man has no use for you at all, as far as I can see; he's

❶他把康妮和克利福德侃晕了。❷她竟敢玩弄男人。❸超过任何性高潮的情感激动。❹我过着非人的生活。a/the deuce of...(口)极厉害的,非常严重的。

entirely wrapped up in himself.'

Connie felt there was truth in this. But she also felt that Mick was hardly making a display of selflessness.

'Aren't all men wrapped up in themselves?' she asked.

'Oh, more or less, I allow. A man's got to be, to get through. But that's not the point. The point is, what sort of a time can a man give a woman? Can he give her a damn good time, or can't he? If he can't he's no right to the woman...' He paused and gazed at her with his full, hazel eyes, almost hypnotic. 'Now I consider,' he added, 'I can give a woman the darndest good time she can ask for. I think I can guarantee myself.'

'And what sort of a good time?' asked Connie, gazing on him still with a sort of amazement, that looked like thrill; and underneath feeling nothing at all.

'Every sort of a good time, damn it, every sort! Dress, jewels up to a point, any nightclub you like, know anybody you want to know, **live the pace**[1]... travel and be somebody wherever you go... Darn it, every sort of good time.'

He spoke it almost in a brilliancy of triumph, and Connie looked at him as if dazzled, and really feeling nothing at all. Hardly even the surface of her mind was tickled at the glowing prospects he offered her. Hardly even her most outside self responded, that at any other time would have been thrilled. She just got no feeling from it, she couldn't 'go off'. She just sat and stared and looked dazzled, and felt nothing, only somewhere she smelt the extraordinarily unpleasant smell of the bitch-goddess.

Mick sat **on tenterhooks**[2], leaning forward in his chair, glaring at her almost hysterically: and whether he was more anxious out of vanity for her to say Yes! or whether he was more panic-stricken for fear she should say Yes! — who can tell?

'I should have to think about it,' she said. 'I couldn't say now. It may seem to you Clifford doesn't count, but he does. When you think how disabled he is...'

'Oh damn it all! If a fellow's going to trade on his disabilities, I might begin to say how lonely I am, and always have been, and all the rest of **the my-eye-Betty-Martin sob-stuff**[3]! Damn it all, if a

[1] go/live the pace，挥霍无度，随便花钱。 [2] 如坐针毡，提心吊胆。 [3] 哭天抹泪的闲淡事。

fellow's got nothing but disabilities to recommend him...'

He turned aside, working his hands furiously in his trousers pockets. That evening he said to her:

'You're coming round to my room tonight, aren't you? I don't darn know where your room is.'

'All right!' she said.

He was a more excited lover that night, with his strange, small boy's frail nakedness. Connie found it impossible to come to her crisis before he had really finished his. And he roused a certain craving passion in her, with his little boy's nakedness and softness; she had to go on after he had finished, **in the wild tumult and heaving of her loins**❶, while he heroically kept himself up, and present in her, with all his will and self-offering, till she brought about her own crisis, with weird little cries.

When at last he drew away from her, he said, in a bitter, almost sneering little voice:

'You couldn't **go off**❷ at the same time as a man, could you? You'd have to bring yourself off! You'd have to run the show!'

This little speech, at the moment, was one of the shocks of her life. Because that passive sort of giving himself was so obviously his only real mode of intercourse.

'What do you mean?' she said.

'You know what I mean. You keep on for hours after I've gone off... and **I have to hang on with my teeth till you bring yourself off by your own exertions**❸.'

She was stunned by this unexpected piece of brutality, at the moment when she was glowing with a sort of pleasure beyond words, and a sort of love for him. Because, after all, like so many modern men, he was finished almost before he had begun. And that forced the woman to be active.

'But you want me to go on, to get my own satisfaction?' she said.

He laughed grimly: 'I want it!' he said. 'That's good! I want to hang on with my teeth clenched, while you go for me!'

'But don't you?' she insisted.

He avoided the question. 'All the darned women are like that,' he said. 'Either they don't go off at all, as if they were dead in there... **or**

❶她的腰疯狂地摇摆起伏。❷(俚)性高潮。❸我不得不咬牙硬挺着,直到把你给彻底伺候爽了。

else they wait till a chap's really done, and then they start in to bring themselves off, and a chap's got to hang on[1]. I never had a woman yet who went off just at the same moment as I did.'

Connie only half heard this piece of novel, masculine information. She was only stunned by his feeling against her...his incomprehensible brutality. She felt so innocent.

'But you want me to have my satisfaction too, don't you?' she repeated.

'Oh, all right! I'm quite willing. But I'm darned if hanging on waiting for a woman to go off is much of a game for a man...'

This speech was one of the crucial blows of Connie's life. It killed something in her. She had not been so very keen on Michaelis; till he started it, she did not want him. It was as if she never positively wanted him. But once he had started her, it seemed only natural for her to come to her own crisis with him. Almost she had loved him for it...almost that night she loved him, and wanted to marry him.

Perhaps instinctively he knew it, and that was why he had to bring down the whole show with a smash; the house of cards. Her whole sexual feeling for him, or for any man, collapsed that night. Her life fell apart from his as completely as if he had never existed.

And she went through the days drearily. There was nothing now but this empty treadmill of what Clifford called the integrated life, the long living together of two people, who are in the habit of being in the same house with one another.

Nothingness! To accept the great nothingness of life seemed to be the one end of living. All the many busy and important little things that make up the grand sum-total of nothingness!

CHAPTER 6

'Why don't men and women really like one another nowadays?' Connie asked Tommy Dukes, who was more or less her oracle.

[1]要么等你完事了她才来劲，让人硬挺着。

'Oh, but they do! I don't think since the human species was invented, there has ever been a time when men and women have liked one another as much as they do today. Genuine liking! Take myself. I really like women better than men; they are braver, one can be more frank with them.'

Connie pondered this.

'Ah, yes, **but you never have anything to do with them**❶!' she said.

'I? What am I doing but talking perfectly sincerely to a woman at this moment?'

'Yes, talking...'

'And what more could I do if you were a man, than talk perfectly sincerely to you?'

'Nothing perhaps. But a woman...'

'A woman wants you to like her and talk to her, and at the same time love her and desire her; and **it seems to me the two things are mutually exclusive**❷.'

'But they shouldn't be!'

'No doubt water ought not to be so wet as it is; it overdoes it in wetness. But there it is! I like women and talk to them, and therefore I don't love them and desire them. The two things don't happen at the same time in me.'

'I think they ought to.'

'All right. **The fact that things ought to be something else than what they are, is not my department**❸.

Connie considered this. 'It isn't true,' she said. 'Men can love women and talk to them. I don't see how they can love them without talking, and being friendly and intimate. How can they?'

'Well,' he said, 'I don't know. What's the use of my generalizing? I only know my own case. I like women, but I don't desire them. I like talking to them; but talking to them, though it makes me intimate in one direction, **sets me poles apart from them as far as kissing is concerned**❹. So there you are! But don't take me as a general example, probably I'm just a special case: one of the men who like

❶可是你和女人从来没有过任何关系。❷在我看来这两件事是互不相干的。❸事情应该是别的样子，而实际上却是这个样子。❹但这和与女人接吻是风马牛不相及的。poles apart/asunder南辕北辙，poles两极。

women, but don't love women, and even hate them if they force me into a pretence of love, or an entangled appearance.'

'But doesn't it make you sad?'

'Why should it? Not a bit! I look at Charlie May, and the rest of the men who have affairs...No, I don't envy them a bit! If fate sent me a woman I wanted, well and good. Since I don't know any woman I want, and never see one...why, I presume I'm cold, and really like some women very much.'

'Do you like me?'

'Very much! And you see there's no question of kissing between us, is there?'

'None at all!' said Connie. 'But oughtn't there to be?'

'Why, in God's name? I like Clifford, but what would you say if I went and kissed him?'

'But isn't there a difference?'

'Where does it lie, as far as we're concerned? We're all intelligent human beings, **and the male and female business is in abeyance**[1]. Just in abeyance. How would you like me to start acting up like a continental male at this moment, and parading the sex thing?'

'I should hate it.'

'Well then! I tell you, if I'm really a male thing at all, I never run across the female of my species. And I don't miss her, I just like women. Who's going to force me into loving or pretending to love them, working up the sex game?'

'No, I'm not. But isn't something wrong?'

'You may feel it, I don't.'

'Yes, I feel something is wrong between men and women. A woman has no glamour for a man any more.'

'Has a man for a woman?'

She pondered the other side of the question.

'Not much,' she said truthfully.

'Then let's leave it all alone, and just be decent and simple, like proper human beings with one another. Be damned to the artificial sex-compulsion! I refuse it!'

Connie knew he was right, really. Yet it left her feeling so forlorn, so forlorn and stray. Like a chip on a dreary pond, she felt. What was the point, of her or anything?

[1]暂且不论男欢女爱之事。in abeyance暂时搁置。

It was her youth which rebelled. These men seemed so old and cold. Everything seemed old and cold. And Michaelis **let one down so**[1]; he was no good. The men didn't want one; they just didn't really want a woman, even Michaelis didn't.

And the bounders who pretended they did, and started working the sex game, they were worse than ever.

It was just dismal, and one had to put up with it. It was quite true, men had no real glamour for a woman: if you could fool yourself into thinking they had, even as she had fooled herself over Michaelis, that was the best you could do. Meanwhile you just lived on and there was nothing to it. She understood perfectly well why people had cocktail parties, and **jazzed, and Charlestoned**[2] till they were ready to drop. You had to take it out some way or other, your youth, or it ate you up. But what a ghastly thing, this youth! **You felt as old as Methuselah**[3], and yet the thing fizzed somehow, and didn't let you be comfortable. A mean sort of life! And no prospect! She almost wished she had gone off with Mick, and made her life one long cocktail party, and jazz evening. Anyhow that was better than just mooning yourself into the grave.

On one of her bad days she went out alone to walk in the wood, ponderously, heeding nothing, not even noticing where she was. The report of a gun not far off startled and angered her.

Then, as she went, she heard voices, and recoiled. People! She didn't want people. But her quick ear caught another sound, and she roused; it was a child sobbing. At once she attended; someone was ill-treating a child. She strode swinging down the wet drive, her sullen resentment uppermost. She felt just prepared to make a scene.

Turning the corner, she saw two figures in the drive beyond her: the keeper, and a little girl in a purple coat and moleskin cap, crying.

'Ah, shut it up, tha false little bitch! ' came the man's angry voice, and the child sobbed louder.

Constance strode nearer, with blazing eyes. The man turned and looked at her, saluting coolly, but he was pale with anger.

'What's the matter? Why is she crying?' demanded Constance,

❶让人非常伤心。 ❷狂跳爵士舞和查尔斯顿。查尔斯顿是二十世纪二十年代流行的一种快节奏舞蹈，其特点是小腿的跳跃扭动。 ❸你感到自己老得如同玛士撒拉。玛士撒拉，据《圣经·旧约全本》记述，他是以诺之子，活了九百六十九岁，是传说中最长寿的人。

peremptory but a little breathless.

A faint smile like a sneer came on the man's face. '**Nay, yo mun ax 'er**[1],' he replied callously, in broad vernacular.

Connie felt as if he had hit her in the face, and she changed colour. Then she gathered her defiance, and looked at him, her dark blue eyes blazing rather vaguely.

'I asked you,' she panted.

He gave a queer little bow, lifting his hat. 'You did, your Ladyship,' he said; then, with a return to the vernacular: 'but I canna tell yer.' And he became a soldier, inscrutable, only pale with annoyance.

Connie turned to the child, a ruddy, black-haired thing of nine or ten. 'What is it, dear? Tell me why you're crying!' she said, with the conventionalized sweetness suitable. More violent sobs, self-conscious. Still more sweetness on Connie's part.

'There, there, don't you cry! Tell me what they've done to you!'...an intense tenderness of tone. At the same time she felt in the pocket of her knitted jacket, and luckily found a sixpence.

'Don't you cry then!' she said, bending in front of the child. 'See what I've got for you!'

Sobs, snuffles, a fist taken from a blubbered face, and a black shrewd eye cast for a second on the sixpence. Then more sobs, but subduing. 'There, tell me what's the matter, tell me!' said Connie, putting the coin into the child's chubb hand, which closed over it.

'It's the...it's the...pussy!'

Shudders of subsiding sobs.

'What pussy, dear?'

After a silence the shy fist, clenching on sixpence, pointed into the bramble brake.

'There!'

Connie looked, and there, sure enough, was a big black cat, stretched out grimly, with a bit of blood on it.

'Oh!' she said in repulsion.

'A poacher, your Ladyship,' said the man satirically.

She glanced at him angrily. 'No wonder the child cried,' she said, 'if you shot it when she was there. No wonder she cried!'

---

[1] 意即"Nay,you must ask her"。

He looked into Connie's eyes, laconic, contemptuous, not hiding his feelings. And again Connie flushed; she felt she had been making a scene, the man did not respect her.

'What is your name?' she said playfully to the child. 'Won't you tell me your name?'

Sniffs; then very affectedly in a piping voice: 'Connie Mellors! '

'Connie Mellors! Well, that's a nice name! And did you come out with your Daddy, and he shot a pussy? But it was a bad pussy! '

The child looked at her, with bold, dark eyes of scrutiny, sizing her up, and her condolence.

'I wanted to stop with my Gran,' said the little girl.

'Did you? But where is your Gran?'

The child lifted an arm, pointing down the drive. 'At th'. cottidge.'

'At the cottage! And would you like to go back to her?'

Sudden, shuddering quivers of reminiscent sobs. 'Yes! '

'Come then, shall I take you? Shall I take you to your Gran? Then your Daddy can do what he has to do.' She turned to the man. 'It is your little girl, isn't it?'

He saluted, and made a slight movement of the head in affirmation.

'I suppose I can take her to the cottage?' asked Connie.

'If your Ladyship wishes.'

Again he looked into her eyes, with that calm, searching detached glance. A man very much alone, and on his own.

'Would you like to come with me to the cottage, to your Gran, dear?'

The child peeped up again. 'Yes! ' she simpered.

Connie disliked her; the spoilt, false little female. Nevertheless she wiped her face and took her hand. The keeper saluted in silence.

'Good morning! ' said Connie.

It was nearly a mile to the cottage, and Connie senior was well red by Connie junior by the time the game-keeper's picturesque little home was in sight. The child was already as full to the brim with tricks as a little monkey, and so self-assured.

At the cottage the door stood open, and there was a rattling heard inside. Connie lingered, the child slipped her hand, and ran indoors.

'Gran! Gran! '

'Why, are yer back a'ready! '

The grandmother had been blackleading the stove, it was Saturday morning. She came to the door in her sacking apron, a blacklead-brush in her hand, and a black smudge on her nose. She was a little, rather dry woman.

'Why, whatever?' she said, hastily wiping her arm across her face as she saw Connie standing outside.

'Good morning!' said Connie. 'She was crying, so I just brought her home.'

The grandmother looked around swiftly at the child:

'Why, wheer was yer Dad?'

The little girl clung to her grandmother's skirts and simpered.

'He was there,' said Connie, 'but he'd shot a poaching cat, and the child was upset.'

'Oh, you'd no right **t'ave**[1] bothered, Lady Chatterley, I'm sure! I'm sure it was very good of you, but you shouldn't 'ave bothered. Why, did ever you see!' — and the old woman turned to the child: 'Fancy Lady Chatterley takin' all that trouble over yer! Why, she shouldn't 'ave bothered!'

'It was no bother, just a walk,' said Connie smiling.

'Why, I'm sure 'twas very kind of you, I must say! So she was crying! I knew there'd be something afore they got far. She's frightened of 'im, that's wheer it is. Seems 'e's almost a stranger to 'er, fair a stranger, and I don't think they're two as'd hit it off very easy. He's got funny ways.'

Connie didn't know what to say.

'Look, Gran!' simpered the child.

The old woman looked down at the sixpence in the little girl's hand.

'An' sixpence an' all! Oh, your Ladyship, you shouldn't, you shouldn't. Why, isn't Lady Chatterley good to yer! **My word**[2], you're a lucky girl this morning!'

She pronounced the name, as all the people did: Chat'ley. — Isn't Lady Chat'ley good to you!' — Connie couldn't help looking at the old woman's nose, and the latter again vaguely wiped her face with the back of her wrist, but missed the smudge.

Connie was moving away 'Well, thank you ever so much, Lady Chat'ley, I'm sure. Say thank you to Lady Chat'ley!' — this last to the

[1] t'ave=to have。 [2] 哎呀!

child.

'Thank you,' piped the child.

'There's a dear!' laughed Connie, and she moved away, saying 'Good morning', heartily relieved to get away from the contact.

Curious, she thought, that that thin, proud man should have that little, sharp woman for a mother!

And the old woman, as soon as Connie had gone, rushed to the bit of mirror in the scullery, and looked at her face. Seeing it, she stamped her foot with impatience. 'Of course she had to catch me in my coarse apron, and a dirty face! Nice idea she'd get of me!'

Connie went slowly home to Wragby. 'Home!'...it was a warm word to use for that great, weary warren. But then it was **a word that had had its day**[1]. It was somehow cancelled. All the great words, it seemed to Connie, were cancelled for her generation: love, joy, happiness, home, mother, father, husband, all these great, dynamic words were half dead now, and dying from day to day. Home was a place you lived in, love was a thing you didn't fool yourself about, joy was a word you applied to a good Charleston, happiness was a term of hypocrisy used to bluff other people, a father was an individual who enjoyed his own existence, a husband was a man you lived with and kept going in spirits. As for sex, the last of the great words, it was just a cocktail term for an excitement that bucked you up for a while, then left you more raggy than ever. Frayed! It was as if the very material you were made of was cheap stuff, and was fraying out to nothing.

All that really remained was a stubborn stoicism: and in that there was a certain pleasure. In the very experience of the nothingness of life, **phase after phase, étape after étape**[2], there was a certain grisly satisfaction. So that's that! Always this was the last utterance: home, love, marriage, Michaelis: So that's that! And when one died, the last words to life would be: So that's that!

Money? Perhaps one couldn't say the same there. Money one always wanted. Money, Success, the bitch-goddess, as Tommy Dukes persisted in calling it, **after Henry James**[3], that was a permanent necessity. You couldn't spend your last sou, and say finally: So that's that! No, if

❶已经过时了的一个词。❷一段又一段，一程又一程。❸依照亨利·詹姆斯的说法。亨利·詹姆斯(1843—1916)，美国小说家。

you lived even another ten minutes, you wanted a few more sous for something or other. Just to keep the business mechanically going, you needed money. You had to have it. Money you have to have. You needn't really have anything else. So that's that!

Since, of course, it's not your own fault you are alive. Once you are alive, money is a necessity, and the only absolute necessity. All the rest you can get along without, **at a pinch**[1]. But not money. Emphatically, that's that!

She thought of Michaelis, and the money she might have had with him; and even that she didn't want. She preferred the lesser amount which she helped Clifford to make by his writing. That she actually helped to make. — 'Clifford and I together, we make twelve hundred a year out of writing'; so she put it to herself. Make money! Make it! Out of nowhere. Wring it out of the thin air! The last feat to be humanly proud of! The rest all-my-eye-Betty-Martin.

So she plodded home to Clifford, to join forces with him again, to make another story out of nothingness: and a story meant money. Clifford seemed to care very much whether his stories were considered first-class literature or not. Strictly, she didn't care. Nothing in it! said her father. Twelve hundred pounds last year! was the retort simple and final.

If you were young, you just set your teeth, and bit on and held on, till the money began to flow from the invisible; it was a question of power. It was a question of will; a subtle, subtle, powerful emanation of will out of yourself brought back to you the mysterious nothingness of money a word on a bit of paper. It was a sort of magic, certainly it was triumph. The bitch-goddess! Well, if one had to prostitute oneself, let it be to a bitch-goddess! One could always despise her even while one prostituted oneself to her, which was good.

Clifford, of course, had still many childish taboos and fetishes. He wanted to be thought 'really good', which was all **cock-a-hoopy nonsense**[2]. What was really good was **what actually caught on**[3]. It was no good being really good and getting left with it. It seemed as if most of the 'really good' men just missed the bus. After all you only lived one life, and if you missed the bus, you were just left on the pavement, along with the rest of the failures.

---

[1] at/in/on a pinch必要时，危机时。 [2] 一派自鸣得意的胡言。 [3] 实际受人欢迎的东西。

Connie was contemplating a winter in London with Clifford, next winter. He and she had caught the bus all right, so they might as well ride on top for a bit, and show it.

The worst of it was, Clifford tended to become vague, absent, and to fall into fits of vacant depression. It was the wound to his psyche coming out. But it made Connie want to scream. Oh God, if the mechanism of the consciousness itself was going to go wrong, then what was one to do? Hang it all, one did one's bit! Was one to be let down absolutely?

Sometimes she wept bitterly, but even as she wept she was saying to herself: Silly fool, wetting hankies! As if that would get you anywhere!

Since Michaelis, she had made up her mind she wanted nothing. That seemed the simplest solution of the otherwise insoluble. She wanted nothing more than what she'd got; only she wanted to get ahead with what she'd got: Clifford, the stories, Wragby, the Lady-Chatterley business, money and fame, such as it was...she wanted to go ahead with it all. Love, sex, all that sort of stuff, just water-ices! Lick it up and forget it. If you don't hang on to it in your mind, it's nothing. Sex especially...nothing! Make up your mind to it, and you've solved the problem. Sex and a cocktail: they both lasted about as long, had the same effect, and amounted to about the same thing.

But a child, a baby! That was still one of the sensations. She would venture very gingerly on that experiment. There was the man to consider, and it was curious, there wasn't a man in the world whose children you wanted. Mick's children! Repulsive thought! **As lief have a child to a rabbit**[1]! Tommy Dukes? he was very nice, but somehow you couldn't associate him with a baby, another generation. He ended in himself. And out of all the rest of Clifford's pretty wide acquaintance, there was not a man who did not rouse her contempt, when she thought of having a child by him. There were several who would have been quite possible as lover, even Mick. But to let them breed a child on you! Ugh! Humiliation and abomination.

So that was that!

Nevertheless, Connie had the child at the back of her mind. Wait! wait! She would sift the generations of men through her sieve, and see

[1] 情愿与兔子下崽子。as lief: gladly, willngly。

if she couldn't find one who would do. — '**Go ye into the streets and by ways of Jerusalem, and see if you can find a man**[1].' It had been impossible to find a man in the Jerusalem of the prophet, though there were thousands of male humans. But a man! **C'est une autre chose**[2]!

She had an idea that he would have to be a foreigner: not an Englishman, still less an Irishman. A real foreigner.

But wait! wait! Next winter she would get Clifford to London; the following winter she would get him abroad to the South of France, Italy. Wait! She was in no hurry about the child. That was her own private affair, and the one point on which, in her own queer, female way, she was serious to the bottom of her soul. She was not going to risk any chance comer, not she! One might take a lover almost at any moment, but a man who should beget a child on one...wait! wait! it's a very different matter. — 'Go ye into the streets and byways of Jerusalem...' It was not a question of love; it was a question of a man. Why, one might even rather hate him, personally. Yet if he was the man, what would one's personal hate matter? This business concerned another part of oneself.

It had rained as usual, and the paths were too sodden for Clifford's chair, but Connie would go out. She went out alone every day now, mostly in the wood, where she was really alone. She saw nobody there.

This day, however, Clifford wanted to send a message to the keeper, and as the boy was laid up with influenza, somebody always seemed to have influenza at Wragby, Connie said she would call at the cottage.

The air was soft and dead, as if all the world were slowly dying. Grey and clammy and silent, even from the shuffling of the collieries, for the pits were working short time, and today they were stopped altogether. The end of all things!

In the wood all was utterly inert and motionless, only great drops fell from the bare boughs, with a hollow little crash. For the rest, among the old trees was depth within depth of grey, hopeless inertia, silence, nothingness.

---

❶"到耶路撒冷的大街小巷走走看，看能否找到一个男子汉"。此句拟套用圣经中一句。❷(法)那是另一回事。

Connie walked dimly on. From the old wood came an ancient melancholy, somehow soothing to her, better than the harsh insentience of the outer world. She liked the inwardness of the remnant of forest, the unspeaking reticence of the old trees. They seemed a very power of silence, and yet a vital presence. They, too, were waiting: obstinately, stoically waiting, and giving off a potency of silence. Perhaps they were only waiting for the end; to be cut down, cleared away, the end of the forest, for them the end of all things. But perhaps their strong and aristocratic silence, the silence of strong trees, meant something else.

As she came out of the wood on the north side, the keeper's cottage, a rather dark, brown stone cottage, with gables and a handsome chimney, looked uninhabited, it was so silent and alone. But a thread of smoke rose from the chimney, and the little railed-in garden in the front of the house was dug and kept very tidy. The door was shut.

Now she was here she felt a little shy of the man, with his curious far-seeing eyes. She did not like bringing him orders, and felt like going away again. She knocked softly, no one came. She knocked again, but still not loudly. There was no answer. She peeped through the window, and saw the dark little room, with its almost sinister privacy, not wanting to be invaded.

She stood and listened, and it seemed to her she heard sounds from the back of the cottage. Having failed to make herself heard, her mettle was roused, she would not be defeated.

So she went round the side of the house. At the back of the cottage the land rose steeply, so the back yard was sunken, and enclosed by a low stone wall. She turned the corner of the house and stopped. In the little yard two paces beyond her, the man was washing himself, utterly unaware. He was naked to the hips, his velveteen breeches slipping down over his slender loins. And his white slim back was curved over a big bowl of soapy water, in which he ducked his head, shaking his head with a queer, quick little motion, lifting his slender white arms, and pressing the soapy water from his ears, quick, subtle as a weasel playing with water, and utterly alone. Connie backed away round the corner of the house, and hurried away to the wood. In spite of herself, she had had a shock. After all, merely a man washing himself, commonplace enough, Heaven knows!

Yet in some curious way it was a visionary experience: it had hit her in the middle of the body. She saw the clumsy breeches slipping down over the pure, delicate, white loins, the bones showing a little, and the sense of aloneness, of a creature purely alone, overwhelmed her. Perfect, white, solitary nudity of a creature that lives alone, and inwardly alone. And beyond that, a certain beauty of a pure creature. Not the stuff of beauty, not even the body of beauty, but a lambency, the warm, white flame of a single life, **revealing itself in contours that one might touch**[1] : a body!

Connie had received the shock of vision in her womb, and she knew it; it lay inside her. But with her mind she was inclined to ridicule. A man washing himself in a back yard! No doubt with evil-smelling yellow soap! She was rather annoyed; why should she be made to stumble on these vulgar privacies?

So she walked away from herself, but after a while she sat down on a stump. She was too confused to think. But in the coil of her confusion, she was determined to deliver her message to the fellow. She would not be balked. She must give him time to dress himself, but not time to go out. He was probably preparing to go out somewhere.

So she sauntered slowly back, listening. As she came near, the cottage looked just the same. A dog barked, and she knocked at the door, her heart beating in spite of herself.

She heard the man coming lightly downstairs. He opened the door quickly, and startled her. He looked uneasy himself, but instantly a laugh came on his face.

'Lady Chatterley!' he said. 'Will you come in?'

His manner was so perfectly easy and good, she stepped over the threshold into the rather dreary little room.

'I only called with a message from Sir Clifford,' she said in her soft, rather breathless voice.

The man was looking at her with those blue, all-seeing eyes of his, which made her turn her face aside a little. He thought her comely, almost beautiful, in her shyness, and he took command of the situation himself at once.

'Would you care to sit down?' he asked, presuming she would not.

[1] 显现出可以触摸到的轮廓。

The door stood open.

'No thanks! Sir Clifford wondered if you would..., and she delivered her message, looking unconsciously into his eyes again. And now his eyes looked warm and kind, particularly to a woman, wonderfully warm, and kind, and at ease.

'Very good, your Ladyship. I will see to it at once.'

Taking an order, his whole self had changed, glazed over with a sort of hardness and distance. Connie hesitated, she ought to go. But she looked round the clean, tidy, rather dreary little sitting-room with something like dismay.

'Do you live here quite alone?' she asked.

'Quite alone, your Ladyship.'

'But your mother...?'

'She lives in her own cottage in the village.'

'With the child?' asked Connie.

'With the child!'

And his plain, rather worn face took on an indefinable look of derision. It was a face that changed all the time, baffling.

'No,' he said, seeing Connie stand at a loss, 'my mother comes and cleans up for me on Saturdays; I do the rest myself.'

Again Connie looked at him. His eyes were smiling again, a little mockingly, but warm and blue, and somehow kind. She wondered at him. He was in trousers and flannel shirt and a grey tie, his hair soft and damp, his face rather pale and worn-looking. When the eyes ceased to laugh they looked as if they had suffered a great deal, still without losing their warmth. **But a pallor of isolation came over him**[1], she was not really there for him.

She wanted to say so many things, and she said nothing. Only she looked up at him again, and remarked:

'I hope I didn't disturb you?'

The faint smile of mockery narrowed his eyes.

'Only combing my hair, if you don't mind. I'm sorry I hadn't a coat on, but then I had no idea who was knocking. Nobody knocks here, and the unexpected sounds ominous.'

[1] 一种苍白的孤寂感占据了他。

He went in front of her down the garden path to hold the gate. In his shirt, without the clumsy velveteen coat, she saw again how slender he was, thin, stooping a little. Yet, as she passed him, there was something young and bright in his fair hair, and his quick eyes. He would be a man about thirty-seven or eight.

She plodded on into the wood, knowing he was looking after her; he upset her so much, in spite of herself.

And he, as he went indoors, was thinking: 'She's nice, she's real! She's nicer than she knows.'

She wondered very much about him; he seemed so unlike a game-keeper, so unlike a working-man anyhow; although he had something in common with the local people. But also something very uncommon.

'The game-keeper, Mellors, is a curious kind of person,' she said to Clifford; 'he might almost be a gentleman.'

'Might he?' said Clifford. 'I hadn't noticed.'

'But isn't there something special about him?' Connie insisted.

'I think he's quite a nice fellow, but I know very little about him. He only came out of the army last year, less than a year ago. From India, I rather think. He may have picked up certain tricks out there, perhaps he was an officer's servant, and improved on his position. Some of the men were like that. But it does them no good, they have to fall back into their old places when they get home again.'

Connie gazed at Clifford contemplatively. She saw in him the peculiar tight rebuff against anyone of the lower classes who might be really climbing up, which she knew was characteristic of his breed.

'But don't you think there is something special about him?' she asked.

'Frankly, no! Nothing I had noticed.'

He looked at her curiously, uneasily, half-suspiciously. And she felt he wasn't telling her the real truth; he wasn't telling himself the real truth, that was it. He disliked any suggestion of a really exceptional human being. People must be more or less at his level, or below it.

Connie felt again the tightness, niggardliness of the men of her generation. They were so tight, so scared of life!

CHAPTER 7

When Connie went up to her bedroom she did what she had not done for a long time: took off all her clothes, and looked at herself naked in the huge mirror. She did not know what she was looking for, or at, very definitely, yet she moved the lamp till it shone full on her.

And she thought, as she had thought so often, what a frail, easily hurt, rather pathetic thing a human body is, naked; somehow a little unfinished, incomplete!

She had been supposed to have rather a good figure, but now she was out of fashion: a little too female, not enough like an adolescent boy. She was not very tall, a bit Scottish and short; but she had a certain fluent, down-slipping grace that might have been beauty. Her skin was faintly tawny, her limbs had a certain stillness, her body should have had a full, down-slipping richness; but it lacked something.

Instead of ripening its firm, down-running curves[1], her body was flattening and going a little harsh. It was as if it had not had enough sun and warmth; it was a little greyish and sapless.

Disappointed of its real womanhood, it had not succeeded in becoming boyish, and unsubstantial, and transparent; instead it had gone opaque.

Her breasts were rather small, and dropping pear-shaped. But they were unripe, a little bitter, without meaning hanging there. And her belly had lost the fresh, round gleam it had had when she was young, in the days of her German boy, who really loved her physically. Then it was young and expectant, with a real look of its own. Now it was going slack, and a little flat, thinner, but with a slack thinness. Her thighs, too, **they used to look so quick and glimpsy in their female roundness**[2], somehow they too were going flat, slack, meaningless.

Her body was going meaningless, going dull and opaque, so much insignificant substance . It made her feel immensely depressed and

❶本应丰满流畅的线条。 ❷女性圆润、光滑的大腿曾经是那样灵活、光鲜。

hopeless. What hope was there? She was old, old at twenty-seven, with no gleam and sparkle in the flesh. Old through neglect and denial, yes, denial. Fashionable women kept their bodies bright like delicate porcelain, by external attention. There was nothing inside the porcelain; but she was not even as bright as that. The mental life! Suddenly she hated it with a rushing fury, the swindle!

She looked in the other mirror's reflection at her back, her waist, her loins. She was getting thinner, but to her it was not becoming. The crumple of her waist at the back, as she bent back to look, was a little weary; and it used to be so gay-looking. And the longish slope of her haunches and her buttocks had lost its gleam and its sense of richness. Gone! Only the German boy had loved it, and he was ten years dead, very nearly. How time went by! Ten years dead, and she was only twenty-seven. The healthy boy with his fresh, **clumsy sensuality that she had then been so scornful of**[1]! Where would she find it now? It was gone out of men. They had their pathetic, two-seconds spasms like Michaelis; but no healthy human sensuality, that warms the blood and freshens the whole being.

Still she thought the most beautiful part of her was the long-sloping fall of the haunches from the socket of the back, and the slumberous, round stillness of the buttocks. Like hillocks of sand, the Arabs say, soft and downward-slipping with a long slope. Here the life still lingered hoping. But here too she was thinner, and going unripe, astringent.

But the front of her body made her miserable. It was already beginning to slacken, with a slack sort of thinness, almost withered, going old before it had ever really lived. She thought of the child she might somehow bear. Was she fit, anyhow?

She slipped into her nightdress, and went to bed, where she sobbed bitterly. And in her bitterness burned a cold indignation against Clifford, and his writings and his talk: against all the men of his sort who defrauded a woman even of her own body.

Unjust! Unjust! The sense of deep physical injustice burned to her very soul.

But in the morning, all the same, she was up at seven, and going downstairs to Clifford. She had to help him in all the intimate things, for

[1]她异常藐视的笨拙的性动作。

he had no man, and refused a woman-servant. The housekeeper's husband, who had known him as a boy, helped him, and did any heavy lifting; but Connie did the personal things, and she did them willingly. It was a demand on her, but she had wanted to do what she could.

So she hardly ever went away from Wragby, and never for more than a day or two; when Mrs Betts, the housekeeper, attended to Clifford. He, as was inevitable in the course of time, took all the service for granted. It was natural he should.

And yet, deep inside herself, a sense of injustice, of being defrauded, had begun to burn in Connie. The physical sense of injustice is a dangerous feeling, once it is awakened. It must have outlet, or it eats away the one in whom it is aroused. Poor Clifford, he was not to blame. His was the greater misfortune. It was all part of the general catastrophe.

And yet was he not in a way to blame? This lack of warmth, this lack of the simple, warm, physical contact, was he not to blame for that? He was never really warm, nor even kind, only thoughtful, considerate, in a well-bred, cold sort of way! But never warm as a man can be warm to a woman, as even Connie's father could be warm to her, with the warmth of a man who did himself well, and intended to, but who still could comfort it woman with a bit of his masculine glow.

But Clifford was not like that. His whole race was not like that. They were all inwardly hard and separate, and warmth to them was just bad taste. You had to get on without it, and hold your own; which was all very well if you were of the same class and race. Then you could keep yourself cold and be very estimable, and hold your own, and enjoy the satisfaction of holding it. But if you were of another class and another race it wouldn't do; there was no fun merely holding your own, and feeling you belonged to the ruling class. What was the point, when even the smartest aristocrats had really nothing positive of their own to hold, and their rule was really a farce, not rule at all? What was the point? It was all cold nonsense.

A sense of rebellion smouldered in Connie. What was the good of it all? What was the good of her sacrifice, her devoting her life to Clifford? What was she serving, after all? A cold spirit of vanity, that had no warm human contacts, and that was as corrupt as any **low-born Jew**,

in craving for prostitution to the bitch-goddess, Success ❶. Even Clifford's cool and contactless assurance that he belonged to the ruling class didn't prevent his tongue lolling out of his mouth, as he panted after the bitch-goddess. After all, Michaelis was really more dignified in the matter, and far, far more successful. Really, if you looked closely at Clifford, he was a buffoon, and **a buffoon is more humiliating than a bounder**❷.

As between the two men, Michaelis really had far more use for her than Clifford had. He had even more need of her. Any good nurse can attend to crippled legs! And as for the heroic effort, Michaelis was a heroic rat, and Clifford was very much of a poodle showing off.

There were people staying in the house, among them Clifford's Aunt Eva, Lady Bennerley. She was a thin woman of sixty, with a red nose, a widow, and still something of "**a grande dame** ❸". She belonged to one of the best families, and had the character to carry it off. Connie liked her, she was so perfectly simple and frank, as far as she intended to be frank, and superficially kind. Inside herself she was a past-mistress in holding her own, and holding other people a little lower, She was not at all a snob: far too sure of herself. She was perfect at the **social sport** ❹ of coolly holding her own, and **making other people defer to her**❺.

She was kind to Connie, and tried to worm into her woman's soul with the sharp gimlet of her well-born observations.

'You're quite wonderful, in my opinion,' she said to Connie. 'You've done wonders for Clifford. I never saw any budding genius myself, and **there he is, all the rage** ❻.' Aunt Eva was quite complacently proud of Clifford's success. **Another feather in the family cap** ❼! She didn't care a straw about his books, but why should she?

'Oh, I don't think it's my doing,' said Connie.

'It must be! Can't be anybody else's. And it seems to me you don't get enough out of it.'

'How?'

'Look at the way you are shut up here. I said to Clifford: If that

❶如同出身低贱的犹太人渴望把自己出卖给婊子女神，成功。❷小丑比无赖更无耻。❸(法)贵妇人。
❹社交才能。❺让别人对她顺从。❻现时他红得发紫。❼家族的另一份荣耀。

child rebels one day **you'll have yourself to thank**[1]!'

'But Clifford never denies me anything,' said Connie.

'Look here, my dear child' — and Lady Bennerley laid her thin hand on Connie's arm. 'A woman has to live her life, or live to repent not having lived it. Believe me!' And she took another sip of brandy, which maybe was her form of repentance.

'But I do live my life, don't I?'

'Not in my idea! Clifford should bring you to London, and let you go about. His sort of friends are all right for him, but what are they for you? If I were you I should think it wasn't good enough. You'll let your youth slip by, and you'll spend your old age, and your middle age too, repenting it.'

Her ladyship lapsed into contemplative silence, soothed by the brandy.

But Connie was not keen on going to London, and being steered into the smart world by Lady Bennerley. She didn't feel really smart, it wasn't interesting. And she did feel the peculiar, withering coldness under it all; **like the soil of Labrador**[2], which his gay little flowers on its surface, and a foot down is frozen.

Tommy Dukes was at Wragby, and another man, Harry Winterslow, and Jack Strangeways with his wife Olive. The talk was much more desultory than when only the cronies were there, and everybody was a bit bored, for the weather was bad, and there was only billiards, and the pianola to dance to.

Olive was reading a book about the future, when babies would be bred in bottles, and women would be '**immunized**[3]'.

'Jolly good thing too!' she said. 'Then a woman can live her own life.' Strangeways wanted children, and she didn't.

'How'd you like to be immunized?' Winterslow asked her, with an ugly smile.

'I hope I am; naturally,' she said. 'Anyhow the future's going to have more sense, and a woman needn't be dragged down by her functions.'

'Perhaps she'll float off into space altogether,' said Dukes.

'I do think sufficient civilization ought to eliminate a lot of the

❶那也全怪你自己。❷如同拉布拉多的土地。拉布拉多位于加拿大东北部，气候寒冷。❸此处指妇女不必怀孕及生产。

physical disabilities,' said Clifford. 'All the love-business for example, it might just as well go. I suppose it would if we could breed babies in bottles.'

'No!' cried Olive. 'That might leave all the more room for fun.'

'I suppose,' said Lady Bennerley, contemplatively, 'if the love-business went, something else would take its place. Morphia, perhaps. A little morphine in all the air. It would be wonderfully refreshing for everybody.'

'The government releasing ether into the air on Saturdays, for a cheerful weekend!' said Jack. 'Sounds all right, but where should we be by Wednesday?'

'So long as you can forget your body you are happy,' said Lady Bennerley. 'And the moment you begin to be aware of your body, you are wretched. So, if civilization is any good, it has to help us to forget our bodies, and then time passes happily without our knowing it.'

'Help us to get rid of our bodies altogether,' said Winterslow. 'It's quite time man began to improve on his own nature, especially the physical side of it.'

'Imagine if we floated like tobacco smoke,' said Connie.

'It won't happen,' said Dukes. 'Our old show will come flop; our civilization is going to fall. It's going down the bottomless pit, down the chasm. And believe me, **the only bridge across the chasm will be the phallus**[1]!'

'Oh do! do be impossible, General!' cried Olive.

'I believe our civilization is going to collapse,' said Aunt Eva.

'And what will come after it?' asked Clifford.

'I haven't the faintest idea, but something, I suppose,' said the elderly lady.

'Connie says people like wisps of smoke, and Olive says immunized women, and babies in bottles, and Dukes says the phallus is the bridge to what comes next. I wonder what it will really be?' said Clifford.

'Oh, don't bother! let's get on with today,' said Olive. '**Only hurry up with the breeding bottle, and let us poor women off**[2].'

❶无底深渊上唯一的桥梁就是男人的阳具。❷"只不过要赶快研究生育管，把我们这些可怜的女人解脱了。"

'There might even be real men, in the next phase,' said Tommy. 'Real, intelligent, wholesome men, and wholesome nice women! Wouldn't that be a change, an enormous change from us? We're not men, and the women aren't women. We're only cerebrating make-shifts, mechanical and intellectual experiments. There may even come a civilization of genuine men and women, **instead of our little lot of clever-jacks**❶, all at the intelligence-age of seven. It would be even more amazing than men of smoke or babies in bottles.'

'Oh, when people begin to talk about real women, I give up,' said Olive.

'Certainly nothing but the spirit in us is worth having,' said Winterslow.

'**Spirits**❷!' said Jack, drinking his whisky and soda.

'Think so? Give me the resurrection of the body!' said Dukes.

'But it'll come, in time, when we've shoved the cerebral stone away a bit, the money and the rest. Then we'll get a democracy of touch, instead of a democracy of pocket.'

Something echoed inside Connie: 'Give me the democracy of touch, the resurrection of the body!' She didn't at all know what it meant, but it comforted her, as meaningless things may do.

Anyhow everything was terribly silly, and she was exasperatedly bored by it all, by Clifford, by Aunt Eva, by Olive and Jack, and Winterslow, and even by Dukes. Talk, talk, talk! What hell it was, the continual rattle of it!

Then, when all the people went, it was no better. She continued plodding on, but exasperation and irritation had got hold of her lower body, she couldn't escape. The days seemed to grind by, with curious painfulness, yet nothing happened. Only she was getting thinner; even the housekeeper noticed it, and asked her about herself. Even Tommy Dukes insisted she was not well, though she said she was all right. Only she began to be afraid of the ghastly white t ombstones, that peculiar loathsome whiteness of **Carrara marble**❸, detestable as false teeth, which stuck up on the hillside, under Tevershall church, and which she saw with such grim pa infulness from the park. The bristling of the

❶来代替我们这群聪明的小丑。 ❷此语双关，兼具"精神"与"烈性酒"之意。 ❸卡拉拉大理石。卡拉拉，意大利西北部一城市，以大理石闻名于世。

hideous false teeth of tombstones on the hill affected her with a grisly kind of horror. She felt the time not far off when she would be buried there, added to the ghastly host under the tombstones and the monuments, in these filthy Midlands.

She needed help, and she knew it: so she wrote a little **cri du coeur**[1] to her sister, Hilda. 'I'm not well lately, and I don't know what's the matter with me.'

Down posted Hilda from Scotland, where she had **taken up her abode**[2]. She came in March, alone, driving herself in a nimble two-seater. Up the drive she came, tooting up the incline, then sweeping round the oval of grass, where the two great wild beech-trees stood, on the flat in front of the house.

Connie had run out to the steps. Hilda pulled up her car, got out, and kissed her sister.

'But Connie!' she cried. 'Whatever is the matter?'

'Nothing!' said Connie, rather shamefacedly; but she knew how she had suffered in contrast to Hilda. Both sisters had the same rather golden, glowing skin, and soft brown hair, and naturally strong, warm physique. But now Connie was thin and earthy-looking, with a scraggy, yellowish neck, that stuck out of her jumper.

'But you're ill, child!' said Hilda, in the soft, rather breathless voice that both sisters had alike. Hilda was nearly, but not quite, two years older than Connie.

'No, not ill. Perhaps I'm bored,' said Connie a little pathetically.

The light of battle glowed in Hilda's face; she was a woman, soft and still as she seemed, of the old amazon sort, not made to fit with men.

'This wretched place!' she said softly, looking at poor, old, lumbering Wragby with real hate. She looked soft and warm herself, as a ripe pear, and **she was an amazon of the real old breed**[3].

She went quietly in to Clifford. He thought how handsome she looked, but also he shrank from her. His wife's family did not have his sort of manners, or his sort of etiquette. He considered them rather

❶(法)抱怨,牢骚。❷居住。❸她真的如同古代的女武士。amazon高大,强壮;有男人气质的女人。

outsiders, but once they got inside they **made him jump through the hoop**[1].

He sat square and well-groomed in his chair, his hair sleek and blond, and his face fresh, his blue eyes pale, and a little prominent, his expression inscrutable, but well-bred. Hilda thought it sulky and stupid, and he waited. He had an air of aplomb, but Hilda didn't care what he had an air of; **she was up in arms**[2], and if he'd been Pope or Emperor it would have been just the same.

'Connie's looking awfully unwell,' she said in her soft voice, fixing him with her beautiful, glowering grey eyes. She looked so maidenly, so did Connie; but he well knew the tone of Scottish obstinacy underneath.

'She's a little thinner,' he said.

'Haven't you done anything about it?'

'Do you think it necessary?' he asked, with his suavest English stiffness, for the two things often go together.

Hilda only glowered at him without replying; **repartee was not her forte**[3], nor Connie's; so she glowered, and he was much more uncomfortable than if she had said things.

'I'll take her to a doctor,' said Hilda at length. 'Can you suggest a good one round here?'

'I'm afraid I can't.'

'Then I'll take her to London, where we have a doctor we trust.'

Though boiling with rage, Clifford said nothing.

'I suppose I may as well stay the night,' said Hilda, pulling off her gloves, 'and I'll drive her to town tomorrow.'

Clifford was yellow at the gills with anger[4], and at evening the whites of his eyes were a little yellow too. **He ran to liver**[5]. But Hilda was consistently modest and maidenly.

'You must have a nurse or somebody, to look after you personally. You should really have a manservant,' said Hilda as they sat, with apparent calmness, at coffee after dinner. She spoke in her soft, seemingly gentle way, but Clifford felt she was hitting him on the head with a bludgeon.

---

[1]这使他很不自在。to jump/go through the hoop:饱尝辛酸,历尽沧桑。[2]她已做好了斗的架势。[3]巧答善辩并不是她的强项。[4]克利福德气得脸色发白。yellow (或white,blue,green,pale) at (around, about) gills 气得脸色发白。[5]肝病发作。

'You think so?' he said coldly.

'I'm sure! It's necessary. Either that, or Father and I must take Connie away for some months. This can't go on.'

'What can't go on?'

'Haven't you looked at the child!' asked Hilda, gazing at him full stare. He looked rather like a huge, boiled crayfish at the moment; or so she thought.

'Connie and I will discuss it,' he said.

'I've already discussed it with her,' said Hilda.

Clifford had been long enough in the hands of nurses; he hated them, because they left him no real privacy. And a manservant! ...he couldn't stand a man hanging round him. Almost better any woman. But why not Connie?

The two sisters drove off in the morning, Connie looking rather like an Easter lamb, rather small beside Hilda, who held the wheel. Sir Malcolm was away, but the Kensington house was open.

The doctor examined Connie carefully, and asked her all about her life. 'I see your photograph, and Sir Clifford's, in the illustrated papers sometimes. Almost notorieties, aren't you? That's how the quiet little girls grow up, though you're only a quiet little girl even now, in spite of the illustrated papers. No, no! There's nothing organically wrong, but it won't do! It won't do! Tell Sir Clifford he's got to bring you to town, or take you abroad, and amuse you. You've got to be amused, got to! Your vitality is much too low; no reserves, no reserves. The nerves of the heart a bit queer already: oh, yes! Nothing but nerves; I'd put you right in a month **at Cannes or Biarritz**①. But it mustn't go on, mustn't, I tell you, or I won't be answerable for consequences. You're spending your life without renewing it. You've got to be amused, properly, healthily amused. **You're spending your vitality without making any**②. Can't go on, you know. Depression! Avoid depression!'

Hilda set her jaw, and that meant something.

Michaelis heard they were in town, and came running with roses. 'Why, whatever's wrong?' he cried. **'You're a shadow of yourself**③. Why, I never saw such a change! Why ever didn't you let me know? Come to Nice with me! Come down to Sicily! Go on, come

①在戛纳或比亚里茨。这两地均为法国南部旅游胜地。②你伤了元气而不补充。③你瘦得像个鬼。

to Sicily with me. It's lovely there just now. You want sun! You want life! Why, you're wasting away! Come away with me! Come to Africa! Oh, hang Sir Clifford! Chuck him, and come along with me. I'll marry you the minute he divorces you. Come along and try a life! God's love! That place Wragby would kill anybody. Beastly place! Foul place! Kill anybody! Come away with me into the sun! It's the sun you want, of course, and a bit of normal life.'

But Connie's heart simply stood still at the thought of abandoning Clifford there and then. She couldn't do it. No...no! She just couldn't. She had to go back to Wragby.

Michaelis was disgusted. Hilda didn't like Michaelis, but she almost preferred him to Clifford. Back went the sisters to the Midlands.

Hilda talked to Clifford, who still had yellow eyeballs when they got back. He, too, in his way, was overwrought; but he had to listen to all Hilda said, to all the doctor had said, not what Michaelis had said, of course, and he sat mum through the ultimatum.

'Here is the address of a good manservant, who was with an invalid patient of the doctor's till he died last month. He is really a good man, and fairly sure to come.'

'But I'm not an invalid, and I will not have a manservant,' said Clifford, poor devil.

'And here are the addresses of two women; I saw one of them, she would do very well; a woman of about fifty, quiet, strong, kind, and in her way cultured...'

Clifford only sulked, and would not answer.

'Very well, Clifford. If we don't settle something by to-morrow, I shall telegraph to Father, and we shall take Connie away.'

'Will Connie go?' asked Clifford.

'She doesn't want to, but she knows she must. Mother died of cancer, brought on by fretting. We're not running any risks.'

So next day Clifford suggested Mrs Bolton, Tevershall parish nurse. Apparently Mrs Betts had thought of her. Mrs Bolton was just retiring from her parish duties to take up private nursing jobs. Clifford had a queer dread of delivering himself into the hands of a stranger, but this Mrs Bolton had once nursed him through scarlet fever, and he knew her.

The two sisters at once called on Mrs Bolton, in a newish house in a row, quite select for Tevershall. They found a rather good-looking woman of forty-odd, in a nurse's uniform, with a white collar and apron, just making herself tea in a small crowded sitting-room.

Mrs Bolton was most attentive and polite, seemed quite nice, spoke with a bit of a broad slur, but in heavily correct English, and from having bossed the sick colliers for a good many years, had a very good opinion of herself, and a fair amount of assurance. In short, in her tiny way, one of the governing class in the village, very much respected.

'Yes, Lady Chatterley's not looking at all well! Why, she used to be that bonny, didn't she now? But she's been failing all winter! Oh, it's hard, it is. Poor Sir Clifford! Eh, that war, it's a lot to answer for.'

And Mrs Bolton would come to Wragby at once, if Dr Shardlow would let her off. She had another fortnight's parish nursing to do, by rights, but they might get a substitute, you know.

Hilda posted off to Dr Shardlow, and on the following Sunday Mrs Bolton drove up in Leiver's cab to Wragby with two trunks. Hilda had talks with her; Mrs Bolton was ready at any moment to talk. And she seemed so young! The way the passion would flush in her rather pale cheek. She was forty-seven.

Her husband, Ted Bolton, had been killed in the pit, twenty-two years ago, twenty-two years last Christmas, just at Christmas time, leaving her with two children, one a baby in arms. Oh, the baby was married now, Edith, to a young man in Boots Cash Chemists in Sheffield. The other one was a schoolteacher in Chesterfield; she came home weekends, when she wasn't asked out somewhere. Young folks enjoyed themselves nowadays, not like when she, Ivy Bolton, was young.

Ted Bolton was twenty-eight when he was killed in an explosion down th' pit. The butty in front shouted to them all to lie down quick, there were four of them. And they all lay down in time, only Ted, and it killed him. Then at the inquiry, on the masters' side they said Ted had been frightened, and trying to run away, and not obeying orders, so it was like his fault really. So the compensation was only three hundred pounds, and they made out as if it was more of a gift than legal compensation, because it was really the man's own fault. And they wouldn't let her have the money down; she wanted to have a little shop. But they said she'd no doubt squander it, perhaps in drink! So she had to draw it thirty shillings a week. Yes, she had to go every Monday morning down to the offices, and stad there a couple of hours waiting her turn; yes, for almost four years she went every Monday. And what could she do with two little children on her hands? But Ted's mother was very good to her. When the baby could toddle she'd keep both the children for the day, while she, Ivy Bolton, went to Sheffield, and attended classes in ambulance, and then the fourth year she even took a nursing course and got qualified. She was determined to be independent and keep her children. So she was assistant at Uthwaite hospital, just a little place, for a while. But when the Company, the Tevershall Colliery Company, really Sir Geoffrey, saw that she could get on by herself, they were very good to her, gave her the parish nursing, and stood by her, she would say that for them. And she'd done it ever since, till now it was getting a bit much for her; she needed something a bit lighter, there was such a lot of traipsing around if you were a district nurse.

'Yes, the Company's been very good to me, I always say it. But I should never forget what they said about Ted, for he was as steady and fearless a chap as ever set foot on the cage, and it was as good as branding him a coward. But there, he was dead, and could say nothing to none of 'em.'

It was a queer mixture of feelings the woman showed as she talked. She liked the colliers, whom she had nursed for so long; but she felt very superior to them. She felt almost upper class; and at the same time a resentment against the ruling class smouldered in her. The masters! In a dispute between masters and men, she was always for the men. But when there was no question of contest, she was pining to be superior, to be one of the upper class. The upper classes fascinated her, appealing to her peculiar English passion for superiority. She was thrilled to come to Wragby; thrilled to talk to Lady Chatterley, my word, different from the common colliers' wives! She said so in so many words. Yet one could see a grudge against the Chatterleys peep out in her; the grudge against the masters.

'Why, yes, of course, it would wear Lady Chatterley out! It's a mercy she had a sister to come and help her. **Men don't think, high and low-alike**[1], they take what a woman does for them for granted. Oh, I've told the colliers off about it many a time. But it's very hard for

[1] 男人们无论高低贵贱都不会这样看。

Sir Clifford, you know, crippled like that. They were always a haughty family, standoffish in a way, as they've a right to be. But then to be brought down like that! And it's very hard on Lady Chatterley, perhaps harder on her. What she misses! I only had Ted three years, but **my word**[1], while I had him I had a husband I could never forget. He was one in a thousand, and jolly as the day. Who'd ever have thought he'd get killed? I don't believe it to this day somehow, I've never believed it, though I washed him with my own hands. But he was never dead for me, he never was. I never took it in.'

This was a new voice in Wragby, very new for Connie to hear; it roused a new ear in her.

For the first week or so, Mrs Bolton, however, was very quiet at Wragby, her assured, bossy manner left her, and she was nervous. With Clifford she was shy, almost frightened, and silent. He liked that, and soon recovered his self-possession, letting her do things for him without even noticing her.

'She's a useful nonentity!' he said. Connie opened her eyes in wonder, but she did not contradict him. So different are impressions on two different people!

And he soon became rather superb, somewhat lordly with the nurse. She had rather expected it, and he played up without knowing. So susceptible we are to what is expected of us! The colliers had been so like children, talking to her, and telling her what hurt them, while she bandaged them, or nursed them. They had always made her feel so grand, almost super-human in her administrations. Now Clifford made her feel small, and like a servant, and she accepted it without a word, adjusting herself to the upper classes.

She came very mute, with her long, handsome face, and downcast eyes, to administer to him. And she said very humbly: 'Shall I do this now, Sir Clifford? Shall I do that?'

'No, leave it for a time. I'll have it done later.'

'Very well, Sir Clifford.'

'Come in again in half an hour.'

'Very well, Sir Clifford.'

'And just take those old papers out, will you?'

'Very well, Sir Clifford.'

[1] 好家伙，真没想到。感叹语，亦做upon/on my word。

She went softly, and in half an hour she came softly again. She was bullied, but she didn't mind. She was experiencing the upper classes. She neither resented nor disliked Clifford; he was just part of a phenomenon, the phenomenon of the high-class folks, so far unknown to her, but now to be known. She felt more at home with Lady Chatterley, and **after all it's the mistress of the house matters most**[1].

Mrs Bolton helped Clifford to bed at night, and slept across the passage from his room, and came if he rang for her in the night. She also helped him in the morning, and soon valeted him completely, even shaving him, in her soft, tentative woman's way. She was very good and competent, and she soon knew how to have him in her power. He wasn't so very different from the colliers after all, when you lathered his chin, and softly rubbed the bristles. The stand-offishness and the lack of frankness didn't bother her; she was having a new experience.

Clifford, however, inside himself, never quite forgave Connie for giving up her personal care of him to a strange hired woman. It killed, he said to himself, the real flower of the intimacy between him and her. But Connie didn't mind that. The fine flower of their intimacy was to her rather like an orchid, **a bulb stuck parasitic on her tree of life**[2], and producing, to her eyes, a rather shabby flower.

Now she had more time to herself she could softly play the piano, up in her room, and sing: 'Touch not the nettle, for the bonds of love are ill to loose.' She had not realized till lately how ill to loose they were, these bonds of love. But thank Heaven she had loosened them! She was so glad to be alone, not always to have to talk to him. When he was alone he tapped-tapped-tapped on a typewriter, to infinity. But when he was not 'working', and she was there, he talked, always talked; infinite small analysis of people and motives, and results, characters and personalities, till now she had had enough. For years she had loved it, until she had enough, and then suddenly it was too much. She was thankful to be alone.

It was as if thousands and thousands of little roots and threads of consciousness in him and her had grown together into a tangled mass, till they could crowd no more, and the plant was dying. Now quietly, subtly, she was unravelling the tangle of his consciousness and hers,

❶毕竟主家的是女人。 ❷寄生在她的生命之树上的球茎之花。

breaking the threads gently, one by one, with patience and impatience to get clear. But **the bonds of such love are more ill to loose even than most bonds**[1]; though Mrs Bolton's coming had been a great help.

But he still wanted the old intimate evenings of talk with Connie: talk or reading aloud. But now she could arrange that Mrs Bolton should come at ten to disturb them. At ten o'clock Connie could go upstairs and be alone. Clifford was in good hands with Mrs Bolton.

Mrs Bolton ate with Mrs Betts in the housekeeper's room, since they were all agreeable. And it was curious how much closer the servants' quarters seemed to have come; right up to the doors of Clifford's study, when before they were so remote. For Mrs Betts would sometimes sit in Mrs Bolton's room, and Connie heard their lowered voices, and felt somehow the strong, other vibration of the working people almost invading the sitting-room, when she and Clifford were alone. So changed was Wragby merely by Mrs Bolton's coming.

And Connie felt herself released, in another world, she felt she breathed differently. But still she was afraid of how many of her roots, perhaps mortal ones, were tangled with Clifford's. Yet still, she breathed freer, a new phase was going to begin in her life.

CHAPTER 8

Mrs Bolton also kept a cherishing eye on Connie, feeling she must extend to her her female and professional protection. She was always urging her ladyship to walk out, to drive to Uthwaite, to be in the air. For Connie had got into the habit of sitting still by the fire, pretending to read; or to sew feebly, and hardly going out at all.

It was a blowy day soon after Hilda had gone, that Mrs Bolton said: 'Now why don't you go for a walk through the wood, and look at the daffs behind the keeper's cottage? They're the prettiest sight you'd see in a day's march. And you could put some in your room; wild daffs are

[1] 爱的纠葛比其他纠葛更难解开。

always so cheerful-looking, aren't they?'

Connie took it in good part[1], even daffs for daffodils. Wild daffodils! After all, one could not **stew in one's own juice**[2]. The spring came back... '**Seasons return, but not to me returns Day, or the sweet approach of Ev'n or Morn**[3].'

And the keeper, his thin, white body, like a lonely pistil of an invisible flower! She had forgotten him in her unspeakable depression. But now something roused... '**Pale beyond porch and portal**[4]'... the thing to do was to pass the porches and the portals.

She was stronger, she could walk better, and in the wood the wind would not be so tiring as it was across the bark, flatten against her. She wanted to forget, to forget the world, and all the dreadful, carrion-bodied people. '**Ye must be born again! I believe in the resurrection of the body! Except a grain of wheat fall into the earth and die, it shall by no means bring forth. When the crocus cometh forth I too will emerge and see the sun**[5]!' In the wind of March endless phrases swept through her consciousness.

Little gusts of sunshine blew, strangely bright, and lit up the celandines at the wood's edge, under the hazel-rods, they spangled out bright and yellow. And the wood was still, stiller, but yet gusty with crossing sun. The first windflowers were out, and all the wood seemed pale with the pallor of endless little anemones, sprinkling the shaken floor. '**The world has grown pale with thy breath**[6].' **But it was the breath of Persephone, this time**[7]; she was out of hell on a cold morning. Cold breaths of wind came, and overhead there was an anger of entangled wind caught among the twigs. It, too, was caught and trying to tear itself free, the wind, like **Absalom**[8]. How cold the anemones looked, bobbing their naked white shoulders over

[1]康妮欣然接受了这个意见。in good part赞成地,欣然地(常与take连用);相反in bad(或ill,evil)part为不情愿地,勉强地。[2]自作自受。[3]"四季轮回,但甜蜜的黄昏或清晨却与我无缘。"引自美国诗人弥尔顿的《失乐园》(*Paradise Lost*,1667)第三部。[4]"门厅与大门外的苍白"。引自美国诗人斯温伯恩(1837—1909)的诗作《珀耳塞福涅的花园》。[5]"你必须重生!我相信肉体之复活!一粒麦子不落在地里死掉,是不会结出许多麦粒的。当春花吐蕊之时,我会再度出现,来看太阳。"语出《新约全本·约翰福音》。[6]"世界在你的呼吸中变白"。此句出自诗人斯温伯恩的《珀耳塞福涅赞歌》。[7]但这次却是珀耳塞福涅的呼吸。Persephone:宙斯的女儿,被冥王哈得斯拐骗后为冥国之王后。[8]押沙龙。据《圣经》载,他是犹太王大卫之子,反叛其父,战败后逃往林中,其长发被树枝所缠绕,不能挣脱,被追兵刺死。

crinoline skirts of green. But they stood it. A few first bleached little primroses too, by the path, and yellow buds unfolding themselves.

The roaring and swaying was overhead, only cold currents came down below. Connie was strangely excited in the wood, and the colour flew in her cheeks, and burned blue in her eyes. She walked ploddingly, picking a few primroses and the first violets, that smelled sweet and cold, sweet and cold. And she drifted on without knowing where she was.

Till she came to the clearing, at the end of the wood, and saw the green-stained stone cottage, looking almost rosy, like the flesh underneath a mushroom, its stone warmed in a burst of sun. And there was a sparkle of yellow jasmine by the door; the closed door. But no sound; no smoke from the chimney; no dog barking.

She went quietly round to the back, where the bank rose up; she had an excuse, to see the daffodils.

And they were there, the short-stemmed flowers, rustling and fluttering and shivering, so bright and alive, but with nowhere to hide their faces, as they turned them away from the wind.

They shook their bright, sunny little rags in bouts of distress. But perhaps they liked it really; perhaps they really liked the tossing.

Constance sat down with her back to a young pine-tree, that wayed against her with curious life, elastic, and powerful, rising up. The erect, alive thing, with its top in the sun! And she watched the daffodils turn golden, in a burst of sun that was warm on her hands and lap. Even she caught the faint, tarry scent of the flowers. And then, being so still and alone, she seemed to bet into the current of her own proper destiny. She had been fastened by a rope, and jagging and snarring like a boat at its moorings; now she was loose and adrift.

The sunshine gave way to chill; the daffodils were in shadow, dipping silently. So they would dip through the day and the long cold night. So strong in their frailty!

She rose, a little stiff, took a few daffodils, and went down. She hated breaking the flowers, but she wanted just one or two to go with her. She would have to go back to Wragby and its walls, and now she hated it, especially its thick walls. Walls! Always walls! Yet one needed them in this wind.

When she got home Clifford asked her:

'Where did you go?'

'Right across the wood! Look, aren't the little daffodils adorable? To think they should come out of the earth! '

'Just as much out of air and sunshine,' he said.

'But modelled in the earth,' she retorted, with a prompt contradiction, that surprised her a little.

The next afternoon she went to the wood again. She followed the broad riding that swerved round and up through the larches to a spring called John's Well. It was cold on this hillside, and not a flower in the darkness of larches. But the icy little spring softly pressed upwards from its tiny well-bed of pure, reddish-white pebbles. How icy and clear it was! Brilliant! The new keeper had no doubt put in fresh pebbles. She heard the faint tinkle of water, as the tiny overflow trickled over and downhill. Even above the hissing boom of the larchwood, that spread its bristling, leafless, wolfish darkness on the down-slope, she heard the tinkle as of tiny water-bells.

This place was a little sinister, cold, damp. Yet the well must have been a drinking-place for hundreds of years. Now no more. Its tiny cleared space was lush and cold and dismal.

She rose and went slowly towards home. As she went she heard a faint tapping away on the right, and stood still to listen. Was it hammering, or a woodpecker? It was surely hammering.

She walked on, listening. And then she noticed a narrow track between young fir-trees, a track that seemed to lead nowhere. But she felt it had been used. She turned down it adventurously, between the thick young firs, which gave way soon to the old oak wood. She followed the track, and the hammering grew nearer, in the silence of the windy wood, for trees make a silence even in their noise of wind.

She saw a secret little clearing, and a secret little hot made of rustic poles. And she had never been here before! She realized it was the quiet place where the growing pheasants were reared; the keeper in his shirt-sleeves was kneeling, hammering. The dog trotted forward with a short, sharp bark, and the keeper lifted his face suddenly and saw her. He had a startled look in his eyes.

He straightened himself and saluted, watching her in silence, as she came forward with weakening limbs. He resented the intrusion; he cherished his solitude as his only and last freedom in life.

'I wondered what the hammering was,' she said, feeling weak and breathless, and a little afraid of him, as he looked so straight at her.

'Ah'm gettin' th' coops ready for th' young bods❶,' he said, in broad vernacular.

She did not know what to say, and she felt weak. 'I should like to sit down a bit,' she said.

'Come and sit 'ere i' th' 'ut❷,' he said, going in front of her to the hut, pushing aside some timber and stuff, and drawing out a rustic chair, made of hazel sticks.

'Am Ah t' light yer a little fire❸?' he asked, with the curious **naïveté**❹ of the dialect.

'Oh, don't bother,' she replied.

But he looked at her hands; they were rather blue. So he quickly took some larch twigs to the little brick fire-place in the corner, and in a moment the yellow flame was running up the chimney. He made a place by the brick hearth.

'Sit 'ere then a bit, and warm yer,' he said.

She obeyed him. He had that curious kind of protective authority she obeyed at once. So she sat and warmed her hands at the blaze, and dropped logs on the fire, whilst outside he was hammering again. She did not really want to sit, poked in a corner by the fire; she would rather have watched from the door, but she was being looked after, so she had to submit.

The hut was quite cosy, panelled with unvarnished deal, having a little rustic table and stool beside her chair, and a carpenter's bench, then a big box, tools, new boards, nails; and many things hung from pegs: axe, hatchet, traps, things in sacks, his coat. It had no window, the light came in through the open door. It was a jumble, but also it was a sort of little sanctuary.

She listened to the tapping of the man's hammer; it was not so happy. He was oppressed. Here was a trespass on his privacy, and a dangerous one! A woman! He had reached the point where all he wanted on earth was to be alone. And yet he was powerless to preserve his privacy; he was a hired man, and these people were his masters.

Especially he did not want to come into contact with a woman again. He feared it; for he had a big wound from old contacts. He felt if he could not be alone, and if he could not be left alone, he would die. His

❶=I'm getting the coops ready for the young birds. ❷=Come and sit here in the hut. ❸=Am I to light you a little fire. ❹幼稚的。

recoil away from the outer world was complete; his last refuge was this wood; to hide himself there!

Connie grew warm by the fire, which she had made too big: then she grew hot. She went and sat on the stool in the doorway, watching the man at work. He seemed not to notice her, but he knew. Yet he worked on, as if absorbedly, and his brown dog sat on her tail near him, and surveyed the untrustworthy world.

Slender, quiet and quick, the man finished the coop he was making, turned it over, tried the sliding door, then set it aside. Then he rose, went for an old coop, and took it to the chopping log where he was working. Crouching, he tried the bars; some broke in his hands; he began to draw the nails. Then he turned the coop over and deliberated, and he gave absolutely no sign of awareness of the woman's presence.

So Connie watched him fixedly. And the same solitary aloneness she had seen in him naked, she now saw in him clothed: solitary, and intent, like an animal that works alone, but also brooding, like a soul that recoils away, away from all human contact. Silently, patiently, he was recoiling away from her even now. It was the stillness, and the timeless sort of patience, in a man impatient and passionate, that touched Connie's womb. She saw it in his bent head, the quick quiet hands, the crouching of his slender, sensitive loins; something patient and withdrawn. She felt his experience had been deeper and wider than her own; much deeper and wider, and perhaps more deadly. And this relieved her of herself; she felt almost irresponsible.

So she sat in the doorway of the hut in a dream, utterly unaware of time and of particular circumstances. She was so drifted away that he glanced up at her quickly, and saw the utterly still, waiting look on her face. To him it was a look of waiting. And a little thin tongue of fire suddenly flickered in his loins, at the root of his back, and he groaned in spirit. He dreaded with a repulsion almost of death, any further close human contact. He wished above all things she would go away, and leave him to his own privacy. He dreaded her will, her female will, and her modern female insistency. And above all he dreaded her cool, upper-class impudence of having her own way. For after all he was only a hired man. He hated her presence there.

Connie came to herself with sudden uneasiness. She rose. The afternoon was turning to evening, yet she could not go away. She went over to the man, who stood up at attention, his worn face stiff and blank, his eyes watching her.

'It is so nice here, so restful,' she said. 'I have never been here before.'

'No?'

'I think I shall come and sit here sometimes.'

'Yes?'

'Do you lock the hut when you're not here?'

'Yes, your Ladyship.'

'Do you think I could have a key too, so that I could sit here sometimes? Are there two keys?'

'**Not as Ah know on, ther' isna**❶.'

He had lapsed into the vernacular. Connie hesitated; he was putting up an opposition. Was it his hut, after all?

'Couldn't we get another key?' she asked in her soft voice, that underneath had the ring of a woman determined to get her way.

'Another!' he said, glancing at her with a flash of anger, touched with derision.

'Yes, a duplicate,' she said, flushing.

'**Appen Sir Clifford 'ud know**❷,' he said, putting her off.

'Yes!' she said, 'he might have another. Otherwise we could have one made from the one you have. It would only take a day or so, I suppose. You could spare your key for so long.'

'Ah canna tell yer, m'Lady! Ah know nob'dy as ma'es keys round 'ere.'

Connie suddenly flushed with anger.

'Very well!' she said. 'I'll see to it.'

'All right, your Ladyship.'

Their eyes met. His had a cold, ugly look of dislike and contempt, and indifference to what would happen. Hers were hot with rebuff.

But her heart sank, she saw how utterly he disliked her, when she went against him. And she saw him in a sort of desperation.

'Good afternoon!'

'Afternoon, my Lady!' He saluted and turned abruptly away. She had wakened the sleeping dogs of old voracious anger in him, anger against the self-willed female. And he was powerless, powerless. He

❶=As far as I know,there is no spare one. ❷=Perhaps Sir Clifford would know.

knew it!

And she was angry against the self-willed male. A servant too! She walked sullenly home.

She found Mrs Bolton under the great beech-tree on the knoll, looking for her.

'I just wondered if you'd be coming, my Lady,' the woman said brightly.

'Am I late?' asked Connie.

'Oh only Sir Clifford was waiting for his tea.'

'Why didn't you make it then?'

'Oh, I don't think it's hardly my place. I don't think Sir Clifford would like it at all, my Lady.'

'I don't see why not,' said Connie.

She went indoors to Clifford's study, where the old brass kettle was simmering on the tray.

'Am I late, Clifford?' she said, putting down the few flowers and taking up the tea-caddy, as she stood before the tray in her hat and scarf. 'I'm sorry! Why didn't you let Mrs Bolton make the tea?'

'I didn't think of it,' he said ironically. 'I don't quite see her presiding at the tea-table.'

'Oh, there's nothing sacrosanct about a silver tea-pot,' said Connie.

He glanced up at her curiously.

'What did you do all afternoon?' he said.

'Walked and sat in a sheltered place. Do you know there are still berries on the big holly-tree?'

She took off her scarf, but not her hat, and sat down to make tea. The toast would certainly be leathery. She put the tea-cosy over the tea-pot, and rose to get a little glass for her violets. The poor flowers hung over, limp on their stalks.

'They'll revive again!' she said, putting them before him in their glass for him to smell.

'**Sweeter than the lids of Juno's eyes**[1],' he quoted.

'I don't see a bit of connexion with the actual violets,' she said. 'The Elizabethans are rather upholstered.'

[1] 比朱诺的眼睑还要温馨。此句出自莎士比亚的戏剧《冬天的故事》(*The Winte's Tale*,1610~1611)。朱诺为罗马神话中的皇后,是主神Jupiter之妻。

She poured him his tea.

'Do you think there is a second key to that little hut not far from John's Well, where the pheasants are reared?' she said.

'There may be. Why?'

'I happened to find it today — and I'd never seen it before. I think it's a darling place. I could sit there sometimes, couldn't I?'

'Was Mellors there?'

'Yes! That's how I found it: his hammering. He didn't seem to like my intruding at all. In fact he was almost rude when I asked about a second key.'

'What did he say?'

'Oh, nothing: just his manner; and he said he knew nothing about keys.'

'There may be one in Father's study. Betts knows them all, they're all there. I'll get him to look.'

'Oh do!' she said.

'So Mellors was almost rude?'

'Oh, nothing, really! But **I don't think he wanted me to have the freedom of the castle**[1], quite.'

'I don't suppose he did.'

'Still, I don't see why he should mind. It's not his home, after all! It's not his private abode. I don't see why I shouldn't sit there if I want to.'

'Quite!' said Clifford. 'He thinks too much of himself, that man.'

'Do you think he does?'

'Oh, decidedly! He thinks he's something exceptional. You know he had a wife he didn't get on with, so he joined up in 1915 and was sent to India, I believe. Anyhow he was blacksmith to the cavalry in Egypt for a time; always was connected with horses, a clever fellow that way. Then **some Indian colonel took a fancy to him**[2], and he was made a lieutenant. Yes, they gave him a commission. I believe he went back to India with his colonel, and up to the north-west frontier. He was ill; he was a pension. He didn't come out of the army till last year, I believe, and then, naturally, it isn't easy for a man like that to get back to his own level. **He's bound to flounder**[3]. But he does his duty all

❶我想他不情愿我在他的王国自由出入。 ❷一位印度上校喜欢上了他。take a fancy to(或for)喜欢，爱上…… ❸他肯定要历尽艰辛。

hank you! I only wanted to be able to sit here sometimes, like today. ut I can sit perfectly well under the porch, so please say no more about .'

He looked at her again, with his wicked blue eyes.

'Why,' he began, in the broad slow dialect. **'Your Ladyship's s welcome as Christmas ter th' hut an' th' key an' erythink as is. On'y this time O' th' year ther's bods r set, an' Ah've got ter be potterin' abaht a good bit, eein' after 'em, an' a'. Winter time Ah ned 'ardly ome nigh th' pleece. But what wi' spring, an' Sir lifford wantin' ter start th' pheasants...An' your adyship'd non want me tinkerin' around an' about hen she was 'ere, all the time**[1].'

She listened with a dim kind of amazement.

'Why should I mind your being here?' she asked.

He looked at her curiously.

'T'nuisance on me[2]!' he said briefly, but significantly. She shed. 'Very well!' she said finally. 'I won't trouble you. But I don't nk I should have minded at all sitting and seeing you look after the ds. I should have liked it. But since you think it interferes with you, I n't disturb you, don't be afraid. You are Sir Clifford's keeper, not e.'

The phrase sounded queer, she didn't know why. But she let it pass.

'Nay, your Ladyship. It's your Ladyship's own 'ut. It's as your yship likes an' pleases, every time. Yer can turn me off at a wik's ce. It wor only...'

'Only what?' she asked, baffled.

He pushed back his hat in an odd comic way.

'On'y as 'appen yo'd like the place ter yersen[3], when id come, an' not me messin' abaht.'

'But why?' she said, angry. 'Aren't you a civilized human being? ou think I ought to be afraid of you? Why should I take any notice

r Ladyship is as welcome as Christmas to the hut and the key and everything as it is. Only this time ar there are binds to set, and I've got to pottering a good bit,seeing after them,and all winter time I rdly come near the place. But what with Spring, and Sir Clifford wanting to start the pheasants... r Ladyship would not want me tinkering about when she was here,all the time. ❷俺自己觉得碍 only as perhaps you would like the place to yourself.

right, as far as I'm concerned. **Only I'm not having any of the Lieutenant Mellors touch**[1].'

'How could they make him an officer when he speaks broad Derbyshire?'

'He doesn't...except **by fits and starts**[2]. He can speak perfectly well, for him. I suppose he has an idea if he's come down to the ranks again, he'd better speak as the ranks speak.'

'Why didn't you tell me about him before?'

'Oh, I've no patience with these romances. They're the ruin of all order. It's a thousand pities they ever happened.'

Connie was inclined to agree. What was the good of discontented people who fitted in nowhere?

In the spell of fine weather Clifford, too, decided to go to the wood. The wind was cold, but not so tiresome, and the sunshine was like life itself, warm and full.

'It's amazing,' said Connie, 'how different one feels when there's a really fresh fine day. Usually one feels the very air is half dead. People are killing the very air.'

'Do you think people are doing it?' he asked.

'I do. The steam of so much boredom, and discontent and anger out of all the people, just kills the vitality in the air. I'm sure of it.'

'Perhaps some condition of the atmosphere lowers the vitality of the people?' he said.

'No, it's man that poisons the universe,' she asserted.

'Fouls his own nest,' remarked Clifford.

The chair puffed on. In the hazel copse catkins were hanging pale gold, and in sunny places the wood-anemones were wide open, as if exclaiming with the joy of life, just as good as in past days, when people could exclaim along with them. They had a faint scent of apple-blossom. Connie gathered a few for Clifford.

He took them and looked at them curiously.

'Thou still unravished bride of quietness[3],' he quoted. 'It seems to fit flowers so much better than Greek vases.'

'Ravished is such a horrid word!' she said. 'It's only people who ravish things.'

❶只不过我不喜欢梅乐士摆出中尉的神气。❷by (或in)fits(and starts)一阵阵地，间歇地。❸"您是未被奸污的娴静新娘"。该句引自美国浪漫主义诗人济慈的诗作《希腊古瓶》。

'Oh, I don't know...snails and things,' he said.

'Even snails only eat them, and bees don't ravish.'

She was angry with him, turning everything into words. Violets were Juno's eyelids, and windflowers were on ravished brides. How she hated words, always coming between her and life: they did the ravishing, if anything did: ready-made words and phrases, sucking all the life-sap out of living things.

The walk with Clifford was not quite a success. Between him and Connie there was a tension that each pretended not to notice, but there it was. Suddenly, with all the force of her female instinct, she was shoving him off. She wanted to be clear of him, and especially of his consciousness, his words, his obsession with himself, his endless treadmill obsession with himself, and his own words.

The weather came rainy again. But after a day or two she went out in the rain, and she went to the wood. And once there, she went towards the hut. It was raining, but not so cold, and the wood felt so silent and remote, inaccessible in the dusk of rain.

She came to the clearing. No one there! The hut was locked. But she sat on the log doorstep, under the rustic porch, and snuggled into her own warmth. So she sat, looking at the rain, listening to the many noiseless noises of it, and to the strange soughings of wind in upper branches, when there seemed to be no wind. Old oak-trees stood around, grey, powerful trunks, rain-blackened, round and vital, throwing off reckless limbs. The ground was fairly free of undergrowth, the anemones sprinkled, there was a bush or two, elder, or guelder-rose, and a purplish tangle of bramble: the old russet of bracken almost vanished under green anemone ruffs. Perhaps this was one of the unravished places. Unravished! The whole world was ravished.

Some things can't be ravished. You can't ravish a tin of sardines. And so many women are like that; and men. But the earth...!

The rain was abating. It was hardly making darkness among the oaks any more. Connie wanted to go; yet she sat on. But she was getting cold; yet the overwhelming inertia of her inner resentment kept her there as if paralysed.

Ravished! How ravished one could be without ever being touched. Ravished by dead words become obscene, and dead ideas become obsessions.

A wet brown dog came running and did not bark, lifting a wet

feather of a tail. The man followed in a wet black oilskin jacke
chauffeur, and face flushed a little. She felt him recoil in his qui
when he saw her. She stood up in the handbreadth of dryness u
rustic porch. He saluted without speaking, coming slowly n
began to withdraw.

'I'm just going,' she said.

'Was yer waitin' to get in?' he asked, looking at the hu
her.

'No, I only sat a few minutes in the shelter,' she said,
dignity.

He looked at her. She looked cold.

'Sir Clifford 'adn't got no other key then?' he asked.

'No, but it doesn't matter. I can sit perfectly dry under
Good afternoon!' She hated the excess of vernacular in his sp

He watched her closely, as she was moving away. Then
up his jacket, and put his hand in his breeches pocket, taking
of the hut.

''Appen yer'd better 'ave this key, **an' Ah min fe**
bods some other road❶.'

She looked at him.

'What do you mean?' she asked.

'I mean as 'appen Ah can find anuther pleece as'll du
th' pheasants. If yer want ter be 'ere, yo'll non want me m
a' th' time.'

She looked at him, getting his meaning through th
dialect.

'Why don't you speak ordinary English?' she said cold

'Me! **Ah thowt it wor ordinary**❷.'

She was silent for a few moments in anger.

'So if yer want t' key, yer'd better tacit. **Or 'a**
better gi'e 't yer termorrer, an' clear all t' stu
Would that du for yer?'

She became more angry.

'I didn't want your key,' she said. 'I don't wa
anything out at all. I don't in the least want to turn you c

❶=I must find some other place for the birds. ❷=I thought it was ordinary. ❸=Or
it to you tomorrow,and clear all the stuff at first.

of you and your being here or not? Why is it important?'

He looked at her, all his face glimmering with wicked laughter.

'It's not, your Ladyship. Not in the very least,' he said.

'Well, why then?' she asked.

'Shall I get your Ladyship another key then?'

'No thank you! I don't want it.'

'Ah'll get it anyhow. We'd best 'ave two keys ter th' place.'

'And I consider you are insolent,' said Connie, with her colour up, panting a little.

'Nay, nay!' he said quickly. '**Dunna yer say that**[1]! Nay, nay! **I niver meant nuthink**[2]. Ah on'y thought as if yo' come 'ere, **Ah s'd ave ter clear out**[3], an' it'd mean a lot of work, settin' up somewheres else. But if your Ladyship isn't going ter take no notice O' me, then...it's Sir Clifford's 'ut, an' everythink is as your Ladyship likes, everythink is as your Ladyship likes an' pleases, barrin' yer take no notice O' me, doin' th' bits of jobs as Ah've got ter do.'

Connie went away completely bewildered. She was not sure whether she had been insulted and mortally offended, or not. Perhaps the man really only meant what he said; that he thought she would expect him to keep away. As if she would dream of it! And as if he could possibly be so important, he and his stupid presence.

She went home in confusion, not knowing what she thought or felt.

CHAPTER 9

Connie was surprised at her own feeling of aversion from Clifford. What is more, she felt she had always really disliked him. Not hate: there was no passion in it. But a profound physical dislike. Almost, it seemed to her, she had married him because she disliked him, in a secret, physical sort of way. But of course, she had married him really because in a mental way he attracted her and excited her. He had seemed, in some way, her master, beyond her.

Now the mental excitement had worn itself out and collapsed, and

[1]=Don't you say that. [2]=I did not mean anything. [3]=I should have to clear out.

she was aware only of the physical aversion. It rose up in her from her depths: and she realized how it had been eating her life away.

She felt weak and utterly forlorn. She wished some help would come from outside. But in the whole world there was no help. Society was terrible because it was insane. Civilized society is insane. **Money and so-called love are its two great manias; money a long way first**[1]. The individual asserts himself in his disconnected insanity in these two modes: money and love. Look at Michaelis! His life and activity were just insanity. His love was a sort of insanity.

And Clifford the same. All that talk! All that writing! All that wild struggling to push himself forwards! It was just insanity. And it was getting worse, really maniacal.

Connie felt washed-out with fear. But at least, Clifford was shifting his grip from her on to Mrs Bolton. He did not know it. Like many insane people, **his insanity might be measured by the things he was not aware of the great desert tracts in his consciousness**[2].

Mrs Bolton was admirable in many ways. But she had that queer sort of bossiness, endless assertion of her own will, which is one of the signs of insanity in modern woman. She thought she was utterly subservient and living for others. Clifford fascinated her because he always, or so often, frustrated her will, as if by a finer instinct. He had a finer, subtler will of self-assertion than herself. This was his charm for her.

Perhaps that had been his charm, too, for Connie.

'It's a lovely day, today!' Mrs Bolton would say in her caressive, persuasive voice. 'I should think you'd enjoy a little run in your chair today, the sun's just lovely.'

'Yes? Will you give me that book — there, that yellow one. And I think I'll have those hyacinths taken out.'

'Why they're so beautiful!' She pronounced it with the 'y' sound: be-yutiful! 'And the scent is simply gorgeous.'

'The scent is what I objcct to,' he said. 'It's a little funereal.'

'Do you think so!' she exclaimed in surprise, just a little offended, but impressed. And she carried the hyacinths out of the room,

❶金钱和所谓的爱情是社会疯狂的热点，而以金钱为最。❷他的癫狂或许由他未意识到的许多事物来度量，那是他意识中的不毛之地。

impressed by his higher fastidiousness.

'Shall I shave you this morning, or would you rather do it yourself?' Always the same soft, caressive, subservient, yet managing voice.

'I don't know. Do you mind waiting a while. I'll ring when I'm ready.'

'Very good, Sir Clifford!' she replied, so soft and submissive, withdrawing quietly. But every rebuff stored up new energy of will in her.

When he rang, after a time, she would appear at once. And then he would say:

'I think I'd rather you shaved me this morning.'

Her heart gave a little thrill, and she replied with extra softness:

'Very good, Sir Clifford!'

She was very deft, with a soft, lingering touch, a little slow. At first he had resented the infinitely soft touch of her lingers on his face. But now he liked it, with a growing voluptuousness. He let her shave him nearly every day: her face near his, her eyes so very concentrated, watching that she did it right. And gradually her fingertips knew his cheeks and lips, his jaw and chin and throat perfectly. He was well-fed and well-liking, his face and throat were handsome enough and he was a gentleman.

She was handsome too, pale, her face rather long and absolutely still, her eyes bright, but revealing nothing. Gradually, with infinite softness, almost with love, **she was getting him by the throat**①, and he was yielding to her.

She now did almost everything for him, and he felt more at home with her, **less ashamed of accepting her menial offices**②, than with Connie. She liked handling him. She loved having his body in her charge, absolutely, to the last menial offices. She said to Connie one day: 'All men are babies, **when you come to the bottom of them**③. Why, I've handled some of the toughest customers as ever went down Tevershall pit. But let anything ail them so that you have to do for them, and they're babies, just big babies. Oh, there's not much

①她牢牢地控制住了他。get/have by the throat控制，战胜…… ②心安理得地接受她卑微的服务。 ③当你彻底地了解了他们后。

difference in men! '

At first Mrs Bolton had thought there really was something different in a gentleman, a real gentleman, like Sir Clifford. So Clifford had got a good start of her. But gradually, as she came to the bottom of him, to use her own term, she found he was like the rest, a baby grown to man's proportions: but a baby with a queer temper and a fine manner and power in its control, and all sorts of odd knowledge that she had never dreamed of, with which he could still bully her.

Connie was sometimes tempted to say to him:

'For God's sake, don't sink so horribly into the hands of that woman! ' But she found she didn't care for him enough to say it, in the long run.

It was still their habit to spend the evening together, till ten o'clock. Then they would talk, or read together, or go over his manuscript. But the thrill had gone out of it. She was bored by his manuscripts. But she still dutifully typed them out for him. But in time Mrs Bolton would do even that.

For Connie had suggested to Mrs Bolton that she should learn to use a typewriter. And Mrs Bolton, always ready, had begun at once, and practised assiduously. So now Clifford would sometimes dictate a letter to her, and she would take it down rather slowly, but correctly. And he was very patient, spelling for her the difficult words, or the occasional phrases in French. She was so thrilled, it was almost a pleasure to instruct her.

Now Connie would sometimes plead a headache as an excuse for going up to her room after dinner.

'**Perhaps Mrs Bolton will play piquet with you**[1],' she said to Clifford.

'Oh, I shall be perfectly all right. You go to your own room and rest, darling.'

But no sooner had she gone, than he rang for Mrs Bolton, and asked her to take a hand at piquet or **bezique**[2], or even chess. He had taught her all these games. And Connie found it curiously objectionable to see Mrs Bolton, flushed and tremulous like a little girl, touching her queen or her knight with uncertain fingers, then drawing away again.

❶博尔顿夫人也许可以和你玩皮克牌。皮克牌,一种两人玩的纸牌,共32张。 ❷齐克牌,一种两人玩的牌,共64张。

And Clifford, faintly smiling with a half-teasing superiority, saying to her:

'You must say **j'adoube**[1]!'

She looked up at him with bright, startled eyes, then murmured shyly, obediently:

'J'adoube!'

Yes, he was educating her. And he enjoyed it, it gave him a sense of power. And she was thrilled. She was coming bit by bit into possession of all that the gentry knew, all that made them upper class: apart from the money. That thrilled her. And at the same time, she was making him want to have her there with him. It was a subtle deep flattery to him, her genuine thrill.

To Connie, **Clifford seemed to be coming out in his true colours**[2]: a little vulgar, a little common, and uninspired; rather fat. Ivy Bolton's tricks and humble bossiness were also only too transparent. But Connie did wonder at the genuine thrill which the woman got out of Clifford. To say she was in love with him would be putting it wrongly. She was thrilled by her contact with a man of the upper class, this titled gentleman, this author who could write books and poems, and whose photograph appeared in the illustrated newspapers. She was thrilled to a weird passion. And his 'educating' her roused in her a passion of excitement and response much deeper than any love affair could have done. In truth, **the very fact that there could be no love affair left her free to thrill to her very marrow with this other passion, the peculiar passion of knowing, knowing as he knew**[3].

There was no mistake that the woman was in some way in love with him: whatever force we give to the word love. She looked so handsome and so young, and her grey eyes were sometimes marvellous. At the same time, there was a lurking soft satisfaction about her, even of triumph, and private satisfaction. Ugh, that private satisfaction. How Connie loathed it!

But no wonder Clifford was caught by the woman! She absolutely adored him, in her persistent fashion, and put herself absolutely at his

❶(法)相当于I adjust. ❷克利福德似在原形毕露。 ❸正是因为不可能产生爱情,她才随心所欲地被另一种热心所陶醉痴迷。这种热情心照不宣,他亦心知肚明。

service, for him to use as he liked. No wonder he was flattered!

Connie heard long conversations going on between the two. Or rather, it was mostly Mrs Bolton talking. She had unloosed to him the stream of gossip about Tevershall village. It was more than gossip. It was Mrs Gaskell and George Eliot and Miss Mitford all rolled in one, with a great deal more, that these women left out. Once started, Mrs Bolton was better than any book, about the lives of the people. She knew them all so intimately, and had such a peculiar, flamey zest in all their affairs, it was wonderful, **if just a trifle humiliating to listen to her**[1]. At first she had not ventured to 'talk Tevershall', as she called it, to Clifford. But once started, it went on. Clifford was listening for 'material', and he found it in plenty. Connie realized that his so-called genius was just this: a perspicuous talent for personal gossip, clever and apparently detached. Mrs Bolton, of course, was very warm when she 'talked Tevershall'. Carried away, in fact. And it was marvellous, the things that happened and that she knew about. She would have run to dozens of volumes.

Connie was fascinated, listening to her. But afterwards always a little ashamed. She ought not to listen with this queer rabid curiosity. After all, one may hear the most private affairs of other people, but only in a spirit of respect for the struggling, battered thing which any human soul is, and in a spirit of fine, discriminative sympathy. For even satire is a form of sympathy. It is the way our sympathy flows and recoils that really determines our lives. And here lies the vast importance of the novel, properly handled. It can inform and lead into new places the flow of our sympathetic consciousness, and it can lead our sympathy away in recoil from things gone dead. **Therefore, the novel, properly handled, can reveal the most secret places of life: for it is in the passional secret places of life, above all, that the tide of sensitive awareness needs to ebb and flow, cleansing and freshening**[2].

But the novel, like gossip, can also excite spurious sympathies and recoils, mechanical and deadening to the psyche. The novel can glorify the most corrupt feelings, so long as they are conventionally 'pure'.

❶听起来尽管有点不作。 ❷因此，撰写恰当的小说，能揭示出生活中最奥秘之处；因为在人生感情的神秘之处，尤其是敏锐的认识之潮需要涨落起伏，净化更新。

Then the novel, like gossip, becomes at last vicious, and, like gossip, **all the more vicious because it is always ostensibly on the side of the angels**❶. Mrs Bolton's gossip was always on the side of the angels. 'And he was such a bad fellow, and she was such a nice woman.' Whereas, as Connie could see even from Mrs Bolton's gossip, the woman had been merely a mealy-mouthed sort, and the man angrily honest. But angry honesty made a 'bad man' of him, and mealy-mouthedness made a 'nice woman' of her, in the vicious, conventional channelling of sympathy by Mrs Bolton.

For this reason, the gossip was humiliating. And for the same reason, most novels, especially popular ones, are humiliating too. The public responds now only to an appeal to its vices.

Nevertheless, one got a new vision of Tevershall village from Mrs Bolton's talk. **A terrible, seething welter of ugly life it seemed**❷: not at all the flat drabness it looked from outside. Clifford of course knew by sight most of the people mentioned, Connie knew only one or two. But it sounded really more like a Central African jungle than an English village.

'I suppose you heard as Miss Allsopp was married last week! Would you ever! Miss Allsopp, old James' daughter, **the boot-and-shoe Allsopp**❸. You know they built a house up at Pye Croft. The old man died last year from a fall; eighty-three, he was, an' nimble as a lad. An' then he slipped on Bestwood Hill, on a slide as the lads 'ad made last winter, an' broke his thigh, and that finished him, poor old man, it did seem a shame. Well, he left all his money to Tattie: didn't leave the boys a penny. An' Tattie, I know, is five years — yes, she's fifty-three last autumn. And you know they were **such Chapel people**❹, my word! She taught Sunday school for thirty years, till her father died. And then she started **carrying on with a fellow**❺ from Kinbrook, I don't know if you know him, an oldish fellow with a red nose, rather dandified, Willcock, as works in Harrison's woodyard. **Well he's sixty-five, if he's a day**❻, yet you'd have thought they were a pair of young turtle-doves, to see them, arm in arm, and kissing at the gate: yes, an' she sitting on his knee right in the bay window on Pye Croft

❶因为它始终披着天使的外衣而更加邪恶。❷它似乎是可怕的不断翻动的丑陋生活的渊源。❸鞋匠奥尔索普。❹虔诚的教徒。❺(口)发生不正当的男女关系。❻他至少65岁。

Road, for anybody to see. And he's got sons over forty: only lost his wife two years ago. If old James Allsopp hasn't risen from his grave, it's because there is no rising: for he kept her that strict! Now they're married and gone to live down at Kinbrook, and they say she goes round in a dressing-gown from morning to night, a veritable sight. I'm sure it's awful, the way the old ones go on! Why they're a lot worse than the young, and a sight more disgusting. **I lay it down to the pictures, myself**❶. But you can't keep them away. I was always saying: go to a good instructive film, but do for goodness sake keep away from these melodramas and love films. Anyhow keep the children away! But there you are, grown-ups are worse than the children: **and the old ones beat the band**❷. Talk about morality! Nobody cares a thing. Folks does as they like, and much better off they are for it, I must say. But **they're having to draw their horns in nowadays**❸, now th' pits are working so bad, and they haven't got the money. And the grumbling they do, it's awful, especially the women. The men are so good and patient! What can they do, poor chaps! But the women, oh, they do carry on! They go and show off, giving contributions for a wedding present for Princess Mary, and then when they see all the grand things that's been given, they simply rave: who's she, any better than anybody else! Why doesn't **Swan & Edgar**❹ give me one fur coat, instead of giving her six. I wish I'd kept my ten shillings! What's she going to give me, I should like to know? Here I can't get a new spring coat, my dad's working that bad, and she gets van-loads. It's time as poor folks had some money to spend, rich ones ' as 'ad it long enough. I want a new spring coat, I do, an' wheer am I going to get it? I say to them, be thankful you're well fed and well clothed, without all the new finery you want! **And they fly back at me**❺: "Why isn't Princess Mary thankful to go about in her old rags, then, an' have nothing! Folks like her get van-loads, an' I can't have a new spring coat. It's a damned shame. Princess! Bloomin' rot about Princess! **It's munney as matters, an' cos she's got lots, they give her more**❻! Nobody's givin' me any, an' I've as much

❶我个人认为这全怪电影。❷姜还是老的辣。beat the and(俚)出众,了不起;异常地。❸现今他们应该收敛了。❹斯万—埃望加百货公司,伦敦一家大百货公司。❺反唇相讥。❻=It's money as matters, and because she's got lots, they gave her more.

right as anybody else. Don't talk to me about education. It's munney as matters. I want a new spring coat, I do, an' I shan't get it, cos there's no munney..." That's all they care about, clothes. They think nothing of **giving seven or eight guineas for a winter coat** ❶ — colliers' daughters, mind you — and two guineas for a child's summer hat. And then they go to **the Primitive Chapel**❷ in their two-guinea hat, girls as would have been proud of a three-and-sixpenny one in my day. I heard that at the Primitive Methodist anniversary this year, when they have a built-up platform for **the Sunday School**❸ children, like a grandstand going almost up to th' ceiling, I heard Miss Thompson, who has the first class of girls in the Sunday School, say there'd be over a thousand pounds in new Sunday clothes sitting on that platform! **And times are what they are**❹! But you can't stop them. They're mad for clothes. And boys the same. The lads spend every penny on themselves, clothes, smoking, drinking in the Miners' Welfare, jaunting off to Sheffield two or three times a week. Why, it's another world. And they fear nothing, and they respect nothing, the young don't. The older men are that patient and good, really, they let the women take everything. And this is what it leads to. The women are positive demons. But the lads aren't like their dads. They're sacrificing nothing, they aren't: they're all for self. If you tell them they ought to **be putting a bit by**❺, for a home, they say: That'll keep, that will, I'm goin' t' enjoy myself while I can. **Owt else'll keep**❻! Oh, they're rough an' selfish, if you like. Everything falls on the older men, an' it's a bad outlook all round.'

Clifford began to get a new idea of his own village. The place had always frightened him, but he had thought it more or less stable. Now — ?

'Is there much Socialism, Bolshevism, among the people?' he asked.

'Oh!' said Mrs Bolton, 'you hear a few loud-mouthed ones. But they're mostly women who've got into debt. The men take no notice. I don't believe you'll ever turn our Tevershall men into **reds**❼. They're too decent for that. But the young ones blether sometimes. Not that they care

❶花七，八个几尼买一件大衣。几尼，1813年停止流通的一种金币，值21先令。❷早期基督教教会。❸主日学校。（指利用星期日对儿童进行宗教教育的学校）。❹这年头就是这样。❺积攒一点钱。❻省钱有啥用。owt，英北部方言=anything。❼信仰布尔什维克主义的赤色分子。

for it really. They only want a bit of money in their pocket, to spend at the Welfare, or go gadding to Sheffield. That's all they care. When they've got no money, they'll listen to the reds spouting. But nobody believes in it, really.'

'So you think there's no danger?'

'Oh no! Not if trade was good, there wouldn't be. But if things were bad for a long spell, **the young ones might go funny**[1]. I tell you, they're a selfish, spoilt lot. But I don't see how they'd ever do anything. They aren't ever serious about anything, except showing off on motor-bikes and dancing at **the Palais-de-danse**[2] in Sheffield. You can't make them serious. The serious ones dress up in evening clothes and go off to the Pally to show off before a lot of girls and dance these new Charlestons and what not. I'm sure sometimes the bus'll be full of young fellows in evening suits, collier lads, off to the Pally: let alone those that have gone with their girls in motors or on motor-bikes. They don't give a serious thought to a thing — **save Doncaster races, and the Derby**[3]: for they all of them bet on every race. And football! But even football's not what it was, not **by a long chalk**[4]. It's too much like hard work, they say. No, they'd rather be off on motor-bikes to Sheffield or Nottingham, Saturday afternoons.'

'But what do they do when they get there?'

'Oh, **hang around**[5] — and have tea in some fine tea-place like the Mikado — and go to the Pally or the pictures or the Empire, with some girl. The girls are as free as the lads. They do just what they like.'

'And what do they do when they haven't the money for these things?'

'They seem to get it, somehow. And they begin talking nasty then. But I don't see how you're going to get bolshevism, when all the lads want is just money to enjoy themselves, and the girls the same, with fine clothes: and they don't care about another thing. They haven't the brains to be socialists. They haven't enough seriousness to take anything really serious, and they never will have.'

Connie thought, how extremely like all the rest of the classes the

❶年轻人便会闹事。❷(法)舞厅。❸除了唐卡斯特和德比的赛马会。唐卡斯特,英格兰北部一工业城镇。德比,自1780年以来每年举行赛马之地,此名是为了纪念创办赛马活动的德比先生(1834年去世)而起的。❹by a long chalk(或by long chalks)在很大程度上。❺闲逛。

lower classes sounded. Just the same thing over again, Tevershall or Mayfair or Kensington. There was only one class nowadays: moneyboys. The moneyboy and the moneygirl, the only difference was how much you'd got, and how much you wanted.

Under Mrs Bolton's influence, Clifford began to take a new interest in the mines. He began to feel he belonged. A new sort of self-assertion came into him. After all, he was the real boss in Tevershall, he was really the pits. It was a new sense of power, something he had till now shrunk from with dread.

Tevershall pits were running thin. There were only two collieries: Tevershall itself, and New London. Tevershall had once been a famous mine, and had made famous money. But its best days were over. New London was never very rich, and in ordinary times just got along decently. But now times were bad, and it was pits like New London that got left.

'There's a lot of Tevershall men left and gone to Stacks Gate and Whiteover,' said Mrs Bolton. 'You've not seen the new works at Stacks Gate, opened after the war, have you, Sir Clifford? Oh, you must go one day, they're something quite new: great big chemical works at the pit-head, doesn't look a bit like a colliery. They say they get more money out of the chemical by-products than out of the coal — I forget what it is. And the grand new houses for the men, fair mansions! of course it's brought a lot of **riff-raff**[1] from all over the country. But a lot of Tevershall men got on there, and doin' well, a lot better than our own men. They say Tevershall's done, finished: only a question of a few more years, and it'll have to shut down. And New London'll go first. My word, won't it be funny when there's no Tevershall pit working. It's bad enough during a strike, but my word, **if it closes for good, it'll be like the end of the world**[2]. Even when I was a girl it was the best pit in the country, and a man counted himself lucky if he could on here. Oh, there's been some money made in Tevershall. And now the men say it's a sinking ship, and it's time they all got out. Doesn't it sound awful! But of course there's a lot as'll never go till they have to. They don't like these new fangled mines, such a depth, and all machinery to work them. Some of them simply dreads those iron men, as they call them, those machines for hewing the coal, where men always

[1] 乌合之众；穷光蛋。 [2] 如果关闭了，那就到了世界末日。for good：永远。

did it before. And they say it's wasteful as well. But what goes in waste is saved in wages, and a lot more. It seems soon there'll be no use for men on the face of the earth, it'll be all machines. But they say that's what folks said when they had to give up the old stocking frames. I can remember one or two. But my word, the more machines, the more people, that's what it looks like! They say you can't get the same chemicals out of Tevershall coal as you can out of Stacks Gate, and that's funny, they're not three miles apart. But they say so. But everybody says it's a shame something can't be started, to keep the men going a bit better, and employ the girls. All the girls traipsing off to Sheffield every day! My word, it would be something to talk about if Tevershall Collieries took a new lease of life, after everybody saying they're finished, and a sinking ship, and the men ought to leave them like rats leave a sinking ship. But folks talk so much, of course there was a boom during the war. When Sir Geoffrey made a trust of himself and got the money safe for ever, somehow. So they say! But they say even the masters and the owners don't get much out of it now. You can hardly believe it, can you! Why I always thought the pits would go on for ever and ever. Who'd have thought, when I was a girl! But New England's shut down, so is Colwick Wood: yes, it's fair haunting to go through that coppy and see Colwick Wood standing there deserted among the trees, and bushes growing up all over the pit-head, and the lines red rusty. It's like death itself, a dead colliery. Why, whatever should we do if Tevershall shut down — ? It doesn't bear thinking of. Always that throng it's been, except at strikes, and even then the fan-wheels didn't stand, except when they fetched the ponies up. I'm sure it's a funny world, you don't know where you are from year to year, you really don't.'

It was Mrs Bolton's talk that really put a new fight into Clifford. His income, as she pointed out to him, was secure, from his father's trust, even though it was not large. The pits did not really concern him. It was the other world he wanted to capture, the world of literature and fame; the popular world, not the working world.

Now he realized the distinction between popular success and working success: the populace of pleasure and the populace of work. He, as a private individual, had been catering with his stories for the populace of pleasure. And he had caught on. **But beneath the**

populace of pleasure lay the populace of work, grim, grimy, and rather terrible[1]. They too had to have their providers. And it was a much grimmer business, providing for the populace of work, than for the populace of pleasure. While he was doing his stories, and 'getting on' in the world, **Tevershall was going to the wall**[2].

He realized now that the bitch-goddess of Success had two main appetites: one for flattery, adulation, stroking and tickling such as writers and artists gave her; but the other a grimmer appetite for meat and bones. And the meat and bones for the bitch-goddess were provided by the men who made money in industry.

Yes, there were two great groups of dogs wrangling for the bitch-goddess: the group of the flatterers, those who offered her amusement, stories, films, plays: and the other, much less showy, much more savage breed, those who gave her meat, the real substance of money. The well-groomed showy dogs of amusement wrangled and snarled among themselves for the favours of the bitch-goddess. But it was nothing to the silent fight-to-the-death that went on among the indispensables, the bone-bringers.

But under Mrs Bolton's influence, Clifford was tempted to enter this other fight, to capture the bitch-goddess by brute means of industrial production. Somehow, he got his pecker up.

In one way, Mrs Bolton made a man of him, as Connie never did. Connie kept him apart, and made him sensitive and conscious of himself and his own states. Mrs Bolton made hint aware only of outside things. Inwardly he began to go soft as pulp. But outwardly he began to be effective.

He even roused himself to go to the mines once more: and when he was there, he went down in a tub, and in a tub he was hauled out into the workings. Things he had learned before the war, and seemed utterly to have forgotten, now came back to him. He sat there, crippled, in a tub, with the underground manager showing him the seam with a powerful torch. And he said little. But his mind began to work.

He began to read again his technical works on the coal-mining

❶但是在娱乐大众之下潜伏的是辛苦、肮脏而相当可怕的劳作大众。❷特弗沙尔在走投无路。go to the wall:被排挤,失败,破产。

industry, he studied the government reports, and he read with care the latest things on mining and the chemistry of coal and of shale which were written in German. Of course the most valuable discoveries were kept secret as far as possible. But once you started a sort of research in the field of coal-mining, a study of methods and means, a study of by-products and the chemical possibilities of coal, **it was astounding the ingenuity and the almost uncanny cleverness of the modern technical mind, as if really the devil himself had lent fiend's wits to the technical scientists of industry**❶. It was far more interesting than art, than literature, poor emotional half-witted stuff, was this technical science of industry. In this field, men were like gods, or demons, inspired to discoveries, and fighting to carry them out. In this activity, men were beyond atty mental age calculable. But Clifford knew that when it did come to the emotional and human life, these self-made men were of a mental age of about thirteen, feeble boys. The discrepancy was enormous and appalling.

But let that be. Let man slide down to general idiocy in the emotional and 'human' mind, Clifford did not care. **Let all that go hang**❷. He was interested in the technicalities of modern coal-mining, and in pulling Tevershall out of the hole.

He went down to the pit day after day, he studied, he put the general manager, and the overhead manager, and the underground manager, and the engineers through a mill they had never dreamed of. Power! He felt a new sense of power flowing through him: power over all these men, over the hundreds and hundreds of colliers. He was finding out: and he was getting things into his grip.

And he seemed verily to be re-born. Now life came into him! He had been gradually dying, with Connie, in the isolated private life of the artist and the conscious being. Now let all that go. Let it sleep. He simply felt life rush into him out of the coal, out of the pit. The very stale air of the colliery was better than oxygen to him. It gave him a sense of power, power. He was doing something: and he was going to do something. He was going to win, to win: not as he had won with his stories, mere

❶现代技术的创新和难以置信的绝妙，似乎魔鬼真的将自己的魔法授予了工业技术专家。❷让所有这一切都见鬼去吧！go hang:被忘却,不关心,(常与let连用)。

publicity, amid a whole sapping of energy and malice. But a man's victory.

At first he thought the solution lay in electricity: convert the coal into electric power. Then a new idea came. The Germans invented a new locomotive engine with a self feeder, that did not need a fireman. And it was to be fed with a new fuel, that burnt in small quantities at a great heat, under peculiar conditions.

The idea of a new concentrated fuel that burnt with a hard slowness at a fierce heat was what first attracted Clifford. There must be some sort of external stimulus of the burning of such fuel, not merely air supply. He began to experiment, and got a clever young fellow, who had proved brilliant in chemistry, to help him.

And he felt triumphant. He had at last got out of himself. He had fulfilled his life-long secret yearning to get out of himself. Art had not done it for him. Art had only made it worse. But now, now he had done it.

He was not aware how much Mrs Bolton was behind him. He did not know how much he depended on her. But for all that, it was evident that when he was with her his voice dropped to an easy rhythm of intimacy, almost a trifle vulgar.

With Connie, he was a little stiff. He felt he owed her everything, and he showed her the utmost respect and consideration, so long as she gave him mere outward respect. But it was obvious he had a secret dread of her. **The new Achilles in him had a heel**[1], and in this heel the woman, the woman like Connie, his wife, could lame him fatally. He went in a certain half-subservient dread of her, and was extremely nice to her. But his voice was a little tense when he spoke to her, and he began to be silent whenever she was present.

Only when he was alone with Mrs Bolton did he really feel a lord and a master, and his voice ran on with her almost as easily and garrulously as her own could run. And he let her shave him or sponge all his body as if he were a child, really as if he were a child.

①他身上的新阿喀琉斯有一个脚后跟。Achilles:阿喀琉斯,希腊神话中的英雄,传说他出生后他的母亲握住其脚浪倒浸在冥河水中,除脚跟外周身刀枪不入,不料在特洛伊战争中他因脚后跟中箭而亡。由此阿喀琉斯的脚后跟喻为致命弱点。

CHAPTER 10

Connie was a good deal alone now, fewer people came to Wragby. Clifford no longer wanted them. He had turned against even the cronies. He was queer. He preferred the radio, which he had installed at some expense, with a good deal of success at last. He could sometimes get Madrid or Frankfurt, even there in the uneasy Midlands.

And he would sit alone for hours listening to the loudspeaker bellowing forth. It amazed and stunned Connie. But there he would sit, with a blank entranced expression on his face, like a person losing his mind, and listen, or seem to listen, to the unspeakable thing.

Was he really listening? **Or was it a sort of soporific he took**[1], whilst something else worked on underneath in him? Connie did now know. She fled up to her room, or out of doors to the wood. A kind of terror filled her sometimes, a terror of the incipient insanity of the whole civilized species.

But now that Clifford was drifting off to this other weirdness of industrial activity, becoming almost a creature, with a hard, efficient shell of an exterior and a pulpy interior, one of the amazing crabs and lobsters of the modern, industrial and financial world, **invertebrates of the crustacean order**[2], with shells of steel, like machines, and inner bodies of soft pulp, Connie herself was really completely stranded.

She was not even free, for Clifford must have her there. He seemed to have a nervous terror that she should leave him. The curious pulpy part of him, the emotional and humanly-individual part, depended on her with terror, like a child, almost like an idiot. She must be there, there at Wragby, a Lady Chatterley, his wife. Otherwise he would be lost like an idiot on a moor.

This amazing dependence Connie realized with a sort of horror. She heard him with his pit managers, with the members of his Board, with young scientists, and she was amazed at his shrewd insight into things,

[1] 或许是他服了种催眠药。 [2] 无脊椎甲壳类动物。

his power, **his uncanny material power over what is called practical men**[1]. He had become a practical man himself and an amazingly astute and powerful one, a master. Connie attributed it to Mrs Bolton's influence upon him, just at the crisis in his life.

But this astute and practical man was almost an idiot when left alone to his own emotional life. He worshipped Connie. She was his wife, a higher being, and he worshipped her with a queer, craven idolatry, like a savage, a worship based on enormous fear, and even hate of the power of the idol, the dread idol. All he wanted was for Connie to swear, to swear not to leave him, not to give him away.

'Clifford,' she said to him — but this was after she had the key to the hut — 'Would you really like me to have a child one day?'

He looked at her with a furtive apprehension in his rather prominent pale eyes.

'I shouldn't mind, if it made no difference between us,' he said.

'No difference to what?' she asked.

'To you and me; to our love for one another. If it's going to affect that, then I'm all against it. Why, I might even one day have a child of my own!'

She looked at him in amazement.

'I mean, **it might come back to me one of these days**[2].'

She still stared in amazement, and he was uncomfortable.

'So you would not like it if I had a child?' she said.

'I tell you,' he replied quickly, like a cornered dog, 'I am quite willing, provided it doesn't touch your love for me. If it would touch that, I am dead against it.'

Connie could only be silent in cold fear and contempt. Such talk was really the gabbling of an idiot. He no longer knew what he was talking about.

'Oh, it wouldn't make any difference to my feeling for you,' she said, with a certain sarcasm.

'There!' he said. 'That is the point! In that case I don't mind in the least. I mean it would be awfully nice to have a child running about the house, and feel one was building up a future for it. I should have something to strive for then, and I should know it was your child,

❶实干家们所具有的奇怪的实质性权力。❷说不定那一天我会康复的。(comeback指生育能力)。

shouldn't I, dear? And it would seem just the same as my own. Because it is you who count in these matters. You know that, don't you, dear? I don't enter, I am a cypher. You are the great I-am! as far as life goes. You know that, don't you? I mean, as far as I am concerned. I mean, but for you I am absolutely nothing. I live for your sake and your future. I am nothing to myself'

Connie heard it all with deepening dismay and repulsion. It was one of the ghastly half-truths that poison human existence. What man in his senses would say such things to a woman! But men aren't in their senses. What man with a spark of honour would put this ghastly burden of life-responsibility upon a woman, and leave her there, in the void?

Moreover, in half an hour's time, Connie heard Clifford talking to Mrs Bolton, in a hot, impulsive voice, revealing himself in a sort of passionless passion to the woman, as if she were half mistress, half foster-mother to him. And Mrs Bolton was carefully dressing him in evening clothes, for there were important business guests in the house.

Connie really sometimes felt she would die at this time. She felt she was being crushed to death by weird lies, and by the amazing cruelty of idiocy. Clifford's strange business efficiency in a way over-awed her, and his declaration of private worship put her into a panic. There was nothing between them. She never even touched him nowadays, and he never touched her. He never even took her hand and held it kindly. No, and because they were so utterly out of touch, he tortured her with his declaration of idolatry. It was the cruelty of utter impotence. And she felt her reason would give way, or she would die.

She fled as much as possible to the wood. One afternoon, as she sat brooding, watching the water bubbling coldly in John's Well, the keeper had strode up to her.

'I got you a key made, my Lady! ' he said, saluting, and he offered her the key.

'Thank you so much! ' she said, startled.

'The hut's not very tidy, if you don't mind,' he said. 'I cleared it what I could.'

'But I didn't want you to trouble! ' she said.

'Oh, it wasn't any trouble. I am setting the hens in about a week. But they won't be scared of you. I s'll have to see to them morning and night, but I shan't bother you any more than I can help.'

'But you wouldn't bother me,' she pleaded. 'I'd rather not go to the hut at all, if I am going to be in the way.'

He looked at her with his keen blue eyes. He seemed kindly, but distant. But at least he was sane, and wholesome, if even he looked thin and ill. A cough troubled him.

'You have a cough,' she said.

'Nothing — a cold! The last pneumonia left me with a cough, but it's nothing.'

He kept distant from her, and would not come any nearer.

She went fairly often to the hut, in the morning or in the afternoon, but he was never there. No doubt he avoided her on purpose. He wanted to keep his own privacy.

He had made the hut tidy, put the little table and chair near the fireplace, left a little pile of kindling and small logs, and put the tools and traps away as far as possible, effacing himself. Outside, by the clearing, he had built a low little roof of boughs and straw, a shelter for the birds, and under it stood the live coops. And, one day when she came, she found two brown hens sitting alert and fierce in the coops, sitting on pheasants' eggs, and fluffed out so proud and deep in all the heat of the pondering female blood. This almost broke Connie's heart. She, herself was so forlorn and unused, not a female at all, just a mere thing of terrors.

Then all the five coops were occupied by hens, three brown and a grey and a black. All alike, they clustered themselves down on the eggs in the soft nestling ponderosity of the female urge, the female nature, fluffing out their feathers. And with brilliant eyes they watched Connie, as she crouched before them, and they gave short sharp clucks of anger and alarm, but chiefly of female anger at being approached.

Connie found corn in the corn-bin in the hut. She offered it to the hens in her hand. They would not eat it. Only one hen pecked at her hand with a fierce little jab, so Connie was frightened. But she was pining to give them something, the brooding mothers who neither fed themselves nor drank. She brought water in a little tin, and was delighted when one of the hens drank.

Now she came every day to the hens, they were the only things in the world that warmed her heart. Clifford's protestations made her go cold from head to foot. Mrs Bolton's voice made her go cold, and the sound of the business men who came. An occasional letter from Michaelis affected her with the same sense of chill. She felt she would surely die if it lasted much longer.

Yet it was spring, and the bluebells were coming in the wood, and the leaf-buds on the hazels were opening like the spatter of green rain. How terrible it was that it should be spring, and everything cold-hearted, cold-hearted. Only the hens, fluffed so wonderfully on the eggs, were warm with their hot, brooding female bodies! Connie felt herself living on the brink of fainting all the time.

Then, one day, a lovely sunny day with great tufts of primroses under the hazels, and many violets dotting the paths, she came in the afternoon to the coops and there was one tiny, tiny perky chicken tinily prancing round in front of a coop, and the mother hen clucking in terror. The slim little chick was greyish brown with dark markings, and it was the most alive little spark of a creature **in seven kingdoms**[1] at that moment. Connie crouched to watch in a sort of ecstasy. Life, life! pure, sparky, fearless new life! New life! So tiny and so utterly without fear! Even when it scampered a little, scrambling into the coop again, and disappeared under the hen's feathers in answer to the mother hen's wild alarm-cries, it was not really frightened, it took it as a game, the game of living. For in a moment a tiny sharp head was poking through the gold-brown feathers of the hen, and eyeing the Cosmos.

Connie was fascinated. And at the same time, never had she felt so acutely the agony of her own female forlornness. It was becoming unbearable.

She had only one desire now, to go to the clearing in the wood. The rest was a kind of painful dream. But sometimes she was kept all day at Wragby, by her duties as hostess. And then she felt as if she too were going blank, just blank and insane.

One evening, guests or no guests, she escaped after tea. It was late, and she fled across the park like one who fears to be called back. The sun was setting rosy as she entered the wood, but she pressed on among the flowers. The light would last long overhead.

She arrived at the clearing flushed and semi-conscious. The keeper was there, in his shirt-sleeves, just closing up the coops for the night, so

[1] 普天之下。(原指基督教中七位守护神庇护的领土)。

the little occupants would be safe. But still one little trio was pattering about on tiny feet, alert drab mites, under the straw shelter, refusing to be called in by the anxious mother.

'I had to come and see the chickens!' she said, panting, glancing shyly at the keeper, almost unaware of him. 'Are there any more?'

'Thurty-six so far!' he said. 'Not bad!'

He too took a curious pleasure in watching the young things come out.

Connie crouched in front of the last coop. The three chicks had run in. But still their cheeky heads came poking sharply through the yellow feathers, then withdrawing, then only one beady little head eyeing forth from the vast mother-body.

'I'd love to touch them,' she said, putting her fingers gingerly through the bars of the coop. But the mother-hen pecked at her hand fiercely, and Connie drew back startled and frightened.

'How she pecks at me! She hates me!' she said in a wondering voice. 'But I wouldn't hurt them!'

The man standing above her laughed, and crouched down beside her, knees apart, and put his hand with quiet confidence slowly into the coop. The old hen pecked at him, but not so savagely. And slowly, softly, with sure gentle fingers, he felt among the old bird's feathers and drew out a faintly-peeping chick in his closed hand.

'There!' he said, holding out his hand to her. She took the little drab thing between her hands, and there it stood, on its impossible little stalks of legs, its atom of balancing life trembling through its almost weightless feet into Connie's hands. But it lifted its handsome, clean-shaped little head boldly, and looked sharply round, and gave a little 'peep'. 'So adorable! So cheeky!' she said softly.

The keeper, squatting beside her, was also watching with an amused face the bold little bird in her hands. Suddenly he saw a tear fall on to her wrist.

And he stood up, and stood away, moving to the other coop. For suddenly he was aware of the old flame shooting and leaping up in his loins, that he had hoped was quiescent for ever. He fought against it, turning his back to her. But it leapt, and leapt downwards, circling in his knees.

He turned again to look at her. She was kneeling and holding her two hands slowly forward, blindly, so that the chicken should run in to the mother-hen again. And there was something so mute and forlorn in her, compassion flamed in his bowels for her.

Without knowing, he came quickly towards her and crouched beside her again, taking the chick from her hands, because she was afraid of the hen, and putting it back in the coop. **At the back of his loins the fire suddenly darted stronger**[1].

He glanced apprehensively at her. Her face was averted, and she was crying blindly, in all the anguish of her generation's forlornness. His heart melted suddenly, like a drop of fire, and he put out his hand and laid his fingers on her knee.

'You shouldn't cry,' he said softly.

But then she put her hands over her face and felt that really her heart was broken and nothing mattered any more.

He laid his hand on her shoulder, and softly, gently, it began to travel down the curve of her back, blindly, with a blind stroking motion, to the curve of her crouching loins. And there his hand softly, softly, stroked the curve of her flank, in the blind instinctive caress.

She had found her scrap of handkerchief and was blindly trying to dry her face.

'Shall you come to the hut?' he said, in a quiet, neutral voice.

And closing his hand softly on her upper arm, he drew her up and led her slowly to the hut, not letting go of her till she was inside. Then he cleared aside the chair and table, and took a brown, soldier's blanket from the tool chest, spreading it slowly. She glanced at his face, as she stood motionless.

His face was pale and without expression, like that of a man submitting to fate.

'You lie there,' he said softly, and he shut the door, so that it was dark, quite dark.

With a queer obedience, she lay down on the blanket. Then she felt the soft, groping, helplessly desirous hand touching her body, feeling for her face. The hand stroked her face softly, softly, with infinite soothing and assurance, and at last there was the soft touch of a kiss on her cheek.

She lay quite still, in a sort of sleep, in a sort of dream. Then she

[1] 他丹田深处之欲火突然升腾起来。

quivered as she felt his hand groping softly, yet with queer thwarted clumsiness, among her 'clothing. Yet the hand knew, too, how to unclothe her where it wanted. He drew down the thin silk sheath, slowly, carefully, right down and over her feet. Then with a quiver of exquisite pleasure he touched the warm soft body, and touched her navel for a moment in a kiss. And he had to come in to her at once, to enter the peace on earth of her soft, quiescent body. It was the moment of pure peace for him, the entry into the body of the woman.

She lay still, in a kind of sleep, always in a kind of sleep. The activity, the orgasm was his, all his; she could strive for herself no more. Even the tightness of his arms round her, even the intense movement of his body, and the springing of his seed in her, was a kind of sleep, from which she did not begin to rouse till he had finished and lay softly panting against her breast.

Then she wondered, just dimly wondered, why? Why was this necessary? Why had it lifted a great cloud from her and given her peace? Was it real? Was it real?

Her tormented modern-woman's brain still had no rest. Was it real? And she knew, if she gave herself to the man, it was real. But if she kept herself for herself it was nothing. She was old; millions of years old, she felt. And at last, she could bear the burden of herself no more. **She was to be had for the taking**[1]. To be had for the taking.

The man lay in a mysterious stillness. What was he feeling? What was he thinking? She did not know. He was a strange man to her, she did not know him. She must only wait, for she did not dare to break his mysterious stillness. He lay there with his arms round her, his body on hers, his wet body touching hers, so close. And completely unknown. Yet not unpeaceful. His very stillness was peaceful.

She knew that, when at last he roused and drew away from her. It was like an abandonment. He drew her dress in the darkness down over her knees and stood a few moments, apparently adjusting his own clothing. Then he quietly opened the door and went out.

She saw a very brilliant little moon shining above the afterglow over the oaks. Quickly she got up and arranged herself; she was tidy. Then she went to the door of the hut.

[1] 她全身都可以奉献出去。

All the lower wood was in shadow, almost darkness. Yet the sky overhead was crystal. But it shed hardly any light. He came through the lower shadow towards her, his face lifted like a pale blotch.

'Shall we go then?' he said.

'Where?'

'I'll go with you to the gate.'

He arranged things his own way. He locked the door of the hut and came after her.

'You aren't sorry, are you?' he asked, as he went at her side.

'No! No! Are you?' she said.

'For that! No!' he said. Then after a while he added: 'But there's the rest of things.'

'What rest of things?' she said.

'Sir Clifford. Other folks. All the complications.'

'Why complications?' she said, disappointed.

'It's always so. For you as well as for me. There's always complications.' He walked on steadily in the dark.

'And are you sorry?' she said.

'In a way!' he replied, looking up at the sky. 'I thought I'd done with it all. Now I've begun again.'

'Begun what?'

'Life.'

'Life!' she re-echoed, with a queer thrill.

'It's life,' he said. '**There's no keeping clear**[1]. And if you do keep clear you might almost as well die. So if I've got to be broken open again, I have.'

She did not quite see it that way, but still 'It's just love,' she said cheerfully.

'Whatever that may be,' he replied.

They went on through the darkening wood in silence, till they were almost at the gate.

'But you don't hate me, do you?' she said wistfully.

'Nay, nay,' he replied. And suddenly he held her fast against his breast again, with the old connecting passion. 'Nay, for me it was good, it was good. Was it for you?'

[1] 规避是做不到的。

'Yes, for me too,' she answered, a little untruthfully, for she had not been conscious of much.

He kissed her softly, softly, with the kisses of warmth.

'If only there weren't so many other people in the world,' he said lugubriously.

She laughed. They were at the gate to the park. He opened it for her.

'I won't come any further,' he said.

'No!' And she held out her hand, as if to shake hands. But he took it in both his.

'Shall I come again?' she asked wistfully.

'Yes! Yes!'

She left him and went across the park.

He stood back and watched her going into the dark, against the pallor of the horizon. Almost with bitterness he watched her go. She had connected him up again, when he had wanted to be alone. She had cost him that bitter privacy of a man who at last wants only to be alone.

He turned into the dark of the wood. All was still, the moon had set. But he was aware of the noises of the night, the engines at Stacks Gate, the traffic on the main road. Slowly he climbed the denuded knoll. And from the top he could see the country, bright rows of lights at Stacks Gate, smaller lights at Tevershall pit, the yellow lights of Tevershall and lights everywhere, here and there, on the dark country, with the distant blush of furnaces, faint and rosy, since the night was clear, the rosiness of the outpouring of white-hot metal. Sharp, wicked electric lights at Stacks Gate! An undefinable quick of evil in them! And all the unease, the ever-shifting dread of the industrial night in the Midlands. He could hear the winding-engines at Stacks Gate turning down the seven-o'clock miners. The pit worked three shifts.

He went down again into the darkness and seclusion of the wood. But he knew that the seclusion of the wood was illusory. The industrial noises broke the solitude, the sharp lights, though unseen, mocked it. A man could no longer be private and withdrawn. The world allows no hermits. And now he had taken the woman, and brought on himself a new cycle of pain and doom. For he knew by experience what it meant.

It was not woman's fault, nor even love's fault, nor the fault of sex. The fault lay there, out there, in those evil electric lights and diabolical rattlings of engines. There, in the world of the mechanical greedy,

greedy mechanism and mechanized greed, sparkling with lights and gushing hot metal and roaring with traffic, there lay the vast evil thing, ready to destroy whatever did not conform. Soon it would destroy the wood, and the bluebells would spring no more. All vulnerable things must perish under the rolling and running of iron.

He thought with infinite tenderness of the woman. Poor forlorn thing, she was nicer than she knew, and oh! **so much too nice for the tough lot she was in contact with**❶. Poor thing, she too had some of the vulnerability of the wild hyacinths, she wasn't all tough rubber-goods and platinum, like the modern girl. And **they would do her in**❷! As sure as life, they would do her in, as they do in all naturally tender life. Tender! Somewhere she was tender, tender with a tenderness of the growing hyacinths, something that has gone out of **the celluloid women of today**❸. But he would protect her with his heart for a little while. For a little while, before the insentient iron world and **the Mammon of mechanized greed**❹ did them both in, her as well as him.

He went home with his gun and his dog, to the dark cottage, lit the lamp, started the fire, and ate his supper of bread and cheese, young onions and beer. He was alone, in a silence he loved. His room was clean and tidy, but rather stark. Yet the fire was bright, the hearth white, the petroleum lamp hung bright over the table, with its white oil-cloth. He tried to read a book about India, but tonight he could not read. He sat by the fire in his shirt-sleeves, not smoking, but with a mug of beer in reach. And he thought about Connie.

To tell the truth, he was sorry for what had happened, perhaps most for her sake. He had a sense of foreboding. No sense of wrong or sin; he was troubled by no conscience in that respect. He knew that conscience was chiefly tear of society, or fear of oneself. He was not afraid of himself. But he was quite consciously afraid of society, **which he knew by instinct to be a malevolent, partly-insane beast**❺.

The woman! If she could be there with him, arid there were nobody else in the world! The desire rose again, his penis began to stir

❶和她接触的那帮粗鲁家伙是配不上她的。 ❷他们会毁掉她。 ❸当今电影里出现的女人,(指丧失了温情脉脉等自然属性的女人)。 ❹机械化的贪婪财神。Mammon:[常做M-](被视为偶像的)财神;贪欲之神。 ❺他本能地知道社会是半疯狂的恶毒野兽。

like a live bird. At the same time an oppression, **a dread of exposing himself and her to that outside Thing that sparkled viciously in the electric lights**[1], weighed down his shoulders. She, poor young thing, was just a young female creature to him; but a young female creature whom he had gone into and whom he desired again.

Stretching with the curious yawn of desire, for he had been alone and apart from man or woman for four years, he rose and took his coat again, and his gun, lowered the lamp and went out into the starry night, with the dog. Driven by desire and by dread of the malevolent Thing outside, he made his round in the wood, slowly, softly. He loved the darkness arid folded himself into it. It fitted the turgidity of his desire which, in spite of all, was like a riches; the stirring restlessness of his penis, the stirring fire in his loins! Oh, if only there were other men to be with, to fight that sparkling electric Thing outside there, to preserve the tenderness of life, the tenderness of women, and the natural riches of desire. If only there were men to fight side by side with! But the men were all outside there, glorying in the Thing, triumphing or being trodden down in the rush of mechanized greed or of greedy mechanism.

Constance, for her part, had hurried across the park, home, almost without thinking. As yet she had no afterthought. She would be in time for dinner.

She was annoyed to find the doors fastened, however, so that she had to ring. Mrs Bolton opened.

'Why there you are, your Ladyship! I was beginning to wonder if you'd gone lost!' she said a little roguishly. 'Sir Clifford hasn't asked for you, though; he's got Mr Linley in with him, talking over something. It looks as if he'd stay to dinner, doesn't it, my Lady?'

'It does rather,' said Connie.

'Shall I put dinner back a quarter of an hour? That would give you time to dress in comfort.'

'Perhaps you'd better.'

Mr Linley was the general manager of the collieries, an elderly man from the north, with not quite enough punch to suit Clifford; **not up to**

[1] 他生怕将自己和她暴露给外面那个在电灯光下闪着邪恶之光的"物"。

post-war conditions, nor post-war colliers either, with their 'ca' canny' creed[1]. But Connie liked Mr Linley, though she was glad to be spared the toadying of his wife.

Linley stayed to dinner, and Connie was the hostess men liked so much, so modest, yet so attentive and aware, with big, wide blue eyes arid a soft repose that sufficiently hid what she was really thinking. Connie had played this woman so much, it was almost second nature to her; but still, decidedly second. Yet it was curious how everything disappeared from her consciousness while she played it.

She waited patiently till she could go upstairs and think her own thoughts. She was always waiting, it seemed to be her forte.

Once in her room, however, she felt still vague and confused. She didn't know what to think. What sort of a man was he, really? Did he really like her? Not much, she felt. Yet he was kind. There was something, a sort of warm naive kindness, curious and sudden, that almost opened her womb to him. But she felt he might be kind like that to any woman. Though even so, it was curiously soothing, comforting. And he was a passionate man, wholesome and passionate. But perhaps he wasn't quite individual enough; he might be the same with any woman as he had been with her. It really wasn't personal. She was only really a female to him.

But perhaps that was better. And after all, he was kind to the female in her, which no man had ever been. Men were very kind to the person she was, but rather cruel to the female, despising her or ignoring her altogether. Men were awfully kind to Constance Reid or to Lady Chatterley; but not to her womb they weren't kind. And he took no notice of Constance or of Lady Chatterley; he just softly stroked her loins or her breasts.

She went to the wood next day. It was a grey, still afternoon, with the dark-green dogs-mercury spreading under the hazel copse, and all the trees making a silent effort to open their buds. Today she could almost feel it in her own body, the huge heave of the sap in the massive trees, upwards, up, up to the bud-tips, there to push into little flamey oak-leaves, bronze as blood. It was like a ride running turgid upward, and spreading on the sky.

[1] 他不能适应战后的情形，同战后的矿工们在一起，而是守着他小心持重的信条。

She came to the clearing, but he was not there. She had only half expected him. The pheasant chicks were running lightly abroad, light as insects, from the coops where the fellow hens clucked anxiously. Connie sat and watched them, and waited. She only waited. Even the chicks she hardly saw. She waited.

The time passed with dream-like slowness, and he did not come. She had only half expected him. He never came in the afternoon. She must go home to tea. But she had to force herself to leave.

As she went home, a fine drizzle of rain fell.

'Is it raining again?' said Clifford, seeing her shake her hat.

'Just drizzle.'

She poured tea in silence, absorbed in a sort of obstinacy. She did want to see the keeper today, to see if it were really real. If it were really real.

'Shall I read a little to you afterwards?' said Clifford.

She looked at him. Had he sensed something?

'The spring makes me feel queer — I thought I might rest a little,' she said.

'Just as you like. Not feeling really unwell, are you?'

'No! Only rather tired — with the spring. Will you have Mrs Bolton to play something with you?'

'No! I think I'll listen in.'

She heard the curious satisfaction in his voice. She went upstairs to her bedroom. There she heard the loudspeaker begin to bellow, in an idiotically velveteen-genteel sort of voice, something about a series of street-cries, the very cream of genteel affectation imitating old criers. She pulled on her old violet coloured mackintosh, and slipped out of the house at the side door.

The drizzle of rain was like a veil over the world, mysterious, hushed, not cold. She got very warm as she hurried across the park. She had to open her light waterproof.

The wood was silent, still and secret in the evening drizzle of rain, full of the mystery of eggs and half-open buds, half unsheathed flowers. In the dimness of it all trees glistened naked and dark as if they had unclothed themselves, and the green things on earth seemed to hum with greenness.

There was still no one at the clearing. The chicks had nearly all gone under the mother-hens, only one or two last adventurous ones still dibbed about in the dryness under the straw roof shelter. And they were doubtful of themselves.

So! He still had not been. He was staying away on purpose. Or perhaps something was wrong. Perhaps she should go to the cottage and see.

But she was born to wait. She opened the hut with her key. It was all tidy, the corn put in the bin, the blankets folded on the shelf, the straw neat in a corner; a new bundle of straw. The hurricane lamp hung on a nail. The table and chair had been put back where she had lain.

She sat down on a stool in the doorway. How still everything was! The fine rain blew very softly, filmily, but the wind made no noise. Nothing made any sound. The trees stood like powerful beings, dim, twilit, silent and alive. How alive everything was!

Night was drawing near again; she would have to go. He was avoiding her.

But suddenly he came striding into the clearing, in his black oilskin jacket like a chauffeur, shining with wet. He glanced quickly at the hut, half-saluted, then veered aside and went on to the coops. There he crouched in silence, looking carefully at everything, then carefully shutting the hens and chicks up safe against the night.

At last he came slowly towards her. She still sat on her stool. He stood before her under the porch.

'You come then,' he said, using the intonation of the dialect.

'Yes,' she said, looking up at him. 'You're late!'

'Ay!' he replied, looking away into the wood.

She rose slowly, drawing aside her stool.

'Did you want to come in?' she asked.

He looked down at her shrewdly.

'Won't folks be thinkin' somethink, you comin' here every night?' he said.

'Why?' She looked up at him, at a loss. 'I said I'd come. Nobody knows.'

'They soon will, though,' he replied. 'An' what then?'

She was at a loss for an answer.

'Why should they know?' she said.

'Folks always does,' he said fatally.

Her lip quivered a little.

'Well I can't help it,' she faltered.

'Nay,' he said. 'You can help it by not comin' — if yer want to,' he added, in a lower tone.

'But I don't want to,' she murmured.

He looked away into the wood, and was silent.

'But what when folks finds out?' he asked at last. 'Think about it! Think how lowered you'll feel, one of your husband's servants.'

She looked up at his averted face.

'Is it,' she stammered, 'is it that you don't want me?'

'Think!' he said. 'Think what if folks find out Sir Clifford an' a' — an' everybody talkin' —'

'Well, I can go away.'

'Where to?'

'Anywhere! I've got money of my own. My mother left me twenty thousand pounds **in trust**[1], and I know Clifford can't touch it. I can go away.'

'But 'appen you don't want to go away.'

'Yes, yes! I don't care what happens to me.'

'Ay, you think that! But you'll care! You'll have to care, everybody has. You've got to remember your Ladyship is carrying on with a game-keeper. It's not as if I was a gentleman. Yes, you'd care. You'd care.'

'I shouldn't. What do I care about my ladyship! I hate it really. I feel people are jeering every time they say it. And they are, they are! Even you jeer when you say it.'

'Me!'

For the first time he looked straight at her, and into her eyes. 'I don't jeer at you,' he said.

As he looked into her eyes she saw his own eyes go dark, quite dark, the pupils dilating.

'Don't you care about a' the risk?' he asked in a husky voice. 'You should care. Don't care when it's too late!'

There was a curious warning pleading in his voice.

'But I've nothing to lose,' she said fretfully. 'If you knew what it is, you'd think I'd be glad to lose it. But are you afraid for yourself?'

'Ay!' he said briefly. 'I am. I'm afraid. I'm afraid. I'm afraid o' things.'

[1] (由银行)托管,保管。

'What things?' she asked.

He gave a curious backward jerk of his head, indicating the outer world.

'Things! Everybody! The lot of 'em.'

Then he bent down and suddenly kissed her unhappy face.

'Nay, I don't care,' he said. 'Let's have it, an' damn the rest. But if you was to feel sorry you'd ever done it — !'

'Don't put me off,' she pleaded.

He put his fingers to her cheek and kissed her again suddenly.

'Let me come in then,' he said softly. 'An' take off your mackintosh.'

He hung up his gun, slipped out of his wet leather jacket, and reached for the blankets.

'I brought another blanket,' he said, 'so we can put one over us if you like.'

'I can't stay long,' she said. 'Dinner is half-past seven.'

He looked at her swiftly, then at his watch.

'All right,' he said.

He shut the door, and lit a tiny light in the hanging hurricane lamp. 'One time we'll have a long time,' he said.

He put the blankets down carefully, one folded for her head. Then he sat down a moment on the stool, and drew her to him, holding her close with one arm, feeling for her body with his free hand. She heard the catch of his intaken breath as he found her. Under her frail petticoat she was naked.

'Eh! what it is to touch thee!' he said, as his finger caressed the delicate, warm, secret skin of her waist and hips. He put his face down and rubbed his cheek against her belly and against her thighs again and again. And again she wondered a little over the sort of rapture it was to him. She did not understand the beauty he found in her, through touch upon her living secret body, almost the ecstasy of beauty. For passion alone is awake to it. And when passion is dead, or absent, then the magnificent throb of beauty is incomprehensible and even a little despicable; **warm, live beauty of contact, so much deeper than the beauty of vision**[1]. She felt the glide of his cheek on her thighs and belly and buttocks, and the close brushing of his moustache

①温暖生动的抚摸之美比视觉之美深刻得多。

and his soft thick hair, and her knees began to quiver. Far down in her she felt a new stirring, a new nakedness emerging. And she was half afraid. Half she wished he would not caress her so. He was encompassing her somehow. Yet she was waiting, waiting.

And when he came into her, with an intensification of relief and consummation that was pure peace to him, still she was waiting. She felt herself a little left out. And she knew, partly it was her own fault. She willed herself into this separateness. Now perhaps she was condemned to it. She lay still, feeling his motion within her, his deep-sunk intentness, the sudden quiver of him at the springing of his seed, then the slow-subsiding thrust. That thrust of the buttocks, surely it was a little ridiculous. If you were a woman, and a part in all the business, surely that thrusting of the man's buttocks was supremely ridiculous. Surely the man was intensely ridiculous in this posture and this act!

But she lay still, without recoil. Even when he had finished, **she did not rouse herself to get a grip on her own satisfaction**[1], as she had done with Michaelis; she lay still, and the tears slowly filled and ran from her eyes.

He lay still, too. But he held her close and tried to cover her poor naked legs with his legs, to keep them warm. He lay on her with a close, undoubting warmth.

'Are yer cold?' he asked, in a soft, small voice, as if she were close, so close. Whereas she was left out, distant.

'No! But I must go,' she said gently.

He sighed, held her closer, then relaxed to rest again.

He had not guessed her tears. **He thought she was there with him**[2].

'I must go,' she repeated.

He lifted himself kneeled beside her a moment, kissed the inner side of her thighs, then drew down her skirts, buttoning his own clothes unthinking, not even turning aside, in the faint, faint light from the lantern.

'Tha mun come ter th' cottage one time,' he said, looking down at her with a warm, sure, easy face.

But she lay there inert, and was gazing up at him thinking: Stranger! Stranger! She even resented him a little.

❶她没有摇动身子以求得到性满足。❷他以为她的感受和他一样。

He put on his coat and looked for his hat, which had fallen, then he slung on his gun.

'Come then!' he said, looking down at her with those warm, peaceful sort of eyes.

She rose slowly. She didn't want to go. She also rather resented staying. He helped her with her thin waterproof and saw she was tidy.

Then he opened the door. The outside was quite dark. The faithful dog under the porch stood up with pleasure seeing him. The drizzle of rain drifted greyly past upon the darkness. It was quite dark.

'Ah mun ta'e th' lantern,' he said. 'The'll be nob'dy.'

He walked just before her in the narrow path, swinging the hurricane lamp low, revealing the wet grass, the black shiny tree-roots like snakes, wan flowers. For the rest, all was grey rain-mist and complete darkness.

'Tha mun come to the cottage one time,' he said, 'shall ta? **We might as well be hung for a sheep as for a lamb**❶.'

It puzzled her, his queer, persistent wanting her, when there was nothing between them, when he never really spoke to her, and in spite of herself she resented the dialect. His 'tha mun come' seemed not addressed to her, but some common woman. She recognized the foxglove leaves of the riding and knew, more or less, where they were.

'It's quarter past seven,' he said, 'you'll do it.' He had changed his voice, seemed to feel her distance. As they turned the last bend in the riding towards the hazel wall and the gate, he blew out the light. 'We'll see from here,' he said, taking her gently by the arm.

But it was difficult, the earth under their feet was a mystery, **but he felt his way by tread**❷: he was used to it. At the gate he gave her his electric torch. 'It's a bit lighter in the park,' he said; 'but take it for fear you get off th' path.'

It was true, there seemed a ghost-glimmer of greyness in the open space of the park. He suddenly drew her to him and whipped his hand under her dress again, feeling her warm body with his wet, chill hand.

'I could die for the touch of a woman like thee,' he said in his throat. 'If tha' would stop another minute.'

She felt the sudden force of his wanting her again.

❶(口)一不做,二不休。 ❷不过他用脚摸索着踩道。

'No, I must run,' she said, a little wildly.

'Ay,' he replied, suddenly changed, letting her go.

She turned away, and on the instant she turned back to him saying: 'Kiss me.'

He bent over her indistinguishable and kissed her on the left eye. She held her mouth and he softly kissed it, but at once drew away. He hated mouth kisses.

'I'll come tomorrow,' she said, drawing away; 'if I can,' she added.

'Ay! not so late,' he replied out of the darkness. Already she could not see him at all.

'Goodnight,' she said.

'Goodnight, your Ladyship,' his voice.

She stopped and looked back into the wet dark. She could just see the bulk of him. 'Why did you say that?' she said.

'Nay,' he replied. 'Goodnight then, run!'

She plunged on in the dark-grey tangible night. She found the side-door open, and slipped into her room unseen. As she closed the door the gong sounded, but she would take her bath all the same — she must take her bath. 'But I won't be late any more,' she said to herself; 'it's too annoying.'

The next day she did not go to the wood. She went instead with Clifford to Uthwaite. He could occasionally go out now in the car, and had got a strong young man as chauffeur, who could help him out of the car if need be. He particularly wanted to see his godfather, Leslie Winter, who lived at Shipley Hall, not far from Uthwaite. Winter was an elderly gentleman now, wealthy, one of the wealthy coal-owners **who had had their hey-day in King Edward's time**[1]. King Edward had stayed more than once at Shipley, for the shooting. It was a handsome old stucco hall, very elegantly appointed, for Winter was a bachelor and prided himself on his style; but the place was beset by collieries. Leslie Winter was attached to Clifford, but personally did not entertain a great respect for him, because of the photographs in illustrated papers and the literature. The old man was **a buck of the King Edward school**[2], who thought life was life and the scribbling fellows

①爱德华国王时代盛极一时,King Edward 这里指爱德华七世(1841—1910)不列颠和爱尔兰国王维多利亚之子。②爱德华国王一派的花花公子。

were something else. Towards Connie the Squire was always rather gallant; he thought her an attractive demure maiden and rather wasted on Clifford, and **it was a thousand pities she stood no chance of bringing forth an heir to Wragby**[1]. He himself had no heir.

Connie wondered what he would say if he knew that Clifford's game-keeper had been having intercourse with her, and saying to her 'tha mun come to th' cottage one time.' He would detest and despise her, for he had come almost to hate the shoving forward of the working classes. A man of her own class he would not mind, for Connie was gifted from nature with this appearance of demure, submissive maidenliness, and perhaps it was part of her nature. Winter called her 'dear child' and gave her a rather lovely miniature of an eighteenth-century lady, rather against her will.

But Connie was preoccupied with her affair with the keeper. After all, Mr Winter, who was really a gentleman and **a man of the world**[2], treated her as a person and a discriminating individual; he did not lump her together with all the rest of his female womanhood in his 'thee' and 'tha'.

She did not go to the wood that day nor the next, nor the day following. She did not go so long as she felt, or imagined she felt, the man waiting for her, wanting her. But the fourth day she was terribly unsettled and uneasy. She still refused to go to the wood and open her thighs once more to the man. She thought of all the things she might do — drive to Sheffield, pay visits, and the thought of all these things was repellent. At last she decided to take a walk, not towards the wood, but in the opposite direction; she would go to Marehay, through the little iron gate in the other side of the park fence. It was a quiet grey day of spring, almost warm. She walked on unheeding, absorbed in thoughts she was not even conscious of She was not really aware of anything outside her, till she was startled by the loud barking of the dog at Marehay Farm. Marehay Farm! Its pastures ran up to Wragby park fence, so they were neighbours, but it was some time since Connie had called.

'Bell! ' she said to the big white bull-terrier. 'Bell! have you forgotten me? Don't you know me?' She was afraid of dogs, and Bell stood back and bellowed, and she wanted to pass through the farmyard

❶令人万分惋惜的是她无法给拉格比生个子嗣。 ❷社会的上流人物。

on to the warren path.

Mrs Flint appeared. She was a woman of Constance's own age, had been a school-teacher, but **Connie suspected her of being rather a false little thing**[1].

'Why, it's Lady Chatterley! Why! ' And Mrs Flint's eyes glowed again, and she flushed like a young girl. 'Bell, Bell. Why! barking at Lady Chatterley! Bell! Be quiet! ' She darted forward and slashed at the dog with a white cloth she held in her hand, then came forward to Connie.

'She used to know me,' said Connie, shaking hands. The Flints were Chatterley tenants.

'Of course she knows your Ladyship! She's just showing off,' said Mrs Flint, glowing and looking up with a sort of flushed confusion, 'but it's so long since she's seen you. I do hope you are better.'

'Yes thanks, I'm all right.'

'We've hardly seen you all winter. Will you come in and look at the baby?'

'Well! ' Connie hesitated. 'Just for a minute.'

Mrs Flint flew wildly in to tidy up, and Connie came slowly after her, hesitating in the rather dark kitchen where the kettle was boiling by the fire. Back came Mrs Flint.

'I do hope you'll excuse me,' she said. 'Will you come in here?'

They went into the living-room, where a baby was sitting on the rag hearth rug, and the table was roughly set for tea. A young servant-girl backed down the passage, shy and awkward.

The baby was a perky little thing of about a year, with red hair like its father, and cheeky pale-blue eyes. It was a girl, and not to be daunted. It sat among cushions and was surrounded with rag dolls and other toys in modern excess.

'Why, what a dear she is! ' said Connie, 'and how she's grown! A big girl! A big girl! '

She had given it a shawl when it was born, and celluloid ducks for Christmas.

'There, Josephine! Who's that come to see you? Who's this, Josephine? Lady Chatterley — you know Lady Chatterley, don't you?'

[1] 康妮怀疑她是个虚伪的小人。

The queer pert little mite gazed cheekily at Connie. Ladyships were still all the same to her.

'Come! Will you come to me?' said Connie to the baby.

The baby didn't care one way or another, so Connie picked her up and held her in her lap. How warm and lovely it was to hold a child in one's lap, and the soft little arms, the unconscious cheeky little legs.

'I was just having a rough cup of tea all by myself. Luke's gone to market, so I can have it when I like. Would you care for a cup, Lady Chatterley? I don't suppose it's what you're used to, but if you would...'

Connie would, though she didn't want to be reminded of what she was used to. There was a great relaying of the table, and the best cups brought and the best tea-pot.

'If only you wouldn't take any trouble,' said Connie.

But if Mrs Flint took no trouble, where was the fun! So Connie played with the child and was amused by its little female dauntlessness, and got a deep voluptuous pleasure out of its soft young warmth. Young life! And so fearless! So fearless, because so defenceless. **All the other people, so narrow with fear**[1]!

She had a cup of tea, which was rather strong, and very good bread and butter, and bottled damsons. Mrs Flint flushed and glowed and bridled with excitement, as if Connie were some gallant knight. And they had a real female chat, and both of them enjoyed it.

'It's a poor little tea, though,' said Mrs Flint.

'It's much nicer than at home,' said Connie truthfully.

'Oh-h!' said Mrs Flint, not believing, of course.

But at last Connie rose.

'I must go,' she said. 'My husband has no idea where I am. He'll be wondering all kinds of things.'

'He'll never think you're here,' laughed Mrs Flint excitedly. 'He'll be sending the crier round.'

'Goodbye, Josephine,' said Connie, kissing the baby and ruffling its red, wispy hair.

Mrs Flint insisted on opening the locked and barred front door. Connie emerged in the farm's little front garden, shut in by a privet hedge. There were two rows of auriculas by the path, very velvety and rich.

[1] 所有其他的人都因为害怕而谨小慎微。

'Lovely auriculas,' said Connie.

'Recklesses, as Luke calls them,' laughed Mrs Flint. 'Have some.'

And eagerly she picked the velvet and primrose flowers.

'Enough! Enough!' said Connie.

They came to the little garden gate.

'Which way were you going?' asked Mrs Flint.

'By the Warren.'

'Let me see! Oh yes, the cows are in the gin close. But they're not up yet. But the gate's locked, you'll have to climb.'

'I can climb,' said Connie.

'Perhaps I can just go down the close with you.'

They went down the poor, rabbit-bitten pasture. Birds were whistling in wild evening triumph in the wood. A man was calling up the last cows, which trailed slowly over the path-worn pasture.

'They're late, milking, tonight,' said Mrs Flint severely. 'They know Luke won't be back till after dark.'

They came to the fence, beyond which the young fir-wood bristled dense. There was a little gate, but it was locked. In the grass on the inside stood a bottle, empty.

'There's the keeper's empty bottle for his milk,' explained Mrs Flint. 'We bring it as far as here for him, and then he fetches it himself'

'When?' said Connie.

'Oh, any time he's around. Often in the morning. Well, goodbye Lady Chatterley! And do come again. It was so lovely having you.'

Connie climbed the fence into the narrow path between the dense, bristling young firs. Mrs Flint went running back across the pasture, in a sun-bonnet, because she was really a schoolteacher. Constance didn't like this dense new part of the wood; it seemed gruesome and choking. She hurried on with her head down, thinking of the Flints' baby. It was a dear little thing, but it would be a bit bow-legged like its father. It showed alrcady, but perhaps it would grow out of it. How warm and fulfilling somehow to have a baby, and how Mrs Flint had showed it off! She had something anyhow that Connie hadn't got, and apparently couldn't have. Yes, Mrs Flint had flaunted her motherhood. And Connie had been just a bit, just a little bit jealous. She couldn't help it.

She started out of her muse, and gave a little cry of fear. A man was there.

It was the keeper. **He stood in the path like Balaam's ass**❶, barring her way.

'How's this?' he said in surprise.

'How did you come?' she panted.

'How did you? Have you been to the hut?'

'No! No! I went to Marehay.'

He looked at her curiously, searchingly, and she hung her head a little guiltily.

'And were you going to the hut now?' he asked rather sternly. 'No! I mustn't. I stayed at Marehay. No one knows where I am. I'm late. I've got to run.'

'Giving me the slip, like?' he said, with a faint ironic smile. 'No! No. Not that. Only —'

'Why, what else?' he said. And he stepped up to her and put his arms around her. She felt the front of his body terribly near to her, and alive.

'Oh, not now, not now,' she cried, trying to push him away.

'Why not? It's only six o'clock. You've got half an hour. Nay! Nay! I want you.'

He held her fast and she felt his urgency. Her old instinct was to fight for her freedom. But something else in her was strange and inert and heavy. His body was urgent against her, and she hadn't the heart any more to fight.

He looked around.

'Come — come here! Through here,' he said, looking penetratingly into the dense fir-trees, that were young and not more than half-grown.

He looked back at her. She saw his eyes, tense and brilliant, fierce, not loving. But her will had left her. A strange weight was on her limbs. She was giving way. She was giving up.

He led her through the wall of prickly trees, that were difficult to come through, to a place where was a little space and a pile of dead boughs. He threw one or two dry ones down, put his coat and waistcoat over them, and she had to lie down there under the boughs of the tree, like an animal, while he waited, standing there in his shirt and breeches,

❶他像巴兰的驴子似的站在路上，巴兰、圣经旧约载他是美索不达米亚的先知，被派去诅咒以色列人，但遭其所骑驴子的责备后，反而祝福以色列人。

watching her with haunted eyes. But still he was provident — he made her lie properly, properly. Yet he broke the band of her underclothes, for she did not help him, only lay inert.

He too had bared the front part of his body and she felt his naked flesh against her as he came into her. For a moment he was still inside her, turgid there and quivering. Then as he began to move, in the sudden helpless orgasm, there awoke in her new strange thrills rippling inside her. Rippling, rippling, rippling, like a flapping overlapping of soft flames, soft as feathers, running to points of brilliance, exquisite, exquisite and melting her all molten inside. It was like bells rippling up and up to a culmination. She lay unconscious of the wild little cries she uttered at the last. But it was over too soon, too soon, and she could no longer force her own conclusion with her own activity. This was different, different. She could do nothing. She could no longer harden and grip for her own satisfaction upon him. She could only wait, wait and moan in spirit as she felt him withdrawing, withdrawing and contracting, coming to the terrible moment when he would slip out of her and be gone. Whilst all her womb was open and soft, and softly clamouring, like a sea-anemone under the tide, clamouring for him to come in again and make a fulfilment for her. She clung to him unconscious in passion, and he never quite slipped from her, and she felt the soft bud of him within her stirring, and strange rhythms flushing up into her with a strange rhythmic growing motion, swelling and swelling till it filled all her cleaving consciousness, and then began again the unspeakable motion that was not really motion, but pure deepening whirlpools of sensation swirling deeper and deeper through all her tissue and consciousness, till she was one perfect concentric fluid of feeling, and she lay there crying in unconscious inarticulate cries. The voice out of the uttermost night, the life! The man heard it beneath him with a kind of awe, as his life sprang out into her. And as it subsided, he subsided too and lay utterly still, unknowing, while her grip on him slowly relaxed, and she lay inert. And they lay and knew nothing, not even of each other, both lost. Till at last he began to rouse and become aware of his defenceless nakedness, and she was aware that his body was loosening its clasp on her. He was coming apart; but in her breast she felt she could not bear him to leave her uncovered. He must cover her now for ever.

But he drew away at last, and kissed her and covered her over, and began to cover himself. She lay looking up to the boughs of the tree, unable as yet to move. He stood and fastened up his breeches, looking round. All was dense and silent, save for the awed dog that lay with its paws against its nose. He sat down again on the brushwood and took Connie's hand in silence.

She turned and looked at him. '**We came off together that time**[1],' he said.

She did not answer.

'It's good when it's like that. Most folks live their lives through and they never know it,' he said, speaking rather dreamily.

She looked into his brooding face.

'Do they?' she said. 'Are you glad?'

He looked back into her eyes. 'Glad,' he said, 'Ay, but never mind.' He did not want her to talk. And he bent over her and kissed her, and she felt, so he must kiss her for ever.

At last she sat up.

'Don't people often come off together?' she asked with naive curiosity.

'A good many of them never. You can see by the raw look of them.' He spoke unwittingly, regretting he had begun.

'Have you come off like that with other women?'

He looked at her amused.

'I don't know,' he said, 'I don't know.'

And she knew he would never tell her anything he didn't want to tell her. She watched his face, and the passion for him moved in her bowels. She resisted it as far as she could, for it was the loss of herself to herself.

He put on his waistcoat and his coat, and pushed a way through to the path again.

The last level rays of the sun touched the wood. 'I won't come with you,' he said; 'better not.'

She looked at him wistfully before she turned. His dog was waiting so anxiously for him to go, and he seemed to have nothing whatever to say. Nothing left.

Connie went slowly home, realizing the depth of the other thing in

---

❶这回我们俩同时达到高潮。

her. Another self was alive in her, burning molten and soft in her womb and bowels, and with this self she adored him. She adored him till her knees were weak as she walked. In her womb and bowels she was flowing and alive now and vulnerable, and helpless in adoration of him as the most naive woman. It feels like a child, she said to herself it feels like a child in me. And so it did, as if her womb, that had always been shut, had opened and filled with new life, almost a burden, yet lovely.

'If I had a child!' she thought to herself; 'if I had him inside me as a child!' — and her limbs turned molten at the thought, and she realized **the immense difference between having a child to oneself and having a child to a man whom one's bowels yearned towards** ❶. The former seemed in a sense ordinary: but to have a child to a man whom one adored in one's bowels and one's womb, it made her feel she was very different from her old self and as if she was sinking deep, deep to the centre of all womanhood and **the sleep of creation**❷.

It was not the passion that was new to her, it was the yearning adoration. She knew she had always feared it, for it left her helpless; she feared it still, **lest if she adored him too much, then she would lose herself become effaced**❸, and she did not want to be effaced, a slave, like a savage woman. She must not become a slave. She feared her adoration, yet she would not at once fight against it. She knew she could fight it. She had a devil of self-will in her breast that could have fought the full soft heaving adoration of her womb and crushed it. She could even now do it, or she thought so, and she could then take up her passion with her own will.

Ah yes, to be passionate like a Bacchante, like a **Bacchanal**❹ fleeing through the woods, **to call on Iacchos**❺, the bright phallos that had no independent personality behind it, but was pure god-servant to the woman! The man, the individual, let him not dare intrude. He was but a temple-servant, the bearer and keeper of the bright phallos, her own.

So, in the flux of new awakening, the old hard passion flamed in

❶有个自己的孩子与怀上个自己全身心爱的男人的孩子之间的天壤之别。❷创造生命的睡眠中。❸她担心太崇拜他,以至于丧失自我,抹杀自己。❹酒神伊阿科司的女仪徒。❺去拜访伊阿科司。伊阿科司,即希腊罗马神话中的酒神狄俄尼索斯(亦称巴克斯)。由于他代表自然之力,受到广大妇女的崇拜,在酒神祭祀中男性生殖器占有重要位置。

her for a time, and **the man dwindled to a contemptible object**[1], the mere phallos-bearer, to be torn to pieces when his service was performed. She felt the force of the Bacchae in her limbs and her body, the woman gleaming and rapid, beating down the male; but while she felt this, her heart was heavy. She did not want it, it was known and barren, birthless; the adoration was her treasure. It was so fathomless, so soft, so deep and so unknown. No, no, she would give up her hard bright female power; she was weary of it, stiffened with it; she would sink in the new bath of life, in the depths of her womb and her bowels that sang the voiceless song of adoration. It was early yet to begin to fear the man.

'I walked over by Marehay, and I had tea with Mrs Flint,' she said to Clifford. 'I wanted to see the baby. It's so adorable, with hair like red cobwebs. Such a dear! Mr Flint had gone to market, so she and I and the baby had tea together. Did you wonder where I was?'

'Well, I wondered, but I guessed you had dropped in somewhere to tea,' said Clifford jealously. With a sort of second sight he sensed something new in her, something to him quite incomprehensible, **but he ascribed it to the baby**[2]. He thought that all that ailed Connie was that she did not have a baby, automatically bring one forth, so to speak.

'I saw you go across the park to the iron gate, my Lady,' said Mrs Bolton; 'so I thought perhaps you'd called at the Rectory.'

'I nearly did, then I turned towards Marehay instead.'

The eyes of the two women met: Mrs Bolton's grey and bright and searching; Connie's blue and veiled and strangely beautiful. Mrs Bolton was almost sure she had a lover, yet how could it be, and who could it be? Where was there a man?

'Oh, it's so good for you, if you go out and see a bit of company sometimes,' said Mrs Bolton. 'I was saying to Sir Clifford, it would do her ladyship a world of good if she'd go out among people more.'

'Yes, I'm glad I went, and such a quaint dear cheeky baby, Clifford,' said Connie. 'It's got hair just like spider-webs, and bright orange, and the oddest, cheekiest, pale-blue china eyes. Of course it's a girl, or it wouldn't be so bold, bolder than any little **Sir Francis Drake**[3].'

❶男人缩小为一种可轻视的东西。❷可是他把这归因于(没有)孩子。❸德雷克爵士(1540—1596),美国海军将军、驾船环行世界的第一个美国人,在与西班牙无敌舰队的战斗中,战功卓著。

'You're right, my Lady — a regular little Flint. They were always a forward sandy-headed family,' said Mrs Bolton.

'Wouldn't you like to see it, Clifford? I've asked them to tea for you to see it.'

'Who?' he asked, looking at Connie in great uneasiness. 'Mrs Flint and the baby, next Monday.'

'You can have them to tea up in your room,' he said.

'Why, don't you want to see the baby?' she cried.

'Oh, I'll see it, but I don't want to sit through a tea-time with them.'

'Oh,' cried Connie, looking at him with wide veiled eyes.

She did not really see him, he was somebody else.

'You can have a nice cosy tea up in your room, my Lady, and Mrs Flint will be more comfortable than if Sir Clifford was there,' said Mrs Bolton.

She was sure Connie had a lover, and something in her soul exulted. But who was he? Who was he? Perhaps Mrs Flint would provide a clue.

Connie would not take her bath this evening. The sense of his flesh touching her, his very stickiness upon her, was dear to her, and in a sense holy.

Clifford was very uneasy. He would not let her go after dinner, and she had wanted so much to be alone. She looked at him, but was curiously submissive.

'Shall we play a game, or shall I read to you, or what shall it be?' he asked uneasily.

'You read to me,' said Connie.

'What shall I read — verse or prose? Or drama?'

'**Read Racine**[1],' she said.

It had been one of his stunts in the past, to read Racine in the real French grand manner, but he was rusty now, and a little self-conscious; he really preferred the loudspeaker. But Connie was sewing, **sewing a little frock silk of primrose silk**[2], cut out of one of her dresses, for Mrs Flint's baby. Between coming home and dinner she had cut it out, and she sat in the soft quiescent rapture of herself sewing, while the noise of the reading went on.

❶读点拉辛的作品吧。拉辛(1639—1699),法国诗人,悲剧作品作家。 ❷用淡黄色的丝线缝一件小斗篷。

Inside herself she could feel the humming of passion, like the after-humming of deep bells.

Clifford said something to her about the Racine. She caught the sense after the words had gone.

'Yes! Yes! ' she said, looking up at him. 'It is splendid.'

Again he was frightened at the deep blue blaze of her eyes, and of her soft stillness, sitting there. She had never been so utterly soft and still. She fascinated him helplessly, as if some perfume about her intoxicated him. So he went on helplessly with his reading, and the throaty sound of the French was like the wind in the chimneys to her. Of the Racine she heard not one syllable.

She was gone in her own soft rapture, like a forest soughing with the dim, glad moan of spring, moving into bud. She could feel in the same world with her the man, the nameless man, moving on beautiful feet, beautiful in the phallic mystery. And in herself in all her veins, she felt him and his child. His child was in all her veins, like a twilight.

'For hands she hath none, nor eyes, nor feet, nor golden Treasure of hair...'

She was like a forest, like the dark interlacing of the oakwood, humming inaudibly with myriad unfolding buds. Meanwhile the birds of desire were asleep in the vast interlaced intricacy of her body.

But Clifford's voice went on, clapping and gurgling with unusual sounds. How extraordinary it was! How extraordinary he was, bent there over the book, queer and rapacious and civilized, with broad shoulders and no real legs! What a strange creature, with the sharp, cold inflexible will of some bird, and no warmth, no warmth at all! One of those creatures of the afterwards, that have no soul, but an extra-alert will, cold will. She shuddered a little, afraid of him. But then, the soft warm flame of life was stronger than he, and the real things were hidden from him.

The reading finished. She was startled. She looked up, and was more startled still to see Clifford watching her with pale, uncanny eyes, like hate.

'Thank you so much! You do read Racine beautifully! ' she said softly.

'Almost as beautifully as you listen to him,' he said cruelly. 'What are you making?' he asked.

'I'm making a child's dress, for Mrs Flint's baby.'

He turned away. A child! A child! That was all her obsession.

'After all,' he said in a declamatory voice, 'one gets all one wants out of Racine. **Emotions that are ordered and given shape are more important than disorderly emotions**❶.

She watched him with wide, vague, veiled eyes. 'Yes, I'm sure they are,' she said.

'**The modern world has only vulgarized emotion by letting it loose**❷. What we need is classic control.'

'Yes,' she said slowly, thinking of him listening with vacant face to the emotional idiocy of the radio. 'People pretend to have emotions, and they really feel nothing. I suppose that is being romantic.'

'Exactly!' he said.

As a matter of fact, he was tired. This evening had tired him. He would rather have been with his technical books, or his pit-manager, or listening-in to the radio.

Mrs Bolton came in with two glasses of malted milk: for Clifford, to make him sleep, and for Connie, to fatten her again. It was a regular **night-cap**❸ she had introduced.

Connie was glad to go, when she had drunk her glass, and thankful she needn't help Clifford to bed. She took his glass and put it on the tray, then took the tray, to leave it outside.

'Goodnight Clifford! Do sleep well! The Racine gets into one like a dream. Goodnight!'

She had drifted to the door. She was going without kissing him goodnight. He watched her with sharp, cold eyes. So! She did not even kiss him goodnight, after he had spent an evening reading to her. Such depths of callousness in her! Even if the kiss was but a formality, **it was on such formalities that life depends**❹. She was a Bolshevik, really. Her instincts were Bolshevistic! He gazed coldly and angrily at the door whence she had gone. Anger!

And again the dread of the night came on him. He was a network of nerves, **and when he was not braced up to work**❺, and so full of energy: or when he was not listening-in, and so utterly neuter:

❶情通理顺的情感比乱七八糟的情感重要得多。❷现代人放荡纵欲只能使感情庸俗不堪。❸（口）夜宵，临睡前喝的饮料。❹而生活是取决于形式的。❺当他未振作起来工作时，brace up：振作精神，鼓起勇气。

then he was haunted by anxiety and a sense of dangerous impending void. He was afraid. And Connie could keep the fear off him, if she would. But it was obvious she wouldn't, she wouldn't. She was callous, cold and callous to all that he did for her. He gave up his life for her, and she was callous to him. She only wanted her own way. 'The lady loves her will.'

Now it was a baby she was obsessed by. Just so that it should be her own, all her own, and not his!

Clifford was so healthy, considering. He looked so well and ruddy in the face, his shoulders were broad and strong, his chest deep, he had put on flesh. And yet, at the same time, he was afraid of death. A terrible hollow seemed to menace him somewhere, somehow, a void, and into this void his energy would collapse. Energyless, he felt at times he was dead, really dead.

So his rather prominent pale eyes had a queer look, furtive, and yet a little cruel, so cold: and at the same time, almost impudent. It was a very odd look, this look of impudence: as if he were triumphing over life in spite of life. 'Who knoweth the mysteries of the will — for it can triumph even against the angels — '

But his dread was the nights when he could not sleep. Then it was awful indeed, when annihilation pressed in on him on every side. Then it was ghastly, to exist without having any life: lifeless, in the night, to exist.

But now he could ring for Mrs Bolton. And she would always come. That was a great comfort. She would come in her dressing gown, with her hair in a plait down her back, curiously girlish and dim, though the brown plait was streaked with grey. And she would make him coffee or **camomile tea**①, and she would play chess or piquet with him. She had a woman's queer faculty of playing even chess well enough, **when she was three parts asleep**②, well enough to make her worth beating. So, in the silent intimacy of the night, they sat, or she sat and he lay on the bed, with the reading-lamp shedding its solitary light on them, she almost gone in sleep, he almost gone in a sort of fear, and they played, played together — then they had a cup of coffee and a biscuit together, hardly speaking, in the silence of night, but being a

①菊花茶。camomie=chamomile。 ②当她在朦朦胧胧的睡眠中。

reassurance to one another.

And this night she was wondering who Lady Chatterley's lover was. And she was thinking of her own Ted, so long dead, yet for her never quite dead. And when she thought of him, the old, old grudge against the world rose up, but especially against the masters, that they had killed him. They had not really killed him. Yet, to her, emotionally, they had. And somewhere deep in herself because of it, she was a nihilist, and really anarchic.

In her half-sleep, thoughts of her Ted and thoughts of Lady Chatterley's unknown lover commingled, and then she felt she shared with the other woman a great grudge against Sir Clifford and all he stood for. At the same time she was playing piquet with him, and they were gambling sixpences. And it was a source of satisfaction to be playing piquet with a baronet, and even losing sixpences to him.

When they played cards, they always gambled. It made him forget himself. And he usually won. Tonight too he was winning. So he would not go to sleep till the first dawn appeared. Luckily it began to appear at half past four or thereabouts.

Connie was in bed, and fast asleep all this time. But the keeper, too, could not rest. He had closed the coops and made his round of the wood, then gone home and eaten supper. But he did not go to bed. Instead he sat by the fire and thought.

He thought of his boyhood in Tevershall, and of his five or six years of married life. He thought of his wife, and always bitterly. She had seemed so brutal. But he had not seen her now since 1915, in the spring when he joined up. Yet there she was, not three miles away, and more brutal than ever. He hoped never to see her again while he lived.

He thought of his life abroad, as a soldier. India, Egypt, then India again: the blind, thoughtless life with the horses: the colonel who had loved him and whom he had loved: the several years that he had been an officer, a lieutenant with a very fair chance of being a captain. Then the death of the colonel from pneumonia, and his own narrow escape from death: his damaged health: his deep restlessness: his leaving the army and coming back to England to be a working man again.

He was temporizing with life. He had thought he would be safe, at least for a time, in this wood. There was no shooting as yet: he had to rear the pheasants. He would have no guns to serve. He would be alone, and apart from life, which was all he wanted. He had to have some sort of a background. And this was his native place. There was even his mother, though she had never meant very much to him. And he could go on in life, existing from day to day, without connexion and without hope. For he did not know what to do with himself.

He did not know what to do with himself. Since he had been an officer for some years, and had mixed among the other officers and civil servants, with their wives and families, he had lost all ambition to 'get on'. There was a toughness, a curious rubbernecked toughness and unlivingness about the middle and upper classes, as he had known them, which just left him feeling cold and different from them.

So, he had come back to his own class. To find there, what he had forgotten during his absence of years, a pettiness and a vulgarity of manner extremely distasteful. He admitted now at last, how important manner was. He admitted, also, how important it was even to pretend not to care about the halfpence and the small things of life. But among the common people there was no pretence. **A penny more or less on the bacon was worse than a change in the Gospel**①. He could not stand it.

And again, there was the wage-squabble. Having lived among the owning classes, he knew the utter futility of expecting any solution of the wage-squabble. There was no solution, **short of death**②. The only thing was not to care, not to care about the wages.

Yet, if you were poor and wretched you had to care. Anyhow, it was becoming the only thing they did care about. The care about money was like a great cancer, eating away the individuals of all classes. He refused to care about money.

And what then? What did life offer apart from the care of money? Nothing.

Yet he could live alone, in the wan satisfaction of being alone, and raise pheasants to be shot ultimately by fat men after breakfast. It was futility, **futility to the nth power**③.

But why care, why bother? And he had not cared nor bothered till now, when this woman had come into his life. He was nearly ten years older than she. And he was a thousand years older in experience, starting

①咸肉的价格多一便士或少一便士比修改福音书都重要。 ②死路一条，short of, except. ③完全徒劳。to the nth power/degree 极端地，极度地，(数)至无限。

from the bottom. The connexion between them was growing closer. He could see the day when it would clinch up and they would have to make a life together. 'For the bonds of love are ill to loose! '

And what then? What then? Must he start again, with nothing to start on? Must he entangle this woman? Must he have the horrible broil with her lame husband? And also some sort of horrible broil with his own brutal wife, who hated him? Misery! Lots of misery! And he was no longer young and merely buoyant. Neither was he the insouciant sort. Every bitterness and every ugliness would hurt him: and the woman!

But even if they got clear of Sir Clifford and of his own wife, even if they got clear, what were they going to do? What was he, himself going to do? What was he going to do with his life? For he must do something. He couldn't be **a mere hanger-on**[1], on her money and his own very small pension.

It was the insoluble. He could only think of going to America, to try a new air. He disbelieved in the dollar utterly. But perhaps, perhaps there was something else.

He could not rest nor even go to bed. After sitting in a stupor of bitter thoughts until midnight, he got suddenly from his chair and reached for his coat and gun.

'Come on, lass,' he said to the dog. 'We're best outside.'

It was a starry night, but moonless. He went on a slow, scrupulous, soft-stepping and stealthy round. The only thing he had to contend with was the colliers setting snares for rabbits, particularly the Stacks Gate colliers, on the Marehay side. But it was breeding season, and even colliers respected it a little. **Nevertheless the stealthy beating of the round in search of poachers**[2] soothed his nerves and took his mind off his thoughts.

But when he had done his slow, **cautious beating of his bounds**[3] — it was nearly a five-mile walk — he was tired. He went to the top of the knoll and looked out. There was no sound save the noise, the faint shuffling noise from Stacks Gate colliery, that never ceased working: and there were hardly any lights, save the brilliant electric rows at the works. The world lay darkly and fumily sleeping. It was half past two. But even in its sleep it was an uneasy, cruel world, stirring with the

①仅仅是个寄生虫。 ②不过,轻手轻脚地巡逻以搜索偷猎者。 ③谨慎地巡逻完一圈之后。

noise of a train or some great lorry on the road, and flashing with some rosy lightning flash from the furnaces. It was a world of iron and coal, the ruelty of iron and the smoke of coal, and the endless, endless greed that drove it all. Only greed, greed stirring in its sleep.

It was cold, and he was coughing. A fine cold draught blew over the knoll. He thought of the woman. Now he would have given all he had or ever might have to hold her warm in his arms, both of them wrapped in one blanket, and sleep. All hopes of eternity and all gain from the past he would have given to have her there, to be wrapped warm with him in one blanket, and sleep, only sleep. It seemed the sleep with the woman in his arms was the only necessity.

He went to the hut, and wrapped himself in the blanket and lay on the floor to sleep. But he could not, he was cold. And besides, he felt cruelly his own unfinished nature. He felt his own unfinished condition of aloneness cruelly. He wanted her, to touch her, to hold her fast against him in one moment of completeness and sleep.

He got up again and went out, towards the park gates this time: then slowly along the path towards the house. It was nearly four o'clock, still clear and cold, but no sign of dawn. He was used to the dark, he could see well.

Slowly, slowly the great house drew him, as a magnet. He wanted to be near her. It was not desire, not that. It was the cruel sense of unfinished aloneness, that needed a silent woman folded in his arms. Perhaps he could find her. Perhaps he could even call her out to him: or find some way in to her. For the need was imperious.

He slowly, silently climbed the incline to the hall. Then he came round the great trees at the top of the knoll, on to the drive, which made a grand sweep round a lozenge of grass in front of the entrance. He could already see the two magnificent beeches which stood in this big level lozenge in front of the house, detaching themselves darkly in the dark air.

There was the house, low and long and obscure, with one light burning downstairs, in Sir Clifford's room. But which room she was in, the woman who held the other end of the frail thread which drew him so mercilessly, that he did not know.

He went a little nearer, gun in hand, and stood motionless on the drive, watching the house. Perhaps even now he could find her, come at her in some way. The house was not impregnable: he was as clever as burglars are. Why not come to her?

He stood motionless, waiting, while the dawn faintly and imperceptibly paled behind him. He saw the light in the house go out. But he did not see Mrs Bolton come to the window and draw back the old curtain of dark-blue silk, and stand herself in the dark room, looking out on the half-dark of the approaching day, looking for the longed-for dawn, waiting, waiting for Clifford to be really reassured that it was daybreak. For when he was sure of daybreak, he would sleep almost at once.

She stood blind with sleep at the window, waiting. And as she stood, she started, and almost cried out. For there was a man out there on the drive, a black figure in the twilight. She woke up greyly, and watched, but without making a sound to disturb Sir Clifford.

The daylight began to rustle into the world, and the dark figure seemed to go smaller and more defined. She made out the gun and gaiters and baggy jacket — it would be Oliver Mellors, the keeper. 'Yes, for there was the dog nosing around like a shadow, and waiting for him'!

And what did the man want? Did he want to rouse the house? What was he standing there for, transfixed, looking up at the house like a love-sick male dog outside the house where the bitch is?

Goodness! The knowledge went through Mrs Bolton like a shot. He was Lady Chatterley's lover! He! He!

To think of it! Why, she, Ivy Bolton, had once been a tiny bit in love with him herself. When he was a lad of sixteen and she a woman of twenty-six. It was when she was studying, and he had helped her a lot with the anatomy and things she had had to learn. He'd been a clever boy, had a scholarship for Sheffield Grammar School, and learned French and things: and then after all had become an overhead blacksmith shoeing horses, because he was fond of horses, he said: but really because he was frightened to go out and face the world, only he'd never admit it.

But he'd been a nice lad, a nice lad, had helped her a lot, so clever at making things clear to you. He was quite as clever as Sir Clifford: and always one for the women. More with women than men, they said.

Till he'd gone and married that Bertha Coutts, as if to spite himself. Some people do marry to spite themselves, because they're disappointed of something. And no wonder it had been a failure. — For years he was gone, all the time of the war: and a lieutenant and all: quite the gentleman, really quite the gentleman! — Then to come back to Tevershall and go as a game-keeper! Really, some people can't take their chances when they've got them! And talking broad Derbyshire again like the worst, when she, Ivy Bolton, knew he spoke like any gentleman, really.

Well, well! So her ladyship had fallen for him! Well her ladyship wasn't the first: there was something about him. But fancy! A Tevershall lad born and bred, and she her ladyship in Wragby Hall! My word, that was a slap back at the high-and-mighty Chatterleys!

But he, the keeper, as the day grew, had realized: it's no good! It's no good trying to get rid of your own aloneness. You've got to stick to it all your life. Only at times, at times, the gap will be filled in. At times! But you have to wait for the times. Accept your own aloneness and stick to it, all your life. And then accept the times when the gap is filled in, when they come. But they've got to come. You can't force them.

With a sudden snap the bleeding desire that had drawn him after her broke. He had broken it, because it must be so. There must be a coming together on both sides. And if she wasn't coming to him, he wouldn't track her down. He mustn't. He must go away, till she came.

He turned slowly, ponderingly, accepting again the isolation. He knew it was better so. She must come to him: it was no use his trailing after her. No use!

Mrs Bolton saw him disappear, saw his dog run after him.

'Well, well!' she said. 'He's the one man I never thought of; and the one man I might have thought of. He was nice to me when he was a lad, after I lost Ted. Well, well! Whatever would he say if he knew!'

And she glanced triumphantly at the already sleeping Clifford, as she stepped softly from the room.

CHAPTER 11

Connie was sorting out one of the Wragby lumber rooms. There were several: the house was a warren, and the family never sold anything. Sir Geoffery's father had liked pictures and Sir Geoffery's mother had liked cinquecento furniture. Sir Geoffery himself had liked old carved oak chests, vestry chests. So it went on through the generations. Clifford collected very modern pictures, at very moderate prices.

So in the lumber room there were bad **Sir Edwin Lands-eers**[1] and pathetic **William Henry Hunt**[2] birds' nests: and other Academy stuff, enough to frighten the daughter of an **R.A.**[3] She determined to look through it one day, and clear it all. And the grotesque furniture interested her.

Wrapped up carefully to preserve it from damage and dry-rot was the old family cradle, of rosewood. She had to unwrap it, to look at it. It had a certain charm: she looked at it a longtime.

'**It's thousand pities it won't be called for**[4],' sighed Mrs Bolton, who was helping. 'Though cradles like that are out of date nowadays.'

'It might be called for. I might have a child,' said Connie casually, as if saying she might have a new hat.

'**You mean if anything happened to Sir Clifford**[5]!' stammered Mrs Bolton.

'No! I mean as things are. It's only muscular paralysis with Sir Clifford — it doesn't affect him,' said Connie, lying as naturally as breathing.

Clifford had put the idea into her head. He had said: 'Of course I may have a child yet. I'm not really mutilated at all. The potency may easily come back, even if the muscles of the hips and legs are paralysed. And then the seed may be transferred.'

He really felt, when he had his periods of energy and worked so

[1]兰西尔(1802—1873),英国绘画家,以画动物闻名。 [2]威廉·亨利·亨特(1827—1910),英国画家。 [3]Royal Academy(皇家艺术学会)的缩写。 [4]非常遗憾,这个摇篮现在用不上了。 [5]您的意思是克利福德男爵康复了?

hard at the question of the mines, as if his sexual potency were returning. Connie had looked at him in terror. But she was quite quick-witted enough to use his suggestion for her own preservation. For she would have a child if she could: but not his.

Mrs Bolton was for a moment breathless, flabbergasted. Then she didn't believe it: **she saw in it a ruse**[1]. Yet doctors could do such things nowadays. They might sort of **graft seed**[2].

'Well, my Lady, I only hope and pray you may. It would be lovely for you: and for everybody. My word, a child in Wragby, what a difference it would make!'

'Wouldn't it!' said Connie.

And she chose three R. A. pictures of sixty years ago, to send to the Duchess of Shortlands for that lady's next charitable bazaar. She was called 'the bazaar duchess', and she always asked all the county to send things for her to sell. She would be delighted with three framed R. A.s. She might even call, **on the strength of**[3] them. How furious Clifford was when she called!

But oh my dear! Mrs Bolton was thinking to herself. Is it Oliver Mellors' child you're preparing us for? Oh my dear, that would be a Tevershall baby in the Wragby cradle, my word! Wouldn't shame it, neither!

Among other monstrosities in this lumber room was a largish blackjapanned box, excellently and ingeniously made some sixty or seventy years ago, and fitted with every imaginable object. On top was a concentrated toilet set: brushes, bottles, mirrors, combs, boxes, even three beautiful little razors in safety sheaths, shaving-bowl and all. Underneath came a sort of **escritoire outfit**[4]: blotters, pens, ink-bottles, paper, envelopes, memorandum books: and then a perfect sewing-outfit, with three different sized scissors, thimbles, needles, silks and cottons, darning egg, all of the very best quality and perfectly finished. Then there was a little medicine store, with **bottles labelled Laudanum, Tincture of Myrrh, Ess. Cloves and so on**[5]: but empty. Everything was perfectly new, and the whole thing, when shut up, was as big as a small, but fat weekend bag. And inside, it fitted together like a puzzle. The bottles could not possibly have spilled:

❶她看这其中有文章。❷移植精子。❸=because of。❹文具用品。❺瓶子上标着各种药名：鸦片酊，没药酊，丁香精等。

there wasn't room.

The thing was wonderfully made and contrived, excellent craftsmanship of the Victorian order. But somehow it was monstrous. **Some Chatterley must even have felt it**[1], for the thing had never been used. It had a peculiar soullessness.

Yet Mrs Bolton was thrilled.

'Look what beautiful brushes, so expensive, even the shaving brushes, three perfect ones! No! and those scissors! They're the best that money could buy. Oh, I call it lovely!'

'Do you?' said Connie. 'Then you have it.'

'Oh no, my Lady!'

'Of course! It will only lie here till Doomsday. If you won't have it, I'll send it to the Duchess as well as the pictures, and she doesn't deserve so much. Do have it!'

'Oh, your Ladyship! Why, **I shall never be able to thank you**[2].'

'You needn't try,' laughed Connie.

And Mrs Bolton sailed down with the huge and very black box in her arms, flushing bright pink in her excitement.

Mr Betts drove her in the trap to her house in the village, with the box. And she had to have a few friends in, to show it: the school-mistress, the chemist's wife, Mrs Weedon the undercashier's wife. They thought it marvellous. And then started the whisper of Lady Chatterley's child.

'Wonders'll never cease!' said Mrs Weedon.

But Mrs Bolton was convinced, if it did come, it would be Sir Clifford's child. So there!

Not long after, the rector said gently to Clifford:

'And may we really hope for an heir to Wragby? Ah, that would be the hand of God in mercy, indeed!'

'Well! We may hope,' said Clifford, with a faint irony, and at the same time, a certain conviction. He had begun to believe it really possible it might even be his child.

Then one afternoon came Leslie Winter, **Squire Winter, as everybody called him**[3]: lean, immaculate, and seventy: and every inch a gentleman, as Mrs Bolton said to Mrs Betts. Every millimetre indeed! And w ith his old-fashioned, rather haw-haw! manner of

[1] 某位查泰莱家的老人肯定有此感受。 [2] 我不知道该如何感谢你才好。 [3] 人们称为“乡绅温特”的他。

speaking, he seemed more out of date than **bag wigs**[1]. Time, in her flight, drops these fine old feathers.

They discussed the collieries. Clifford's idea was, that his coal, even the poor sort, could be made into hard concentrated fuel that would burn at great heat if fed with certain damp, acidulated air at a fairly strong pressure. It had long been observed that in a particularly strong, wet wind the pit-bank burned very vivid, gave off hardly any fumes, and left a fine powder of ash, instead of the slow pink gravel.

'But where will you find the proper engines for burning your fuel?' asked Winter.

'I'll make them myself. And I'll use my fuel myself. And I'll sell electric power. I'm certain I could do it.'

'If you can do it, then splendid, splendid, my dear boy. Haw! Splendid! If I can be of any help, I shall be delighted. I'm afraid I am a little out of date, and my collieries are like me. But who knows, when I'm gone, there may be men like you. Splendid! It will employ all the men again, and you won't have to sell your coal, or fail to sell it. A splendid idea, and I hope it will be a success. If I had sons of my own, no doubt they would have up-to-date ideas for Shipley: no doubt! By the way, dear boy, is there any foundation to the rumour that we may entertain hopes of an heir to Wragby?'

'Is there a rumour?' asked Clifford.

'Well, my dear boy, Marshall from Fillingwood asked me, that's all I can say about a rumour. **Of course I wouldn't repeat it for the world, if there were no foundation**[2].'

'Well, Sir,' said Clifford uneasily, but with strange bright eyes. 'There is a hope. There is a hope.'

Winter came across the room and wrung Clifford's hand.

'My dear boy, my dear lad, can you believe what it means to me, to hear that! And to hear you are working in the hopes of a son: and that you may again employ every man at Tevershall. Ah, my boy! **to keep up the level of the race**[3], and to have work waiting for any man who cares to work! —'

The old man was really moved.

Next day Connie was arranging tall yellow tulips in a glass vase.

①戴假发的人。 ②当然,如果这是无事生非,我不会满世界地去说。 ③保持竞争的领先地位。

'Connie,' said Clifford, 'did you know there was a rumour that you are going to supply Wragby with a son and heir?'

Connie felt dim with terror, yet she stood quite still, touching the flowers.

'No!' she said. 'Is it a joke? Or malice?'

He paused before he answered:

'Neither, I hope. I hope it may be a prophecy.'

Connie went on with her flowers.

'I had a letter from Father this morning,' She said. 'He wants to know if I am aware he has accepted Sir Alexander Cooper's Invitation for me for July and August, to the Villa Esmeralda in Venice.'

'July and August?' said Clifford.

'Oh, I wouldn't stay all that time. Are you sure you wouldn't come?'

'I won't travel abroad,' said Clifford promptly. She took her flowers to the window.

'Do you mind if I go?' she said. You know it was promised, for this summer.

'For how long would you go?'

'Perhaps three weeks.'

There was silence for a time.

'Well,' said Clifford slowly, and a little gloomily. 'I suppose I could stand it for three weeks: if I were absolutely sure you'd want to come back.'

'I should want to come back,' she said, with a quiet simplicity, heavy with conviction. She was thinking of the other man.

Clifford felt her conviction, and somehow he believed her, he believed it was for him. He felt immensely relieved, joyful at once.

'In that case,' he said,

'I think it would be all right, don't you?'

'I think so,' she said.

'You'd enjoy the change?' She looked up at him with strange blue eyes.

'I should like to see Venice again,' she said, 'and **to bathe from one of the shingle islands across the lagoon**①. But you know I loathe **the Lido**②! And I don't fancy I shall like Sir Alexander Cooper and Lady Cooper. But if Hilda is there, and we have a gondola of our own:

①在泻湖对面的大砾沙岛上沐浴。 ②丽都岛:威尼斯的著名的海滨浴场。

yes, it will be rather lovely. I do wish you'd come.'

She said it sincerely. She would so love to make him happy, in these ways.

'Ah, but think of me, though, at **the Gare du Nord**[1]: at Calais quay!'

'But why not? I see other men carried in litter-chairs, who have been wounded in the war. Besides, we'd motor all the way.'

'We should need to take two men.'

'Oh no! We'd manage with Field. There would always be another man there.'

But Clifford shook his head.

'Not this year, dear! Not this year! Next year probably I'll try.'

She went away gloomily. Next year! What would next year bring? She herself did not really want to go to Venice: not now, now there was the other man. But she was going as a sort of discipline: and also because, if she had a child, Clifford could think she had a lover in Venice.

It was already May, and in June they were supposed to start. Always these arrangements! Always one's life arranged for one! Wheels that worked one and drove one, and over which one had no real control!

It was May, but cold and wet again. A cold wet May, good for corn and hay! Much the corn and hay matter nowadays! Connie had to go into Uthwaite, which was their little town, **where the Chatterleys were still the Chatterleys**[2]. She went alone, Field driving her.

In spite of May and a new greenness, the country was dismal. It was rather chilly, and there was smoke on the rain, and a certain sense of exhaust vapour in the air. One just had to live from one's resistance. No wonder these people were ugly and tough.

The car ploughed uphill through the long squalid straggle of Tevershall, the blackened brick dwellings, the black slate roofs glistening their sharp edges, the mud black with coal-dust, the pavements wet and black. It was as if dismalness had soaked through and through everything. The utter negation of natural beauty, the utter negation of the gladness of life, the utter absence of the instinct for shapely beauty which every bird

❶(法)巴黎北站。 ❷在这里查泰莱家族声名依旧显赫。

and beast has, the utter death of the human intuitive faculty was appalling. The stacks of soap in the grocers' shops, the rhubarb and lemons in the greengrocers! The awful hats in the milliners! all went by ugly, ugly, ugly, followed **by the plaster-and-gilt horror of the cinema**① with its wet picture announcements, 'A Woman's Love!', and the new big Primitive chapel, primitive enough in its stark brick and big panes of greenish and raspberry glass in the windows. **The Wesleyan chapel**②, higher up, was of blackened brick and stood behind iron railings and blackened shrubs. **The Congregational chapel**③, which thought itself superior, was built of rusticated sandstone and had a steeple, but not a very high one. Just beyond were the new school buildings, expensive pink brick, and gravelled playground inside iron railings, all very imposing, and fixing the suggestion of a chapel and a prison. Standard Five girls were having a singing lesson, just finishing the la-me-doh-la exercises and beginning a 'sweet children's song'. Anything more unlike song, spontaneous song, would be impossible to imagine: **a strange bawling yell that followed the outlines of a tune**④. It was not like savages: savages have subtle rhythms. It was not like animals: animals mean something when they yell. It was like nothing on earth, and it was called singing. **Connie sat and listened with her heart in her boots**⑤, as Field was filling petrol. What could possibly become of such a people, **a people in whom the living intuitive faculty was dead as nails, and only queer mechanical yells and uncanny will-power remained**⑥?

A coal-cart was coming downhill, clanking in the rain. Field started upwards, past the big but weary-looking drapers and clothing shops, the post-office, into the little market-place of forlorn space, where Sam Black was peering out of the door of the Sun, that called itself an inn, not a pub, and where the commercial travellers stayed, and was bowing to Lady Chatterley's car.

The church was away to the left among black trees. The car slid on downhill, past the Miners' Arms. It had already passed the Wellington, the Nelson, the Three Tuns, and the Sun, now it passed the Miners'

①用泥灰和镀金材料建造的俗气的影院。 ②卫斯理小教堂：查尔斯·卫斯理(1707—1788)和其兄约翰·卫斯理(1703—1791)为英国基督教卫斯理教的创始人。 ③(基督教)公理会教堂。 ④稍带曲调的奇怪呼号。 ⑤康妮心情抑郁地坐在那儿听着。 ⑥这个民族生存的直觉机能已死亡殆尽，只留下古怪的机械呼号不可思议的意志力。

Arms, then the Mechanics' Hall, then the new and almost gaudy Miners' Welfare and so, past a few new 'villas', out into the blackened road between dark hedges and dark green fields, towards Stacks Gate.

Tevershall! That was Tevershall! Merrie England! Shakespeare's England! No, but the England of today, as Connie had realized since she had come to live in it. It was producing a new race of mankind, over-conscious in the money and social and political side, on the spontaneous, intuitive side dead, but dead. Half-corpses, all of them: but with a terrible insistent consciousness in the other half. There was something uncanny and underground about it all. It was an under-world. And quite incalculable. How shall we understand the reactions in half-corpses? When Connie saw the great lorries full of steel-workers from Sheffield, weird, distorted smallish beings like men, off for an excursion to Matlock, her bowels fainted and she thought: Ah God, what has man done to man? What have the leaders of men been doing to their fellow men? **They have reduced them to less than humanness**[1]; and now there can be no fellowship any more! It is just a nightmare.

She felt again in a wave of terror the grey, gritty hopelessness of it all. With such creatures for the industrial masses, and the upper classes as she knew them, there was no hope, no hope any more. Yet she was wanting a baby, and an heir to Wragby! An heir to Wragby! She shuddered with dread.

Yet Mellors had come out of all this! — Yes, but he was as apart from it all as she was. Even in him there was no fellowship left. It was dead. The fellowship was dead. There was only apartness and hopelessness, as far as all this was concerned. And this was England, the vast bulk of England: as Connie knew, since she had motored from the centre of it.

The car was rising towards Stacks Gate. The rain was holding off, and in the air came a queer pellucid gleam of May. The country rolled away in long undulations, south towards the Peak, east towards Mansfield and Nottingham. Connie was travelling South.

As she rose on to the high country, she could see on her left, on a height above the rolling land, the shadowy, powerful bulk of Warsop

[1] 领导者使人们丧失人性。

Castle, dark grey, with below it the reddish plastering of miners' dwellings, newish, and below those the plumes of dark smoke and white steam from the great colliery which **put so many thousand pounds per annum into the pockets of the Duke and the other shareholders**❶. The powerful old castle was a ruin, yet it hung its bulk on the low sky-line, over the black plumes and the white that waved on the damp air below.

A turn, and they ran on the high level to Stacks Gate. Stacks Gate, as seen from the highroad, was just a huge and gorgeous new hotel, the Coningsby Arms, standing red and white and gilt in barbarous isolation off the road. But if you looked, you saw on the left rows of handsome 'modern' dwellings, set down like a game of dominoes, with spaces and gardens, a queer game of dominoes that some weird 'masters' were playing on the surprised earth. And beyond these blocks of dwellings, at the back, rose all the astonishing and frightening overhead erections of a really modern mine, chemical works and long galleries, enormous, and of shapes not before known to man. The head-stock and pit-bank of the mine itself were insignificant among the huge new installations. And in front of this, the game of dominoes stood forever in a sort of surprise, waiting to be played.

This was Stacks Gate, new on the face of the earth, since the war. But as a matter of fact, though even Connie did not know it, downhill half a mile below the 'hotel' was old Stacks Gate, with a little old colliery and blackish old brick dwellings, and a chapel or two and a shop or two and a little pub or two.

But that didn't count any more. The vast plumes of smoke and vapour rose from the new works up above, and this was now Stacks Gate: no chapels, no pubs, even no shops. Only the great works', which are the modern **Olympia**❷ with temples to all the gods; then the model dwellings: then the hotel. The hotel in actuality was nothing but a miners' pub though it looked first-classy.

Even since Connie's arrival at Wragby this new place had arisen on the face of the earth, and **the model dwellings had filled with riff-raff drifting in from anywhere**❸, to poach Clifford's rabbits among other occupations.

❶每年把数千英镑送入公爵和其他股东的腰包。 ❷奥林匹亚：希腊伯罗奔尼撒半岛西部的古迹，古希腊著名圣地。 ❸这些格式化的建筑里住满了从各地流落来的贱民。

The car ran on along the uplands, seeing the rolling county spread out. The county! It had once been a proud and lordly county. In front, looming again and hanging on the brow of the sky-line, was the huge and splendid bulk of Chadwick Hall, more window than wall, one of the most famous Elizabethan houses. Noble it stood alone above a great park, but out of date, passed over. It was still kept up, but as a show place. 'Look how our ancestors lorded it!'

That was the past. The present lay below. God alone knows where the future lies. The car was already turning, between little old blackened miners' cottages, to descend to Uthwaite. And Uthwaite, on a damp day, was sending up a whole array of smoke plumes and steam, to whatever gods there be. Uthwaite down in the valley, with all the steel threads of the railways to Sheffield drawn through it, and the coal-mines and the steel-works sending up smoke and glare from long tubes, and the pathetic little corkscrew spire of the church, that is going to tumble down, still pricking the fumes, always affected Connie strangely. It was an old market-town, centre of the dales. One of the chief inns was the Chatterley Arms. There, in Uthwaite, Wragby was known as Wragby, as if it were a whole place, not just a house, as it was to outsiders: Wragby Hall, near Tevershall: Wragby, a 'seat'.

The miners' cottages, blackened, stood flush on the pavement, with that intimacy and smallness of colliers' dwellings over a hundred years old. They lined all the way. The road had become a street, and as you sank, you forgot instantly the open, rolling country where the castles and big houses still dominated, but like ghosts. Now you were just above the tangle of naked railway-lines, and foundries and other 'works' rose about you, so big you were only aware of walls. And iron clanked with a huge reverberating clank, and huge lorries shook the earth, and whistles screamed.

Yet again, once you had got right down and into the twisted and crooked heart of the town, behind the church, you were in the world of two centuries ago, in the crooked streets where the Chatterley Arms stood, and the old pharmacy, streets which used to lead out to the wild open world of the castles and stately couchant houses.

But at the corner a policeman held up his hand as three lorries loaded with iron rolled past, shaking the poor old church. And not till the lorries were past could he salute her ladyship.

So it was. Upon the old crooked burgess streets hordes of oldish blackened miners' dwellings crowded, lining the roads out. And immediately after these came the newer, pinker rows of rather larger houses, plastering the valley: the homes of more modern workmen. And beyond that again, in the wide rolling regions of the castles, smoke waved against steam, and patch after patch of raw reddish brick showed the newer mining settlements, sometimes in the hollows, sometimes gruesomely ugly along the sky-line of the slopes. And between, in between, were the tattered remnants of the old coaching and cottage England, even the England of Robin Hood, where the miners prowled with the dismalness of suppressed sporting instincts, when they were not at work.

England, my England! But which is my England? The stately homes of England make good photographs, and create the illusion of a connexion with the Elizabethans. The handsome old halls are there, from the days of **Good Queen Anne**① and **Tom Jones**②. But smuts fall and blacken on the drab stucco, that has long ceased to be golden. And one by one, like the stately homes, they were abandoned. Now they are being pulled down. As for the cottages of England — there they are — great plasterings of brick dwellings on the hopeless countryside.

'Now they are pulling down the stately homes, the Georgian halls are going. Fritchley, a perfect old Georgian mansion, was even now, as Connie passed in the car, being demolished. It was in perfect repair: till the war the Weatherleys had lived in style there. But now it was too big, too expensive, and the country had become too uncongenial. The gentry were departing to pleasanter places, where they could spend their money **without having to see how it was made**③.'

This is history. One England blots out another. The mines had made the halls wealthy. Now they were blotting them out, as they had already blotted out the cottages. The industrial England blots out the agricultural England. One meaning blots out another. The new England blots out the old England. And the continuity is not organic, but mechanical.

Connie, belonging to the leisured classes, had clung to the remnants of the old England. It had taken her years to realize that it was really

①慈爱安妮女王。安妮女王(1665—1714),斯图加特王朝最后一位君主。 ②汤姆·琼斯:英国小说家亨利·菲尔丁(Henry Fielding,1707—1754)的代表作《弃婴汤姆·琼斯的事故》中的主人公名。 ③而无须明白金钱是怎么样攒的。

blotted out by this terrifying new and gruesome England, and that the blotting out would go on till it was complete. Fritchley was gone, Eastwood was gone, Shipley was going: Squire Winter's beloved Shipley.

Connie called for a moment at Shipley. The park gates, at the back, opened just near the level crossing of the colliery railway; the Shipley colliery itself stood just beyond the trees. The gates stood open, because through the park was **a right-of-way**[1] that the colliers used. They hung around the park.

The car passed the ornamental ponds, in which the colliers threw their newspapers, and took the private drive to the house. It stood above, aside, a very pleasant stucco building from the middle of the eighteenth century. It had a beautiful alley of yew trees, that had approached an older house, and the hall stood serenely spread out, winking its Georgian panes as if cheerfully. Behind, there were really beautiful gardens.

Connie liked the interior much better than Wragby. It was much lighter, more alive, shapen and elegant. The rooms were panelled with creamy painted panelling, the ceilings were touched with gilt, and everything was kept in exquisite order, all the appointments were perfect, regardless of expense. Even the corridors managed to be ample and lovely, softly curved and full of life.

But Leslie Winter was alone. He had adored his house. But his park was bordered by three of his own collieries. He had been a generous man in his ideas. He had almost welcomed the colliers in his park. Had the miners not made him rich! So, when he saw the gangs of unshapely men lounging by his ornamental waters — not in the private part of the park, no, he drew the line there — he would say: 'the miners are perhaps not so ornamental as deer, but they are far more profitable.'

But that was **in the golden — monetarily — latter half of Queen Victoria's reign**[2]. Miners were then 'good working men'.

Winter had made this speech, half apologetic, to his guest, the then Prince of Wales. And the Prince had replied, in his rather guttural English:

'You are quite right. If there were coal under Sandringham, I would

❶道路行驶权。 ❷维多利亚执政的后半期——金钱充溢的黄金时代。维多利亚(1819—1901),英国女王,其统治时代被认为是英国历史上的"黄金时代"。

open a mine on the lawns, and think it first-rate landscape gardening. Oh, I am quite willing to exchange roe-deer for colliers, at the price. Your men are good men too, I hear.'

But then, the Prince had perhaps an exaggerated idea of the beauty of money, and the blessings of industrialism.

However, the Prince had been a King, and the King had died, and now there was another King, whose chief function seemed to be **to open soup-kitchens**[1].

And the good working men were somehow hemming Shipley in. New mining villages crowded on the park, and the squire felt somehow that the population was alien. He used to feel, in a good-natured but quite grand way, lord of his own domain and of his own colliers. Now, by a subtle pervasion of the new spirit, he had somehow been pushed out. It was he who did not belong any more. There was no mistaking it. The mines, the industry, had a will of its own, and this will was against the gentleman-owner. All the colliers took part in the will, and it was hard to live up against it. It either shoved you out of the place, or out of life altogether.

Squire Winter, a soldier, **had stood it out**[2]. But he no longer cared to walk in the park after dinner. He almost hid, indoors. Once he had walked, bare-headed, and in his patent-leather shoes and purple silk socks, with Connie down to the gate, talking to her in his well-bred rather haw-haw fashion. But when it came to passing the little gangs of colliers who stood and stared without either salute or anything else, Connie felt how the lean, well-bred old man winced, winced as an elegant antelope stag in a cage winces from the vulgar stare. The colliers were not personally hostile: not at all. But their spirit was cold, and shoving him out. And, deep down, there was a profound grudge. They 'worked for him'. And in their ugliness, they resented his elegant, well-groomed, well-bred existence. 'Who's he! ' It was the difference they resented.

And somewhere, in his secret English heart, being a good deal of a soldier, he believed they were right to resent the difference. He felt himself a little in the wrong, for having all the advantages. Nevertheless he represented a system, and he would not be shoved out.

[1] 开设施粥场。[2] 坚持了下来。

Except by death. Which came on him soon after Connie's call, suddenly. And **he remembered Clifford handsomely in his will**[1].

The heirs at once gave out the order for the demolishing of Shipley. It cost too much to keep up. No one would live there. So it was broken up. The avenue of yews was cut down. The park was denuded of its timber, and divided into lots. It was near enough to Uthwaite. In the strange, bald desert of **this still-one-more no-man's-land**[2], new little streets of semi-detacheds were run up, very desirable! The Shipley Hall Estate!

Within a year of Connie's last call, it had happened. There stood Shipley Hall Estate, an array of red-brick semi-detached 'villas' in new streets. No one would have dreamed that the stucco hall had stood there twelve months before.

But this is a later stage of **King Edward's**[3] landscape gardening, the sort that has an ornamental coal-mine on the lawn.

One England blots out another. The England of the Squire Winters and the Wragby Halls was gone, dead. The blotting out was only not yet complete.

What would come after? Connie could not imagine. She could only see the new brick streets spreading into the fields, the new erections rising at the collieries, the new girls in their silk stockings, the new collier lads lounging into the Pally or the Welfare. The younger generation were utterly unconscious of the old England. There was a gap in the continuity of consciousness, almost American: but industrial really. What next?

Connie always felt there was no next. She wanted to hide her head in the sand: or, at least, in the bosom of a living man.

The world was so complicated and weird and gruesome! The common people were so many, and really so terrible. So she bought as she was going home, and saw the colliers trailing from the pits, grey-black, distorted, one shoulder higher than the other, slurring their heavy ironshod boots. Underground grey faces, whites of eyes rolling, necks cringing from the pit roof, shoulders out of shape. Men! Men! Alas, in

❶在他的遗嘱中，他给克利福德留下了一笔不小的遗产。❷又一块无主的土地上。❸爱德华国王的风景园艺，此处指爱德华七世，维多利亚女王之子。

some ways patient and good men. In other ways, non-existent. Something that men should have was bred and killed out of them. Yet they were men. They begot children. One might bear a child to them. Terrible, terrible thought! They were good and kindly. But they were only half, only the grey half of a human being. As yet, they were 'good'. But even that was the goodness of their halfness. Supposing the dead in them ever rose up! But no, it was too terrible to think of. Connie was absolutely afraid of the industrial masses. They seemed so weird to her. A life with utterly no beauty in it, no intuition, always 'in the pit'.

Children from such men! Oh God, oh God!

Yet Mellors had come from such a father. Not quite. Forty years had made a difference, an appalling difference in manhood. The iron and the coal had eaten deep into the bodies and souls of the men.

Incarnate ugliness, and yet alive! What would become of them all? Perhaps with the passing of the coal they would disappear again, off the face of the earth. They had appeared out of nowhere in their thousands, when the coal had called for them. Perhaps they were only weird fauna of the coal-seams. Creatures of another reality, they were elementals, serving the elements of coal, as the metal-workers were elementals, serving the element of iron. Men not men, but animas of coal and iron and clay. Fauna of the elements, carbon, iron, silicon: elementals. They had perhaps some of the weird, inhuman beauty of minerals, the lustre of coal, the weight and blueness and resistance of iron, the transparency of glass. Elemental creatures, weird and distorted, of the mineral world! They belonged to the coal, the iron, the clay, as fish belong to the sea and worms to dead wood. The anima of mineral disintegration!

Connie was glad to be home, to bury her head in the sand. She was glad even to babble to Clifford. For her fear of the mining and iron Midlands affected her with a queer feeling that went all over her, like influenza.

'Of course I had to have tea in Miss Bentley's shop,' she said.

'Really! Winter would have given you tea.'

'Oh yes, but I daren't disappoint Miss Bentley.' Miss Bentley was a shallow old maid with a rather large nose and romantic disposition who served tea with a careful intensity worthy of a sacrament.

'Did she ask after me?' said Clifford.

'Of course! — . May I ask your Ladyship how Sir Clifford is! — I believe she ranks you even higher than **Nurse Cavell**[1]! '

'And I suppose you said I was blooming.'

'Yes! And she looked as rapt as if I had said the heavens had opened to you. I said if she ever came to Tevershall she was to come to see you.'

'Me! Whatever for! See me!'

'Why yes, Clifford. **You can't be so adored without making some slight return**[2]. **Saint George of Cappadocia**[3] was nothing to you, in her eyes.'

'And do you think she'll come?'

'Oh, she blushed! and looked quite beautiful for a moment, poor thing! Why don't men marry the women who would really adore them?'

'The women start adoring too late. But did she say she'd come?'

'Oh! ' Connie imitated the breathless Miss Bentley, 'your Ladyship, **if ever I should dare to presume**[4]! '

'Dare to presume! how absurd! But I hope to God she won't turn up. And how was her tea?'

'Oh, **Lipton's**[5] and very strong. But Clifford, do you realize you are **the Roman de la rose**[6] of Miss Bentley and lots like her?'

'I'm not flattered, even then.'

'They treasure up every one of your pictures in the illustrated papers, and probably pray for you every night. It's rather wonderful.'

She went upstairs to change.

That evening he said to her:

'You do think, don't you, that there is something eternal in marriage?'

She looked at him.

'But Clifford, you make eternity sound like a lid or a long, long chain that trailed after one, no matter how far one went.'

He looked at her, annoyed.

'What I mean,' he said, 'is that if you go to Venice, you won't go in the hopes of some love affair that you can take **au grand sérieux**[7], will you?'

---

❶Edith Louisa卡维尔(1865—1915),第一次世界大战中被德国人处死的英国护士。 ❷你总不能让人如此崇拜而不做出些表示。 ❸卡帕多西亚的圣乔治:四世纪的基督教教士,因对正统派和异教徒迫害惨烈,被亚历山大城的暴民杀害。 ❹我哪儿敢如此造次。 ❺利普顿茶叶。利普顿,英国商人,1898年创立利普顿公司。 ❻《玫瑰史》,欧洲中世纪情诗。 ❼(法)大艳遇。

'A love affair in Venice au grand sérieux? No. I assure you! No, **I'd never take a love affair in Venice more than au très petit sérieux**[1].'

She spoke with a queer kind of contempt. He knitted his brows, look-ing at her.

Coming downstairs in the morning, she found the keeper's dog Flossie sitting in the corridor outside Clifford's room, and whimpering very faintly.

'Why, Flossie!' she said softly. 'What are you doing here?'

And she quietly opened Clifford's door. Clifford was sitting up in bed, with the bed-table and typewriter pushed aside, and the keeper was standing at attention at the foot of the bed. Flossie ran in. With a faint gesture of head and eyes, Mellors ordered her to the door again, and she slunk out.

'Oh, good morning, Clifford!' Connie said. 'I didn't know you were busy.' Then she looked at the keeper, saying good morning to him. He murmured his reply, looking at her as if vaguely. But **she felt a whiff of passion touch her**[2], from his mere presence.

'Did I interrupt you, Clifford? I'm sorry.'

'No, it's nothing of any importance.'

She slipped out of the room again, and up to the blue boudoir on the first floor. She sat in the window, and saw him go down the drive, with his curious, silent motion, effaced. He had a natural sort of quiet distinction, an aloof pride, and also a certain look of frailty. A hireling! One of Clifford's hirelings! '**The fault, dear Brutus, is not in our stars, but in ourselves, that we are underlings**[3].'

Was he an underling? Was he? What did he think of her?

It was a sunny day, and Connie was working in the garden, and Mrs Bolton was helping her. For some reason, the two women had drawn together, in one of the unaccountable flows and ebbs of sympathy that exist between people. They were pegging down carnations, and putting in small plants for the summer. It was work they both liked. Connie especially felt a delight in putting the soft roots of young plants into a soft black puddle, and cradling them down. On this spring morning she felt a quiver in her womb too, as if the sunshine had touched it and made

❶我在威尼斯绝不会有什么艳遇，更不用说小艳遇了。 ❷她感到一阵激情在向她袭来。 ❸亲爱的布鲁特斯，我们是下人，这并不是命运不济，而是因为自己不争气。引自莎士比亚剧作《裘利斯·恺撒》。

it happy.

'It is many years since you lost your husband?' she said to Mrs Bolton as she took up another little plant and laid it in its hole.

'Twenty-three! ' said Mrs Bolton, as she carefully separated the young columbines into single plants. 'Twenty-three years since they brought him home.'

Connie's heart gave a lurch, at the terrible finality of it. 'Brought him home! '

'Why did he get killed, do you think?' she asked. 'He was happy with you?'

It was a woman's question to a woman. Mrs Bolton put aside a strand of hair from her face, with the back of her hand.

'I don't know, my Lady! He sort of wouldn't give in to things: he wouldn't really go with the rest. And then he hated ducking his head for anything on earth. A sort of obstinacy, that gets itself killed. You see he didn't really care. **I lay it down to the pit**[1]. He ought never to have been down pit. But his dad made him go down, as a lad; and then, when you're over twenty, it's not very easy to come out.'

'Did he say he hated it?'

'Oh no! Never! He never said he hated anything. He just made a funny face. He was one of those who wouldn't take care: like some of the first lads as went off so blithe to the war and got killed right away. He wasn't really wezzle-brained. But he wouldn't care. I used to say to him: "You care for nought nor nobody! " But he did! The way he sat when my first baby was born, motionless, and the sort of fatal eyes he looked at me with, when it was over! I had a bad time, but I had to comfort him. "It's all right, lad, it's all right! " I said to him. And he gave me a look, and that funny sort of smile. He never said anything. But I don't believe he had any right pleasure with me at nights after; **he'd never really let himself go**[2]. I used to say to him: Oh, let thysen go, lad! — **I'd talk broad to him sometimes**[3]. And he said nothing. But he wouldn't let himself go, or he couldn't. He didn't want me to have any more children. I always blamed his mother, for letting him in th' room. He'd no right t'ave been there. Men makes so much more of things than they should, once they start brooding.'

[1]我认为这全是矿井的缘故。[2]他不再让自己尽情发泄。[3]有时候我给他讲粗话。

'Did he mind so much?' said Connie in wonder.

'Yes, he sort of couldn't take it for natural, all that pain. And it spoilt his pleasure in his bit of married love. I said to him: If I don't care, why should you? It's my look-out! — But all he'd ever say was: It's not right!'

'Perhaps he was too sensitive,' said Connie.

'That's it! When you come to know men, that's how they are: too sensitive in the wrong place. And I believe, unbeknown to himself he hated the pit, just hated it. He looked so quiet when he was dead, as if he'd got free. He was such a nice-looking lad. It just broke my heart to see him, so still and pure looking, as if he'd wanted to die. Oh, it broke my heart, that did. But it was the pit.'

She wept a few bitter tears, and Connie wept more. It was a warm spring day, with a perfume of earth and of yellow flowers, many things rising to bud, and the garden still with the very sap of sunshine.

'It must have been terrible for you!' said Connie.

'Oh, my Lady! I never realized at first. I could only say: Oh my lad, what did you want to leave me for! — That was all my cry. But somehow I felt he'd come back.'

'But he didn't want to leave you,' said Connie.

'Oh no, my Lady! That was only my silly cry. And I kept expecting him back. Especially at nights. I kept waking up thinking: Why he's not in bed with me! — It was as if my feelings wouldn't believe he'd gone. I just felt he'd have to come back and lie against me, so I could feel him with me. That was all I wanted, to feel him there with me, warm. And it took me a thousand shocks before I knew he wouldn't come back, it took me years.'

'The touch of him,' said Connie.

'That's it, my Lady, the touch of him! I've never got over it to this day, and never shall. And if there's a heaven above, he'll be there, and will lie up against me so I can sleep.'

Connie glanced at the handsome, brooding face in fear. Another passionate one out of Tevershall! The touch of him! For the bonds of love are ill to loose!

'It's terrible, once you've got a man into your blood!' she said.

'Oh, my Lady! And that's what makes you feel so bitter. You feel folks wanted him killed. You feel the pit fair wanted to kill him. Oh, I felt, if it hadn't been for the pit, an' them as runs the pit, there'd have been no leaving me. But they all want to separate a woman and a man, if they're together.'

'If they're physically together,' said Connie.

'That's right, my Lady! There's a lot of hard-hearted folks in the world. And every morning when he got up and went to th' pit, I felt it was wrong, wrong. But what else could he do? What can a man do?'

A queer hate flared in the woman.

'But can a touch last so long?' Connie asked suddenly. 'That you could feel him so long?'

'Oh my Lady, what else is there to last? Children grows away from you. But the man, well! But even that they'd like to kill in you, the very thought of the touch of him. Even your own children! Ah well! We might have drifted apart, who knows. But the feeling's something different. It's 'appen better never to care. But there, when I look at women who's never really been warmed through by a man, well, they seem to me poor dool-owls after all, no matter how they may dress up and gad. No, I'll abide by my own. I've not much respect for people.'

CHAPTER 12

Connie went to the wood directly after lunch. It was really a lovely day, the first dandelions making suns, the first daisies so white. The hazel thicket was a lace-work, of half-open leaves, and the last dusty perpendicular of the catkins. Yellow celandines now were in crowds, flat open, pressed back in urgency, and the yellow glitter of themselves. It was the yellow, the powerful yellow of early summer. And primroses were broad, and full of pale abandon, thick-clustered primroses no longer shy. The lush, dark green of hyacinths was a sea, with buds rising like pale corn, while in the riding the forget-me-nots were fluffing up, and columbines were unfolding their ink-purple ruches, and there were bits of blue bird's eggshell under a bush. Everywhere the bud-knots and the leap of life!

The keeper was not at the hut. Everything was serene, brown chickens running lustily. Connie walked on towards the cottage, because she wanted to find him.

The cottage stood in the sun, off the wood's edge. In the little garden the double daffodils rose in tufts, near the wide-open door, and red double daisies made a border to the path. There was the bark of a dog, and Flossie came running.

The wide-open door! so he was at home. And the sunlight falling on the red-brick floor! As she went up the path, she saw him through the window, sitting at the table in his shirt-sleeves, eating. The dog wuffed softly, slowly wagging her tail.

He rose, and came to the door, wiping his mouth with a red handkerchief still chewing.

'May I come in?' she said.

'Come in!'

The sun shone into the bare room, which still smelled of a mutton chop, done in a dutch oven before the fire, because the dutch oven still stood on the fender, with the black potato-saucepan on a piece of paper, beside it on the white hearth. The fire was red, rather low, the bar dropped, the kettle singing.

On the table was his plate, with potatoes and the remains of the chop; also bread in a basket, salt, and a blue mug with beer. The table-cloth was white oil-cloth, he stood in the shade.

'You are very late,' she said. 'Do go on eating!'

She sat down on a wooden chair, in the sunlight by the door.

'I had to go to Uthwaite,' he said, sitting down at the table but not eating.

'Do eat,' she said. But he did not touch the food.

'Shall y'ave something?' he asked her. 'Shall y'ave a cup of tea? t' kettle's on t' boil'— he half rose again from his chair.

'If you'll let me make it myself,' she said, rising. He seemed sad, and she felt she was bothering him.

'Well, tea-pot's in there' — he pointed to a little, drab corner cupboard; 'an' cups. An' tea's on t' mantel ower yer 'ead,'

She got the black tea-pot, and the tin of tea from the mantel-shelf. She rinsed the tea-pot with hot water, and stood a moment wondering where to empty it.

'Throw it out,' he said, aware of her. 'It's clean.'

She went to the door and threw the drop of water down the path. How lovely it was here, so still, so really woodland. The oaks were putting out ochre yellow leaves: in the garden the red daisies were like red plush buttons. She glanced at the big, hollow sandstone slab of the threshold, now crossed by so few feet.

'But it's lovely here,' she said. 'Such a beautiful stillness, everything alive and still.'

He was eating again, rather slowly and unwillingly, and she could feel he was discouraged. She made the tea in silence, and set the tea-pot on the hob, as she knew the people did. He pushed his plate aside and went to the back place; she heard a latch click, then he came back with cheese on a plate, and butter.

She set the two cups on the table; there were only two. 'Will you have a cup of tea?' she said.

'If you like. Sugar's in th' cupboard, an' there's a little cream jug. Milk's in a jug in th' pantry.'

'Shall I take your plate away?' she asked him. He looked up at her with a faint ironical smile.

'Why...if you like,' he said, slowly eating bread and cheese. She went to the back, into the pent-house scullery, where the pump was. On the left was a door, no doubt the pantry door. She unlatched it, and almost smiled at the place he called a pantry; a long narrow white-washed slip of a cupboard. But it managed to contain a little barrel of beer, as well as a few dishes and bits of food. She took a little milk from the yellow jug.

'How do you get your milk?' she asked him, when she came back to the table.

'Flints! They leave me a bottle at the warren end. You know, where I met you!'

But he was discouraged. She poured out the tea, poising the cream-jug.

'No milk,' he said; then he seemed to hear a noise, and looked keenly through the doorway.

'Appen we'd better shut,' he said.

'It seems a pity,' she replied. 'Nobody will come, will they?'

'Not unless it's one time in a thousand, but you never know.'

'And even then it's no matter,' she said. 'It's only a cup of tea.'

'Where are the spoons?'

He reached over, and pulled open the table drawer. Connie sat at the table in the sunshine of the doorway.

'Flossie! ' he said to the dog, who was lying on a little mat at the stair foot. 'Go an' hark, hark! '

He lifted his finger, and his 'hark!' was very vivid. The dog trotted out to reconnoitre.

'Are you sad today?' she asked him.

He turned his blue eyes quickly, and gazed direct on her.

'Sad! no, bored! I had to go getting summonses for two poachers I caught, and, oh well, I don't like people.'

He spoke cold, good English, and there was anger in his voice. 'Do you hate being a game-keeper?' she asked.

'Being a game-keeper, no! So long as I'm left alone. But when I have to go messing around at the police-station, and various other places, and waiting for a lot of fools to attend to me...oh well, I get mad...' and he smiled, with a certain faint humour.

'Couldn't you be really independent?' she asked.

'Me? I suppose I could, if you mean manage to exist on my pension. I could! But I've got to work, or I should die. That is, I've got to have something that keeps me occupied. And I'm not in a good enough temper to work for myself. It's got to be a sort of job for somebody else, **or I should throw it up in a month, out of bad temper**[1]. So altogether I'm very well off here, especially lately...'

He laughed at her again, with mocking humour.

'But why are you in a bad temper?' she asked. 'Do you mean you are always in a bad temper?'

'Pretty well,' he said, laughing. '**I don't quite digest my bile**[2].'

'But what bile?' she said.

'Bile! ' he said. 'Don't you know what that is?' She was silent, and disappointed. He was taking no notice of her.

'I'm going away for a while next month,' she said.

'You are! Where to?'

'Venice! With Sir Clifford? For how long?'

'For a month or so,' she replied. 'Clifford won't go.'

'He'll stay here?' he asked.

'Yes! He hates to travel as he is.'

'Ay, poor devil! ' he said, with sympathy. There was a pause.

①否则,由于脾气坏,不出一个月我就会扔下不干了。②我控制不住自己的脾气。bile 胆汁,脾气。

'You won't forget me when I'm gone, will you?' she asked. Again he lifted his eyes and looked full at her.

'Forget?' he said. 'You know nobody forgets. It's not a question of memory;'

She wanted to say: 'When then?' but she didn't. Instead, she said in a mute kind of voice: 'I told Clifford I might have a child.'

Now he really looked at her, intense and searching.

'You did?' he said at last. 'And what did he say?'

'Oh, he wouldn't mind. He'd be glad, really, so long as it seemed to be his.' She dared not look up at him.

He was silent a long time, then he gazed again on her face.

'No mention of me, of course?' he said.

'No. No mention of you,' she said.

'No, **he'd hardly swallow me as a substitute breeder**[1]. Then where are you supposed to be getting the child?'

'I might have a love-affair in Venice,' she said.

'You might,' he replied slowly. 'So that's why you're going?'

'Not to have the love-affair,' she said, looking up at him, pleading.

'Just the appearance of one,' he said.

There was silence. He sat staring out the window, with a faint grin, half mockery, half bitterness, on his face. She hated his grin.

'You've not taken any precautions against having a child then?' he asked her suddenly. 'Because I haven't.'

'No,' she said faintly. 'I should hate that.'

He looked at her, then again with the peculiar subtle grin out of the window. There was a tense silence.

At last he turned his head and said satirically:

'That was why you wanted me, then, to get a child?'

She hung her head.

'No. Not really,' she said. 'What then, really?' he asked rather bitingly.

She looked up at him reproachfully, saying: 'I don't know.'

He broke into a laugh.

'Then I'm damned if I do,' he said.

There was a long pause of silence, a cold silence.

---

[1] 他知道我替他下种的话会掐死我。

'Well,' he said at last. 'It's as your Ladyship likes. If you get the baby, Sir Clifford's welcome to it. I shan't have lost anything. On the contrary, I've had a very nice experience, very nice indeed!' — and he stretched in a half-suppressed sort of yawn. 'If you've made use of me,' he said, 'it's not the first time I've been made use of; and I don't suppose it's ever been as pleasant as this time; though of course one can't feel tremendously dignified about it.' — He stretched again, curiously, his muscles quivering, and his jaw oddly set.

'But I didn't make use of you,' she said, pleading.

'At your Ladyship's service,' he replied.

'No,' she said. 'I liked your body.'

'Did you?' he replied, and he laughed. 'Well, then, **we're quits**[1], because I liked yours.'

He looked at her with queer darkened eyes.

'Would you like to go upstairs now?' he asked her, in a strangled sort of voice.

'No, not here. Not now!' she said heavily, though if he had used any power over her, she would have gone, for she had no strength against him.

He turned his face away again, and seemed to forget her. 'I want to touch you like you touch me,' she said. 'I've never really touched your body.'

He looked at her, and smiled again. 'Now?' he said. 'No! No! Not here! At the hut. Would you mind?'

'How do I touch you?' he asked.

'When you feel me.'

He looked at her, and met her heavy, anxious eyes.

'And do you like it when I feel you?' he asked, laughing at her still.

'Yes, do you?' she said.

'Oh, me!' Then he changed his tone. 'Yes,' he said. 'You know without asking.' Which was true.

She rose and picked up her hat. 'I must go,' she said.

'Will you go?' he replied politely.

She wanted him to touch her, to say something to her, but he said nothing, only waited politely.

---

[1]你我扯平了。

'Thank you for the tea,' she said.

'I haven't thanked your Ladyship for doing me the honours of my tea-pot,' he said.

She went down the path, and he stood in the doorway, faintly grinning. Flossie came running with her tail lifted. And Connie had to plod dumbly across into the wood, knowing he was standing there watching her, with that incomprehensible grin on his face.

She walked home very much downcast and annoyed. She didn't at all like his saying he had been made use of because, in a sense, it was true. But he oughtn't to have said it. Therefore, again, she was divided between two feelings: resentment against him, and a desire to make it up with him.

She passed a very uneasy and irritated tea-time, and at once went up to her room. But when she was there it was no good; she could neither sit nor stand. She would have to do something about it. She would have to go back to the hut; if he was not there, **well and good**[1].

She slipped out of the side door, and took her way direct and a little sullen. When she came to the clearing she was terribly uneasy. But there he was again, in his shirt-sleeves, stooping, letting the hens out of the coops, among the chicks that were now growing a little gawky, but were much more trim than hen-chickens.

She went straight across to him. 'You see I've come!' she said.

'Ay, I see it!' he said, straightening his back, and looking at her with a faint amusement.

'Do you let the hens out now?' she asked.

'Yes, **they've sat themselves to skin and bone**[2],' he said. 'An' now they're not all that anxious to come out an' feed. **There's no self in a sitting hen; she's all in the eggs or the chicks**[3].'

The poor mother-hens; such blind devotion! even to eggs not their own! Connie looked at them in compassion. A helpless silence fell between the man and the woman.

'Shall us go i' th' 'ut?' he asked.

'Do you want me?' she asked, in a sort of mistrust.

'Ay, if you want to come.'

❶(口)那当然也好。 ❷他们坐窝都坐到皮包骨头了。 ❸坐窝的母鸡是忘我的,他们的心思都在蛋上,在小鸡身上。

She was silent.

'Come then!' he said.

And she went with him to the hut. It was quite dark when he had shut the door, so he made a small light in the lantern, as before.

'Have you left your underthings off?' he asked her.

'Yes!'

'Ay, well, then I'll take my things off too.'

He spread the blankets, putting one at the side for a coverlet. She took off her hat, and shook her hair. He sat down, taking off his shoes and gaiters, and undoing his cord breeches.

'Lie down then!' he said, when he stood in his shirt. She obeyed in silence, and he lay beside her, and pulled the blanket over them both.

'There!' he said.

And he lifted her dress right back, till he came even to her breasts. He kissed them softly, taking the nipples in his lips in tiny caresses.

'Eh, but tha'rt nice, tha'rt nice!' he said, suddenly rubbing his face with a snuggling movement against her warm belly.

And she put her arms round him under his shirt, but she was afraid, afraid of his thin, smooth, naked body, that seemed so powerful, afraid of the violent muscles. She shrank, afraid.

And when he said, with a sort of little sigh: 'Eh, tha'rt nice!' something in her quivered, and something in her spirit stiffened in resistance: stiffened from the terribly physical intimacy, and from the peculiar haste of his possession. And this time the sharp ecstasy of her own passion did not overcome her; she lay with her ends inert on his striving body, and do what she might, her spirit seemed to look on from the top of her head, and the butting of his haunches seemed ridiculous to her, and the sort of anxiety of his penis to come to its little evacuating crisis seemed farcical. Yes, this was love, this ridiculous bouncing of the buttocks, and the wilting of the poor, insignificant, moist little penis. This was the divine love! After all, the moderns were right when they felt contempt for the performance; for it was a performance. It was quite true, as some poets said, that the God who created man must have had a sinister sense of humour, creating him a reasonable being, yet forcing him to take this ridiculous posture, and driving him with blind craving for this ridic ulous performance. Even a **Maupassant** [1] found it a

[1] 莫泊桑(1850—1893),法国长篇和短篇小说家。

humiliating anti-climax. Men despised the intercourse act, and yet did it.

Cold and derisive her queer female mind stood apart, and though she lay perfectly still, her impulse was to heave her loins, and throw the man out, escape his ugly grip, and the butting over-riding of his absurd haunches. His body was a foolish, impudent, imperfect thing, a little disgusting in its unfinished clumsiness. For surely a complete evolution would eliminate this performance, this 'function'.

And yet when he had finished, soon over, and lay very very still, receding into silence, and a strange motionless distance, far, farther than the horizon of her awareness, her heart began to weep. She could feel him ebbing away, ebbing away, leaving her there like a stone on a shore. He was withdrawing, his spirit was leaving her. He knew.

And in real grief, tormented by her own double consciousness and reaction, she began to weep. He took no notice, or did not even know. The storm of weeping swelled and shook her, and shook him.

'Ay!' he said. 'It was no good that time. You wasn't there.' — So he knew! Her sobs became violent.

'But what's amiss?' he said. 'It's once in a while that way.'

'I...I can't love you,' she sobbed, suddenly feeling her heart breaking.

'Canna ter? Well, dunna fret! There's no law says as tha's got to. Ta'e it for what it is.'

He still lay with his hand on her breast. But she had drawn both her hands from him.

His words were small comfort. She sobbed aloud.

'Nay, nay!' he said. **'Ta'e the thick wi' th' thin. This wor a bit o' thin for once[1].'**

She wept bitterly, sobbing. 'But I want to love you, and I can't. It only seems horrid.'

He laughed a little, half bitter, half amused.

'It isna horrid,' he said, 'even if tha thinks it is. An' tha canna ma'e it horrid. Dunna fret thysen about lovin' me. Tha'lt niver force thysen to 't. There's sure to be a bad nut in a basketful. **Tha mun ta'e th' rough wi' th' smooth[2].'**

He took his hand away from her breast, not touching her. And now

❶事情有苦也有甜,这次稍微有些苦。 ❷即 take the rough with the smooth 既能享乐也能吃苦,顺境逆境一样承受,泰然对待人世的沉浮。

she was untouched she took an almost perverse satisfaction in it. She hated the dialect: the thee and the tha and the thysen. He could get up if he liked, and stand there, above her, buttoning down those absurd corduroy breeches, straight in front of her. After all, Michaelis had had the decency to turn away. This man was so assured in himself he didn't know what a clown other people found him, a half-bred fellow.

Yet, as he was drawing away, to rise silently and leave her, she clung to him in terror.

'Don't! Don't go! Don't leave me! Don't be cross with me! Hold me! Hold me fast!' she whispered in blind frenzy, not even knowing what she said, and clinging to him with uncanny force. It was from herself she wanted to be saved, from her own inward anger and resistance. Yet how powerful was that inward resistance that possessed her!

He took her in his arms again and drew her to him, and suddenly she became small in his arms, small and nestling. It was gone, the resistance was gone, and she began to melt in a marvellous peace. And as she melted small and wonderful in his arms, she became infinitely desirable to him, all his blood-vessels seemed to scald with intense yet tender desire, for her, for her softness, for the penetrating beauty of her in his arms, passing into his blood. And softly, with that marvellous swoon-like caress of his hand in pure soft desire, softly he stroked the silky slope of her loins, down, down between her soft warm buttocks, coming nearer and nearer to the very quick of her. And she felt him like a flame of desire, yet tender, and she felt herself melting in the flame. She let herself go. She felt his penis risen against her with silent amazing force and assertion and she let herself go to him. She yielded with a quiver that was like death, she went all open to him. And oh, if he were not tender to her now, how cruel, for she was all open to him and helpless!

She quivered again at the potent inexorable entry inside her, so strange and terrible. It might come with the thrust of a sword in her softly-opened body, and that would be death. She clung in a sudden anguish of terror. But it came with a strange slow thrust of peace, the dark thrust of peace and a ponderous, primordial tenderness, such as made the world in the beginning. And her terror subsided in her breast, her breast dared to be gone in peace, she held nothing. She dared to let go everything, all herself and be gone in the flood.

And it seemed she was like the sea, nothing but dark waves rising and heaving, heaving with a great swell, so that slowly her whole darkness was in motion, and she was ocean rolling its dark, dumb mass. Oh, and far down inside her the deeps parted and rolled asunder, in long, fair-travelling billows, and ever, at the quick of her, the depths parted and rolled asunder, from the centre of soft plunging, as the plunger went deeper and deeper, touching lower, and she was deeper and deeper and deeper disclosed, the heavier the billows of her rolled away to some shore, uncovering her, and closer and closer plunged the palpable unknown, and further and further rolled the waves of herself away from herself leaving her, till suddenly, in a soft, shuddering convulsion, the quick of all her plasm was touched, she knew herself touched, the consummation was upon her, and she was gone. She was gone, she was not, and she was born: a woman.

Ah, too lovely, too lovely! In the ebbing she realized all the loveliness. Now all her body clung with tender love to the unknown man, and blindly to the wilting penis, as it so tenderly, frailly, unknowingly withdrew, after the fierce thrust of its potency. As it drew out and left her body, the secret, sensitive thing, she gave an unconscious cry of pure loss, and she tried to put it back. It had been so perfect! And she loved it so!

And only now she became aware of the small, bud-like reticence and tenderness of the penis, and a little cry of wonder and poignancy escaped her again, her woman's heart crying out over the tender frailty of that which had been the power.

'It was so lovely!' she moaned. 'It was so lovely!' But he said nothing, only softly kissed her, lying still above her. And she moaned with a sort of bliss, as a sacrifice, and a newborn thing.

And now in her heart the queer wonder of him was awakened. A man! The strange potency of manhood upon her! Her hands strayed over him, still a little afraid. Afraid of that strange, hostile, slightly repulsive thing that he had been to her, a man. And now she touched him, and it was the sons of god with the daughters of men. How beautiful he felt, how pure in tissue! How lovely, how lovely, strong, and yet pure and delicate, such stillness of the sensitive body! Such utter stillness of potency and delicate flesh. How beautiful! How beautiful! Her hands came timorously down his back, to the soft, smallish globes of the buttocks. Beauty! What beauty! a sudden little flame of new awareness went through her. How was it possible, this beauty here, where she had previously only been repelled? The unspeakable beauty to the touch of the warm, living buttocks! The life within life, the sheer warm, potent loveliness. And the strange weight of the balls between his legs! What a mystery! What a strange heavy weight of mystery, that could lie soft and heavy in one's hand! The roots, root of all that is lovely, the primeval root of all full beauty.

She clung to him, with a hiss of wonder that was almost awe, terror. He held her close, but he said nothing. He would never say anything. She crept nearer to him, nearer, only to be near to the sensual wonder of him. And out of his utter, incomprehensible stillness, she felt again the slow momentous, surging rise of the phallus again, the other power. And her heart melted out with a kind of awe.

And this time his being within her was all soft and iridescent, purely soft and iridescent, such as no consciousness could seize. Her whole self quivered unconscious and alive, like plasm. She could not know what it was. She could not remember what it had been. Only that it had been more lovely than anything ever could be. Only that. And afterwards she was utterly still, utterly unknowing, she was not aware for how long. And he was still with her, in an unfathomable silence along with her. And of this, they would never speak.

When awareness of the outside began to come back, she clung to his breast, murmuring 'My love! My love!' And he held her silently. And she curled on his breast, perfect.

But his silence was fathomless. His hands held her like flowers, so still aid strange. 'Where are you?' she whispered to him.

'Where are you? Speak to me! Say something to me!'

He kissed her softly, murmuring: 'Ay, my lass!'

But she did not know what he meant, she did not know where he was. In his silence he seemed lost to her.

'You love me, don't you?' she murmured.

'Ay, tha knows!' he said. 'But tell me!' she pleaded.

'Ay! Ay! 'asn't ter felt it?' he said dimly, but softly and surely. And she clung close to him, closer. He was so much more peaceful in love than she was, and she wanted him to reassure her.

'You do love me!' she whispered, assertive. And his hands stroked her softly, as if she were a flower, without the quiver of desire, but with delicate nearness. And still there haunted her a restless necessity to get a grip on love.

'Say you'll always love me!' she pleaded.

'Ay!' he said, abstractedly. And she felt her questions driving him away from her.

'Mustn't we get up?' he said at last.

'No!' she said.

But she could feel his consciousness straying, listening to the noises outside.

'It'll be nearly dark,' he said. And she heard the pressure of circumstances in his voice. She kissed him, **with a woman's grief at yielding up her hour**[1].

He rose, and turned up the lantern, then began to pull on his clothes, quickly disappearing inside them. Then he stood there, above her, fastening his breeches and looking down at her with dark, wide-eyes, his face a little flushed and his hair ruffled, curiously warm and still and beautiful in the dim light of the lantern, so beautiful, she would never tell him how beautiful. It made her want to cling fast to him, to hold him, for there was a warm, half-sleepy remoteness in his beauty that made her want to cry out and clutch him, to have him. She would never have him. So she lay on the blanket with curved, soft naked haunches, and he had no idea what she was thinking, but to him too she was beautiful, the soft, marvellous thing he could go into, beyond everything.

'I love thee that I call go into thee,' he said.

'Do you like me?' she said, her heart beating.

'It heals it all up, that I can go into thee. I love thee that tha opened to me. I love thee that I came into thee like that.'

He bent down and kissed her soft flank, rubbed his cheek against it, then covered it up.

'And will you never leave me?' she said.

'Dunna ask them things,' he said.

'But you do believe I love you?' she said.

'Tha loved me just now, wider than iver tha thout tha would. But who knows what'll 'appen, once tha starts thinkin' about it!'

'No, don't say those things! — And you don't really think that I wanted to make use of you, do you?'

---

[1] 带着女人放弃自己欢乐时刻的悲伤心情。

'How?'

'To have a child — ?'

'Now anybody can 'ave any childt i' th' world,' he said, as he sat down fastening on his leggings.

'Ah no!' she cried. 'You don't mean it?'

'Eh well!' he said, looking at her under his brows. 'This wort' best.'

She lay still. He softly opened the door. The sky was dark blue, with crystalline, turquoise rim. He went out, to shut up the hens, speaking softly to his dog. And she lay and wondered at the wonder of life, and of being.

When he came back she was still lying there, glowing like a gipsy. He sat on the stool by her.

'Tha mun come one naight ter th' cottage, afore tha goos; sholl ter?' he asked, lifting his eyebrows as he looked at her, his hands dangling between his knees.

'Sholl ter?' she echoed, teasing.

He smiled. 'Ay, sholl ter?' he repeated.

'Ay!' she said, imitating the dialect sound.

'Yi!' he said.

'Yi!' she repeated.

'An' slaip wi' me,' he said. 'It needs that. When sholt come?'

'When sholl I?' she said.

'Nay,' he said, 'tha canna do't. When sholt come then?'

''Appen Sunday,' she said.

''Appen a' Sunday! Ay!'

He laughed at her quickly.

'Nay, tha canna,' he protested.

'Why canna I?' she said.

CHAPTER 13

On Sunday Clifford wanted to go into the wood. It was a lovely morning, the pear-blossom and plum had suddenly appeared in the world in a wonder of white here and there.

It was cruel for Clifford, while the world bloomed, to have to be helped from chair to bath-chair. But he had forgotten, and even seemed to have a certain conceit of himself in his lameness. Connie still suffered, having to lift his inert legs into place. Mrs Bolton did it now, or Field.

She waited for him at the top of the drive, at the edge of the screen of beeches. His chair came puffing along **with a sort of valetudinarian slow importance**❶. As he joined his wife he said:

'Sir Clifford on his roaming steed!'

'Snorting, at least!' she laughed.

He stopped and looked round at the facade of the long, low old brown house.

'Wragby doesn't wink an eyelid!' he said. 'But then why should it! I ride upon the achievements of the mind of man, and **that beats a horse**❷.'

'I suppose it does. And **the souls in Plato riding up to heaven in a two-horse chariot**❸ would go in a Ford car now,' she said.

'Or a Rolls-Royce: Plato was an aristocrat!'

'Quite! No more black horse to thrash and maltreat. Plato never thought we'd go one better than his black steed and his white steed, and have no steeds at all, only an engine!'

'Only an engine and gas!' said Clifford.

'I hope I can have some repairs done to the old place next year. I think I shall have about a thousand to spare for that: but work costs so much!' he added.

'Oh, good!' said Connie. 'If only there aren't more strikes!'

'What would be the use of their striking again! Merely ruin the industry, what's left of it: and surely the owls are beginning to see it!'

'Perhaps they don't mind ruining the industry,' said Connie.

'Ah, don't talk like a woman! The industry fills their bellies, even if it can't keep their pockets quite so flush,' he said, using turns of speech that oddly had a twang of Mrs Bolton.

'But didn't you say the other day that you were a conservative-anarchist,' she asked innocently.

---

❶轮椅走得如同病人似的缓慢。❷这胜于骑任何骏马。❸柏拉图的神灵骑着双马之辇赴天堂。柏拉图(公元前427—347),希腊哲学家。

'And did you understand what I meant?' he retorted. 'All I meant is, people can be what they like and feel what they like and do what they like, strictly privately, so long as they keep the form of life intact, and the apparatus.'

Connie walked on in silence a few paces. Then she said, obstinately: 'It sounds like saying an egg may go as addled as it likes, so long as it keeps its shell on whole. But addled eggs do break of themselves.'

'I don't think people are eggs,' he said. 'Not even angels' eggs, my dear little evangelist.'

He was in rather high feather this bright morning①. The larks were trilling away over the park, the distant pit in the hollow was fuming silent steam. It was almost like old days, before the war. Connie didn't really want to argue. But then she did not really want to go to the wood with Clifford either. So she walked beside his chair in a certain obstinacy of spirit.

'No,' he said. 'There will be no more strikes, if the thing is properly managed.'

'Why not?'

'Because strikes will be made as good as impossible.'

'But will the men let you?' she asked.

'We shan't ask them. We shall do it while they aren't looking: for their own good, to save the industry.'

'For your own good too,' she said.

'Naturally! For the good of everybody. But for their good even more than mine. I can live without the pits. They can't. They'll starve if there are no pits. I've got other provision.'

They looked up the shallow valley at the mine, and beyond it, at the black-lidded houses of Tevershall crawling like some serpent up the hill. From the old brown church the bells were ringing: Sunday, Sunday, Sunday!

'But will the men let you dictate terms?' she said. 'My dear, they will have to: if one does it gently.'

'But mightn't there be a mutual understanding?'

'Absolutely: when they realize that **the industry comes before the individual**②.'

'But must you own the industry?' she said.

①在这明媚的清晨，他情绪饱满。 ②煤矿业比个人重要。

'I don't. But to the extent I do own it, yes, most decidedly. The ownership of property has now become a religious question: as it has been **since Jesus and St Francis**[1]. The point is not: **take all thou hast and give to the poor**[2], but use all thou hast to encourage the industry and give work to the poor. It's the only way to feed all the mouths and clothe all the bodies. Giving away all we have to the poor spells starvation for the poor just as much as for us. And universal starvation is no high aim. Even general poverty is no lovely thing. Poverty is ugly.'

'But the disparity?'

'That is fate. Why is the star **Jupiter bigger than the star Neptune**[3]? You can't start altering the make-up of things!'

'But when this envy and jealousy and discontent has once started,' she began.

'Do, your best to stop it. Somebody's got to be boss of the show.'

'But who is boss of the show?' she asked.

'The men who own and run the industries.'

There was a long silence.

'It seems to me they're a bad boss,' she said.

'Then you suggest what they should do.'

'They don't take their boss-ship seriously enough,' she said.

'They take it far more seriously than you take your ladyship,' he said.

'**That's thrust upon me**[4]. I don't really want it,' she blurted out. He stopped the chair and looked at her.

'Who's shirking their responsibility now!' he said. 'Who is trying to get away now from the responsibility of their own boss-ship, as you call it?'

'But I don't want any boss-ship,' she protested.

'Ah! But that is funk. You've got it: fated to it. And you should live up to it. Who has given the colliers all they have that's worth having: all their political liberty, and their education, such as it is, their sanitation, their health-conditions, their books, their music, everything.

❶自从耶稣和圣方济各以来就这样。耶稣：基督教信奉的救世主；圣方济各(1506—1552)，西班牙传教士。 ❷将你新拥有的一切赐予穷人，语出《圣经·马太福音》第19章。 ❸木星比海王星大，木星：太阳系中最大的行星，以太阳照至的距离来说排在第5。Neptune：海王星，太阳系的第8大行星。 ❹那个身份是别人强加给我的。

Who has given it them? Have colliers given it to colliers? No! All the Wragbys and Shipleys in England have given their part, and must go on giving. There's your responsibility.'

Connie listened, and flushed very red.

'I'd like to give something,' she said. 'But I'm not allowed. Everything is to be sold and paid for now; and all the things you mention now, Wragby and Shipley sells them to the people, at a good prof it. Everything is sold. You don't give one heart-beat of real sympathy. And besides, who has taken away from the people their natural life and manhood, and given them this industrial horror? Who has done that?'

'And what must I do?' he asked, **green**[1]. 'Ask them to come and pillage me?'

'Why is Tevershall so ugly, so hideous? Why are their lives so hopeless?'

'They built their own Tevershall, that's part of their display of freedom. They built themselves their pretty Tevershall, and they live their own pretty lives. I can't live their lives for them. Every beetle must live its own life.'

'But you make them work for you. They live the life of your coal-mine.'

'Not at all. Every beetle finds its own food. Not one man is forced to work for me.

'Their lives are industrialized and hopeless, and so are ours,' she cried.

'I don't think they are. **That's just a romantic figure of speech**[2], a relic of the swooning and die-away romanticism. You don't look at all a hopeless figure standing there, Connie my dear.'

Which was true. For her dark-blue eyes were flashing, her colour was hot in her cheeks, she looked full of a rebellious passion **far from the dejection of hopelessness**[3]. She noticed, ill the tussocky places of the grass, cottony young cowslips standing up still bleared in their down. And she wondered with rage, why it was she felt Clifford was so wrong, yet she couldn't say it to him, she could not say exactly where he was wrong.

'No wonder the men hate you,' she said.

---

❶脸色铁青。❷那仅仅是个不切实际的比喻修辞。❸全然没有无情的沮丧。

'They don't!' he replied. 'And don't fall into errors: in your sense of the word, they are not men. They are animals you don't understand, and never could. Don't thrust your illusions on other people. The masses were always the same, and will always be the same. **Nero's slaves**[1] were extremely little different from our colliers or the Ford motor-car workmen. I mean Nero's mine slaves and his field slaves. It is the masses: they are the unchangeable. An individual may emerge from the masses. But the emergence doesn't alter the mass. The masses are unalterable. It is one of the most momentous facts of social science. **Panem et circenses**[2]! Only today education is one of the bad substitutes for a circus. What is wrong today is that we've made a profound hash of the circuses part of the programme, and poisoned our masses with a little education.'

When Clifford became really roused in his feelings about the common people, Connie was frightened. There was something devastatingly true in what he said. But it was a truth that killed.

Seeing her pale and silent, Clifford started the chair again, and no more was said till he halted again at the wood gate, which she opened.

'And what we need to take up now,' he said, 'is whips, not swords. The masses have been ruled since time began, and till time ends, ruled they will have to be. It is sheer hypocrisy and farce to say they can rule themselves.'

'But can you rule them?' she asked.

'I? Oh yes! Neither my mind nor my will is crippled, and I don't rule with my legs. I can do my share of ruling: absolutely, my share; and give me a son, and he will be able to rule his portion after me.'

'But he wouldn't be your own son, of your own ruling class; or perhaps not,' she stammered.

'I don't care who his father may be, so long as he is a healthy man not below normal intelligence. Give me the child of any healthy, normally intelligent man, and I will make a perfectly competent Chatterley of him. It is not who begets us, that matters, but where fate places us. Place any child among the ruling classes, and he will grow up, to his own extent, a ruler. Put kings' and dukes' children among the masses, and they'll

①尼禄的奴隶们。尼禄(37—68),古罗马皇帝(54—68在位),以独裁和残暴而臭名昭著。据传是他纵火焚毁了大半个罗马城。 ②(意)面包和马戏。

be little plebeians, mass products. It is the overwhelming pressure of environment.'

'Then the common people aren't a race, and the aristocrats aren't blood,' she said.

'No, my child! All that is romantic illusion. Aristocracy is a function, a part of fate. And the masses are a functioning of another part of fate. The individual hardly matters. It is a question of which function you are brought up to and adapted to. It is not the individuals that make an aristocracy: it is the functioning of the aristocratic whole. And it is the functioning of the whole mass that makes the common man what he is.'

'Then there is no common humanity between us all!'

'Just as you like. We all need to fill our bellies. But when it comes to expressive or executive functioning, I believe there is a gulf and an absolute one, between the ruling and the serving classes. The two functions are opposed. And the function determines the individual.'

Connie looked at him with dazed eyes.

'Won't you come on?' she said.

And he started his chair. He had said his say. Now he lapsed into his peculiar and rather vacant apathy, that Connie found so trying. In the wood, anyhow, she was determined not to argue.

In front of them ran the open cleft of the riding, between the hazel walls and the gay grey trees. The chair puffed slowly on, slowly surging into the forget-me-nots that rose up in the drive like milk froth, beyond the hazel shadows. Clifford steered the middle course, where feet passing had kept a channel through the flowers. But Connie, walking behind, had watched the wheels jolt over the wood-ruff and the bugle, and squash the little yellow cups of the creeping-jenny. Now they made a wake through the forget-me-nots.

All the flowers were there, the first bluebells in blue pools, like standing water.

'You are quite right about its being beautiful,' said Clifford. 'It is so amazingly. What is quite so lovely as an English spring!'

Connie thought it sounded as if even the spring bloomed by act of Parliament. An English spring! Why not an Irish one? or Jewish? The chair moved slowly ahead, past tufts of sturdy bluebells that stood up like wheat and over grey burdock leaves. When they came to the open place where the trees had been felled, the light flooded in rather stark. And the bluebells made sheets of bright blue colour, here and there, sheering off into lilac and purple. And between, the bracken was lifting its brown curled heads, **like legions of young snakes with a new secret to whisper to Eve**①.

Clifford kept the chair going till he came to the brow of the hill; Connie followed slowly behind. The oak-buds were opening soft and brown. Everything came tenderly out of the old hardness. Even the snaggy craggy oak-trees put out the softest young leaves, spreading thin, brown little wings like young bat-wings in the light. Why had men never any newness in them, any freshness to come forth with! Stale men!

Clifford stopped the chair at the top of the rise and looked down. The bluebells washed blue like flood-water over the broad riding, and lit up the downhill with a warm blueness.

'It's a very fine colour in itself,' said Clifford, 'but useless for making a painting.'

'Quite!' said Connie, completely uninterested.

'Shall I venture as far as the spring?' said Clifford.

'Will the chair get up again?' she said.

'We'll try; **nothing venture, nothing win**②!'

And the chair began to advance slowly, joltingly down the beautiful broad riding washed over with blue encroaching hyacinths. O last of all ships, through the hyacinthian shallows! O pinnace on the last wild waters, sailing in the last voyage of our civilization! Whither, O weird wheeled ship, your slow course steering. Quiet and complacent, Clifford sat at the wheel of adventure: in his old black hat and tweed jacket, motionless and cautious. O Captain, my Captain, our splendid trip is done! Not yet though! Downhill, **in the wake**③, came Constance in her grey dress, watching the chair jolt downwards.

They passed the narrow track to the hut. Thank heaven it was not wide enough for the chair: hardly wide enough for one person. The chair reached the bottom of the slope, and swerved round, to disappear. And Connie heard a low whistle behind her. She glanced sharply round: the keeper was striding downhill towards her, his dog keeping behind him.

'Is Sir Clifford going to the cottage?' he asked, looking into

①像无数条幼蛇，想要向夏娃吐露新的秘密。夏娃，亚当之妻，世界上第一位女人《创世纪》3:20中描述她被蛇引诱偷食禁果，而被逐出伊甸园。 ②不入虎穴，焉得虎子，亦作nothing venture,nothing have。 ③紧跟，随后。

her eyes.

'No, only to the well.'

'Ah! Good! Then I can keep out of sight. But I shall see you tonight. I shall wait for you at the park-gate about ten.'

He looked again direct into her eyes.

'Yes,' she faltered.

They heard the Papp! Papp! of Clifford's horn, tooting for Connie. She 'Coo-eed!' in reply. The keeper's face flickered with a little grimace, and with his hand he softly brushed her breast upwards, from underneath. She looked at him, frightened, and started running down the hill, calling Coo-ee! again to Clifford. The man above watched her, then turned, grinning faintly, back into his path.

She found Clifford slowly mounting to the spring, which was halfway up the slope of the dark larch-wood. He was there by the time she caught him up.

'She did that all right,' he said, referring to the chair.

Connie looked at the great grey leaves of burdock that grew out ghostly from the edge of the larch-wood. The people call it Robin Hood's Rhubarb. How silent and gloomy it seemed by the well! Yet the water bubbled so bright, wonderful! And there were bits of eye-bright and strong blue bugle...And there, under the bank, the yellow earth was moving. A mole! It emerged, rowing its pink hands, and waving its blind gimlet of a face, with the tiny pink nose-tip uplifted.

'It seems to see with the end of its nose,' said Connie.

'Better than with its eyes!' he said. 'Will you drink?'

'Will you?'

She took an enamel mug from a twig on a tree, and stooped to fill it for him. He drank in sips. Then she stooped again, and drank a little herself.

'So icy!' she said gasping.

'Good, isn't it! Did you wish?'

'Did you?'

'Yes, I wished. But I won't tell.'

She was aware of the rapping of a woodpecker, then of the wind, soft and eerie through the larches. She looked up. White clouds were crossing the blue.

'Clouds!' she said.

'White lambs only,' he replied.

A shadow crossed the little clearing. The mole had swum out on to the soft yellow earth.

'Unpleasant little beast, we ought to kill him,' said Clifford.

'Look! he's like a parson in a pulpit,' she said.

She gathered some sprigs of woodruff and brought them to him.

'New-mown hay!' he said. 'Doesn't it smell like the romantic ladies of the last century, who **had their heads screwed on the right way after all**[1]!'

She was looking at the white clouds.

'I wonder if it will rain,' she said.

'Rain! Why! Do you want it to?'

They started on the return journey, Clifford jolting cautiously downhill. They came to the dark bottom of the hollow, turned to the right, and after a hundred yards swerved up the foot of the long slope, where bluebells stood in the light.

'Now, old girl!' said Clifford, putting the chair to it.

It was a steep and jolty climb. The chair pugged slowly, in a struggling unwilling fashion. Still, she nosed her way up unevenly, till she came to where the hyacinths were all around her, then she balked, struggled, jerked a little way out of the flowers, then stopped

'We'd better sound the horn and see if the keeper will come,' said Connie. 'He could push her a bit. For that matter, I will push. It helps.'

'We'll let her breathe,' said Clifford. 'Do you mind putting a scotch under the wheel?'

Connie found a stone, and they waited. After a while Clifford started his motor again, then set the chair in motion. It struggled and faltered like a sick thing, with curious noises.

'Let me push!' said Connie, coming up behind.

'No! Don't push!' he said angrily. 'What's the good of the damned thing, if it has to be pushed! Put the stone under!'

There was another pause, then another start; but more ineffectual than before.

'You must let me push,' said she. 'Or sound the horn for the keeper.'

---

[1] 毕竟她们聪明能干。to have (have got) head screwed on the right way,亦作have a (good) head on one's shoulders 有才能,有见识,精明能干。

'Wait! '

She waited; and he had another try, doing more harm than good.

'Sound the horn then, if you won't let me push,' she said. 'Hell! Be quiet a moment! '

She was quiet a moment: he made shattering efforts with the little motor.

'You'll only break the thing down altogether, Clifford,' she remonstrated; 'besides wasting your nervous energy.'

'If I could only get out and look at the damned thing! ' he said, exasperated. And he sounded the horn stridently. 'Perhaps Mellors can see what's wrong.'

They waited, among the mashed flowers under a sky softly curdling with cloud. In the silence a wood-pigeon began to coo roo-hoo hoo! roo-hoo hoo! Clifford shut her up with a blast on the horn.

The keeper appeared directly, striding inquiringly round the corner. He saluted.

'Do you know anything about motors?' asked Clifford sharply.

'I am afraid I don't. Has she gone wrong?'

'Apparently! ' snapped Clifford.

The man crouched solicitously by the wheel, and peered at the little engine.

'I'm afraid I know nothing at all about these mechanical things, Sir Clifford,' he said calmly. 'If she has enough petrol and oil — '

'Just look carefully and see if you can see anything broken,' snapped Clifford.

The man laid his gun against a tree, took oil his coat, and threw it beside it. The brown dog sat guard. Then he sat down on his heels and peered under the chair, poking with his finger at the greasy little engine, and resenting the grease-marks on his clean Sunday shirt.

'Doesn't seem anything broken,' he said. And he stood up, pushing back his hat from his forehead, rubbing his brow and apparently studying.

'Have you looked at the rods underneath?' asked Clifford. 'See if they are all right! '

The man lay flat on his stomach on the floor, his neck pressed back, wriggling under the engine and poking with his finger. Connie thought what a pathetic sort of thing a man was, feeble and small-looking, when he was lying on his belly on the big earth.

'Seems all right as far as I can see,' came his muffled voice.

'I don't suppose you can do anything,' said Clifford.

'Seems as if I can't!' And he scrambled up and sat on his heels, collier fashion. 'There's certainly nothing obviously broken.'

Clifford started his engine, then put her in gear. She would not move.

'**Run her a bit hard, like**①,' suggested the keeper.

Clifford resented the interference: but he made his engine buzz like a blue-bottle. Then she coughed and snarled and seemed to go better.

'**Sounds as if she'd come clear**②,' said Mellors.

But Clifford had already jerked her into gear. She gave a sick lurch and ebbed weakly forwards.

'If I give her a push, she'll do it,' said the keeper, going behind.

'Keep off!' snapped Clifford. 'She'll do it by herself.'

'But Clifford!' put in Connie from the bank, 'you know it's too much for her. Why are you so obstinate!'

Clifford was pale with anger. He jabbed at his levers. The chair gave a sort of scurry, reeled on a few more yards, and came to her end amid a particularly promising patch of bluebells.

'She's done!' said the keeper. 'Not power enough.'

'She's been up here before,' said Clifford coldly.

'She won't do it this time,' said the keeper.

Clifford did not reply. He began doing things with his engine, running her fast and slow as if to get some sort of tune out of her. The wood re-echoed with weird noises. Then he put her in gear with a jerk, having jerked off his brake.

'You'll rip her inside out,' murmured the keeper.

The chair charged in a sick lurch sideways at the ditch.

'Clifford!' cried Connie, rushing forward.

But the keeper had got the chair by the rail. Clifford, however, putting on all his pressure, managed to steer into the riding, and with a strange noise the chair was fighting the hill. Mellors pushed steadily behind, and up she went, as if to retrieve herself.

'You see, she's doing it!' said Clifford, victorious, glancing over

①看来得加大一点马力。②听起来好像故障没了。

his shoulder. There he saw the keeper's face.

'Are you pushing her?'

'She won't do it without.'

'Leave her alone. I asked you not.

'She won't do it.'

'Let her try!' snarled Clifford, with all his emphasis.

The keeper stood back: then turned to fetch his coat and gun. The chair seemed to strange immediately. She stood inert. Clifford, seated a prisoner, was white with vexation. He jerked at the levers with his hand, his feet were no good. He got queer noises out of her. In savage impatience he moved little handles and got more noises out of her. But she would not budge. No, she would not budge. He stopped the engine and sat rigid with anger.

Constance sat on the bank arid looked at the wretched and trampled bluebells. 'Nothing quite so lovely as an English spring.' 'I can do my share of ruling.' 'What we need to take up now is whips, not swords.' 'The ruling classes!'

The keeper strode up with his coat and gun, Flossie cautiously at his heels. Clifford asked the man to do something or other to the engine. Connie, who understood nothing at all of the technicalities of motors, and who had had experience of breakdowns, **sat patiently on the bank as if she were a cipher**[1]. The keeper lay on his stomach again. The ruling classes and the serving classes!

He got to his feet and said patiently:

'Try her again, then.'

He spoke in a quiet voice, almost as if to a child.

Clifford tried her, and Mellors stepped quickly behind and began to push. She was going, the engine doing about half the work, the man the rest.

Clifford glanced round, yellow with anger.

'Will you get off there!'

The keeper dropped his hold at once, and Clifford added: 'How shall I know what she is doing!'

The man put his gun down and began to pull on his coat. He'd done.

The chair began slowly to run backwards.

[1] 她耐心地坐在一旁，似乎自己是个无足轻重的人。

'Clifford, your brake!' cried Connie.

She, Mellors, and Clifford moved at once, Connie and the keeper jostling lightly. The chair stood. There was a moment of dead silence.

'**It's obvious I'm at everybody's mercy**[1]!' said Clifford. He was yellow with anger.

No one answered. Mellors was slinging his gun over his shoulder, his face queer and expressionless, save for an abstracted look of patience. The dog Flossie, standing on guard almost between her master's legs, moved uneasily, eyeing the chair with great suspicion and dislike, and very much perplexed between the three human beings. The **tableau vivant**[2] remained set among the squashed bluebells, nobody proffering a word.

'I expect she'll have to be pushed,' said Clifford at last, with an affectation of **sang froid**[3].

No answer. Mellors' abstracted face looked as if he had heard nothing. Connie glanced anxiously at him. Clifford too glanced round.

'Do you mind pushing her home, Mellors!' he said in a cool superior tone. 'I hope I have said nothing to offend you,' he added, in a tone of dislike.

'Nothing at all, Sir Clifford! Do you want me to push that chair?'

'If you please.'

The man stepped up to it: but this time it was without effect. The brake was jammed. They poked and pulled, and the keeper took off his gun and his coat once more. And now Clifford said never a word. At last the keeper heaved the back of the chair off the ground and, with an instantaneous push of his foot, tried to loosen the wheels. He failed, the chair sank. Clifford was clutching the sides. The man gasped with the weight.

'Don't do it!' cried Connie to him.

'If you'll pull the wheel that way, so!' he said to her, showing her how.

'No! You mustn't lift it! You'll strain yourself,' she said, flushed now with anger.

But he looked into her eyes and nodded. And she had to go and take hold of the wheel, ready. He heaved and she tugged, and the chair reeled.

---

❶显然,我得让人摆布了。❷(法)生动的情景。❸(法)镇定沉着。

'For God's sake! ' cried Clifford in terror.

But it was all right, and the brake was off. The keeper put a stone under the wheel, and went to sit on the bank, his heart beat and his face white with the effort, semi-conscious. Connie looked at him, and almost cried with anger. There was a pause and a dead silence. She saw his hands trembling on his thighs.

'Have you hurt yourself?' she asked, going to him.

'No. No! ' He turned away almost angrily.

There was dead silence. The back of Clifford's fair head did not move. Even the dog stood motionless. The sky had clouded over.

At last he sighed, and blew his nose on his red handkerchief.

'**That pneumonia took a lot out of me**[1],' he said.

No one answered. Connie calculated the amount of strength it must have taken to heave up that chair and the bulky Clifford: too much, far too much! If it hadn't killed him!

He rose, and again picked up his coat, slinging it through the handle of the chair.

'Are you ready, then, Sir Clifford?'

'When you are! '

He stooped and took out the scotch, then put his weight against the chair. He was paler than Connie had ever seen him: and more absent. Clifford was a heavy man: and the hill was steep. Connie stepped to the keeper's side.

'I'm going to push too! ' she said.

And she began to shove with a woman's turbulent energy of anger. The chair went faster. Clifford looked round.

'Is that necessary?' he said.

'Very! Do you want to kill the man! If you'd let the motor work while it would — '

But she did not finish. She was already panting. She slackened off a little, for it was surprisingly hard work.

'Ay! slower! ' said the man at her side, with a faint smile of his eyes.

'Are you sure you've not hurt yourself?' she said fiercely.

He shook his head. She looked at his smallish, short, alive hand, browned by the weather. It was the hand that caressed her. She had never

[1] 肺炎使我虚弱了许多。

even looked at it before. It seemed so still, like him, with a curious inward stillness that made her want to clutch it, as if she could not reach it. All her soul suddenly swept towards him: he was so silent, and out of reach! And he felt his limbs revive. Shoving with his left hand, he laid his right on her round white wrist, softly enfolding her wrist, with a caress. And the flame of strength went down his back and his loins, reviving him. And she bent suddenly and kissed his hand. Meanwhile the back of Clifford's head was held sleek and motionless, just in front of them.

At the top of the hill they rested, and Connie was glad to let go. She had had fugitive dreams of friendship between these two men: one her husband, the other the father of her child. Now she saw the screaming absurdity of her dreams. The two males were as hostile as fire and water. They mutually exterminated one another. And she realized for the first time what a queer subtle thing hate is. For the first time, she had consciously and definitely hated Clifford, with vivid hate: as if he ought to be obliterated from the face of the earth. And it was strange, how free and full of life it made her feel, to hate him and to admit it fully to herself. — 'Now I've hated him, I shall never be able to go on living with him,' came the thought into her mind.

On the level the keeper could push the chair alone. Clifford made a little conversation with her, to show his complete composure: about Aunt Eva, who was at Dieppe, and about Sir Malcolm, who had written to ask would Connie drive with him in his small car, to Venice, or would she and Hilda go by train.

'I'd much rather go by train,' said Connie. 'I don't like long motor drives, especially when there's dust. But I shall see what Hilda wants.'

'She will want to drive her own car, and take you with her,' he said.

'Probably! — I must help up here. You've no idea how heavy this chair is.'

She went to the back of the chair, and plodded side by side with the keeper, shoving up the pink path. She did not care who saw.

'Why not let me wait, and fetch Field? He is strong enough for the job,' said Clifford.

'It's so near,' she panted.

But both she and Mellors wiped the sweat from their faces when they came to the top. It was curious, but this bit of work together had brought them much closer than they had been before.

'Thanks so much, Mellors,' said Clifford, when they were at the house door. 'I must get a different sort of motor, that's all. Won't you go to the kitchen and have a meal? It must be about time.'

'Thank you, Sir Clifford. I was going to my mother for dinner today, Sunday.'

'As you like.'

Mellors slung into his coat, looked at Connie, saluted, and was gone. Connie, furious, went upstairs.

At lunch she could not contain her feeling.

'Why are you so abominably inconsiderate, Clifford?' she said to him.

'Of whom?'

'Of the keeper! If that is what you call ruling classes, I'm sorry for you.'

'Why?'

'A man who's been ill, and isn't strong! My word, if I were the serving classes, I'd let you wait for service. I'd let you whistle.'

'I quite believe it.'

'If he'd been sitting in a chair with paralysed legs, and behaved as you behaved, what would you have done for him?'

'My dear evangelist, this confusing of persons and personalities is in bad taste.'

'And your nasty, sterile want of common sympathy is in the worst taste imaginable. **Noblesse oblige**[1]! You and your ruling class!'

'And to what should it oblige me? To have a lot of unnecessary emotions about my game-keeper? I refuse. I leave it all to my evangelist.'

'As if he weren't a man as much as you are, my word!'

'My game-keeper to boot, and I pay him two pounds a week and give him a house.'

'Pay him! What do you think you pay for, with two pounds a week and a house?'

'His services.'

'Bah! I would tell you to keep your two pounds a week and your house.'

[1] (法谚)位高者责任重。

'Probably he would like to: but can't afford the luxury!'

'You, and rule!' she said. 'You don't rule, don't flatter yourself. You have only got more than your share of the money, and make people work for you for two pounds a week, or threaten them with starvation. Rule! **What do you give forth of rule**[1]? Why, **you're dried up**[2]! You only bully with your money, like any Jew or any Schieber!'

'You are very elegant in your speech, Lady Chatterley!'

'I assure you, you were very elegant altogether out there in the wood. I was utterly ashamed of you. Why, my father is ten times the human being you are: you gentleman!'

He reached and rang the bell for Mrs Bolton. But he was yellow at the gills.

She went up to her room, furious, saying to herself: 'Him and buying people! Well, he doesn't buy me, and therefore there's no need for me to stay with him. Dead fish of a gentleman, with his celluloid soul! And **how they take one in**[3], with their manners and their mock wistfulness and gentleness. **They've got about as much feeling as celluloid has**[4].'

She made her plans for the night, and determined to get Clifford off her mind. She didn't want to hate him. She didn't want to be mixed up very intimately with him in any sort of feeling. She wanted him not to know anything at all about herself: and especially, not to know anything about her feeling for the keeper. This squabble of her attitude to the servants was an old one. He found her too familiar, she found him stupidly insentient, tough and indiarubbery where other people were concerned.

She went downstairs calmly, with her old demure bearing, at dinner-time. He was still yellow at the gills: in for one of his liver bouts, when he was really very queer. — He was reading a French book.

'Have you ever read **Proust**[5]?' he asked her.

'I've tried, but he bores me.'

'He's really very extraordinary.'

'Possibly! But he bores me: all that sophistication! He doesn't

---

❶你统治的内容都是些什么？ ❷你理屈词穷了吧。 ❸他们多会骗人。 ❹他们像赛璐珞一样毫无感情。 ❺普鲁斯特(1871—1922)，法国小说家。

have feelings, he only has streams of words about feelings. I'm tired of self-important mentalities.'

'Would you prefer self-important animalities?'

'Perhaps! But one might possibly get something that wasn't self-important.'

'Well, I like Proust's subtlety and his well-bred anarchy.'

'It makes you very dead, really.'

'There speaks my evangelical little wife.'

They were at it again, at it again! But she couldn't help fighting him. He seemed to sit there like a skeleton, sending out a skeleton's cold grizzly will against her. Almost she could feel the skeleton clutching her and pressing her to its cage of ribs. He too was really up in arms: and she was a little afraid of him.

She went upstairs as soon as possible, and went to bed quite early. But at half past nine she got up, and went outside to listen. There was no sound. She slipped on a dressing-gown and went downstairs. Clifford and Mrs Bolton were playing cards, gambling. They would probably go on until midnight.

Connie returned to her room, threw her pyjamas on the tossed bed, put on a thin tennis-dress and over that a woollen day-dress, put on rubber tennis-shoes, and then a light coat. And she was ready. If she met anybody, she was just going out for a few minutes. And in the morning, when she came in again, she would just have been for a little walk in the dew, as she fairly often did before breakfast. For the rest, the only danger was that someone should go into her room during the night. But that was most unlikely: not one chance in a hundred.

Betts had not locked up. He fastened up the house at ten o'clock, and unfastened it again at seven in the morning. She slipped out silently and unseen. There was a half-moon shining, enough to make a little light in the world, not enough to show her up in her dark-grey coat. She walked quickly across the park, **not really in the thrill of the assignation**[1], but with a certain anger and rebellion burning in her heart. It was not the right sort of heart to take to a love-meeting. But **à la guerre comme à la guerre**[2]!

[1]实际上并无情人幽会的那种兴奋。 [2](法)战争时期就有战争时期的心境。

CHAPTER 14

When she got near the park-gate, she heard the click of the latch. He was there, then, in the darkness of the wood, and had seen her!

'You are good and early,' he said out of the dark. 'Was everything all right?'

'Perfectly easy.'

He shut the gate quietly after her, and made a spot of light on the dark ground, showing the pallid flowers still standing there open in the night. They went on apart, in silence.

'Are you sure you didn't hurt yourself this morning with that chair?' she asked.

'No, no!'

'When you had that pneumonia, what did it do to you?'

'Oh nothing! it left my heart not so strong and the lungs not so elastic. But it always does that.'

'And you ought not to make violent physical efforts?'

'Not often.'

She plodded on in an angry silence.

'Did you hate Clifford?' she said at last.

'Hate him, no! I've met too many like him to upset myself hating him. I know beforehand I don't care for his sort, and I let it go at that.'

'What is his sort?'

'Nay, you know better than I do. The sort of youngish gentleman a bit like a lady, and no balls.'

'What balls?'

'Balls! A man's balls!'

She pondered this.

'But is it a question of that?' she said, a little annoyed.

'You say a man's got no brain, when he's a fool: and no heart, when he's mean; and no stomach when he's a funker. And when he's got none of that spunky wild bit of a man in him, you say he's got no balls. When he's a sort of tame.'

She pondered this.

'And is Clifford tame?' she asked.

'Tame, and nasty with it: like most such fellows, when you come up against 'em.'

'And do you think you're not tame?'

'Maybe not quite!'

At length she saw in the distance a yellow light.

She stood still.

'There is a light!' she said.

'I always leave a light in the house,' he said.

She went on again at his side, but not touching him, wondering why she was going with him at all.

He unlocked, and they went in, he bolting the door behind them. As if it were a prison, she thought! The kettle was singing by the red fire, there were cups on the table.

She sat in the wooden arm-chair by the fire. It was warm after the chill outside.

'I'll take off my shoes, they are wet,' she said.

She sat with her stockinged feet on the bright steel fender. He went to the pantry, bringing food: bread and butter and **pressed tongue**[1]. She was warm: she took off her coat. He hung it on the door.

'Shall you have cocoa or tea or coffee to drink?' he asked.

'I don't think I want anything,' she said, looking at the table. 'But you eat.'

'Nay, I don't care about it. I'll just feed the dog.'

He tramped with a quiet inevitability over the brick floor, putting food for the dog in a brown bowl. The spaniel looked up at him anxiously.

'Ay, this is thy supper, tha **nedna**[2] look as if tha wouldna get it!' he said.

He set the bowl on the stairfoot mat, and sat himself on a chair by the wall, to take off his leggings and boots. The dog instead of eating, came to him again, and sat looking up at him, troubled.

He slowly unbuckled his leggings. The dog edged a little nearer.

'What's amiss wi' thee then? Art upset because there's somebody else here? Tha'rt a female, tha art! Go an' eat thy supper.'

[1] 卤腌口条。 [2] =need not。

He put his hand on her head, and the bitch leaned her head sideways against him. He slowly, softly pulled the long silky ear.

'There!' he said. 'There! Go an' eat thy supper! Go!'

He tilted his chair towards the pot on the mat, and the dog meekly went, and fell to eating.

'Do you like dogs?' Connie asked him.

'No, not really. They're too tame and clinging.'

He had taken off his leggings and was unlacing his heavy boots. Connie had turned from the fire. How bare the little room was! Yet over his head on the wall hung a hideous enlarged photograph of a young married couple, apparently him and a bold-faced young woman, no doubt his wife.

'Is that you?' Connie asked him.

He twisted and looked at the enlargement above his head.

'Ay! Taken just afore we was married, when I was twenty-one.' He looked at it impassively.

'Do you like it?' Connie asked him.

'Like it? No! I never liked the thing. But she fixed it all up to have it done, like.'

He returned to pulling off his boots.

'If you don't like it, why do you keep it hanging there? Perhaps your wife would like to have it,' she said.

He looked up at her with a sudden grin.

'She carted off iverything as was worth taking from th' 'ouse,' he said. 'But she left that!'

'Then why do you keep it? for sentimental reasons?'

'Nay, I niver look at it. I hardly knowed it wor theer. It's bin theer sin' we come to this place.'

'Why don't you burn it?' she said.

He twisted round again and looked at the enlarged photograph. It was framed in a brown-and-gilt frame, hideous. It showed a clean-shaven, alert, very young-looking man in a rather high collar, and a somewhat plump, bold young woman with hair fluffed out and crimped, and wearing a dark satin blouse.

'It wouldn't be a bad idea, would it?' he said.

He had pulled off his boots, and put on a pair of slippers. He stood up on the chair, and lifted down the photograph. It left a big pale place on the greenish wall-paper.

'No use dusting it now,' he said, setting the thing against the wall.

He went to the scullery, and returned with hammer and pincers. Sitting where he had sat before, he started to tear off the back-paper from the big frame, and to pull out the sprigs that held the backboard in position, working with the immediate quiet absorption that was characteristic of him.

He soon had the nails out: then he pulled out the backboards, then the enlargement itself, in its solid white mount. He looked at the photograph with amusement.

'Shows me for what I was, a young curate, and her for what she was, a bully,' he said. 'The prig and the bully!'

'Let me look!' said Connie.

He did look indeed very clean-shaven and very clean altogether, one of the clean young men of twenty years ago. But even in the photograph his eyes were alert and dauntless. And the woman was not altogether a bully, though her jowl was heavy. There was a touch of appeal in her.

'One never should keep these things,' said Connie. 'That one shouldn't! One should never have them made!'

He broke the cardboard photograph and mount over his knee, and when it was small enough, put it on the fire.

'It'll spoil the fire though,' he said.

The glass and the backboard he carefully took upstairs.

The frame he knocked asunder with a few blows of the hammer, making the stucco fly. Then he took the pieces into the scullery.

'We'll burn that tomorrow,' he said. 'There's too much plaster-moulding on it.'

Having cleared away, he sat down.

'Did you love your wife?' she asked him.

'Love?' he said. 'Did you love Sir Clifford?'

But she was not going to be put off.

'But you cared for her?' she insisted.

'Cared?' He grinned.

'Perhaps you care for her now,' she said.

'Me!' His eyes widened. 'Ah no, I can't think of her,' he said quietly.

'Why?'

But he shook his head.

'Then why don't you get a divorce? She'll come back to you one day,' said Connie.

He looked up at her sharply.

'She wouldn't come within a mile of me. She hates me a lot worse than I hate her.'

'You'll see she'll come back to you.'

'That she never will. That's done! It would make me sick to see her.'

'You will see her. And you're not even legally separated, are you?'

'No.'

'Ah well, then she'll come back, and you'll have to take her in.'

He gazed at Connie fixedly. Then he gave the queer toss of his head.

'You might be right. I was a fool ever to come back here. But I felt stranded and had to go somewhere. A man's a poor bit of a wastrel blown about. But you're right. I'll get a divorce and get clear. I hate those things like death, officials and courts and judges. But I've got to get through with it. I'll get a divorce.'

And she saw his jaw set. Inwardly she exulted. 'I think I will have a cup of tea now,' she said. He rose to make it. But his face was set. As they sat at table she asked him:

'Why did you marry her? She was commoner than yourself. Mrs Bolton told me about her. She could never understand why you married her.'

He looked at her fixedly.

'I'll tell you,' he said. 'The first girl I had, I began with when I was sixteen. She was a school-master's daughter over at Ollerton, pretty, beautiful really. I was supposed to be a clever sort of young fellow from Sheffield Grammar School, with a bit of French and German, very much up aloft. She was the romantic sort that hated commonness. **She egged me on to poetry and reading**[1]: in a way, she made a man of me. I read and I thought **like a house on fire**[2], for her. And I was a clerk in Butterley offices, thin, white-faced fellow fuming with all the things I read. And about everything I talked to her: but everything. We talked

①她鼓励我读书吟诗。 ②拼命地，热切地。

ourselves into **Persepolis and Timbuctoo**❶. We were the most literary-cultured couple in ten counties. I **held forth with rapture to her**❷, positively with rapture. **I simply went up in smoke**❸. And she adored me. The serpent in the grass was sex. She somehow didn't have any; at least, not where it's supposed to be. I got thinner and crazier. Then I said we'd got to be lovers. I talked her into it, as usual. So she let me. I was excited, and she never wanted it. She just didn't want it. She adored me, she loved me to talk to her and kiss her: in that way she had a passion for me. But the other, she just didn't want. And there are lots of women like her. And it was just the other that I did want. So there we split. I was cruel, and left her. Then I took on with another girl, a teacher, who had made a scandal by carrying on with a married man and driving him nearly out of his mind. She was a soft, white-skinned, soft sort of a woman, older than me, and played the fiddle. And she was a demon. She loved everything about love, except the sex. Clinging, caressing, creeping into you in every way: but if you forced her to the sex itself, she just ground her teeth and sent out hate. I forced her to it, and she could simply numb me with hate because of it. So I was balked again. I loathed all that. I wanted a woman who wanted me, and wanted it.

'Then came Bertha Coutts. They'd lived next door to us when I was a little lad, so I knew 'em all right. And they were common. Well, Bertha went away to some place or other in Birmingham; she said, as a lady's companion; everybody else said, as a waitress or something in a hotel. Anyhow just when I was more than fed up with that other girl, when I was twenty-one, back comes Bertha, with airs and graces and smart clothes and a sort of bloom on her: a sort of sensual bloom that you'd see sometimes on a woman, or on a trolly. Well, **I was in a state of murder**❹. I chucked up my job at Butterley because I thought I was a weed, clerking there: and I got on as overhead blacksmith at Tevershall: shoeing horses mostly. It had been my dad's job, and I'd always been with him. It was a job I liked: handling horses: and it came natural to me. So I stopped talking "fine", as they call it, talking proper English, and went back to talking broad. I still read books, at home: but I blacksmithed and had a pony-trap of my own, and

❶波斯波利斯：古波斯帝国都城之一；廷巴克图：历史名城，在撒哈拉沙漠之南。 ❷我和她谈得心醉神迷。 ❸我简直飘飘欲仙，忘乎所以。 ❹我的心情糟透了。

was My Lord Duckfoot. My dad left me three hundred pounds when he died. So I took on with Bertha, and I was glad she was common. I wanted her to be common. I wanted to be common myself. Well, I married her, and she wasn't bad. **Those other "pure" women had nearly taken all the balls out of me**❶, but she was all right that way. She wanted me, and **made no bones about it**❷. And I was as pleased as punch. That was what I wanted: a woman who wanted me to fuck her. So I fucked her like **a good un**❸. And I think she despised me a bit, for being so pleased about it, and bringin' her her breakfast in bed sometimes. She sort of let things go, didn't get me a proper dinner when I came home from work, and if I said anything, flew out at me. And I flew back, **hammer and tongs**❹. She flung a cup at me and I took her by the scruff of the neck and squeezed the life out of her. That sort of thing! But she treated me with insolence. And she got so's she'd never have me when I wanted her: never. **Always put me off, brutal as you like**❺. And then when she'd put me right off, and I didn't want her, she'd come **all lovey-dovey**❻, and get me. And **I always went**❼. But when I had her, she'd never come off when I did. Never! She'd just wait. If I kept back for half an hour, she'd keep back longer. And when I'd come and really finished, then she'd start on her own account, and I had to stop inside her till she brought herself off, wriggling and shouting, she'd clutch clutch with herself down there, an' then she'd come off, fair in ecstasy. And then she'd say: That was lovely! Gradually I got sick of it: and she got worse. She sort of got harder and harder to bring off, and she'd sort of tear at me down there, as if it was a beak tearing at me. By God, you think a woman's soft down there, like a fig. But I tell you **the old rampers**❽ have beaks between their legs, and they tear at you with it till you're sick. Self! Self! Self! all self! tearing and shouting! They talk about men's selfishness, but I doubt if it can ever touch a woman's blind beakishness, once she's gone that way. Like an old trull! And she couldn't help it. I told her about it, I told her how I hated it. And she'd even try. She'd try to lie still and let me work the business. She'd try. But it was no good. She got no feeling off it, from my working. She had to work the thing

❶那些"纯洁"的女人几乎把我的睾丸都玩完了。❷make no bones about (of):(口)对……毫不犹豫;对……毫无顾忌。❸好人;真家伙。❹针锋相对,大闹一场。❺总是粗暴地拒绝我。❻(口)情意绵绵地。❼我总让着她。❽老娼妇。

herself, **grind her own coffee**[1]. And it came back on her like a raving necessity, she had to let herself go, and tear, tear, tear, as if she had no sensation in her except in the top of her beak, the very outside top tip, that rubbed and tore. That's how old whores used to be, so men used to say. It was a low kind of self-will in her, a raving sort of self-will: like in a woman who drinks. Well in the end I couldn't stand it. We slept apart. She herself had started it, in her bouts when she wanted to be clear of me, when she said I bossed her. She had started having a room for herself. But the time came when I wouldn't have her coming to my room. I wouldn't.

'I hated it. And she hated me. My God, how she hated me before that child was born! I often think she conceived it out of hate. Anyhow, after the child was born I left her alone. And then came the war, and I joined up. And I didn't come back till I knew she was with that fellow at Stacks Gate.

He broke off, pale in the face.

'And what is the man at Stacks Gate like?' asked Connie.

'A big baby sort of fellow, **very low-mouthed**[2]. She bullies him, and they both drink.'

'My word, if she came back!'

'My God, yes! I should just go, disappear again.'

There was a silence. The pasteboard in the fire had turned to grey ash.

'So when you did get a woman who wanted you,' said Connie, 'you got a bit too much of a good thing.'

'Ay! Seems so! Yet even then I'd rather have her than **the never-never ones**[3]: **the white love of my youth**[4], and that other poison-smelling lily, and the rest.'

'What about the rest?' said Connie.

'The rest? There is no rest. Only to my experience the mass of women are like this: most of them want a man, but don't want the sex, but they put up with it, as part of the bargain. The more old-fashioned sort just lie there like nothing and let you go ahead. They don't mind afterwards: then they like you. But the actual thing itself is nothing to them, a bit distasteful. Add most men like it that way. I hate it. But the

---

❶借喻，意思是她要用自己的方式满足自己的私欲。 ❷满嘴脏话。 ❸老不愿做爱的女人。 ❹我青春时的纯洁情人。

sly sort of women who are like that pretend they're not. They pretend they're passionate and have thrills. But it's all cockaloopy. They make it up. Then there's the ones that love everything, every kind of feeling and cuddling and going off, every kind except the natural one. They always make you go off when you're not in the only place you should be, when you go off. — Then there's the hard sort, that are the devil to bring off at all, and bring themselves off, like my wife. They want to be the active party. — Then there's the sort that's just dead inside: but dead: and they know it. Then there's the sort that puts you out before you really "come", and go on writhing their loins till they bring themselves off against your thighs. But they're mostly **the Lesbian sort**❶. It's astonishing how Lesbian women are, consciously or unconsciously. Seems to me they're nearly all Lesbian.'

'And do you mind?' asked Connie.

'I could kill them. When I'm with a woman who's really Lesbian, I fairly howl in my soul, wanting to kill her.'

'And what do you do?'

'Just go away as fast as I can.'

'But do you think Lesbian women any worse than homosexual men?'

'I do! Because I've suffered more from them. In the abstract, I've no idea. When I get with a Lesbian woman, whether she knows she's one or not, **I see red**❷. No, no! But I wanted to have nothing to do with any woman any more. I wanted to keep to myself: keep my privacy and my decency.'

He looked pale, and his brows were sombre.

'And were you sorry when I came along?' she asked.

'I was sorry and I was glad.'

'And what are you now?'

'I'm sorry, from the outside: all the complications and the ugliness and recrimination that's bound to come, sooner or later. That's when my blood sinks, and I'm low. But when my blood comes up, I'm glad. I'm even triumphant. I was really getting bitter. I thought there was no real sex left: never a woman who'd really "come" naturally with a man: except black women, and somehow, well, we're white men: and they're a bit like mud.'

'And now, are you glad of me?' she asked.

❶女性同性恋者。 ❷我都会发怒。

'Yes! When I can forget the rest. When I can't forget the rest, I want to get under the table and die.'

'Why under the table?'

'Why?' he laughed. 'Hide, I suppose. Baby!'

'You do seem to have had awful experiences of women,' she said.

'You see, I couldn't fool myself. That's **where most men manage**[1]. They take an attitude, and accept a lie. I could never fool myself. I knew what I wanted with a woman, and I could never say I'd got it when I hadn't.'

'But have you got it now?'

'Looks as if I might have.'

'Then why are you so pale and gloomy?'

'Bellyful of remembering: and perhaps afraid of myself.'

She sat in silence. It was growing late.

'And do you think it's important, a man and a woman?' she asked him.

'For me it is. For me it's the core of my life: if I have a right relation with a woman.'

'And if you didn't get it?'

'Then I'd have to do without.'

Again she pondered, before she asked:

'And do you think you've always been right with women?'

'God, no! I let my wife get to what she was: my fault a good deal. I spoilt her. And I'm very mistrustful. You'll have to expect it. It takes a lot to make me trust anybody, inwardly. So perhaps I'm a fraud too. I mistrust. And tenderness is not to be mistaken.'

She looked at him.

'You don't mistrust with your body, when your blood comes up,' she said. 'You don't mistrust then, do you?'

'No, alas! That's how I've got into all the trouble. And that's why my mind mistrusts so thoroughly.'

'Let your mind mistrust. What does it matter!'

The dog sighed with discomfort on the mat. The ash-clogged fire sank.

'**We are a couple of battered warriors**[2],' said Connie.

'Are you battered too?' he laughed. 'And here we are returning to the fray!'

[1]大多数男人都能设法糊弄自己。[2]我们是一对饱经忧患的战士。

'Yes! I feel really frightened.'

'Ay!'

He got up, and put her shoes to dry, and wiped his own and set them near the fire. In the morning he would grease them. He poked the ash of pasteboard as much as possible out of the fire. 'Even burnt, it's filthy,' he said. Then he brought sticks and put them on the hob for the morning. Then he went out a while with the dog.

When he came back, Connie said:

'I want to go out too, for a minute.'

She went alone into the darkness. There were stars overhead. She could smell flowers on the night air. And she could feel her wet shoes getting wetter again. But she felt like going away, right away from him and everybody.

It was chilly. She shuddered, and returned to the house. He was sitting in front of the low fire.

'Ugh! Cold!' she shuddered.

He put the sticks on the fire, and fetched more, till they had a good crackling chimneyful of blaze. The rippling running yellow flame made them both happy, warmed their faces and their souls.

'Never mind!' she said, taking his hand as he sat silent and remote. 'One does one's best.'

'Ay!' He sighed, with a twist of a smile.

She slipped over to him, and into his arms, as he sat there before the fire.

'Forget then!' she whispered. 'Forget!'

He held her close, in the running warmth of the fire. The flame itself was like a forgetting. And her soft, warm, ripe weight! Slowly his blood turned, and began to ebb back into strength and reckless vigour again.

'And perhaps the women really wanted to be there and love you properly, only perhaps they couldn't. Perhaps it wasn't all their fault,' she said.

'I know it. Do you think I don't know what a broken-backed snake that's been trodden on I was myself!'

She clung to him suddenly. She had not wanted to start all this again. Yet some perversity had made her.

'But you're not now,' she said. 'You're not that now: a broken-backed snake that's been trodden on.'

'I don't know what I am. There's black days ahead.'

'No!' she protested, clinging to him. 'Why? Why?'

'There's black days coming for us all and for everybody,' he repeated with a prophetic gloom.

'No! You're not to say it!'

He was silent. But **she could feel the black void of despair inside him**[1]. That was the death of all desire, the death of all love: this despair that was like the dark cave inside the men, in which their spirit was lost.

'And you talk so coldly about sex,' she said. 'You talk as if you had only wanted your own pleasure and satisfaction.'

She was protesting nervously against him.

'Nay!' he said. 'I wanted to have my pleasure and satisfaction of a woman, and I never got it: because I could never get my pleasure and satisfaction of her unless she got hers of me at the same time. And it never happened. It takes two.'

'But you never believed in your women. You don't even believe really in me,' she said.

'I don't know what believing in a woman means.'

'That's it, you see!'

She still was curled on his lap. But his spirit was grey and absent, he was not there for her. And everything she said drove him further.

'But what do you believe in?' she insisted.

'I don't know.'

'Nothing, like all the men I've ever known,' she said.

They were both silent. Then he roused himself and said:

'Yes, I do believe in something. I believe in being warm-hearted. I believe especially in being warm-hearted in love, in fucking with a warm heart. I believe if men could fuck with warm hearts, and the women take it warm-heartedly, everything would come all right. It's all this cold-hearted fucking that is death and idiocy.'

'But you don't fuck me cold-heartedly,' she protested.

'I don't want to fuck you at all. My heart's as cold as cold potatoes just now.'

'Oh!' she said, kissing him mockingly. 'Let's **have them sautées**[2].' He laughed, and sat erect.

[1]她可以感到他内心深处那绝望的黑洞。[2](法)煎。

'It's a fact!' he said. 'Anything for a bit of warm-heartedness. But the women don't like it. Even you don't really like it. You like good, sharp, piercing cold-hearted fucking, and then pretending it's all sugar. Where's your tenderness for me? You're as suspicious of me as a cat is of a dog. I tell you it takes two even to be tender and warm-hearted. You love fucking all right: but you want it to be called something grand and mysterious, just to flatter your own self-importance. Your own self-importance is more to you, fifty times more, than any man, or being together with a man.'

'But that's what I'd say of you. Your own self-importance is everything to you.'

'Ay! Very well then!' he said, moving as if he wanted to rise. 'Let's keep apart then. I'd rather die than do any more cold-hearted fucking.'

She slid away from him, and he stood up.

'And do you think I want it?' she said.

'I hope you don't,' he replied. 'But anyhow, you go to bed an' I'll sleep down here.'

She looked at him. He was pale, his brows were sullen, he was as distant in recoil as the cold pole. Men were all alike.

'I can't go home till morning,' she said.

'No! Go to bed. It's a quarter to one.'

'I certainly won't,' she said.

He went across and picked up his boots.

'Then I'll go out!' he said.

He began to put on his boots. She stared at him.

'Wait!' she faltered. 'Wait! What's come between us?'

He was bent over, lacing his boot, and did not reply. The moments passed. A dimness came over her, like a swoon. All her consciousness died, and she stood there wide-eyed, looking at him from the unknown, knowing nothing any more.

He looked up, because of the silence, and saw her wide-eyed and lost. And as if a wind tossed him he got up and hobbled over to her, one shoe off and one shoe on, and took her in his arms, pressing her against his body, which somehow felt hurt right through. And there he held her, and there she remained.

Till his hands reached blindly down and felt for her, and felt under the clothing to where she was smooth and warm.

'Ma lass!' he murmured. 'Ma little lass! Dunna let's light! Dunna let's niver light! I love thee an' th' touch on thee. Dunna argue wi' me! Dunna! Dunna! Dunna! Let's be together.'

She lifted her face and looked at him.

'Don't be upset,' she said steadily. 'It's no good being upset. Do you really want to be together with me?'

She looked with wide, steady eyes into his face. He stopped, and went suddenly still, turning his face aside. All his body went perfectly still, but did not withdraw.

Then he lifted his head and looked into her eyes, with his odd, faintly mocking grin, saying: 'Ay-ay! Let's be together on oath.'

'But really?' she said, her eyes filling with tears. 'Ay really! Heart an' belly an' cock.'

He still smiled faintly down at her, with the flicker of irony in his eyes, and a touch of bitterness.

She was silently weeping, and he lay with her and went into her there on the hearthrug, and so **they gained a measure of equanimity**[1]. And then they went quickly to bed, for it was growing chill, and they had tired each other out. And she nestled up to him, feeling small and enfolded, and they both went to sleep at once, fast in one sleep. And so they lay and never moved, till the sun rose over the wood and day was beginning.

Then he woke up and looked at the light. The curtains were drawn. He listened to the loud wild calling of blackbirds and thrushes in the wood. It would be a brilliant morning, about half past five, his hour for rising. He had slept so fast! It was such a new day! The woman was still curled asleep and tender. His hand moved on her, and she opened her blue wondering eyes, smiling unconsciously into his face.

'Are you awake?' she said to him.

He was looking into her eyes. He smiled, and kissed her. And suddenly she roused and sat up.

'Fancy that I am here!' she said.

She looked round the whitewashed little bedroom with its sloping ceiling and gable window where the white curtains were closed. The room was bare save for a little yellow-painted chest of drawers, and a

[1] 他们才安静下来。

chair: and the smallish white bed in which she lay with him.

'Fancy that we are here! ' she said, looking down at him. He was lying watching her, stroking her breasts with his fingers, under the thin nightdress. When he was warm and smoothed out, he looked young and handsome. His eyes could look so warm. And she was fresh and young like a flower.

'I want to take this off! ' she said, gathering the thin batiste nightdress and pulling it over her head. She sat there with bare shoulders and longish breasts faintly golden. He loved to make her breasts swing softly, like bells.

'You must take off your pyjamas too,' she said.

'Eh, nay! '

'Yes! Yes! ' she commanded.

And he took off his old cotton pyjama-jacket, and pushed down the trousers. Save for his hands and wrists and face and neck he was white as milk, with fine slender muscular flesh. To Connie he was suddenly piercingly beautiful again, as when she had seen him that afternoon washing himself.

Gold of sunshine touched the closed white curtain. She felt it wanted to come in.

'Oh, do let's draw the curtains! The birds are singing so! Do let the sun in,' she said.

He slipped out of bed with his back to her, naked and white and thin, and went to the window, stooping a little, drawing the curtains and looking out for a moment. The back was white and fine, the small buttocks beautiful with an exquisite, delicate manliness, the back of the neck ruddy and delicate and yet strong.

here was an inward, not an outward strength in the delicate fine body.

'But you are beautiful! ' she said. 'So pure and fine! Come! ' She held her arms out.

He was ashamed to turn to her, because of his aroused nakedness.

He caught his shirt off the floor, and held it to him, coming to her.

'No! ' she said still holding out her beautiful slim arms from her dropping breasts. 'Let me see you! '

He dropped the shirt and stood still looking towards her. The sun through the low window sent in a beam that lit up his thighs and slim belly and the erect phallos rising darkish and hot-looking from the little cloud of vivid gold-red hair. She was startled and afraid.

'How strange!' she said slowly. 'How strange he stands there! So big! and so dark and cock-sure! Is he like that?'

The man looked down the front of his slender white body, and laughed. Between the slim breasts the hair was dark, almost black. But at the root of the belly, where the phallos rose thick and arching, it was gold-red, vivid in a little cloud.

'So proud!' she murmured, uneasy. 'And so lordly! Now I know why men are so overbearing! But he's lovely, really. Like another being! A bit terrifying! But lovely really! And he comes to me! —' She caught her lower lip between her teeth, in fear and excitement.

The man looked down in silence at the tense phallos, that did not change. — 'Ay!' he said at last, in a little voice. 'Ay ma lad! tha're theer right enough. Yi, tha mun rear thy head! Theer on thy own, eh? an' **ta'es no count o' nob'dy**[1]! **Tha ma'es nowt o' me, John Thomas**[2]. Art boss? of me? Eh well, tha're more cocky than me, an' tha says less. John Thomas! Dost want her? Dost want my lady Jane? **Tha's dipped me in again**[3], tha hast. Ay, an' tha comes up smilin'. — Ax 'er then! Ax lady Jane! Say: Lift up your heads, o ye gates, that the king of glory may come in. Ay, **th' cheek on thee**[4]! Cunt, that's what tha're after. Tell lady Jane tha wants cunt. John Thomas, an' th' cunt o' lady Jane! —'

'Oh, don't tease him,' said Connie, crawling on her knees on the bed towards him and putting her arms round his white slender loins, and drawing him to her so that her hanging, swinging breasts touched the tip of the stirring, erect phallos, and caught the drop of moisture. She held the man fast.

'Lie down!' he said. 'Lie down! Let me come!'

He was in a hurry now.

And afterwards, when they had been quite still, the woman had to uncover the man again, to look at the mystery of the phallos.

'And now he's tiny, and soft like a little bud of life!' she said, taking the soft small penis in her hand. 'Isn't he somehow lovely! so on his own, so strange! And so innocent! And he comes so far into me!

❶把谁都不放在眼里。 ❷你使我相形见绌，约翰·托马斯是梅乐士对自己阳具的谑称。 ❸你又使我在你里面充涨起来。 ❹(口)你真不害臊。

You must never insult him, you know. He's mine too. He's not only yours. He's mine! And so lovely and innocent!' And she held the penis soft in her hand.

He laughed.

'Blest be the tie that binds our hearts in kindred love,' he said.

'Of course!' she said. 'Even when he's soft and little I feel my heart simply tied to him. And how lovely your hair is here! quite, quite different!'

'That's John Thomas's hair, not mine!' he said.

'John Thomas! John Thomas!' and she quickly kissed the soft penis, that was beginning to stir again.

'Ay!' said the man, stretching his body almost painfully. 'He's got his root in my soul, has that gentleman! An' sometimes I don' know what ter do wi' him. Ay, he's got a will of his own, an' it's hard to suit him. Yet I wouldn't have him killed.'

'No wonder men have always been afraid of him!' she said. 'He's rather terrible.'

The quiver was going through the man's body, as the stream of consciousness again changed its direction, turning downwards. And he was helpless, as the penis in slow soft undulations filled and surged and rose up, and grew hard, standing there hard and overweening, in its curious towering fashion. The woman too trembled a little as she watched.

'There! Take him then! He's thine,' said the man.

And she quivered, and her own mind melted out. Sharp soft waves of unspeakable pleasure washed over her as he entered her, and started the curious molten thrilling that spread and spread till she was carried away with the last, blind flush of extremity.

He heard the distant hooters of Stacks Gate for seven o'clock. It was Monday morning. He shivered a little, and with his face between her breasts pressed her soft breasts up over his ears, to deafen him.

She had not even heard the hooters. She lay perfectly still, her soul washed transparent.

'You must get up, mustn't you?' he muttered.

'What time?' came her colourless voice.

'Seven-o'clock blowers a bit sin'.'

'I suppose I must.'

She was resenting as she always did, the compulsion from outside.

He sat up and looked blankly out of the window. 'You do love me, don't you?' she asked calmly. He looked down at her.

'Tha knows what tha knows. What dost ax for!' he said, a little fretfully.

'I want you to keep me, not to let me go,' she said.

His eyes seemed full of a warm, soft darkness that could not think.

'When? Now?'

'Now in your heart. Then I want to come and live with you, always, soon.'

He sat naked on the bed, with his head dropped, unable to think.

'Don't you want it?' she asked.

'Ay!' he said.

Then with the same eyes darkened with another flame of consciousness, almost like sleep, he looked at her.

'Dunna ax me nowt now,' he said. 'Let me be. I like thee. I luv thee when tha lies theer. A woman's a lovely thing when 'er's deep ter fuck, and cunt's good. Ah luv thee, thy legs, an' th' shape on thee, an' th' womanness on thee. Ah luv th' womanness on thee. Ah luv thee wi' my bas an' wi' my heart. But dunna ax me nowt. Dunna ma'e me say nowt. Let me stop as I am while I can. Tha can ax me iverything after. Now let me be, let me be!'

And softly, he laid his hand over her mound of Venus, on the soft brown maiden-hair, and himself-sat still and naked on the bed, his face motionless in physical abstraction, almost like the face of Buddha. Motionless, and in the invisible flame of another consciousness, he sat with his hand on her, and waited for the turn.

After a while, he reached for his shirt and put it on, dressed himself swiftly in silence, looked at her once as she still lay naked and faintly golden like **a Gloire de Dijon**[1] rose on the bed, and was gone. She heard him downstairs opening the door.

And still she lay musing, musing. It was very hard to go: to go out of his arms. He called from the foot of the stairs: 'Half past seven!' She sighed, and got out of bed. The bare little room! Nothing in it at all but the small chest of drawers and the smallish bed. But the board floor was

①生长在法国第戏的玫瑰花。

scrubbed clean. And in the corner by the window gable was a shelf with some books, and some from a circulating library. She looked. There were books about Bolshevist Russia, books of travel, a volume about the atom and the electron, another about the composition of the earth's core, and the causes of earthquakes: then a few novels: then three books on India. So! He was a reader after all.

The sun fell on her naked limbs through the gable window. Outside she saw the dog Flossie roaming round. The hazel-brake was misted with green, and dark-green dogs-mercury under. It was a clear clean morning with birds flying and triumphantly singing. If only she could stay! If only there weren't the other ghastly world of smoke and iron! If only he would make her a world.

She came downstairs, down the steep, narrow wooden stairs. Still she would be content with this little house, if only it were in a world of its own.

He was washed and fresh, and the fire was burning. 'Will you eat anything?' he said.

'No! Only lend me a comb.'

She followed him into the scullery, and combed her hair before the handbreadth of mirror by the back door. Then she was ready to go.

She stood in the little front garden, looking at the dewy flowers, the grey bed of pinks in bud already.

'I would like to have all the rest of the world disappear,' she said, 'and live with you here.'

'It won't disappear,' he said.

They went almost in silence through the lovely dewy wood. But they were together in a world of their own.

It was bitter to her to go on to Wragby.

'I want soon to come and live with you altogether,' she said as she left him.

He smiled, unanswering.

She got home quietly and unremarked, and went up to her room.

CHAPTER 15

There was a letter from Hilda on the breakfast-tray. 'Father is going to London this week, and I shall call for you on Thursday week, June 17th. You must be ready so that we can go at once. I don't want to waste time at Wragby, it's an awful place. I shall probably stay the night at Retford with the Colemans, so I should be with you for lunch, Thursday. Then we could start at teatime, and sleep perhaps in Grantham. It is no use our spending an evening with Clifford. If he hates your going, it would be no pleasure to him.'

So! She was being pushed round on the chess-board again.

Clifford hated her going, but it was only because he didn't feel safe in her absence. Her presence, for some reason, made him feel safe, and free to do the things he was occupied with. He was a great deal at the pits, and wrestling in spirit with the almost hopeless problems of getting out his coal in the most economical fashion and then selling it when he'd got it out. He knew he ought to find some way of using it, or converting it, so that he needn't sell it, or **needn't have the chagrin of failing to sell it**[1]. But if he made electric power, could he sell that or use it? And to convert into oil was as yet too costly and too elaborate. To keep industry alive there must be more industry, like a madness.

It was a madness, and it required a madman to succeed in it. Well, he was a little mad. Connie thought so. His very intensity and acumen in the affairs of the pits seemed like a manifestation of madness to her, his very inspirations were the inspirations of insanity.

He talked to her of all his serious schemes, and she listened in a kind of wonder, and let him talk. Then the flow ceased, and he turned on the loudspeaker, and became a blank, while apparently his schemes coiled on inside him like a kind of dream.

And every night now he played **pontoon, that game of the Tommies**[2], with Mrs Bolton, gambling with sixpences. And again, in

❶无须因没有销路而烦恼。 ❷英国兵们玩的那种潘东牌游，潘东在美国称21点。

the gambling he was gone in a kind of unconsciousness, or blank intoxication, or intoxication of blankness, whatever it was. Connie could not bear to see him. But when she had gone to bed, he and Mrs Bolton would gamble on till two and three in the morning, safely, and with strange lust. **Mrs Bolton was caught in the lust as much as Clifford**[1]: the more so, as she nearly always lost.

She told Connie one day: 'I lost twenty-three shillings to Sir Clifford last night.'

'And did he take the money from you?' asked Connie aghast.

'Why of course, my Lady! Debt of honour!'

Connie expostulated roundly, and was angry with both of them. The upshot was, Sir Clifford raised Mrs Bolton's wages a hundred a year, and she could gamble on that. Meanwhile, it seemed to Connie, Clifford was really going deader.

She told him at length she was leaving on the seventeenth.

'Seventeenth!' he said. 'And when will you be back?'

'By the twentieth of July at the latest.'

'Yes! the twentieth of July.'

Strangely and blankly he looked at her, with the vagueness of a child, but with the queer blank cunning of an old man.

'You won't let me down, now, will you?' he said.

'How?'

'While you're away, I mean, you're sure to come back?'

'I'm as sure as I can be of anything, that I shall come back.'

'Yes! Well! Twentieth of July!'

He looked at her so strangely.

Yet he really wanted her to go. That was so curious. He wanted her to go, positively, to have her little adventures and perhaps come home pregnant, and all that. At the same time, he was afraid of her going.

She was quivering, watching her real opportunity for leaving him altogether, waiting till the time, herself himself should be ripe.

She sat and talked to the keeper of her going abroad.

'And then when I come back,' she said, 'I can tell Clifford I must leave him. And you and I can go away. They never need even know it is you. We can go to another country, shall we? To Africa or Australia. Shall we?'

---

[1] 博尔顿太太和克利福德一样沉溺于情欲。

She was quite thrilled by her plan.

'You've never been to the Colonies, have you?' he asked her.

'No! Have you?'

'I've been in India, and South Africa, and Egypt.'

'Why shouldn't we go to South Africa?'

'We might!' he said slowly.

'Or don't you want to?' she asked.

'I don't care. I don't much care what I do.'

'Doesn't it make you happy? Why not? We shan't be poor. I have about six hundred a year, I wrote and asked. It's not much, but it's enough, isn't it?'

'It's riches to me.'

'Oh, how lovely it will be!'

'But I ought to get divorced, and so ought you, unless we're going to have complications.'

There was plenty to think about.

Another day she asked him about himself. They were in the hut, and there was a thunderstorm.

'And weren't you happy, when you were a lieutenant and an officer and a gentleman?'

'Happy? All right. I liked my Colonel.'

'Did you love him?'

'Yes! I loved him.'

'And did he love you?'

'Yes! In a way, he loved me.'

'Tell me about him.'

'What is there to tell? **He had risen from the ranks**[1]. He loved the army. And he had never married. He was twenty years older than me. He was a very intelligent man: and alone in the army, as such a man is: a passionate man in his way: and a very clever officer. **I lived under his spell**[2] while I was with him. I sort of let him run my life. And I never regret it.'

'And did you mind very much when he died?'

'I was as near death myself. But when I came to, I knew another part of me was finished. But then I had always known it would finish in death. All things do, as far as that goes.'

[1]他行伍出身。 [2]我被他迷住了。

She sat and ruminated. The thunder crashed outside. It was like being in **a little ark in the Flood**①.

'You seem to have such a lot behind you,' she said.

'Do I? It seems to me I've died once or twice already. Yet here I am, pegging on, and in for more trouble.'

She was thinking hard, yet listening to the storm.

'And weren't you happy as an officer and a gentleman, when your Colonel was dead?'

'No! They were a mingy lot.' He laughed suddenly. 'The Colonel used to say: Lad, the English middle classes have to chew every mouthful thirty times because their guts are so narrow, a bit as big as a pea would give them a stoppage. They're the mingiest set of ladylike snipe ever invented: full of conceit of themselves, frightened even if their boot-laces aren't correct, **rotten as high game, and always in the right**②. That's what finishes me up. Kow-tow, kow-tow, arse-licking till their tongues are tough: yet they're always in the right. Prigs on top of everything. Prigs! **A generation of ladylike prigs with half a ball each** —③'

Connie laughed. The rain was rushing down.

'He hated them!'

'No,' said he. 'He didn't bother. He just disliked them. There's a difference. Because, as he said, the Tommies are getting just as priggish and half-balled and narrow-gutted. It's the fate of mankind, to go that way.'

'The common people too, the working people?'

'All the lot. Their spunk is gone dead. Motor-cars and cinemas and aeroplanes suck that last bit out of them. I tell you, every generation breeds a more rabbity generation, with india rubber tubing for guts and tin legs and tin faces. Tin people! It's all a steady sort of bolshevism just killing off the human thing, and worshipping the mechanical thing. Money, money, money! **All the modern lot get their real kick out of killing the old human feeling out of man**④, making mincemeat of the old Adam and the old Eve. They're all alike. The world is all alike: kill off the human reality, a quid for every

①大洪水中的一叶方舟，Flood指基督教《圣经》中说的大洪水。②腐败透顶，自以为永远正确。③一代婆娘似的假道学先生。④所有的现代人都从扼杀人类的古老感情中取乐。to get kick out of... 从……中得到快乐。

foreskin, two quid for each pair of balls. What is cunt but machine-fucking! — It's all alike. Pay 'em money to cut off the world's cock. Pay money, money, money to them that will take spunk out of mankind, and leave 'em all little twiddling machines.'

He sat there in the hut, his face pulled to mocking irony. Yet even then, he had one ear set backwards, listening to the storm over the wood. It made him feel so alone.

'But won't it ever come to an end?' she said.

'Ay, it will. It'll achieve its own salvation. When the last real man is killed, and they're all tame: white, black, yellow, all colours of tame ones: then they'll all be insane. Because the root of sanity is in the balls. Then they'll all be insane, and they'll make their grand *auto da fe*. You know *auto da fe means act of faith*? Ay, well, they'll make their own grand little act of faith. **They'll offer one another up**[1].'

'You mean kill one another?'

'I do, duckie! If we go on at our present rate then in a hundred years' time there won't be ten thousand people in this island: there may not be ten. They'll have lovingly wiped each other out. The thunder was rolling further away.

'How nice! ' she said.

'Quite nice! To contemplate the extermination of the human species and the long pause that follows before some other species crops up, it calms you more than anything else. And if we go on in this way, with everybody, intellectuals, artists, government, industrialists and workers all frantically killing off the last human feeling, the last bit of their intuition, the last healthy instinct; if it goes on in algebraical progression, as it is going on: then ta-tah! to the human species! Goodbye! darling! the serpent swallows itself and leaves a void, considerably messed up, but not hopeless. Very nice! When savage wild dogs bark in Wragby, and savage wild pit-ponies stamp on Tevershall pit-bank! **te deum laudamus**[2]! '

Connie laughed, but not very happily.

'Then you ought to be pleased that they are all bolshevists,' she said. 'You ought to be pleased that they hurry on towards the end.'

'So I am. I don't stop 'em. Because I couldn't if I would.'

'Then why are you so bitter?'

[1]他们将相互把对方作为祭品。 [2](拉)赞美诗。

'I'm not! If my cock gives its last crow, I don't mind.'

'But if you have a child?' she said.

He dropped his head.

'Why,' he said at last. 'It seems to me a wrong and bitter thing to do, to bring a child into this world.'

'No! Don't say it! Don't say it!' she pleaded. 'I think I'm going to have one. Say you'll he pleased.' She laid her hand on his.

'I'm pleased for you to be pleased,' he said. 'But for me it seems a ghastly treachery to the unborn creature.

'Ah no!' she said, shocked. 'Then you can't ever really want me! You can't want me, if you feel that!'

Again he was silent, his face sullen. Outside there was only the threshing of the rain.

'It's not quite true!' she whispered. 'It's not quite true! There's another truth.' She felt he was bitter now partly because she was leaving him, deliberately going away to Venice. And this half pleased her.

She pulled open his clothing and uncovered his belly, and kissed his navel. Then she laid her cheek on his belly and pressed her arm round his warm, silent loins. They were alone in the flood.

'Tell me you want a child, in hope!' she murmured, pressing her face against his belly. 'Tell me you do!'

'Why!' he said at last: and she felt the curious quiver of changing consciousness and relaxation going through his body. 'Why I've thought sometimes if one but tried, here among th' colliers even! They're workin' bad now, an' not earnin' much. If a man could say to 'em: Dunna think o' nowt but th' money. When it comes ter wants, we want but little. Let's not live for money —'

She softly rubbed her cheek on his belly, and gathered his balls in her hand. The penis stirred softly, with strange life, but did not rise up. The rain beat bruisingly outside.

'Let's live for summat else. Let's not live ter make money, neither for us-selves nor for anybody else. Now we're forced to. We're forced to make a bit for us-selves, an' a fair lot for th' bosses. Let's stop it! Bit by bit, let's stop it. We needn't rant an' rave. Bit by bit, let's drop the whole industrial life an' go back. The least little bit o' money'll do. For everybody, me an' you, bosses an' masters, even th' king. The least little bit o' money'll really do. Just make up your mind to it, an' you've got out o' th' mess.' He paused, then went on:

'An' I'd tell 'em: Look! Look at Joe! He moves lovely! Look how he moves, alive and aware. He's beautiful! An' look at Jonah! He's clumsy, he's ugly, because he's niver willin' to rouse himself. I'd tell 'em: Look! look at yourselves! one shoulder higher than t'other, legs twisted, feet all lumps! What have yer done ter yerselves, wi' the blasted work? Spoilt yerselves. No need to work that much. Take yer clothes off an' look at yourselves. Yer ought ter be alive an' beautiful, an' yer ugly an' half dead. So I'd tell 'em. An' I'd get my men to wear different clothes: appen close red trousers, bright red, an' little short white jackets. Why, if men had red, fine legs, that alone would change them in a month. They'd begin to be men again, to be men! An' the women could dress as they liked. Because if once the men walked with legs close bright scarlet, and buttocks nice and showing scarlet under a little white jacket: then the women 'ud begin to be women. It's because th' men aren't men, that th' women have to be. — An' in time pull down Tevershall and build a few beautiful buildings, that would hold us all. An' clean the country up again. An' not have many children, because the world is overcrowded.

'But I wouldn't preach to the men: only strip 'em an' say: Look at yourselves! That's workin' for money! — Hark at yourselves! That's working for money. You've been working for money! Look at Tevershall! It's horrible. That's because it was built while you was working for money. Look at your girls! They don't care about you, you don't care about them. It's because you've spent your time working an' caring for money. You can't talk nor move nor live, you can't properly be with a woman. You're not alive. Look at yourselves!'

There fell a complete silence. Connie was half listening, and threading in the hair at the root of his belly a few forget-me-nots that she had gathered on the way to the hut. Outside, the world had gone still, and a little icy.

'You've got four kinds of hair,' she said to him. 'On your chest it's nearly black, and your hair isn't dark on your head: but your moustache is hard and dark red, and your hair here, your love-hair, is like a little brush of bright red-gold mistletoe. It's the loveliest of all!'

He looked down and saw the milky bits of forget-me-nots in the hair on his groin.

'Ay! That's where to put forget-me-nots, in the man-hair, or the maiden-hair. But don't you care about the future?'

She looked up at him.

'Oh, I do, terribly!' she said.

'Because when I feel the human world is doomed, has doomed itself by its own mingy beastliness, then I feel the Colonies aren't far enough. The moon wouldn't be far enough, because even there you could look back and see the earth, dirty, beastly, unsavoury among all the stars: made foul by men. Then I feel I've swallowed gall, and it's eating my inside out, and nowhere's far enough away to get away. But when I get a turn, I forget it all again. Though it's a shame, what's been done to people these last hundred years: men turned into nothing but labour-insects, and all their manhood taken away, and all their real life. I'd wipe the machines off the face of the earth again, and end the industrial epoch absolutely, like a black mistake. But since I can't, an' nobody can, I'd better hold my peace, an' try an' live my own life: if I've got one to live, which I rather doubt.'

The thunder had ceased outside, but the rain which had abated, suddenly came striking down, with a last blench of lightning and mutter of departing storm. Connie was uneasy. He had talked so long now, and he was really talking to himself not to her. Despair seemed to come down on him completely, and she was feeling happy, she hated despair. She knew her leaving him, which he had only just realized inside himself had plunged him back into this mood. And she triumphed a little.

She opened the door and looked at the straight heavy rain, like a steel curtain, and had a sudden desire to rush out into it, to rush away. She got up, and began swiftly pulling off her stockings, then her dress and underclothing, and he held his breath. Her pointed keen animal breasts tipped and stirred as she moved. She was ivory-coloured in the greenish light. She slipped on her rubber shoes again and ran out with a wild little laugh, holding up her breasts to the heavy rain and spreading her arms, and running blurred in the rain with the eurhythmic dance movements she had learned so long ago in Dresden. It was a strange pallid figure lifting and falling, bending so the rain beat and glistened on the full haunches, swaying up again and coming belly-forward through the rain, then stooping again so that only the full loins and buttocks were offered in a kind of homage towards him, repeating a wild obeisance.

He laughed wryly, and threw off his clothes. It was too much. He jumped out, naked and white, with a little shiver, into the hard slanting rain. Flossie sprang before him with a frantic little bark. Connie, her hair all wet and sticking to her head, turned her hot face and saw him. Her blue eyes blazed with excitement as she turned and ran fast, with a strange charging movement, out of the clearing and down the path, the wet boughs whipping her. She ran, and he saw nothing but the round wet head, the wet back leaning forward in flight, the rounded buttocks twinkling: a wonderful cowering female nakedness in flight.

She was nearly at the wide riding when he came up and flung his naked arm round her soft, naked-wet middle. She gave a shriek and straightened herself and the heap of her soft, chill flesh came up against his body. He pressed it all up against him, madly, the heap of soft, chilled female flesh that became quickly warm as flame, in contact. The rain streamed on them till they smoked. He gathered her lovely, heavy posteriors one in each hand and pressed them in towards him in a frenzy, quivering motionless in the rain. Then suddenly he tipped her up and fell with her on the path, in the roaring silence of the rain, and short and sharp, he took her, short and sharp and finished, like an animal.

He got up in an instant, wiping the rain from his eyes.

'Come in,' he said, and they started running back to the hut. He ran straight and swift: he didn't like the rain. But she came slower, gathering forget-me-nots and campion and bluebells, running a few steps and watching him fleeing away from her.

When she came with her flowers, panting to the hut, he had already started a fire, and the twigs were crackling. Her sharp breasts rose and fell, her hair was plastered down with rain, her face was flushed ruddy and her body glistened and trickled. Wide-eyed and breathless, with a small wet head and full, trickling, naive haunches, she looked another creature.

He took the old sheet and rubbed her down, she standing like a child. Then he rubbed himself having shut the door of the hut. The fire was blazing up. She ducked her head in the other end of the sheet, and rubbed her wet hair.

'We're drying ourselves together on the same towel, we shall quarrel!' he said.

She looked up for a moment, her hair all odds and ends.

'No!' she said, her eyes wide. 'It's not a towel, it's a sheet.' And she went on busily rubbing her head, while he busily rubbed his.

Still panting with their exertions, each wrapped in an army blanket, but the front of the body open to the fire, they sat on a log side by side before the blaze, to get quiet. Connie hated the feel of the blanket against her skin. But now the sheet was all wet.

She dropped her blanket and kneeled on the clay hearth, holding her head to the fire, and shaking her hair to dry it. He watched the beautiful curving drop of her haunches. That fascinated him today. How it sloped with a rich down-slope to the heavy roundness of her buttocks! And in between, folded in the secret warmth, the secret entrances!

He stroked her tail with his hand, long and subtly taking in the curves and the globe-fullness.

'Tha's got such a nice tail on thee,' he said, in the throaty caressive dialect. 'Tha's got the nicest arse of anybody. It's the nicest, nicest woman's arse as is! An' ivery bit of it is woman, woman sure as nuts. Tha'rt not one o' them button-arsed lasses as should be lads, are ter! Tha's got a real soft sloping bottom on thee, as a man loves in 'is guts. It's a bottom as could hold the world up, it is!'

All the while he spoke he exquisitely stroked the rounded tail, till it seemed as if a slippery sort of fire came from it into his hands. And his finger-tips touched the two secret openings to her body, time after time, with a soft little brush of fire.

'An' if tha shits an' if tha pisses, I'm glad. I don't want a woman as couldna shit nor piss.'

Connie could not help a sudden snort of astonished laughter, but he went on unmoved.

'Tha'rt real, tha art! Tha'art real, even a bit of a bitch. Here tha shits an' here tha pisses: an' I lay my hand on 'em both an' like thee for it. I like thee for it. Tha's got a proper, woman's arse, proud of itself. It's none ashamed of itself this isna.'

He laid his hand close and firm over her secret places, in a kind of close greeting.

'I like it,' he said. 'I like it! An' if I only lived ten minutes, an' stroked thy arse an' got to know it, I should reckon I'd lived one life, see ter! Industrial system or not! Here's one o' my lifetimes.'

She turned round and climbed into his lap, clinging to him. 'Kiss me!' she whispered.

And she knew the thought of their separation was latent in both their minds, and at last she was sad.

She sat on his thighs, her head against his breast, and her ivory-gleaming legs loosely apart, the fire glowing unequally upon them. Sitting with his head dropped, he looked at the folds of her body in the fire-glow, and at the fleece of soft brown hair that hung down to a point between her open thighs. He reached to the table behind, and took up her bunch of flowers, still so wet that drops of rain fell on to her.

'Flowers stops out of doors all weathers,' he said. 'They have no houses.'

'Not even a hut!' she murmured.

With quiet fingers he threaded a few forget-me-not flowers in the fine brown fleece of the mount of Venus.

'There!' he said. 'There's forget-me-nots in the right place!'

She looked down at the milky odd little flowers among the brown maiden-hair at the lower tip of her body.

'Doesn't it look pretty!' she said.

'Pretty as life,' he replied.

And he stuck a pink campion-bud among the hair.

'There! That's me where you won't forget me! **That's Moses in the bull-rushes**[1].'

'You don't mind, do you, that I'm going away?' she asked wistfully, looking up into his face.

But his face was inscrutable, under the heavy brows. He kept it quite blank.

'You do as you wish,' he said.

And he spoke in good English.

'But I won't go if you don't wish it,' she said, clinging to him.

There was silence. He leaned and put another piece of wood on the fire. The flame glowed on his silent, abstracted face. She waited, but he said nothing.

'Only I thought it would be a good way to begin a break with Clifford. I do want a child. And it would give me a chance to, to — ,' she resumed.

'To let them think a few lies,' he said.

'Yes, that among other things. Do you want them to think the truth?'

---

[1] 那就是放在大灯芯草丛中的摩西，摩西是《圣经》中记载的犹太民族的伟大先知，摩西出生后，为防止被埃及王杀害，其父母将其藏于一蒲草箱内，后为法老之女发现并收养。

'I don't care what they think.'

'I do! I don't want them handling me with their unpleasant cold minds, not while I'm still at Wragby. They can think what they like when I'm finally gone.'

He was silent.

'But Sir Clifford expects you to come back to him?'

'Oh, I must come back,' she said: and there was silence.

'And would you have a child in Wragby?' he asked.

She closed her arm round his neck.

'If you wouldn't take me away, I should have to,' she said.

'Take you where to?'

'Anywhere! away! But right away from Wragby.'

'When?'

'Why, when I come back.'

'But what's the good of coming back, doing the thing twice, if you're once gone?' he said.

'Oh, I must come back. I've promised! I've promised so faithfully. Besides, I come back to you, really.'

'To your husband's game-keeper?'

'I don't see that that matters,' she said.

'No?' He mused a while. 'And when would you think of going away again, then; finally? When exactly?'

'Oh, I don't know. I'd come back from Venice. And then we'd prepare everything.'

'How prepare?'

'Oh, I'd tell Clifford. I'd have to tell him.'

'Would you!'

He remained silent. She put her arms round his neck.

'Don't make it difficult for me,' she pleaded.

'Make what difficult?'

'For me to go to Venice and arrange things.'

A little smile, half a grin, flickered on his face.

'I don't make it difficult,' he said. 'I only want to find out just what you are after. But you don't really know yourself. You want to take time: get away and look at it. I don't blame you. I think you're wise. You may prefer to stay mistress of Wragby. I don't blame you. I've no Wragbys to offer. In fact, you know what you'll get out of me. No, no,

I think you're right! I really do! And I'm not keen on coming to live on you, being kept by you. There's that too.'

She felt somehow as if **he were giving her tit for tat**[1].

'But you want me, don't you?' she asked.

'Do you want me?'

'You know I do. That's evident.'

'Quite! And when do you want me?'

'You know we can arrange it all when I come back. Now I'm out of breath with you. I must get calm and clear.'

'Quite! Get calm and clear!'

She was a little offended.

'But you trust me, don't you?' she said.

'Oh, absolutely!'

She heard the mockery in his tone.

'Tell me then,' she said flatly; 'do you think it would be better if I don't go to Venice?'

'I'm sure it's better if you do go to Venice,' he replied in the cool, slightly mocking voice.

'You know it's next Thursday?' she said.

'Yes!'

She now began to muse. At last she said:

'And we shall know better where we are when I come back, shan't we?'

'Oh surely!'

The curious gulf of silence between them!

'I've been to the lawyer about my divorce,' he said, a little constrainedly.

She gave a slight shudder.

'Have you!' she said. 'And what did he say?'

'He said I ought to have done it before; that may be a difficulty. But since I was in the army, he thinks it will go through all right. **If only it doesn't bring her down on my head**[2]!'

'Will she have to know?'

'Yes! **she is served with a notice**[3]: so is the man she lives with, the co-respondent.'

'Isn't it hateful, all the performances! I suppose I'd have to go

[1]他的话和她针锋相对。[2]但愿别因离婚又让她和你纠缠上。[3]她将收到一些传票。

through it with Clifford.'

There was a silence.

'And of course,' he said, 'I have to live an exemplary life for the next six or eight months. So if you go to Venice, there's temptation removed for a week or two, at least.'

'Am I temptation!' she said, stroking his face. 'I'm so glad I'm temptation to you! Don't let's think about it! You frighten me when you start thinking: you roll me out flat. Don't let's think about it. We can think so much when we are apart. That's the whole point! I've been thinking, I must come to you for another night before I go. I must come once more to the cottage. Shall I come on Thursday night?'

'Isn't that when your sister will be there?'

'Yes! But she said we would start at tea-time. So we could start at tea-time. But she could sleep somewhere else and I could sleep with you.

'But then she'd have to know.'

'Oh, I shall tell her. I've more or less told her already. I must talk it all over with Hilda. She's a great help, so sensible.'

He was thinking of her plan.

'So you'd start off from Wragby at tea-time, as if you were going to London? Which way were you going?'

'By Nottingham and Grantham.'

'And then your sister would drop you somewhere and you'd walk or drive back here? Sounds very risky, to me.'

'Does it? Well, then, Hilda could bring me back. She could sleep at Mansfield, and bring me back here in the evening, and fetch me again in the morning. It's quite easy.'

'And the people who see you?'

'I'll wear goggles and a veil.'

He pondered for some time.

'Well,' he said. 'You please yourself as usual.'

'But wouldn't it please you?'

'Oh yes! It'd please me all right,' he said a little grimly. '**I might as well smite while the iron's hot**[1].'

'Do you know what I thought?' she said suddenly. 'It suddenly came to me. You are the "**Knight of the Burning Pestle**[2]"!'

❶我也不妨趁热打铁。 ❷"骑士的燃烧杵"是法国作家博蒙特·弗朗西斯写的一部讽刺剧中的人物，该剧类似于《堂·吉诃德》。

'Ay! And you? Are you the Lady of the Red-Hot Mortar?'

'Yes!' she said. 'Yes! You're Sir Pestle and I'm Lady Mortar.'

'All right, then I'm knighted. John Thomas is Sir John, to your Lady Jane.'

'Yes! John Thomas is knighted! I'm my-lady-maiden-hair, and you must have flowers too. Yes!'

She threaded two pink campions in the bush of red-gold hair above his penis.

'There!' she said. 'Charming! Charming! Sir John!'

And she pushed a bit of forget-me-not in the dark hair of his breast.

'And you won't forget me there, will you?' She kissed him on the breast, and made two bits of forget-me-not lodge one over each nipple, kissing him again.

'**Make a calendar of me**[1]!' he said. He laughed, and the flowers shook from his breast.

'Wait a bit!' he said.

He rose, and opened the door of the hut. Flossie, lying in the porch, got up and looked at him.

'Ay, it's me!' he said.

The rain had ceased. There was a wet, heavy, perfumed stillness. Evening was approaching.

He went out and down the little path in the opposite direction from the riding. Connie watched his thin, white figure, and it looked to her like a ghost, an apparition moving away from her.

When she could see it no more, her heart sank. She stood in the door of the hut, with a blanket round her, looking into the drenched, motionless silence.

But he was coming back, trotting strangely, and carrying flowers. She was a little afraid of him, as if he were not quite human. And when he came near, his eyes looked into hers, but she could not understand the meaning.

He had brought columbines and campions, and new-mown hay, and oak-tufts and honeysuckle in small bud. He fastened fluffy young oak-sprays round her breasts, sticking in tufts of bluebells and campion: and in her navel he poised a pink campion flower, and in her maiden-hair were forget-me-nots and woodruff.

[1] 就当我是你的日历吧。

'That's you in all your glory!' he said. 'Lady Jane, at her wedding with John Thomas.'

And he stuck flowers in the hair of his own body, and wound a bit of creeping-jenny round his penis, and stuck a single bell of a hyacinth in his navel. She watched him with amusement, his odd intentness. And she pushed a campion flower in his moustache, where it stuck, dangling under his nose.

'This is John Thomas marryin' Lady Jane,' he said. 'An' we mun let Constance an' Oliver go their ways. Maybe —'

He spread out his hand with a gesture, and then he sneezed, sneezing away the flowers from his nose and his navel. He sneezed again.

'Maybe what?' she said, waiting for him to go on.

He looked at her a little bewildered.

'Eh?' he said.

'Maybe what? Go on with what you were going to say,' she insisted.

'Ay, what was I going to say?'

He had forgotten. And it was one of the disappointments of her life, that he never finished.

A yellow ray of sun shone over the trees.

'Sun!' he said. 'And time you went. Time, my Lady, time! What's that as flies without wings, your Ladyship? Time! Time!'

He reached for his shirt.

'Say goodnight! to John Thomas,' he said, looking down at his penis. 'He's safe in the arms of creeping Jenny! Not much burning pestle about him just now.'

And he put his flannel shirt over his head.

'A man's most dangerous moment,' he said, when his head had emerged, 'is when he's getting into his shirt. Then he puts his head in a bag. That's why I prefer those American shirts, that you put on like a jacket.' She still stood watching him. He stepped into his short drawers, and buttoned them round the waist.

'Look at Jane!' he said. 'In all her blossoms! Who'll put blossoms on you next year, Jinny? Me, or somebody else? "Good-bye, my bluebell, farewell to you!" I hate that song, it's early war days.' He then sat down, and was pulling on his stockings. She still stood unmoving.

He laid his hand on the slope of her buttocks. 'Pretty little Lady Jane!' he said. 'Perhaps in Venice you'll find a man who'll put jasmine in your maiden-hair, and a pomegranate flower in your navel. Poor little lady Jane!'

'Don't say those things!' she said. 'You only say them to hurt me.'

He dropped his head. Then he said, in dialect:

'Ay, maybe I do, maybe I do! Well then, I'll say nowt, an' ha' done wi't. But tha mun dress thysen, all' go back to thy stately homes of England, how beautiful they stand. Time's up! Time's up for Sir John, an' for little Lady Jane! Put thy shimmy on, Lady Chatterley! Tha might be anybody, standin' there be-out even a shimmy, an' a few rags o' flowers. There then, there then, I'll undress thee, tha bob-tailed young throstle.' And he took the leaves from her hair, kissing her damp hair, and the flowers from her breasts, and kissed her breasts, and kissed her navel, and kissed her maiden-hair, where he left the flowers threaded. 'They mun stop while they will,' he said. 'So! There tha'rt bare again, nowt but a bare-arsed lass an' a bit of a Lady Jane! Now put thy shimmy on, for tha mun go, or else Lady Chatterley's goin' to be late for dinner, an' where 'ave yer been to my pretty maid!'

She never knew how to answer him when he was in this condition of the vernacular. So she dressed herself and prepared to go a little ignominiously home to Wragby. Or so she felt it: a little ignominiously home.

He would accompany her to the broad riding. His young pheasants were all right under the shelter.

When he and she came out on to the riding, there was Mrs Bolton faltering palely towards them.

'Oh, my Lady, we wondered if anything had happened!'

'No! Nothing has happened.'

Mrs Bolton looked into the man's face, that was smooth and new-looking with love. She met his half-laughing, half-mocking eyes. He always laughed at mischance. But he looked at her kindly.

'Evening, Mrs Bolton! Your Ladyship will be all right now, so I can leave you. Good-night to your Ladyship! Good-night, Mrs Bolton!'

He saluted and turned away.

CHAPTER 16

Connie arrived home to an ordeal of cross-questioning. Clifford had been out at tea-time, had come in just before the storm, and where was her ladyship? Nobody knew, only Mrs Bolton suggested she had gone for a walk into the wood. Into the wood, in such a storm! Clifford for once let himself get into a state of nervous frenzy. He started at every flash of lightning, and blenched at every roll of thunder. He looked at the icy thunder-rain as if it dare the end of the world. He got more and more worked up.

Mrs Bolton tried to soothe him.

'She'll be sheltering in the hut, till it's over. Don't worry, her Ladyship is all right.'

'I don't like her being in the wood in a storm like this! I don't like her being in the wood at all! She's been gone now more than two hours. When did she go out?'

'A little while before you came in.'

'I didn't see her in the park. God knows where she is and what has happened to her.'

'Oh, nothing's happened to her. You'll see, she'll be home directly after the rain stops. It's just the rain that's keeping her.'

But her ladyship did not come home directly the rain stopped. In fact time went by, the sun came out for his last yellow glimpse, and there still was no sign of her. The sun was set, it was growing dark, and the first dinner-gong had rung.

'It's no good!' said Clifford in a frenzy. 'I'm going to send out Field and Betts to find her.'

'Oh don't do that!' cried Mrs Bolton. 'They'll think there's a suicide or something. Oh don't start a lot of talk going. Let me slip over to the hut and see if she's not there. I'll find her all right.'

So, after some persuasion, Clifford allowed her to go.

And so Connie had come upon her in the drive, alone and palely loitering.

'You mustn't mind me coming to look for you, my Lady! But Sir Clifford worked himself up into such a state. He made sure you were struck by lightning, or killed by a falling tree. And he was determined to send Field and Betts to the wood to find the body. So I thought I'd better come, rather than set all the servants agog.

She spoke nervously. She could still see on Connie's face the smoothness and the half-dream of passion, and she could feel the irritation against herself.

'Quite! ' said Connie. And she could say no more.

The two women plodded on through the wet world, in silence, while great drops splashed like explosions in the wood. When they came to the park, Connie strode ahead, and Mrs Bolton panted a little. She was getting plumper.

'How foolish of Clifford to make a fuss! ' said Connie at length, angrily, really speaking to herself.

'Oh, you know what men are! They like working themselves up. But he'll be all right as soon as he sees your Ladyship.'

Connie was very angry that Mrs Bolton knew her secret: for certainly she knew it.

Suddenly Constance stood still on the path.

'It's monstrous that I should have to be followed! ' she said, her eyes flashing.

'Oh! your Ladyship, don't say that! He'd certainly have sent the two men, and they'd have come straight to the hut. I didn't know where it was, really.'

Connie flushed darker with rage, at the suggestion. Yet, while her passion was on her, she could not lie. She could not even pretend there was nothing between herself and the keeper. She looked at the other woman, who stood so sly, with her head dropped: yet somehow, in her femaleness, an ally.

'Oh well! ' she said. 'If it is so it is so. I don't mind! '

'Why, you're all right, my Lady! You've only been sheltering in the hut. It's absolutely nothing.'

They went on to the house. Connie marched in to Clifford's room, furious with him, furious with his pale, over-wrought face and prominent eyes.

'I must say, I don't think you need send the servants after me,' she burst out.

'My God! ' he exploded. 'Where have you been, woman, You've been gone hours, hours, and in a storm like this! What the hell do you go to that-bloody wood for? What have you been up to? It's hours even since the rain stopped, hours! Do you know what time it is? You're enough to drive anybody mad. Where have you been? What in the name of hell have you been doing?'

'And what if I don't choose to tell you?' She pulled her hat from her head and shook her hair.

He lied at her with his eyes bulging, and yellow coming into the whites. It was very bad for him to get into these rages: Mrs Bolton had a weary time with him, for days after. Connie felt a sudden qualm.

But really!' she said, milder. 'Anyone would think I'd been I don't know where! I just sat in the hut during all the storm, and made myself a little fire, and was happy.'

She spoke now easily. After all, why work him up any more!

He looked at her suspiciously.

And look at your hair! ' he said; 'look at yourself! '

'Yes! ' she replied calmly. 'I ran out in the rain with no clothes on.'

He stared at her speechless.

'You must be mad! ' he said.

'Why? To like a shower bath from the rain?'

'And how did you dry yourself?'

'On an old towel and at the fire.'

He still stared at her in a dumbfounded way.

'And supposing anybody came,' he said.

'Who would come?'

'Who? Why, anybody! And Mellors. Does he come? He must come in the evenings.'

'Yes, he came later, when it had cleared up, to feed the pheasants with corn.'

She spoke with amazing nonchalance. Mrs Bolton, who was listening in the next room, heard in sheer admiration. **To think a woman could carry it off so naturally**[1]!

'And suppose he'd come while you were running about in the rain with nothing on, like a maniac?'

'I suppose **he'd have had the fright of his life, and cleared out as fast as he could**[2].'

Clifford still stared at her transfixed. What he thought in his under-

[1]设想一个女人应对得竟如此自然。[2]他会吓得失魂落魄，拔腿逃命。

consciousness he would never know. And he was too much taken aback to form one clear thought in his upper consciousness. He just simply accepted what she said, in a sort of blank. And he admired her. He could not help admiring her. She looked so flushed and handsome and smooth: love smooth.

'At least,' he said, subsiding, 'you'll be lucky if you've got off without a severe cold.'

'Oh, I haven't got a cold,' she replied. She was thinking to herself of the other man's words: Tha's got the nicest woman's arse of anybody! She wished, she dearly wished she could tell Clifford that this had been said her, during the famous thunderstorm. However! **She bore herself rather like an offended queen**[1], and went upstairs to change.

That evening, Clifford wanted to be nice to her. He was reading one of the latest scientific-religious books: **he had a streak of a spurious sort of religion in him**[2], and was egocentrically concerned with the future of his own ego. It was like his habit to make conversation to Connie about some book, since the conversation between them had to be made, almost chemically. They had almost chemically to concoct it in their heads.

'What do you think of this, by the way?' he said, reaching for his book. 'You'd have no need to cool your ardent body by running out in the rain, if only we have a few more aeons of evolution behind us. Ah, here it is! — "The universe shows us two aspects: on one side it is physically wasting, on the other it is spiritually ascending."'

Connie listened, expecting more. But Clifford was waiting. She looked at him in surprise.

'And if it spiritually ascends,' she said, 'what does it leave down below, in the place where its tail used to be?'

'Ah!' he said. **'Take the man for what he means. Ascending is the opposite of his wasting**[3], I presume.'

'Spiritually blown out, so to speak!'

'No, but seriously, without joking: do you think there is anything in it?'

She looked at him again.

❶她摆出了颇似被冒犯了的王后的样子。 ❷他身上具有一丝似是而非的宗教气质。 ❸从作者的意思来看,"上升"即是"浪费"的反义。

'Physically wasting?' she said. 'I see you getting fatter, and I'm not wasting myself. Do you think the sun is smaller than he used to be? He's not to me. And I suppose the apple Adam offered Eve wasn't really much bigger, if any, than one of our orange pippins. Do you think it was?'

'Well, hear how he goes on: "It is thus slowly passing, with a slowness inconceivable in our measures of time, to new creative conditions, amid which the physical world, as we at present know it, **will be represented by a ripple barely to be disting uished from nonentity**❶."'

She listened with a glisten of amusement. All sorts of improper things suggested themselves. But she only said:

'What silly hocus-pocus! As if his little conceited consciousness could know what was happening as slowly as all that! It only means he's a physical failure on the earth, so he wants to make the whole universe a physical failure. Priggish little impertinence!'

'Oh, but listen! Don't interrupt the great man's solemn words! — "The present type of order in the world has risen from an unimaginable part, and will find its grave in an unimaginable future. **There remains the inexhaustive realm of abstract forms, and creativity with its shifting character ever determined afresh by its own creatures**❷, and God, upon whose wisdom all forms of order depend." — There, that's how he winds up!'

Connie sat listening contemptuously.

'He's spiritually blown out,' she said. 'What a lot of stuff! Unimaginables, and types of order in graves, and realms of abstract forms, and creativity with a shifty character, and God mixed up with forms of order! Why, it's idiotic!'

'I must say, it is a little vaguely conglomerate, a mixture of gases, so to speak,' said Clifford. 'Still, I think there is something in the idea that the universe is physically wasting and spiritually ascending.'

'Do you? Then let it ascend, so long as it leaves me safely and solidly physically here below.'

'Do you like your physique?' he asked.

'I love it!' And through her mind went the words: It's the nicest,

❶(物质世界)将被一个与虚无几乎没有什么区别的涟漪所取代。❷尚存的是耗之不尽的抽象王国以及自我更新,变化无穷的创造力。

nicest woman's arse as is!

'But that is really rather extraordinary, because there's no denying it's an encumbrance. But then I suppose a woman doesn't take a supreme pleasure in the life of the mind.'

'Supreme pleasure?' she said, looking up at him. 'Is that sort of idiocy the supreme pleasure of the life of the mind? No thank you! Give me the body. I believe the life of the body is a greater reality than the life of the mind: when the body is really wakened to life. But so many people, like your famous wind-machine, have only got minds tacked on to their physical corpses.'

He looked at her in wonder.

'The life of the body,' he said, 'is just the life of the animals.'

'And that's better than the life of professional corpses. But it's not true! the human body is only just coming to real life. With the Greeks it gave a lovely flicker, then Plato and Aristotle killed it, and Jesus finished it off. But now the body is coming really to life, it is really rising from the tomb. And It will be a lovely, lovely life in the lovely universe, the life of the human body.'

'My dear, you speak as if you were ushering it all in! True, you am going away on a holiday: but don't please be quite so indecently elated about it. Believe me, whatever God there is is slowly eliminating the guts and alimentary system from the human being, to evolve a higher, more spiritual being.'

'Why should I believe you, Clifford, when I feel that whatever God there is has at last wakened up in my guts, as you call them, and is rippling so happily there, like dawn. Why should I believe you, when I feel so very much the contrary?'

'Oh, exactly! And what has caused this extraordinary change in you? Running out stark naked in the rain, and playing Bacchante? Desire for sensation, or the anticipation of going to Venice?'

'Both! Do you think it is horrid of me to be so thrilled at going off?' she said.

'Rather horrid to show it so plainly.'

'Then I'll hide it.'

'Oh, don't trouble! You almost communicate a thrill to me. I almost feel that it is I who am going off.'

'Well, why don't you come?'

'We've gone over all that. And as a matter of fact, I suppose your greatest thrill comes from being able to say a temporary farewell to all this. Nothing so thrilling, for the moment, as Good-bye-to-all! — But every parting means a meeting elsewhere. And every meeting is a new bondage.'

'I'm not going to enter any new bondages.'

'Don't boast, while the gods are listening,' he said.

She pulled up short[1].

'No! I won't boast!' she said.

But she was thrilled, none the less, to be going off: to feel bonds snap. She couldn't help it.

Clifford, who couldn't sleep, gambled all night with Mrs Bolton, till she was too sleepy almost to live.

And the day came round for Hilda to arrive. Connie had arranged with Mellors that if everything promised well for their night together, she would hang a green shawl out of the window. If there were frustration, a red one.

Mrs Bolton helped Connie to pack.

'It will be so good for your Ladyship to have a change.'

'I think it will. You don't mind having Sir Clifford on your hands alone for a time, do you?'

'Oh no! I can manage him quite all right. I mean, I can do all he needs me to do. Don't you think he's better than he used to be?'

'Oh much! You do wonders with him.'

'Do I though! But men are all alike: just babies, and you have to flatter them and wheedle them and let them think they're having their own way. Don't you find it so, my Lady?'

'I'm afraid I haven't much experience.'

Connie paused in her occupation.

'Even your husband, did you have to manage him, and wheedle him like a baby?' she asked, looking at the other woman.

Mrs Bolton paused too.

'Well!' she said. 'I had to do a good bit of coaxing, with him too. But he always knew what I was after, I must say that. But he generally gave in to me.'

'He was never the lord and master thing?'

'No! At least there'd be a look in his eyes sometimes, and then I

[1] 她突然停了下来。

knew I'd got to give in. But usually he gave in to me. No, he was never lord and master. But neither was I. I knew when I could go no further with him, and then I gave in: though it cost me a good bit, sometimes.'

'And what if you had held out against him?'

'Oh, I don't know, I never did. Even when he was in the wrong, if he was fixed, I gave in. You see, I never wanted to break what was between us. And if you really set your will against a man, that finishes it. If you care for a man, you have to give in to him once he's really determined; whether you're in the right or not, you have to give in. Else you break something. But I must say, Ted 'ud give in to me sometimes, when I was set on a thing, and in the wrong. So I suppose it cuts both ways.'

'And that's how you are with all your patients?' asked Connie.

'Oh, That's different. I don't care at all, in the same way. I know what's good for them, or I try to, and then I just contrive to manage them for their own good. It's not like anybody as you're really fond of. It's quite different. Once you've been really fond of a man, you can be affectionate to almost any man, if he needs you at all. But it's not the same thing. You don't really care. I doubt, once you've really cared, if you can ever really care again.'

These words frightened Connie.

'Do you think one can only care once?' she asked.

'Or never. Most women never care, never begin to. They don't know what it means. Nor men either. But **when I see a woman as cares**[1], my heart stands still for her.'

'And do you think men easily take offence?'

'Yes! If you wound them on their pride. But aren't women the same? Only our two prides are a bit different.'

Connie pondered this. She began again to have some misgiving about her gag away. After all, was she not giving her man the go-by, if only for a short time? And he knew it. That's why he was so queer and sarcastic.

Still! the human existence is a good deal controlled by the machine of external circumstance. She was in the power of this machine. She couldn't extricate herself all in five minutes. She didn't even want to.

Hilda arrive d in good time on Thursday morning, in a nimble

[1]当我看见一个女人在恋爱时。

two-seater car, with her suit-case strapped firmly behind. She looked as demure and maidenly as ever, but she had the same will of her own. **She had the very hell of a will of her own**❶, as her husband had found out. But the husband was now divorcing her.

Yes, she even made it easy for him to do that, though she had no lover. For the time being, she was 'off' men. She was very well content to be quite her own mistress: and mistress of her two children, whom she was going to bring up 'properly', whatever that may mean.

Connie was only allowed a suit-case, also. But she had sent on a trunk to her father, who was going by train. No use taking a car to Venice. And Italy much too hot to motor in, in July. He was going comfortably by train. He had just come down from Scotland.

So, **like a demure arcadian field-marshal**❷, Hilda arranged the material part of the journey. She and Connie sat in the upstairs room, chatting.

'But Hilda!' said Connie, a little frightened. 'I want to stay near here tonight. Not here: near here!'

Hilda fixed her sister with grey, inscrutable eyes. She seemed so calm: and she was so often furious.

'Where, near here?' she asked softly.

'Well, you know I love somebody, don't you?'

'I gathered there was something.'

'Well he lives near here, and I want to spend this last night with him. Imust! I've promised.'

Connie became insistent.

Hilda bent her Minerva-like head in silence❸. Then she looked up.

'Do you want to tell me who he is?' she said.

'He's our game-keeper,' faltered Connie, and she flushed vividly, like a shamed child.

'Connie!' said Hilda, lifting her nose slightly with disgust: a motion she had from her mother.

'I know: but he's lovely really. He really understands tenderness,' said Connie, trying to apologize for him.

❶她有她自己的老主意。very hell加强语气,强调。 ❷一本正经地宛若一约阿卡迪亚大元帅,阿卡迪亚:古希腊伯罗奔尼撒中部田园牧歌式的地区。 ❸希尔达低着她那密涅瓦般的头颅,默不作声。密涅瓦:古罗马神话传说中执掌各行技艺和战争的女神。

Hilda, like a ruddy, rich-coloured **Athena**[1], bowed her head and pondered. She was really violently angry. But she dared not show it, because Connie, taking after her father, would straight away become obstreperous and unmanageable.

It was true, Hilda did not like Clifford: his cool assurance that he was somebody! She thought he made use of Connie shamefully and impudently. She had hoped her sister would leave him. But, being solid Scotch middle class, she loathed any 'lowering' of oneself or the family. She looked up at last.

'You'll regret it,' she said,

'I shan't,' cried Connie, flushed red. 'He's quite the exception. I really love him. He's lovely as a lover.'

Hilda still pondered.

'**You'll get over him quite soon**[2],' she said, 'and live to be ashamed of yourself because of him.'

'I shan't! I hope I'm going to have a child of his.'

'Connie!' said Hilda, hard as a hammer-stroke, and pale with anger.

'I shall if I possibly can. I should be fearfully proud if I had a child by him.'

It was no use talking to her. Hilda pondered.

'And doesn't Clifford suspect?' she said.

'Oh no! Why should he?'

'I've no doubt you've given him plenty of occasion for suspicion,' said Hilda.

'Not it all.'

'And tonight's business seems quite gratuitous folly. Where does the man live?'

'In the cottage at the other end of the wood.'

'Is he a bachelor?'

'No! His wife left him.'

'How old?'

'I don't know. Older than me.'

Hilda became more angry at every reply, angry as her mother used to be, in a kind of paroxysm. But still she hid it.

'I would give up tonight's escapade if I were you,' she advised calmly.

---

①阿茜娜:智慧女神，相当于罗马神话中的密涅瓦。②你和他会很快分手。

'I can't! I must stay with him tonight, or I can't go to Venice at all. I just can't.'

Hilda heard her father over again, and she gave way, out of mere diplomacy. And she consented to drive to Mansfield, both of them, to dinner, to bring Connie back to the lane-end after dark, and to fetch her from the lane-end the next morning, herself sleeping in Mansfield, only half an hour away, good going. But she was furious. **She stored it up against her sister**[1], this balk in her plans.

Connie flung an emerald-green shawl over her window-sill.

On the strength of her anger, Hilda warmed toward Clifford.

After all, he had a mind. And if he had no sex, functionally, all the better: so much the less to quarrel about! Hilda wanted no more of that sex business, where men became nasty, selfish little horrors. Connie really had less to put up with than many women if she did but know it.

And Clifford decided that Hilda, after all, was a decidedly intelligent woman, and **would make a man a first-rate helpmate**[2], if he were going in for politics for example. Yes, she had none of Connie's silliness, Connie was more a child: you had to make excuses for her, because she was not altogether dependable.

There was an early cup of tea in the hall, where doors were open to let in the sun. Everybody seemed to be panting a little.

'Good-bye, Connie girl! Come back to me safely.'

'Good-bye, Clifford! Yes, I shan't be long.' Connie was almost tender.

'Good-bye, Hilda! You will keep an eye on her, won't you?'

'I'll even keep two!' said Hilda. 'She shan't go very far astray.'

'It's a promise!'

'Good-bye, Mrs Bolton! I know you'll look after Sir Clifford nobly.'

'I'll do what I can, your Ladyship.'

'And write to me if there is any news, and tell me about Sir Clifford, how he is.'

'Very good, your Ladyship, I will. And have a good time, and come back and cheer us up.'

Everybody waved. The car went off. Connie looked back and saw

❶她把对妹妹的气愤藏在了心里。❷会成为男人最好的帮手。

Clifford, sitting at the top of the steps in his house-chair. After all, he was her husband: Wragby was her home: circumstance had done it.

Mrs Chambers held the gate and wished her ladyship a happy holiday. The car slipped out of the dark spinney that masked the park, on to the highroad where the colliers were trailing home. Hilda turned to the Crosshill Road, that was not a main road, but ran to Mansfield. Connie put on goggles. They ran beside the railway, which was in a cutting below them. Then they crossed the cutting on a bridge.

'That's the lane to the cottage!' said Connie.

Hilda glanced at it impatiently.

'It's a frightful pity we can't go straight off!' she said. We could have been in Pall Mall by nine o'clock.'

'I'm sorry for your sake,' said Connie, from behind her goggles.

They were soon at Mansfield, that once-romantic, now utterly disheartening colliery town. Hilda stopped at the hotel named in the motor-car book, and took a room. The whole thing was utterly uninteresting, and she was almost too angry to talk. However, Connie had to tell her something of the man's history.

'He! He! What name do you call him by? You only say he,' said Hilda.

'I've never called him by any name: nor he me: which is curious, when you come to think of it. Unless we say Lady Jane and John Thomas. But his name is Oliver Mellors.'

'And how would you like to be Mrs Oliver Mellors, instead of Lady Chatterley?'

'I'd love it.'

There was nothing to be done with Connie. And anyhow, if the man had been a lieutenant in the army in India for four or five years, he must be more or less presentable. **Apparently he had character**[1]. Hilda began to relent a little.

'But you'll be through with him in a while,' she said, 'and then you'll be ashamed of having been connected with him. One can't mix up with the working people.'

'But you are such a socialist! You're always on the side of the working classes.'

---

[1]显然他很有个性。

'I may be on their side in a political crisis, but being on their side makes me know how impossible it is to mix one's life with theirs. Not out of snobbery, but just because the whole rhythm is different.'

Hilda had lived among the real political intellectuals, so she was disastrously unanswerable.

The nondescript evening in the hotel dragged out, and at last they had a nondescript dinner. Then Connie slipped a few things into a little silk bag, and combed her hair once more.

'After all, Hilda,' she said, 'love can be wonderful: when you feel you live, and are in the very middle of creation.' It was almost like bragging on her part.

'I suppose every mosquito feels the same,' said Hilda. 'Do you think it does? How nice for it!'

The evening was wonderfully clear and long-lingering, even in the small town. It would be half-light all night. With a face like a mask, from resentment, Hilda started her car again, and the two sped back on their traces, taking the other road, through Bolsover.

Connie wore her goggles and disguising cap, and she sat in silence. Because of Hilda's opposition, she was fiercely on the sidle of the man, **she would stand by him through thick and thin**[1].

They had their head-lights on, by the time they passed Crosshill, and the small lit-up train that chuffed past in the cutting made it seem like real night. Hilda had calculated the turn into the lane at the bridge-end. She slowed up rather suddenly and swerved off the road, the lights glaring white into the grassy, overgrown lane. Connie looked out. She saw a shadowy figure, and she opened the door.

'Here we are!' she said softly.

But Hilda had switched off the lights, and was absorbed backing, making the turn.

'Nothing on the bridge?' she asked shortly. 'You're all right,' said the mall's voice. She backed on to the bridge, reversed, let the car run forwards a few yards along the road, then backed into the lane, under a wych-elm tree, crushing the grass and bracken. Then all the lights went out. Connie stepped down. The man stood under the trees.

'Did you wait long?' Connie asked.

❶无论遇到什么艰难险阻她都会站在他一边。

'Not so very,' he replied.

They both waited for Hilda to get out. But Hilda shut the door of the car and sat tight.

'This is my sister Hilda. Won't you come and speak to her? Hilda! This is Mr Mellors.'

The keeper lifted his hat, but went no nearer.

'Do walk down to the cottage with us, Hilda,' Connie pleaded. 'It's not far.'

'What about the car?'

'People do leave them on the lanes. You have the key.'

Hilda was silent, deliberating. Then she looked backwards down the lane.

'Can I back round the bush?' she said.

'Oh yes!' said the keeper.

She backed slowly round the curve, out of sight of the road, locked the car, and got down. It was night, but luminous dark. The hedges rose high and wild, by the unused lane, and very dark seeming. There was a fresh sweet scent on the air. The keeper went ahead, then came Connie, then Hilda, and in silence. He lit up the difficult places with a flash-light torch, and they went on again, while an owl softly hooted over the oaks, and Flossie padded silently around. Nobody could speak. There was nothing to say.

At length Connie saw the yellow light of the house, and her heart beat fast. She was a little frightened. They trailed on, **still in Indian file**[1].

He unlocked the door and preceded them into the warm but bare little room. The fire burned low and red in the grate. The table was set with two plates and two glasses on a proper white table-cloth for once. Hilda shook her hair and looked round the bare, cheerless room. Then she summoned her courage and looked at the man.

He was moderately tall, and thin, and she thought him good-looking. He kept a quiet distance of his own, and seemed absolutely unwilling to speak.

'Do sit down, Hilda,' said Connie.

'Do!' he said. 'Can I make you tea or anything, or will you drink

[1] 仍然一路纵队地走。Indian file：一前一后单走(源出印第安人在森林中的走法)。

a glass of beer? It's moderately cool.'

'Beer!' said Connie.

'Beer for me, please!' said Hilda, with a mock sort of shyness. He looked at her and blinked.

He took a blue jug and tramped to the scullery. When he came back with the beer, his face had changed again.

Connie sat down by the door, and Hilda sat in his seat, with the back to the wall, against the window corner.

'That is his chair,' said Connie softly. And Hilda rose as if it had burnt her.

'Sit yer still, sit yer still! Ta'e ony cheer as yo'n a mind to, none of us is th' big bear,' he said, with complete equanimity.

And he brought Hilda a glass, and poured her beer first from the blue jug.

'As for cigarettes,' he said, 'I've got none, but 'appen you've got your own. I dunna smoke, mysen. Shall y' eat summat?' He turned direct to Connie. 'Shall t'eat a smite o' summat, if I bring it thee? Tha can usually do wi' a bite.' He spoke the vernacular with a curious calm assurance, as if he were the landlord of the inn.

'What is there?' asked Connie, flushing.

'Boiled ham, cheese, pickled wa'nuts, if yer like. — Nowt much.'

'Yes,' said Connie. 'Won't you, Hilda?'

Hilda looked up at him.

'Why do you speak Yorkshire?' she said softly.

'That! That's non Yorkshire, that's Derby.'

He looked back at her with that faint, distant grin.

'Derby, then! Why do you speak Derby? You spoke natural English at first.'

'Did Ah though? An' canna Ah change if Ah'm a mind to 't? Nay, nay, let me talk Derby if it suits me. If yo'n nowt against it.'

'It sounds a little affected,' said Hilda.

'Ay, 'appen so! An' up i' Tevershall yo'd sound affected.' He looked again at her, **with a queer calculating distance, along his cheek-bone**[1]: as if to say: Yi, an' who are you?

He tramped away to the pantry for the food.

[1] 脸颊部呈现出故作疏远的奇怪神色。

The sisters sat in silence. He brought another plate, and knife and fork. Then he said,

'An' if it's the same to you, I s'll ta'e my coat off like I allers do.'

And he took off his coat, and hung it on the peg, then sat down to table in his shirt-sleeves: a shirt of thin, cream-coloured flannel.

''Elp yerselves!' he said. ''**Elp yerselves! Dunna wait f'r axin**[1]'!' He cut the bread, then sat motionless. Hilda felt, as Connie once used to, his power of silence and distance. She saw his smallish, sensitive, loose hand on the table. He was no simple working man, not he: he was acting! acting!

'Still!' she said, as she took a little cheese. 'It would be more natural if you spoke to us in normal English, not in vernacular.'

He looked at her, feeling her devil of a will.

'Would it?' he said in the normal English. 'Would it? Would anything that was said between you and me be quite natural, unless you said you wished me to hell before your sister ever saw me again: and unless I said something almost as unpleasant back again? Would anything else be natural?'

'Oh yes!' said Hilda. 'Just good manners would be quite natural.'

'Second nature, so to speak!' he said: then he began to laugh. 'Nay,' he said. '**I'm weary o' manners. Let me be**[2]!'

Hilda was frankly baffled and furiously annoyed. After all, he might show that he realized he was being honoured. Instead of which, with his play-acting and lordly airs, he seemed to think it was he who was conferring the honour. Just impudence! Poor misguided Connie, in the man's clutches!

The three ate in silence. Hilda looked to see what his table-manners were like. She could not help realizing that he was instinctively much more delicate and well-bred than herself. She had a certain Scottish clumsiness. And moreover, he had all the quiet self-contained assurance of the English, **no loose edges**[3]. It would be very difficult to get the better of him.

But neither would he get the better of her[4].

'And do you really think,' she said, a little more humanly, 'it's worth the risk.'

❶随意吧，甭等人来请(=help yourself! Don't wait for asking!) ❷我厌倦了这些所谓礼貌，让我随我的天性好了。 ❸无懈可击。 ❹而他也不会胜过她。

'Is what worth what risk?'

'This escapade with my sister.'

He flickered his irritating grin.

'Yo' maun ax 'er!' Then he looked at Connie.

'**Tha comes o' thine own accord**[1], lass, doesn't ter? It's non me as forces thee?'

Connie looked at Hilda.

'I wish you wouldn't cavil, Hilda.'

'Naturally I don't want to. But someone has to think about things. You've got to have some sort of continuity in your life. You can't just go making a mess.'

There was a moment's pause.

'Eh, continuity!' he said. 'An' what by that? What continuity ave yer got i' your life? I thought you was gettin' divorced. What continuity's that? Continuity o' yer own stubbornness. I can see that much. An' what good's it goin' to do yer? You'll be sick o' yer continuity **afore yer a fat sight older**[2]. A stubborn woman an er own self-will: ay, they make a fast continuity, they do. **Thank heaven, it isn't me as 'as got th' 'andlin' of yer**[3]!'

'What right have you to speak like that to me?' said Hilda.

'Right! What right ha' yo' ter start harnessin' other folks i' your continuity? Leave folks to their own continuities.'

'My dear man, do you think I am concerned with you?' said Hilda softly.

'Ay,' he said. 'Yo' are. **For it's a force-put**[4]. Yo' more or less my sister-in-law.'

'Still far from it, I assure you.

'Not a' that far, I assure you. **I've got my own sort o' continuity**[5], back your life! Good as yours, any day. An' if your sister there comes ter me for a bit o' cunt an' tenderness, she knows what she's after. She's been in my bed afore: which you 'aven't, thank the Lord, with your continuity.' There was a dead pause, before he added: ' — Eh, **I don't wear me breeches arse-forrards. An' if I get a windfall, I thank my stars**[6]. A man gets a lot of

[1]那是你自己愿意的。 [2](俚)意思是"不久","很快"。 [3]谢天谢地,多亏和你打交道的不是俺。 [4]你不管都不行。 [5]拿你的话来说,俺有自己的连续性。 [6]我不会让人笑我是个大笨蛋,倘若天鹅肉掉到我嘴里,那是我吉星高照。

enjoyment out o' that lass theer, which is more than anybody gets out o' th' likes o' you. Which is a pity, for you might appen a' bin a good apple, 'stead of a handsome crab. Women like you needs proper graftin'.'

He was looking at her with an odd, flickering smile, faintly sensual and appreciative.

'And men like you,' she said, 'ought to be segregated: **justifying their own vulgarity and selfish lust**[1].'

'Ay, ma'am! It's a mercy there's a few men left like me. But you deserve what you get: to be left severely alone.'

Hilda had risen and gone to the door. He rose and took his coat from the peg.

'I can find my way quite well alone,' she said.

'I doubt you can't,' he replied easily.

They tramped in ridiculous file down the lane again, in silence. An owl still hooted. He knew he ought to shoot it.

The car stood untouched, a little dewy. Hilda got in and started the engine. The other two waited.

'All I mean,' she said from her entrenchment, 'is that I doubt if you'll find it's been worth it, either of you!'

'**One man's meat is another man's poison**[2],' he said, out of the darkness. 'But it's meat an' drink to me.

The lights flared out.

'Don't make me wait in the morning,'

'No, I won't. Goodnight!'

The car rose slowly on to the highroad, then slid swiftly away, leaving the night silent.

Connie timidly took his arm, and they went down the lane. He did not speak. At length she drew him to a standstill.

'Kiss me!' she murmured.

'Nay, wait a bit! **Let me simmer down**[3],' he said.

That amused her. She still kept hold of his arm, and they went quickly down the lane, in silence. She was so glad to be with him, just now. She shivered, knowing that Hilda might have snatched her away. He was inscrutably silent.

When they wer e in the cottage again, she almost jumped with

[1]这是对他们的粗俗和私欲应得的惩罚。 [2]一个人的美味佳肴是另一个人的毒药。 [3]让我静一静。

pleasure, that she should be free of her sister.

'But you were horrid to Hilda,' she said to him.

'She should ha' been slapped in time.'

'But why? and she's so nice.'

He didn't answer, went round doing the evening chores, with a quiet, inevitable sort of motion. He was outwardly angry, but not with her. So Connie felt. And his anger gave him a peculiar handsomeness, an inwardness and glisten that thrilled her and made her limbs go molten.

Still he took no notice of her.

Till he sat down and began to unlace his boots. Then he looked up at her from under his brows, on which the anger still sat firm.

'Shan't you go up?' he said. 'There's a candle!'

He jerked his head swiftly to indicate the candle burning on the table. She took it obediently, and he watched the full curve of her hips as she went up the first stairs.

It was a night of sensual passion, in which she was a little startled and almost unwilling: yet pierced again with piercing thrills of sensuality, different, sharper, more terrible than the thrills of tenderness, but, at the moment, more desirable. Though a little frightened, she let him have his way, and the reckless, shameless sensuality shook her to her foundations, stripped her to the very last, and made a different woman of her. It was not really love. It was not voluptuousness. It was sensuality sharp and searing as fire, burning the soul to tinder.

Burning out the shames, the deepest, oldest shames, in the most secret places. It cost her an effort to let him have his way and his will of her. She had to be a passive, consenting thing, like a slave, a physical slave. Yet the passion licked round her, consuming, and when the sensual flame of it pressed through her bowels and breast, she really thought she was dying: yet a poignant, marvellous death.

She had often wondered what **Abélard**[1] meant, when he said that in their year of love he and Héloise had passed through all the stages and refinements of passion. The same thing, a thousand years ago: ten thousand years ago! The same on the Greek vases, everywhere! The refinements of passion, the extravagances of sensuality! And necessary,

①阿贝拉与爱洛绮斯的故事。中世纪法国神学家与自己的学生爱洛绮斯相爱,二人秘密生有一子,为此阿贝拉遭受宫刑。爱洛绮斯被迫出家当修女,死后二人合葬在巴黎雪拉兹神父公墓,一九二一年小说《爱洛绮斯和阿贝拉》发表,作者为爱尔兰人穆尔。

forever necessary, to burn out false shames and smelt out the heaviest ore of the body into purity. With the fire of sheer sensuality.

In the short summer night she learnt so much. She would have thought a woman would have died of shame. Instead of which, the shame died. Shame, which is fear: the deep organic shame, the old, old physical fear which crouches in the bodily roots of us, and can only be chased away by the sensual fire, at last it was roused up and routed by the phallic hunt of the man, and she came to the very heart of the jungle of herself. She felt, now, she had come to the real bed-rock of her nature, and was essentially shameless. She was her sensual self, naked and unashamed. She felt a triumph, almost a vainglory. So! That was how it was! That was life! That was how oneself really was! There was nothing left to disguise or be ashamed of. She shared her ultimate nakedness with a man, another being.

And what a reckless devil the man was! really like a devil! One had to be strong to bear him. But it took some getting at, the core of the physical jungle, the last and deepest recess of organic shame. The phallos alone could explore it. And how he had pressed in on her!

And how, in fear, she had hated it. But how she had really wanted it! She knew now. At the bottom of her soul, fundamentally, she had needed this phallic hunting out, she had secretly wanted it, and she had believed that she would never get it. Now suddenly there it was, and a man was sharing her last and final nakedness, she was shameless.

What liars poets and everybody were! They made one think one wanted sentiment. When what one supremely wanted was this piercing, consuming, rather awful sensuality. To find a man who dared do it, without shame or sin or final misgiving! If he had been ashamed afterwards, and made one feel ashamed, how awful! What a pity most men are so doggy, a bit shameful, like Clifford! Like Michaelis even! Both sensually a bit doggy and humiliating. The supreme pleasure of the mind! And what is that to a woman? What is it, really, to the man either! He becomes merely messy and doggy, even in his mind. It needs sheer sensuality even to purify and quicken the mind. Sheer fiery sensuality, not messiness.

Ah, God, how rare a thing a man is! They are all dogs that trot and sniff and copulate. To have found a man who was not afraid and not ashamed! She looked at him now, sleeping so like a wild animal asleep, gone, gone in the remoteness of it. She nestled down, not to be away from him.

Till his rousing waked her completely. He was sitting up in bed, looking down at her. She saw her own nakedness in his eyes, immediate knowledge of her. And the fluid, male knowledge of herself seemed to flow to her from his eyes and wrap her voluptuously. Oh, how voluptuous and lovely it was to have limbs and body half-asleep, heavy and suffused with passion.

'Is it time to wake up?' she said.

'Half past six.'

She had to be at the lane-end at eight. Always, always, always this compulsion on one!

'I might make the breakfast and bring it up here; should I?' he said.

'Oh yes!'

Flossie whimpered gently below. He got up and threw off his pyjamas, and rubbed himself with a towel. When the human being is full of courage and full of life, how beautiful it is! So she thought, as she watched him in silence.

'Draw the curtain, will you?'

The sun was shining already on the tender green leaves of morning, and the wood stood bluey-fresh, in the nearness. She sat up in bed, looking dreamily out through the dormer window, her naked arms pushing her naked breasts together. He was dressing himself. She was half-dreaming of life, a life together with him: just a life.

He was going, fleeing from her dangerous, crouching nakedness.

'Have I lost my nightie altogether?' she said.

He pushed his hand down in the bed, and pulled out the bit of flimsy silk.

'I knowed I felt silk at my ankles,' he said.

But the night-dress was slit almost in two.

'Never mind!' she said. 'It belongs here, really. I'll leave it.'

'Ay, leave it, I can put it between my legs at night, for company. There's no name nor mark on it, is there?'

She slipped on the torn thing, and sat dreamily looking out of the window. The window was open, the air of morning drifted in, and the sound of birds. Birds flew continuously past. Then she saw Flossie roaming out. It was morning.

Downstairs she heard him making the fire, pumping water, going out at the back door. By and by came the smell of bacon, and at length he came upstairs with a huge black tray that would only just go through the door. He set the tray on the bed, and poured out the tea. Connie squatted in her torn nightdress, and fell on her food hungrily. He sat on the one chair, with his plate on his knees.

'How good it is!' she said. 'How nice to have breakfast together.'

He ate in silence, his mind on the time that was quickly passing. That made her remember.

'Oh, how I wish I could stay here with you, and Wragby were a million miles away! It's Wragby I'm going away from really. You know that, don't you?'

'Ay!'

'And you promise we will live together and have a life together, you and me! You promise me, don't you?'

'Ay! When we can.'

'Yes! And we will! we will, won't we?' she leaned over, making the tea spill, catching his wrist.

'Ay!' he said, tidying up the tea.

'We can't possibly not live together now, can we?' she said appealingly.

He looked up at her with his flickering grin.

'No!' he said. 'Only you've got to start in twenty-five minutes.'

'Have I?' she cried. Suddenly he held up a warning finger, and rose to his feet.

Flossie had given a short bark, then three loud sharp yaps of warning.

Silent, he put his plate on the tray and went downstairs. Constance heard him go down the garden path. A bicycle bell tinkled outside there.

'Morning, Mr Mellors! Registered letter!'

'Oh ay! Got a pencil?'

'Here y'are!'

There was a pause.

'Canada!' said the stranger's voice.

'Ay! That's a mate o' mine out there in **British Columbia**[1]. Dunno what he's got to register.'

---

[1] 不列颠哥伦比亚(加拿大省名)。

''Appen sent y'a fortune, like.'

'More like wants summat.'

Pause.

'Well! Lovely day again!'

'Ay!'

'Morning!'

'Morning!'

After a time he came upstairs again, looking a little angry.

'Postman,' he said.

'Very early!' she replied.

'Rural round; he's mostly here by seven, when he does come.

'Did your mate send you a fortune?'

'No! Only some photographs and papers about a place out there in British Columbia.'

'Would you go there?'

'I thought perhaps we might.'

'Oh yes! I believe it's lovely!' **But he was put out by the postman's coming**[1].

'Them damn bikes, they're on you afore you know where you are. I hope he twigged nothing.'

'After all, what could he twig!'

'You must get up now, and get ready. I'm just goin' ter look round outside.'

She saw him go reconnoitring into the lane, with dog and gun. She went downstairs and washed, and was ready by the time he came back, with the few things in the little silk bag.

He locked up, and they set off, but through the wood, not down the lane. He was being wary.

'Don't you think one lives for times like last night?' she said to him.

'Ay! But there's the rest o'times to think on,' he replied, rather short.

They plodded on down the overgrown path, he in front, in silence.

'And we will live together and make a life together, won't we?' she pleaded.

'Ay!' he replied, striding on without looking round. 'When t' time

---

[1]可是邮差的到来使他不安。

comes! Just now you're off to Venice or somewhere.'

She followed him dumbly, with sinking heart. Oh, now she was wae to go!

At last he stopped.

'I'll just strike across here,' he said, pointing to the right.

But she flung her arms round his neck, and clung to him.

'But you'll keep the tenderness for me, won't you?' she whispered. 'I loved last night. But you'll keep the tenderness for me, won't you?'

He kissed her and held her close for a moment. Then he sighed, and kissed her again.

'I must go an' look if th' car's there.'

He strode over the low brambles and bracken, leaving a trail through the fern. For a minute or two he was gone. Then he came striding back.

'Car's not there yet,' he said. 'But there's the baker's cart on t' road.'

He seemed anxious and troubled.

'Hark!'

They heard a car softly hoot as it came nearer. It slowed up on the bridge.

She plunged with utter mournfulness in his track through the fern, and came to a huge holly hedge. He was just behind her.

'Here! Go through there!' he said, pointing to a gap. 'I shan't come out.

She looked at him in despair. But he kissed her and made her go. She crept in sheer misery through the holly and through the wooden fence, stumbled down the little ditch and up into the lane, where Hilda was just getting out of the car in vexation.

'Why you're there!' said Hilda. 'Where's he?'

'He's not coming.'

Connie's face was running with tears as she got into the car with her little bag. Hilda snatched up the motoring helmet with the disfiguring goggles.

'Put it on!' she said. And Connie pulled on the disguise, then the long motoring coat, and she sat down, a goggling inhuman, unrecognizable creature. Hilda started the car with a businesslike motion. They heaved out of the lane, and were away down the road. Connie had looked round, but there was no sight of him. Away! Away! She sat in bitter tears. The parting had come so suddenly, so unexpectedly. It was like death.

'Thank goodness you'll be away from him for some time!' said Hilda, turning to avoid Crosshill village.

CHAPTER 17

'You see, Hilda,' said Connie after lunch, when they were nearing London, 'you have never known either real tenderness or real sensuality: and if you do know them, with the same person, it makes a great difference.'

'For mercy's sake don't brag about your experiences!' said Hilda. 'I've never met the man yet who was capable of intimacy with a woman, giving himself up to her. That was what I wanted. I'm not keen on their self-satisfied tenderness, and their sensuality. I'm not content to be any man's little petsy-wetsy, nor his **chair à plaisir**① either. I wanted a complete intimacy, and I didn't get it. That's enough for me.'

Connie pondered this. Complete intimacy! She supposed that meant revealing everything concerning yourself to the other person, and his revealing everything concerning himself. But that was a bore. And all that weary self-consciousness between a man and a woman! a disease!

'I think you're too conscious of yourself all the time, with everybody,' she said to her sister.

'I hope at least I haven't a slave nature,' said Hilda.

'But perhaps you have! Perhaps you are a slave to your own idea of yourself.'

Hilda drove in silence for some time after this piece of unheard of insolence from that chit Connie.

'**At least I'm not a slave to somebody else's idea of me**②: and the somebody else a servant of my husband's,' she retorted at last, in crude anger.

'You see, it's not so,' said Connie calmly.

①(法)池欲器,玩偶。 ②至少我不是别人对我的看法的奴隶。

She had always let herself be dominated by her elder sister. Now, though somewhere inside herself she was weeping, she was free of the dominion of other women. Ah! that in itself was a relief, like being given another life: to be free of the strange dominion and obsession of other women. How awful they were, women!

She was glad to be with her father, whose favourite she had always been. She and Hilda stayed in a little hotel off Pall Mall, and Sir Malcolm was in his club. But he took his daughters out in the evening, and they liked going with him.

He was still handsome and robust, though just a little afraid of the new world that had sprung up around him. He had got a second wife in Scotland, younger than himself and richer. But he had as many holidays away from her as possible: just as with his first wife.

Connie sat next to him at the opera. He was moderately stout, and had stout thighs, but they were still strong and well-knit, the thighs of a healthy man who had taken his pleasure in life. His good-humoured selfishness, his dogged sort of independence, his unrepenting sensuality, it seemed to Connie she could see them all in his well-knit straight thighs. Just a man! And now becoming an old man, which is sad. **Because in his strong, thick male legs there was none of the alert sensitiveness and power of tenderness which is the very essence of youth, that which never dies, once it is there**[1].

Connie woke up to the existence of legs. They became more important to her than faces, which are no longer very real. How few people had live, alert legs! She looked at the men in the stalls. Great puddingy thighs in black pudding-cloth, or lean wooden sticks in black funeral stuff, or well-shaped young legs without any meaning whatever, either sensuality or tenderness or sensitiveness, just mere leggy ordinariness that pranced around. Not even any sensuality like her father's. They were all daunted, daunted out of existence.

But the women were not daunted. **The awful mill-posts of most females! really shocking, really enough to justify murder**[2]! Or the poor thin pegs! or the trim neat things in silk stockings, without the slightest look of life! Awful, the millions of meaningless legs prancing meaninglessly around!

---

[1]因为在他那粗壮结实的男性大腿上，已经没有了警觉的敏感和柔韧的力量，而这些正是青春的精华所在，只要青春在，它们便不会消失。 [2]多数女人的腿那么粗笨，让人吃惊，真能把人吓死。

But she was not happy in London. The people seemed so spectral and blank. They had no alive happiness, no matter how brisk and good-looking they were. It was all barren. And Connie had a woman's blind craving for happiness, to be assured of happiness.

In Paris at any rate she felt a bit of sensuality still. But what a weary, tired, worn-out sensuality. Worn-out for lack of tenderness. Oh! Paris was sad. One of the saddest towns: weary of its now-mechanical sensuality, weary of the tension of money, money, money, weary even of resentment and conceit, just weary to death, and still not sufficiently Americanized or Londonized to hide the weariness under a mechanical jig-jig-jig! Ah, these manly he-men, these flaneurs, the oglers, these eaters of good dinners! How weary they were! weary, worn-out for lack of a little tenderness, given and taken. The efficient, sometimes charming women knew a thing or two about the sensual realities: **they had that pull over their jigging English sisters**[1]. But they knew even less of tenderness. Dry, with the endless dry tension of will, they too were wearing out. The human world was just getting worn out. Perhaps it would turn fiercely destructive. A sort of anarchy! Clifford and his conservative anarchy! Perhaps it wouldn't be conservative much longer. Perhaps it would develop into a very radical anarchy.

Connie found herself shrinking and afraid of the world. Sometimes she was happy for a little while in the Boulevards or in **the Bois**[2] or the Luxembourg Gardens. But already Paris was full of Americans and English, strange Americans in the oddest uniforms, and the usual dreary English that are so hopeless abroad.

She was glad to drive on. It was suddenly hot weather, so Hilda was going through Switzerland and over **the Brenner**[3], then through **the Dolomites**[4] down to Venice. Hilda loved all the managing and the driving and being mistress of the show. Connie was quite content to keep quiet.

And the trip was really quite nice. Only Connie kept saying to herself: Why don't I really care! Why am I never really thrilled? How awful, that I don't really care about the landscape any more! But I don't. It's rather awful. I'm like **Saint Bernard**[5], who could sail

❶她们比那些跳快步舞的美国姐妹们略胜一筹。❷(法)林子。❸即Brenner Pass 布伦纳山口,意大利和奥地利边界间的阿尔卑斯山口。❹多洛迈茨山(在阿尔卑斯山的分界处)。❺圣伯尔纳(1090—1153),法国基督教神学家。

down the lake of **Lucerne**[1] without ever noticing that there were even mountain and green water. I just don't care for landscape any more. Why should one stare at it? Why should one? I refuse to.

No, she found nothing vital in France or Switzerland or the **Tyrol**[2] or Italy. She just was carted through it all. And it was all less real than Wragby. Less real than the awful Wragby! She felt she didn't care if she never saw France or Switzerland or Italy again. They'd keep. Wragby was more real.

As for people! people were all alike, with very little difference. They all wanted to get money out of you: or, if they were travellers, they wanted to get enjoyment, perforce, like squeezing blood out of a stone. Poor mountains! poor landscape! it all had to be squeezed and squeezed and squeezed again, to provide a thrill, to provide enjoyment. What did people mean, with their simply determined enjoying of themselves?

No! said Connie to herself. I'd rather be at Wragby, where I can go about and be still, and not stare at anything or do any performing of any sort. This tourist performance of enjoying oneself is too hopelessly humiliating: it's such a failure.

She wanted to go back to Wragby, even to Clifford, even to poor crippled Clifford. He wasn't such a fool as this swarming holidaying lot, anyhow.

But in her inner consciousness she was keeping touch with the other man. She mustn't let her connexion with him go: oh, she mustn't let it go, or she was lost, lost utterly in this world of riff-raffy expensive people and joy-hogs. Oh, the joy-hogs! Oh 'enjoying oneself'! Another modern form of sickness.

They left the car in Mestre, in a garage, and took the regular steamer over to Venice. It was a lovely summer afternoon, the shallow lagoon rippled, the full sunshine made Venice, turning its back to them across the water, look dim.

At the station quay they changed to a gondola, giving the man the address. He was a regular gondolier in a white-and-blue blouse, not very good-looking, not at all impressive.

'Yes! The Villa Esmeralda! Yes! I know it! I have been the gondolier for a gentleman there. But a fair distance out!'

He seemed a rather childish, impetuous fellow. He rowed with a

[1]卢塞恩(瑞士中部城市)。 [2]提罗尔:奥地利西部和意大利北部一地区。

certain exaggerated impetuosity, through the dark side-canals with the horrible, slimy green walls, the canals that go through the poorer quarters, where the washing hangs high up on ropes, and there is a slight, or strong, odour of sewage.

But at last he came to one of the open canals with pavement on either side, and looping bridges, that run straight, at right-angles to the Grand Canal. The two women sat under the little awning, the man was perched above, behind them.

'Are the signorine staying long at the Villa Esmeralda?' he asked, rowing easy, and wiping his perspiring face with a white-and-blue handkerchief.

'Some twenty days: we are both married ladies,' said Hilda, in her curious hushed voice, that made her Italian sound so foreign.

'Ah! Twenty days!' said the man. There was a pause. After which he asked: 'Do the **signore**[1] want a gondolier for the twenty days or so that they will stay at the Villa Esmeralda? Or by the day, or by the week?'

Connie and Hilda considered. In Venice, it is always preferable to have one's own gondola, as it is preferable to have one's own car on land.

'What is there at the Villa? what boats?'

'There is a motor-launch, also a gondola. But — ' The but meant: they won't be your property.

'How much do you charge?'

It was about thirty shillings a day, or ten pounds a week.

'Is that the regular price?' asked Hilda.

'Less, Signora, less. The regular price — '

The sisters considered.

'Well,' said Hilda, 'come tomorrow morning, and we will arrange it. What is your name?'

His name was Giovanni, and he wanted to know at what time he should come, and then for whom should he say he was waiting. Hilda had no card. Connie gave him one of hers. He glanced at it swiftly, with his hot, southern blue eyes, then glanced again.

'Ah!' he said, lighting up. '**Milady**[2]! Milady, isn't it?'

'Milady **Costanza**[3]!' said Connie.

---

[1](意大利语)对已婚女子的尊称。 [2]昔时欧洲大陆人对英国贵妇人的尊称。 [3]是Connie的名字,念成意大利语的发音。

He nodded, repeating: 'Milady Costanza!' and putting the card carefully away in his blouse.

The Villa Esmeralda was quite a long way out, on the edge of the lagoon looking towards Chioggia. It was not a very old house, and pleasant, with the terraces looking seawards, and below, quite a big garden with dark trees, walled in from the lagoon.

Their host was a heavy, rather coarse Scotchman who had made a good fortune in Italy before the war, and had been knighted for his ultrapatriotism during the war. His wife was a thin, pale, sharp kind of person with no fortune of her own, and the misfortune of having to regulate her husband's rather **sordid amorous exploits**❶. He was terribly tiresome with the servants. But having had a slight stroke during the winter, he was now more manageable.

The house was pretty full. Besides Sir Malcolm and his two daughters, there were seven more people, a Scotch couple, again with two daughters; a young Italian Contessa, a widow; a young Georgian prince, and a youngish English clergyman who had had pneumonia and was being chaplain to Sir Alexander for his health's sake. The prince was penniless, good-looking, would make an excellent chauffeur, with the necessary impudence, and **basta**❷! The Contessa was a quiet little puss with a game on somewhere. The clergyman was a raw simple fellow from a Bucks vicarage: luckily he had left his wife and two children at home. And the Guthries, the family of four, were good solid Edinburgh middle class, enjoying everything in a solid fashion, and daring everything while risking nothing.

Connie and Hilda ruled out the prince at once. The Guthries were more or less their own sort, substantial, but boring: and the girls wanted husbands. The chaplain was not a bad fellow, but too deferential. Sir Alexander, after his slight stroke, had a terrible heaviness his joviality, but he was still thrilled at the presence of so many handsome young women. Lady Cooper was a quiet, catty person who **had a thin time of it**❸, poor thing, and who watched every other woman with a cold watchfulness that had become her second nature, and who said cold, nasty little things which showed what an utterly low opinion she had of all human nature. She was also quite venomously overbearing with the

❶肮脏的招蜂引蝶的行为。❷(意大利语)够了。❸(俚)指过得不愉快。

servants, Connie found: but in a quiet way. And she skilfully behaved so that Sir Alexander should think that he was lord and monarch of the whole caboosh, with his stout, would-be-genial paunch, and his utterly boring jokes, his humourosity, as Hilda called it.

Sir Malcolm was painting. Yes, he still would do a Venetian lagoonscape, now and then, in contrast to his Scottish landscapes. So in the morning he was rowed off with a huge canvas, to his 'site'. A little later, Lady Cooper would he rowed off into the heart of the city, with sketching-block and colours. She was an inveterate watercolour painter, and the house was full of rose-coloured palaces, dark canals, swaying bridges, medieval facades, and so on. A little later the Guthries, the prince, the countess, Sir Alexander, and sometimes Mr Lind, the chaplain, would go off to the Lido, where they would bathe; coming home to a late lunch at half past one.

The house-party, as a house-party, was distinctly boring. But this did not trouble the sisters. They were out all the time. Their father took them to the exhibition, miles and miles of weary paintings. He took them to all the cronies of his in the Villa Lucchese, he sat with them on warm evenings in the piazza, having got a table at Florian's: he took them to the theatre, to the **Golodi**[1] plays. There were illuminated **water-fêtes**[2], there were dances. This was a holiday-place of all holiday-places. The Lido, with its acres of sun-pinked or pyjamaed bodies, was like a strand with an endless heap of seals come up for mating. Too many people in the piazza, too many limbs and trunks of humanity on the Lido, too many gondolas, too many motor-launches, too many steamers, too many pigeons, too many ices, too many cocktails, too many menservants wanting tips, too many languages rattling, too much, too much sun, too much smell of Venice, too many cargoes of strawberries, too many silk shawls, too many huge, raw-beef slices of watermelon on stalls: too much enjoyment, altogether far too much enjoyment!

Connie and Hilda went around in their sunny frocks. There were dozens of people they knew, dozens of people knew them. Michaelis turned up **like a bad penny**[3]. 'Hullo! Where you staying? Come and have an ice-cream or something! Come with me somewhere in my

❶哥尔多尼(1707—1793),意大利现实主义喜剧奠基人,喜剧作家。❷水上游艺会。❸指不想看见时一再出现,而想忘记又忘不掉的东西。

gondola.' Even Michaelis almost sun-burned: though sun-cooked is more appropriate to the look of the mass of human flesh.

It was pleasant in a way. It was almost enjoyment. But anyhow, with all the cocktails, all the lying in warmish water and sunbathing on hot sand in hot sun, jazzing with your stomach up against some fellow in the warm nights, cooling off with ices, it was a complete narcotic. And that was what they all wanted, a drug: the slow water, a drug; the sun, a drug; jazz, a drug; cigarettes, cocktails, ices, vermouth. To be drugged! Enjoyment! Enjoyment!

Hilda half liked being drugged. She liked looking at all the women, speculating about them. The women were absorbingly interested in the women. How does she look! what man has she captured? what fun is she getting out of it? — The men were like great dogs in white flannel trousers, waiting to be patted, waiting to wallow, waiting to plaster some woman's stomach against their own, in jazz.

Hilda liked jazz, because she could plaster her stomach against the stomach of some so-called man, and let him control her movement from the visceral centre, here and there across the floor, and then she could break loose and ignore 'the creature'. He had been merely made use of. Poor Connie was rather unhappy. She wouldn't jazz, because she simply couldn't plaster her stomach against some 'creature's' stomach. She hated the conglomerate mass of nearly nude flesh on the Lido: there was hardly enough water to wet them all. She disliked Sir Alexander and Lady Cooper. She did not want Michaelis or anybody else trailing her.

The happiest times were when she got Hilda to go with her away across the lagoon, far across to some lonely shingle-bank, where they could bathe quite alone, the gondola remaining on the inner side of the reef.

Then Giovanni got another gondolier to help him, because it was a long way and he sweated terrifically in the sun. Giovanni was very nice: affectionate, as the Italians are, and quite passionless. The Italians are not passionate: passion has deep reserves. They are easily moved, and often affectionate, but they rarely have any abiding passion of any sort.

So Giovanni was already devoted to his ladies, as he had been devoted to cargoes of ladies in the past. He was perfectly ready to prostitute himself to them, if they wanted hint: he secretly hoped they would want him. They would give him a handsome present, and it would come in very handy, as he was just going to be married. He told them about his marriage, and they were suitably interested.

He thought this trip to some lonely bank across the lagoon probably meant business: business being **l'amore**[1], love. So he got a mate to help him, for it was a long way; and after all, they were two ladies. Two ladies, two mackerels! Good arithmetic! Beautiful ladies, too! He was justly proud of them. And though it was the Signora who paid him and gave him orders, he rather hoped it would be the young milady who would select hint for l'amore. She would give more money too.

The mate he brought was called Daniele. He was not a regular gondolier, so he had none of the cadger and prostitute about him. He was a sandola man, a sandola being a big boat that brings in fruit and produce from the islands.

Daniele was beautiful, tall and well-shapen, with a light round head of little, close, pale-blond curls, and a good-looking man's face, a little like a lion, and long-distance blue eyes. He was not effusive, loquacious, and bibulous like Giovanni. He was silent and he rowed with a strength and ease as if he were alone on the water. The ladies were ladies, remote from him. He did not even look at them. He looked ahead.

He was a real man, a little angry when Giovanni drank too much wine and rowed awkwardly, with effusive shoves of the great oar. He was a man as Mellors was a man, unprostituted. Connie pitied the wife of the easily-overflowing Giovanni. But Daniele's wife would be one of those sweet Venetian women of the people whom one still sees, modest and flower-like in the back of that labyrinth of a town.

Ah, how sad that man first prostitutes woman, then woman prostitutes man. Giovanni was pining to prostitute himself, dribbling like a dog, wanting to give himself to a woman. And for money!

Connie looked at Venice far off, low and rose-coloured upon the water. Built of money, blossomed of money, and dead with money. The money-deadness! Money, money, money, prostitution and deadness.

Yet Daniele was still a man capable of a man's free allegiance. He did not wear the gondolier's blouse: only the knitted blue jersey. He was a little wild, uncouth and proud. So he was hireling to the rather doggy

[1](法语)爱。

Giovanni who was hireling again to two women. So it is! When Jesus refused the devil's money, he left the devil like a Jewish banker, master of the whole situation.

Connie would come home from the blazing light of the lagoon in a kind of stupor, to lind letters from home. Clifford wrote regularly. He wrote very good letters: they might all have been printed in a book. And for this reason Connie found them not very interesting.

She lived in the stupor of the light of the lagoon, the lapping saltiness of the water, the space, the emptiness, the nothingness: but health, health, complete stupor of health. It was gratifying, and **she was lulled away in it**❶, not caring for anything. Besides, she was pregnant. She knew now. So the stupor of sunlight and lagoon salt and sea-bathing and lying on shingle and finding shells and drifting away, away in a gondola, was completed by the pregnancy inside her, another fullness of health, satisfying and stupefying.

She had been at Venice a fortnight, and she was to stay another ten days or a fortnight. **The sunshine blazed over any count of time**❷, and the fullness of physical health made forgetfulness complete. She was in a sort of stupor of well-being.

From which a letter of Clifford roused her.

We too have had our mild local excitement. It appears the truant wife of Mellors, the keeper, turned up at the cottage and found herself unwelcome. He packed her off, and locked the door. Report has it, however, that when he returned from the wood he found the no longer fair lady firmly established in his bed, **in puris naturalibus**❸; or one should say, in **impuris naturalibus**❹. She had broken a window and got in that way. Unable to evict the **somewhat man-handled Venus**❺ from his couch, he beat a retreat and retired, it is said, to his mother's house in Tevershall. Meanwhile the Venus of Stacks Gate is established in the cottage, which she claims is her home, and Apollo, apparently, is domiciled in Tevershall.

I repeat this from hearsay, as Mellors has not come to me personally. I had this particular bit of local garbage from our garbage bird, our ibis, our scavenging turkey-buzzard, Mrs Bolton. I would not

❶她沉醉其中。 ❷阳光照得人忘却了时间的流逝。 ❸纯洁地赤裸裸。 ❹淫猥地赤裸裸。 ❺指 Mellors 的妻子,有讥讽之意。

have repeated it had she not exclaimed: her Ladyship will go no more to the wood if that woman's going to be about!

I like your picture of Sir Malcolm striding into the sea with white hair blowing and pink flesh glowing. I envy you that sun. Here it rains. But I don't envy Sir Malcolm his inveterate mortal carnality. However, it suits his age. Apparently one grows more carnal and more mortal as one grows older. Only youth has a taste of immortality —

This news affected Connie in her state of semi-stupefied well-being with vexation amounting to exasperation. Now she had got to be bothered by that beast of a woman! Now she must start and fret! She had no letter from Mellors. They had agreed not to write at all, but now she wanted to hear from him personally. After all, he was the father of the child that was coming. Let him write!

But how hateful! Now everything was messed up. How foul those low people were! How nice it was here, in the sunshine and the indolence, compared to that dismal mess of that English Midlands! After all, a clear sky was almost the most important thing in life.

She did not mention the fact of her pregnancy, even to Hilda. She wrote to Mrs Bolton for exact information.

Duncan Forbes, an artist friend of theirs, had arrived at the Villa Esmeralda, coming north from Rome. Now he made a third in the gondola, and he bathed with them across the lagoon, and was their escort: a quiet, almost taciturn young man, very advanced in his art.

She had a letter from Mrs Bolton:

You will be pleased, I am sure, my Lady, when you see Sir Clifford. He's looking quite blooming and working very hard, and very hopeful. Of course he is looking forward to seeing you among us again. It is a dull house without my Lady, and we shall all welcome her presence among us once more.

About Mr Mellors, I don't know how much Sir Clifford told you. It seems his wife came back all of a sudden one afternoon, and he found her sitting on the doorstep when he came in from the wood. She said she was come back to him and wanted to live with him again, as she was his legal wife, and he wasn't going to divorce her. But he wouldn't have anything to do with her, and wouldn't let her in the house, and did not go in himself; he went back into the wood without ever opening the door.

But when he came back after dark, he found the house broken into, so he went upstairs to see what she'd done, and he found her in bed without a rag on her. He offered her money, but she said she was his wife and he must take her back. I don't know what sort of a scene they had. His mother told me about it, she's terribly upset. Well, he told her he'd die rather than ever live with her again, so he took his things and went straight to his mother's on Tevershall hill. He stopped the night and went to the wood next day through the park, never going near the cottage. It seems he never saw his wife that day. But the day after she was at her brother Pan's at Beggarlee, swearing and carrying on, saying she was his legal wife, and that he'd been having women at the cottage, because she'd found a scent-bottle in his drawer, and gold-tipped cigarette-ends on the ash-heap, and I don't know what all. Then it seems the postman Fred Kirk says he heard somebody talking in Mr Mellors' bedroom early one morning, and a motor-car had been in the lane.

Mr Mellors stayed on with his mother, and went to the wood through the park, and it seems she stayed on at the cottage. Well, there was no end of talk. So at last Mr Mellors and Tom Phillips went to the cottage and fetched away most of the furniture and bedding, and unscrewed the handle of the pump, so she was forced to go. But instead of going back to Stacks Gate she went and lodged with that Mrs Swain at Beggarlee, because her brother Dan's wife wouldn't have her. And she kept going to old Mrs Mellors' house, to catch him, and she began swearing he'd got in bed with her in the cottage and she went to a lawyer to make him pay her an allowance. She's grown heavy, and more common than ever, and as strong as a bull. And she goes about saying the most awful things about him, how he has women at the cottage, and how he behaved to her when they were married, the low, beastly things he did to her, and I don't know what all. I'm sure it's awful, the mischief a woman can do, once she starts talking. And no matter how low she may be, there'll be some as will believe her, and some of the dirt will stick. I'm sure the way she makes out that Mr Mellors was one of those low, beastly men with women, is simply shocking. And people are only too ready to believe things against anybody, especially things like that. She declared she'll never leave him alone while he lives. Though what I say is, if he was so beastly to her, why is she so anxious to go back to him? But of course **she's coming near her change of life**[1], for she's years older than he is. And these common, violent women always go partly insane when the change of life comes upon them —

This was a nasty blow to Connie. Here she was, sure as life, coming in for her share of the lowness and dirt. She felt angry with him for not having got clear of a Bertha Coutts: nay, for ever having married her. Perhaps he had a certain hankering after lowness. Connie remembered the last night she had spent with him, and shivered. He had known all that sensuality, even with a Bertha Coutts! It was really rather disgusting. It would be well to be rid of him, clear of him altogether. He was perhaps really common, really low.

She had a revulsion against the whole affair, and almost envied the Guthrie girls their gawky inexperience and crude maidenliness. And she now dreaded the thought that anybody would know about herself and the keeper. How unspeakably humiliating! She was weary, afraid, and felt a craving for utter respectability, even for the vulgar and deadening respectability of the Guthrie girls. If Clifford knew about her affair, how unspeakably humiliating! She was afraid, terrified of society and its unclean bite. She almost wished she could get rid of the child again, and be quite clear. In short, she fell into a state of funk.

As for the scent-bottle, that was her own folly. She had not been able to refrain from perfuming his one or two handkerchiefs and his shirts in the drawer, just out of childishness, and she had left a little bottle of Coty's Wood-violet perfume, half empty, among his things. She wanted him to remember her in the perfume. As for the cigarette-ends, they were Hilda's.

She could not help confiding a little in Duncan Forbes. She didn't say she had been the keeper's lover, she only said she liked him, and told Forbes the history of the man.

'Oh,' said Forbes, 'you'll see, they'll never rest till they've pulled the man down and done him in. If he has refused to creep up into the middle classes, when he had a chance; and if he's a man who stands up for his own sex, then they'll do him in. It's the one thing they won't let you be, straight and open in your sex. You can be as dirty as you like. In fact the more dirt you do on sex the better they like it. But if you believe

[1]她快到更年期了。

in your own sex, and won't have it done dirt to: they'll down you. It's the one insane taboo left: sex as a natural and vital thing. They won't have it, and they'll kill you before they'll let you have it. You'll see, they'll hound that man down. And what's he done, after all? If he's made love to his wife all ends on, hasn't he a right to? She ought to be proud of it. But you see, even a low bitch like that turns on him, and uses the hyena instinct of the mob against sex, to pull him down. You have a snivel and feel sinful or awful about your sex, before you're allowed to have any. Oh, they'll hound the poor devil down.'

Connie had a revulsion in the opposite direction now. What had he done, after all? what had he done to herself, Connie, but give her an exquisite pleasure and a sense of freedom and life? He had released her warm, natural sexual flow. And for that they would hound him down.

No no, it should not be. She saw the image of him, naked white with tanned face and hands, looking down and addressing his erect penis as if it were another being, the odd grin flickering on his face. And she heard his voice again: Tha's got the nicest woman's arse of anybody! And she felt his hand warmly and softly closing over her tail again, over her secret places, like a benediction. And the warmth ran through her womb, and the little flames flickered in her knees, and she said: Oh, no! I mustn't go back on it! I must not go back on him. I must stick to him and to what I had of him, through everything. I had no warm, flamy life till he gave it me. And I won't go back on it.

She did a rash thing. She sent a letter to Ivy Bolton, enclosing a note to the keeper, and asking Mrs Bolton to give it him. And she wrote to him:

I am very much distressed to hear of all the trouble your wife is making for you, but don't mind it, it is only a sort of hysteria. It will all blow over as suddenly as it came. But I'm awfully sorry about it, and I do hope you are not minding very much. After all, it isn't worth it. She is only a hysterical woman who wants to hurt you. I shall be home in ten days' time, and I do hope everything will be all right.

A few days later came a letter from Clifford. He was evidently upset.

I am delighted to hear you are prepared to leave Venice on the sixteenth. But if you are enjoying it, don't hurry home. We miss you, Wragby misses you. But it is essential that you should get your full amount of sunshine, sunshine and pyjamas, as the advertisements of the Lido say. So please do stay on a little longer, if it is cheering you up and preparing you for our sufficiently awful winter. Even today, it rains.

I am assiduously, admirably looked after by Mrs Bolton. She is a queer specimen. The more I live, the more I realize what strange creatures human beings are. Some of them might just as well have a hundred legs, like a centipede, or six, like a lobster. The human consistency and dignity one has been led to expect from one's fellow-men seem actually nonexistent. One doubts if they exist to any startling degree even is oneself.

The scandal of the keeper continues and gets bigger like a snowball. Mrs Bolton keeps me informed. She reminds me of a fish which, though dumb, seems to be breathing silent gossip through its gills, while ever it lives. All goes through the sieve of her gills, and nothing surprises her. It is as if the events of other people's lives were the necessary oxygen of her own.

She is preoccupied with the Mellors scandal, and if I will let her begin, she takes me down to the depths. Her great indignation, which even then is like the indignation of an actress playing a role, is against the wife of Mellors, whom she persists in calling Bertha Courts. I have been to the depths of the muddy lives of the Bertha Couttses of this world, and when, released from the current of gossip, I slowly rise to the surface again, I look at the daylight its wonder that it ever should be.

It seems to me absolutely true, that our world, which appears to us the surface of all things, is really the bottom of a deep ocean: all our trees are submarine growths, and we are weird, **scaly-clad submarine fauna**[1], feeding ourselves on offal like shrimps. Only occasionally the soul rises gasping through the fathomless fathoms under which we live, far up to the surface of the ether, where there is true air. I am convinced that the air we normally breathe is a kind of water, and men and women are a species of fish.

But sometimes the soul does come up, shoots like a kittiwake into the light, with ecstasy, after having preyed on the submarine depths. It is our mortal destiny, I suppose, to prey upon the ghastly subaqueous life of our fellow-men, in the submarine jungle of mankind. But our immortal

[1] 海底的鳞甲动物。

destiny is to escape, once we have swallowed our swimmy catch, up again into the bright ether, bursting out from the surface of Old Ocean into real light. Then one realizes one's eternal nature.

When I hear Mrs Bolton talk, I feel myself plunging down, down, to the depths where the fish of human secrets wriggle and swim. Carnal appetite makes one seize a beakful of prey: then up, up again, out of the dense into the ethereal, from the wet into the dry. To you I can tell the whole process. But with Mrs Bolton I only feel the downward plunge, down, horribly, among the sea-weeds and the pallid monsters of the very bottom.

I am afraid we are going to lose our game-keeper. The scandal of the truant wife, instead of dying down, has reverberated to greater and greater dimensions. He is accused of all unspeakable things and curiously enough, the woman has managed to get the bulk of the colliers' wives behind her, gruesome fish, and the village is putrescent with talk.

I hear this Bertha Coutts besieges Mellors in his mother's house, having ransacked the cottage and the hut. She seized one day upon her own daughter, as that chip of the female block was returning from school; but the little one, instead of kissing the loving mother's hand, bit it firmly, and so received from the other hand a smack in the face which sent her reeling into the gutter: whence she was rescued by an indignant and harassed grandmother.

The woman has blown off an amazing quantity of poison-gas. She has aired in detail all those incidents of her conjugal life which are usually buried down in the deepest grave of matrimonial silence, between married couples. Having chosen to exhume them, after ten years of burial, she has a weird array. I hear these details from Linley and the doctor: the latter being amused. Of course there is really nothing in it. Humanity has always had a strange avidity for unusual sexual postures, and if a man likes to use his wife, as **Benvenuto Cellini**[1] says, 'in the Italian way', well that is a matter of taste. But I had hardly expected our game-keeper to be up to so many tricks. No doubt Bertha Coutts herself first put him up to them. In any case, it is a matter of their own personal squalor, and nothing to do with anybody else.

However, everybody listens: as I do myself. A dozen years ago,

[1] 切利尼(1500—1571),意大利雕塑家,金匠。

common decency would have hushed the thing. But common decency no longer exists, and the colliers' wives are all up in arms and unabashed in voice. One would think every child in Tevershall, for the last fifty years, had been an immaculate conception, and every one of our nonconformist females was a shining **Joan of Arc**[1]. That our estimable game-keeper should **have about him a touch of Rabelais**[2] seems to make him more monstrous and shocking than a murderer like **Crippen**[3]. Yet these people in Tevershall are a loose lot, if one is to believe all accounts.

The trouble is, however, the execrable Bertha Coutts has not confined herself to her own experiences and sufferings. She has discovered, at the top of her voice, that her husband has been 'keeping' women down at the cottage, and has made a few random shots at naming the women. This has brought a few decent names trailing through the mud, and the thing has gone quite considerably too far. An injunction has been taken out against the woman.

I have had to interview Mellors about the business, as it was impossible to keep the woman away from the wood. He goes about as usual, with his **Miller-of-the-Dee air**[4], I care for nobody, no not I, if nobody care for me! Nevertheless, I shrewdly suspect he feels like a dog with a tin can tied to its tail: though he makes a very good show of pretending the tin can isn't there. But I heard that in the village the women call away their children if he is passing, as if he were **the Marquis de Sade**[5] in person. He goes on with a certain impudence, but I am afraid the tin can is firmly tied to his tail, and that inwardly he repeats, like Don Rodrigo in the Spanish ballad: 'Ah, now it bites me where I most have sinned!'

I asked him if it he thought he would be able to attend to his duty in the wood, and he said he did not think he had neglected it. I told him it was a nuisance to have the woman trespassing: to which he replied that he had no power to arrest her. Then I hinted at the scandal and its unpleasant course. 'Ay,' he said. 'folks should do their own fuckin', then they wouldn't want to listen to a lot of clatfart about another man's.'

[1]圣女贞佳(1412—1431),法国民族英雄,百年战争时解除英军对奥尔良城之围后被俘,受火刑而死。[2]身上带有拉伯雷的气质(即富于幻想和热情),拉伯雷(1483—1553),法国作家,人文主义者。[3]英国二十世纪初的残暴杀害女性而闻名的罪犯。[4]一副漠不关心的神情。典出一首十九世纪英国民歌。[5]法国作家(1740—1814),军人出身,著有长篇小说《美德的厄运》等,以擅长色情描写著称,曾因变态性虐待行为多次遭监禁。sadism(施虐狂)一词即源于其姓氏。

He said it with some bitterness, and no doubt it contains the real germ of truth. The mode of putting it, however, is neither delicate nor respectful. I hinted as much, and then I heard the tin can rattle again. 'It's not for a man the shape you're in, Sir Clifford, to twit me for havin' a cod atween my legs.'

These things, said indiscriminately to **all and sundry**[1], of course do not help him at all, and the rector, and Finley, and Burroughs all think it would be as well if the man left the place.

I asked him if it was true that he entertained ladies down at the cottage, and all he said was: 'Why, what's that to you, Sir Clifford?' I told him I intended to have decency observed on my estate, to which he replied: 'Then you mun button the mouths o' a' th' women.' — When I pressed him about his manner of life at the cottage, he said: 'Surely you might ma'e a scandal out o' me an' my bitch Flossie. You've missed summat there.' As a matter of fact, for an example of impertinence he'd be hard to beat.

I asked him fit would be easy for him to find another job. He said: 'If you're hintin' that you'd like to shunt me out of this job, it'd be easy as wink.' So he made no trouble at all about leaving at the end of next week, and apparently is willing to initiate a young fellow, Joe Chambers, into as many mysteries of the craft as possible. I told him I would give him a month's wages extra, when he left. He said he'd rather I kept my money, as I'd no occasion to ease my conscience. I asked him what he meant, and he said: 'You don't owe me nothing extra, Sir Clifford, so don't pay me nothing extra. **If you think you see my shirt hanging out, just tell me**[2].'

Well, there is the end of it for the time being. The woman has gone away: we don't know where to: but she is liable to arrest if she shows her face in Tevershall. And I heard she is mortally afraid of gaol, because she merits it so well. Mellors will depart on Saturday week, and the place will soon become normal again.

Meanwhile, my dear Connie, if you would enjoy to stay in Venice or in Switzerland till the beginning of August, I should be glad to think you were out of all this buzz of nastiness, which will have died quite away by the end of the month.

[1]各种各样的人。 [2]如果你还有什么不满的话要说,就尽管告诉我。

So you see, we are deep-sea monsters, and when the lobster walks on mud, he stirs it up for everybody. We must perforce take it philosophically.

The irritation, and the lack of any sympathy in any direction, of Clifford's letter, had a bad effect on Connie. But she understood it better when she received the following from Mellors:

The cat is out of the bag, along with various other pussies. You have heard that my wife Bertha came back to my unloving arms, and took up her abode in the cottage: where, to speak disrespectfully, she smelled a rat, in the shape of a little bottle of Coty. Other evidence she did not find, at least for some days, when she began to howl about the burnt photograph. She noticed the glass and the back-board in the square bedroom. Unfortunately, on the back-board somebody had scribbled little sketches, and the initials, several times repeated: C. S. R. This, however, afforded no clue until she broke into the hut, and found one of your books, an autobiography of the actress Judith, with your name, Constance Stewart Reid, on the front page. After this, for some days she went round loudly saying that my paramour was no less a person than Lady Chatterley herself. The news came at last to the rector, Mr Burroughs, and to Sir Clifford. They then proceeded to take legal steps against my liege lady, who for her part disappeared, having always had a mortal fear of the police.

Sir Clifford asked to see me, so I went to him. He talked around things and seemed annoyed with me. Then he asked if I knew that even her ladyship's name had been mentioned. I said I never listened to scandal, and was surprised to hear this bit from Sir Clifford himself. He said, of course it was a great insult, and I told him there was Queen Mary on a calendar in the scullery, no doubt because Her Majesty formed part of my harem. But he didn't appreciate the sarcasm. He as good as told me I was a disreputable character also walked about with my breeches' buttons undone, and I as good as told him he'd nothing to unbutton anyhow, so he **gave me the sack**[1], and I leave on Saturday week, and the place thereof shall know me no more.

I shall go to London, and my old landlady, Mrs Inger, 17 Coburg Square, will either give me a room or will find one for me.

[1] 解雇了我。

Be sure **your sins will find you out**[1], especially if you're married and her name's Bertha —

There was not a word about herself, or to her. Connie resented this. He might have said some few words of consolation or reassurance. But she knew he was leaving her free, free to go back to Wragby and to Clifford. She resented that too. **He need not to be so falsely chivalrous**[2]. She wished he had said to Clifford: 'Yes, she is my lover and my mistress and I am proud of it!' But his courage wouldn't carry him so far.

So her name was coupled with his in Tevershall! It was a mess. But that would soon die down.

She was angry, with the complicated and confused anger that made her inert. She did not know what to do nor what to say, so she said and did nothing. She went on at Venice just the same, rowing out in the gondola with Duncan Forbes, bathing, letting the days slip by. Duncan, who had been rather depressingly in love with her ten years ago, was in love with her again. But she said to him: 'I only want one thing of men, and that is, that they should leave me alone.'

So Duncan left her alone: really quite pleased to be able to. All the same, he offered her a soft stream of a queer, inverted sort of love. He wanted to be with her.

'Have you ever thought,' he said to her one day, 'how very little people are connected with one another. Look at Daniele! He is handsome as a son of the sun. But see how alone he looks in his handsomeness. Yet I bet he has a wife and family, and couldn't possibly go away from them.'

'Ask him,' said Connie.

Duncan did so. Daniele said he was married, and had two children, both male, aged seven and nine. But he betrayed no emotion over the fact.

'Perhaps only people who are capable of real togetherness have that look of being alone in the universe,' said Connie. 'The others have a certain stickiness, they stick to the mass, like Giovanni.' 'And,' she thought to herself, 'like you, Duncan.'

❶你所犯的罪过将会受到报应。 ❷他不必如此故作神勇。

CHAPTER 18

She had to make up her mind what to do. She would leave Venice on the Saturday that he was leaving Wragby: in six days' time. This would bring her to London on the Monday following, and she would then see him. She wrote to him to the London address, asking him to send her a letter to Hartland's hotel, and to call for her on the Monday evening at seven.

Inside herself she was curiously and complicatedly angry, and all her responses were numb. She refused to confide even in Hilda, and Hilda, offended by her steady silence, had become rather intimate with a Dutch woman. Connie hated these rather stifling intimacies between women, intimacy into which Hilda always entered ponderously.

Sir Malcolm decided to travel with Connie, and Duncan could come on with Hilda. The old artist always did himself well: he took berths on the Orient Express, in spite of Connie's dislike of **trains de luxe**[1], the atmosphere of vulgar depravity there is aboard them nowadays. However, it would make the journey to Paris shorter.

Sir Malcolm was always uneasy going back to his wife. It was habit carried over from the first wife. But there would be a house-party for the grouse, and he wanted to be well ahead. Connie, sunburnt and handsome, sat in silence, forgetting all about the landscape.

'A little dull for you, going back to Wragby,' said her father, noticing her glumness.

'I'm not sure I shall go back to Wragby,' she said, with startling abruptness, looking into his eyes with her big blue eyes. His big blue eyes took on the frightened look of **a man whose social conscience is not quite clear**[2].

'You mean you'll stay on in Paris a while?'

'No! I mean never go back to Wragby.'

He was bothered by his own little problems, and sincerely hoped he

❶豪华列车。❷一个内心有歉疚的人。

was getting none of hers to shoulder.

'How's that, all at once?' he asked.

'I'm going to have a child.'

It was the first time she had uttered the words to any living soul, and it seemed to mark a cleavage in her life.

'How do you know?' said her father.

She smiled.

'How should I know?'

'But not Clifford's child, of course?'

'No! Another man's.'

She rather enjoyed tormenting him.

'Do I know the man?' asked Sir Malcolm.

'No! You've never seen him.'

There was a long pause.

'And what are your plans?'

'I don't know. That's the point.'

'**No patching it up with Clifford**[1]?'

'I suppose Clifford would take it,' said Connie. 'He told me, after last time you talked to him, he wouldn't mind if I had a child, so long as I went about it discreetly.'

'Only sensible thing he could say, under the circumstances. Then I suppose it'll be all right.'

'In what way?' said Connie, looking into her father's eyes. They were big blue eyes rather like her own, but with a certain uneasiness in them, a look sometimes of an uneasy little boy, sometimes a look of sullen selfishness, usually good-humoured and wary.

'You can present Clifford with an heir to all the Chatterleys, and put another baronet in Wragby.'

Sir Malcolm's face smiled with a half-sensual smile.

'But I don't think I want to,' she said.

'Why not? Feeling entangled with the other man? Well! If you want the truth from me, my child, it's this. The world goes on. Wragby stands and will go on standing. The world is more or less a fixed thing and, externally, we have to adapt ourselves to it. Privately, in my private opinion, we can please ourselves. Emotions change. You may like

[1] 不能和 Clifford 商量解决吗?

one man this year and another next. But Wragby still stands. Stick by Wragby as far as Wragby sticks by you. Then please yourself. But you'll get very little out of making a break. You can make a break if you wish. You have an independent income, the only thing that never lets you down. But you won't get much out of it. Put a little baronet in Wragby. It's an amusing thing to do.'

And Sir Malcolm sat back and smiled again. Connie did not answer.

'I hope you had a real man at last,' he said to her after a while, sensually alert.

'I did. That's the trouble. There aren't many of them about,' she said.

'No, by God!' he mused. 'There aren't! Well, my dear, to look at you, he was a lucky man. Surely he wouldn't make trouble for you?'

'Oh no! He leaves me my own mistress entirely.'

'Quite! Quite! A genuine man would.'

Sir Malcolm was pleased. Connie was his favourite daughter, he had always liked the female in her. Not so much of her mother in her as in Hilda. And he had always disliked Clifford. So he was pleased, and very tender with his daughter, as if the unborn child were his child.

He drove with her to Hartland's hotel, and saw her installed: then went round to his club. She had refused his company for the evening.

She found a letter from Mellors.

I won't come round to your hotel, but I'll wait for you outside the Golden Cock in Adam Street at seven.

There he stood, tall and slender, and so different, in a formal suit of thin dark cloth. He had a natural distinction, but he had not the **cut-to-pattern**[1] look of her class. Yet, she saw at once, he could go anywhere. He had a native breeding which was really much nicer than the cut-to-pattern class thing.

'Ah, there you are! How well you look!'

'Yes! But not you.'

She looked in his face anxiously. It was thin, and the cheekbones showed. But his eyes smiled at her, and she felt at home with him. There it was: suddenly, the tension of keeping up her appearances fell from her. Something flowed out of him physically, that made her feel inwardly at

[1] 典型的。

ease and happy, at home. With a woman's now alert instinct for happiness, she registered it at once. 'I'm happy when he's there!' Not all the sunshine of Venice had given her this inward expansion and warmth.

'Was it horrid for you?' she asked as she sat opposite him at table. He was too thin; she saw it now. His hand lay as she knew it, with the curious loose forgottenness of a sleeping animal. She wanted so much to take it and kiss it. But she did not quite dare.

'People are always horrid,' he said.

'And did you mind very much?'

'I minded, as I always shall mind. And I knew I was a fool to mind.'

'Did you feel like a dog with a tin can tied to its tail? Clifford said you felt like that.'

He looked at her. It was cruel of her at that moment: for his pride had suffered bitterly.

'I suppose I did,' he said.

She never knew the fierce bitterness with which he resented insult.

There was a long pause.

'And did you miss me?' she asked.

'I was glad you were out of it.'

Again there was a pause.

'But did people believe about you and me?' she asked.

'No! I don't think so for a moment.'

'Did Clifford?'

'I should say not. He put it off without thinking about it. But naturally it made him **want to see the last of me**[1].'

'I'm going to have a child.'

The expression died utterly out of his face, out of his whole body. He looked at her with darkened eyes, whose look she could not understand at all: like some dark-flamed spirit looking at her.

'Say you're glad!' she pleaded, groping for his hand. And she saw a certain exultance spring up in him. But it was netted down by things she could not understand.

'It's the future,' he said.

[1]不想再见到我。

'But aren't you glad?' she persisted.

'I have such a terrible mistrust of the future.'

'But you needn't be troubled by any responsibility. Clifford would have it as his own, he'd be glad.'

She saw him go pale, and recoil under this. He did not answer.

'Shall I go back to Clifford and put a little baronet into Wragby?' she asked.

He looked at her, pale and very remote. The ugly little grin flickered on his face.

'You wouldn't have to tell him who the father was?'

'Oh!' she said; 'he'd take it even then, if I wanted him to.'

He thought for a time.

'Ay!' he said at last, to himself. 'I suppose he would.'

There was silence. A big gulf was between them.

'But you don't want me to go back to Clifford, do you?' she asked him.

'What do you want yourself?' he replied.

'I want to live with you,' she said simply.

In spite of himself, little flames ran over his belly as he heard her say it, and he dropped his head. Then he looked up at her again, with those haunted eyes.

'If it's worth it to you,' he said. 'I've got nothing.'

'You've got more than most men. Come, you know it,' she said.

'In one way, I know it.' He was silent for a time, thinking. Then he resumed: 'They used to say I had too much of the woman in me. But it's not that. I'm not a woman not because I don't want to shoot birds, neither because I don't want to make money, or get on. I could have got on in the army, easily, but I didn't like the army. Though I could manage the men all right: they liked me and they had a bit of a holy fear of me when I got mad. No, it was stupid, dead-handed higher authority that made the army dead: absolutely fool-dead. I like men, and men like me. But I can't stand the twaddling bossy impudence of the people who run this world. That's why I can't get on. I hate the impudence of money, and I hate the impudence of class. So in the world as it is, what have I to offer a woman?'

'But why offer anything? It's not a bargain. It's just that we love one another,' she said.

'Nay, nay! It's more than that. Living is moving and moving on. My life won't go down the proper gutters, it just won't. So I'm a bit of a waste ticket by myself. And I've no business to take a woman into my life, unless my life does something and gets somewhere, inwardly at least, to keep us both fresh. A man must offer a woman some meaning in his life, if it's going to be an isolated life, and if she's a genuine woman. I can't be just your male concubine.'

'Why not?' she said.

'Why, because I can't. And you would soon hate it.'

'As if you couldn't trust me,' she said.

The grin flickered on his face.

'The money is yours, the position is yours, the decisions will lie with you. I'm not just my Lady's fucker, after all.'

'What else are you?'

'You may well ask. It no doubt is invisible. Yet I'm something to myself at least. I can see the point of my own existence, though I can quite understand nobody else's seeing it.'

'And will your existence have less point, if you live with me?'

He paused a long time before replying:

'It might.'

She too stayed to think about it.

'And what is the point of your existence?'

'I tell you, it's invisible. I don't believe in the world, not in money, nor in advancement, nor in the future of our civilization. If there's got to be a future for humanity, there'll have to be a very big change from what now is.'

'And what will the real future have to be like?'

'God knows! I can feel something inside me, all mixed up with a lot of rage. But what it really amounts to, I don't know.'

'Shall I tell you?' she said, looking into his face. 'Shall I tell you what you have that other men don't have, and that will make the future? Shall I tell you?'

'Tell me then,' he replied.

'It's the courage of your own tenderness, that's what it is: like when you put your hand on my tail and say I've got a pretty tail.'

The grin came flickering on his face.

'That! ' he said.

Then he sat thinking.

'Ay!' he said. 'You're right. It's that really. It's that all the way through. I knew it with the men. I had to be in touch with them, physically, and not go back on it. I had to be bodily aware of them and a bit tender to them, even if I put 'em through hell. It's a question of awareness, as Buddha said. But even he fought shy of the bodily awareness, and that natural physical tenderness, which is the best, even between men; in a proper manly way. Makes 'em really manly, not so monkeyish. Ay! it's tenderness, really; it's cunt-awareness. Sex is really only touch, the closest of all touch. And it's touch we're afraid of. We're only half-conscious, and half alive. We've got to come alive and aware. Especially the English have got to get into touch with one another, a bit delicate and a bit tender. It's our **crying need**[1].'

She looked at him.

'Then why are you afraid of me?' she said.

He looked at her a long time before he answered.

'It's the money, really, and the position. It's the world in you.'

'But isn't there tenderness in me?' she said wistfully.

He looked down at her, with darkened, abstract eyes.

'Ay! It comes an' goes, like in me.'

'But can't you trust it between you and me?' she asked, gazing anxiously at him.

She saw his face all softening down, losing its armour. 'Maybe!' he said. They were both silent.

'I want you to hold me in your arms,' she said. 'I want you to tell me you are glad we are having a child.'

She looked so lovely and warm and wistful, his bowels stirred towards her.

'I suppose we can go to my room,' he said. 'Though it's scandalous again.'

But she saw the forgetfulness of the world coming over him again, his face taking the soft, pure look of tender passion.

They walked by the remoter streets to Coburg Square, where he had a room at the top of the house, an attic room where he cooked for himself on a gas ring. It was small, but decent and tidy.

---

[1] 迫切的需要。

She took off her things, and made him do the same. She was lovely in the soft first flush of her pregnancy.

'I ought to leave you alone,' he said.

'No!' she said. 'Love me! Love me, and say you'll keep me. Say you'll keep me! Say you'll never let me go, to the world nor to anybody.'

She crept close against him, clinging fast to his thin, strong naked body, the only home she had ever known.

'Then I'll keep thee,' he said. 'If tha wants it, then I'll keep thee.'

He held her round and fast.

'And say you're glad about the child,' she repeated.

'Kiss it! Kiss my womb and say you're glad it's there.'

But that was more difficult for him.

'I've a dread of puttin' children i' th' world,' he said. 'I've such a dread o' th' future for 'em.'

'But you've put it into me. Be tender to it, and that will be its future already. Kiss it!'

He quivered, because it was true. 'Be tender to it, and that will be its future.' — At that moment he felt a sheer love for the woman. He kissed her belly and her mound of Venus, to kiss close to the womb and the foetus within the womb.

'Oh, you love me! You love me!' she said, in a little cry like one of her blind, inarticulate love cries. And he went in to her softly, feeling the stream of tenderness flowing in release from his bowels to hers, the bowels of compassion kindled between them.

And he realized as he went into her that this was the thing he had to do, to come into tender touch, without losing his pride or his dignity or his integrity as a man. After all, if she had money and means, and he had none, he should be too proud and honourable to hold back his tenderness from her on that account. 'I stand for the touch of bodily awareness between human beings,' he said to himself, 'and the touch of tenderness. And she is my mate. And it is a battle against the money, and the machine, and the insentient ideal monkeyishness of the world. And she will stand behind me there. Thank God I've got a woman! Thank God I've got a woman who is with me, and tender and aware of me. Thank God she's not a bully, nor a fool. Thank God she's a tender, aware woman.' And as his seed sprang in her, his soul sprang towards her too, in the creative act that is far more than procreative.

She was quite determined now that there should be no parting between him and her. But the ways and means were still to settle.

'Did you hate Bertha Coutts?' she asked him.

'Don't talk to me about her.'

'Yes! You must let me. Because once you liked her. And once you were as intimate with her as you are with me. So you have to tell me. Isn't it rather terrible, when you've been intimate with her, to hate her so? Why is it?'

'I don't know. She sort of kept her will ready against me, always, always: her ghastly female will: her freedom! A woman's ghastly freedom that ends in the most beastly bullying! Oh, she always kept her freedom against me, like vitriol in my face.'

'But she's not free of you even now. Does she still love you?'

'No, no! If she's not free of me, it's because she's got that mad rage, she must try to bully me.'

'But she must have loved you.'

'No! Well, in specks she did. She was drawn to me. And I think even that she hated. She loved me in moments. But she always took it back, and started bullying. Her deepest desire was to bully me, and there was no altering her. Her will was wrong, from the first.'

'But perhaps she felt you didn't really love her, and she wanted to make you.'

'My God, it was bloody making.'

'But you didn't really love her, did you? You did her that wrong.'

'How could I? I began to. I began to love her. But somehow, she always ripped me up. No, don't let's talk of it. It was a doom, that was. And she was a doomed woman. This last time, I'd have shot her like I shoot a stoat, if I'd but been allowed: a raving, doomed thing in the shape of a woman! If only I could have shot her, and ended the whole misery! It ought to be allowed. When a woman gets absolutely possessed by her own will, her own will set against everything, then it' fearful, and she should be shot at last.'

'And shouldn't men be shot at last, if they get possessed by their own will?'

'Ay! — the same! But I must get free of her, or she'll be at me again. I wanted to tell you. I must get a divorce if I possibly can. So we must be careful. We mustn't really be seen together, you and I. I never,

never could stand it if she came down on me and you.'

Connie pondered this.

'Then we can't be together?' she said.

'Not for six months or so. But I think my divorce will go through in September; then till March.'

'But the baby will probably be born at the end of February,' she said.

He was silent.

'I could wish the Cliffords and Berthas all dead,' he said.

'It's not being very tender to them,' she said.

'Tender to them? Yea, even then the tenderest thing you could do for them, perhaps, would be to give them death. They can't live! They only frustrate life. Their souls are awful inside them. Death ought to be sweet to them. And I ought to be allowed to shoot them.'

'But you wouldn't do it,' she said.

'I would though! and with less qualms than I shoot a weasel. It anyhow has a prettiness and a loneliness. But they are legion. Oh, I'd shoot them.'

'Then perhaps it is just as well you daren't.'

'Well.'

Connie had now plenty to think of. It was evident he wanted absolutely to be free of Bertha Coutts. And she felt he was right. The last attack had been too grim. — This meant her living alone, till spring. Perhaps she could get divorced from Clifford. But how? If Mellors were named, then there was an end to his divorce. How loathsome! Couldn't one go right away, to the far ends of the earth, and be free from it all?

One could not. The far ends of the world are not five minutes from **Charing Cross**[1], nowadays. While the wireless is active, there are no far ends of the earth. Kings of **Dahomey**[2] and Lamas of Tibet listen in to London and New York.

Patience! Patience! The world is a vast and ghastly intricacy of mechanism, and one has to be very wary, not to get mangled by it.

Connie confided in her father.

'You see, Father, he was Clifford's game-keeper: but he was an officer in the army in India. Only he is like Colonel C. E. Florence, who

[1]伦敦的一条街道。 [2]达荷美是西非国家贝宁的旧称。

preferred to become a private soldier again.'

Sir Malcolm, however, had no sympathy with the unsatisfactory mysticism of the famous C. E. Florence. He saw too much advertisement behind all the humility. It looked just like the sort of conceit the knight most loathed, the conceit of self-abasement.

'Where did your game-keeper spring from?' asked Sir Malcolm irritably.

'He was a collier's son in Tevershall. But he's absolutely presentable.'

The knighted artist became more angry.

'Looks to me like a gold-digger,' he said. 'And you're a pretty easy gold-mine, apparently.'

'No, Father, it's not like that. You'd know if you saw him. He's a man. Clifford always detested him for not being humble.'

'Apparently he had a good instinct, for once.'

What Sir Malcolm could not bear was the scandal of his daughter's **having an intrigue with**[1] a game-keeper. He did not mind the intrigue: he minded the scandal.

'I care nothing about the fellow. He's evidently been able to get round you all right. But, by God, think of all the talk. Think of your step-mother how she'll take it!'

'I know,' said Connie. '**Talk is beastly: especially if you live in society**[2]. And he wants so much to get his own divorce. I thought we might perhaps say it was another man's child, and not mention Mellors' name at all.'

'Another man's! What other man's?'

'Perhaps Duncan Forbes. He has been our friend all his life.'

'And he's a fairly well-known artist. And he's fond of me.'

'Well I'm damned! Poor Duncan! And what's he going to get out of it?'

'I don't know. But he might rather like it, even.'

'He might, might he? Well, he's a funny man if he does. Why, you've never even had an affair with him, have you?'

'No! But he doesn't really want it. He only loves me to be near him, but not to touch him.'

'My God, what a generation!'

---

❶与某人有私情。 ❷闲话是可怕的，尤其对于生活在上流社会的人来说。

'He would like me most of all to be a model for him to paint from. Only I never wanted to.'

'God help him! **But he looks down-trodden enough for anything**[1].'

'Still, you wouldn't mind so much the talk about him?'

'My God, Connie, all the bloody contriving!'

'I know! It's sickening! But what can I do?'

'Contriving, conniving; conniving, contriving! Makes a man think he's lived too long.'

'Come, Father, if you haven't done a good deal of contriving and conniving in your time, you may talk.'

'But it was different, I assure you.'

'It's always different.'

Hilda arrived, also furious when she heard of the new developments. And she also simply could not stand the thought of a public scandal about her sister and a game-keeper. Too, too humiliating!

'Why should we not just disappear, separately, to British Columbia, and have no scandal?' said Connie.

But that was no good. The scandal would come out just the same. And if Connie was going with the man, she'd better be able to marry him. This was Hilda's opinion. Sir Malcolm wasn't sure. The affair might still blow over.

'But will you see him, Father?'

Poor Sir Malcolm! he was by no means keen on it. And poor Mellors, he was still less keen. Yet the meeting took place: a lunch in a private room at the club, the two men alone, looking one another up and down.

Sir Malcolm drank a fair amount of whisky, Mellors also drank. And they talked all the while about India, on which the young man was well informed.

This lasted during the meal. Only when coffee was served, and the waiter had gone, Sir Malcolm lit a cigar and said, heartily:

'Well, young man, and what about my daughter?'

The grin flickered on Mellors' face.

'Well, Sir, and what about her?'

'You've got a baby in her all right.'

'I have that honour!' grinned Mellors.

[1] 但像他这样一个没有骨气的人什么事都干得出来。

'Honour, by God!' Sir Malcolm **gave a little squirting laugh**[1], and became Scotch and lewd. 'Honour! How was the going, eh? Good, my boy, what?'

'Good!'

'I'll bet it was! Ha-ha! My daughter, chip of the old block, what! I never went back on a good bit of fucking, myself. Though her mother, oh, holy saints!' He rolled his eyes to heaven. 'But you warmed her up, oh, you warmed her up, I can see that. Ha-ha! My blood in her! You set fire to her haystack all right. Ha-ha-ha! I was jolly glad of it, I can tell you. She needed it. Oh, she's a nice girl, she's a nice girl, and I knew she'd be good going, if only some damned man would set her stack on fire! Ha-ha-ha! A game-keeper, eh, my boy! Bloody good poacher, if you ask me. Ha-ha! But now, look here, speaking seriously, what are we going to do about it? Speaking seriously, you know!'

Speaking seriously, they didn't get very far. Mellors, though a little tipsy, was much the soberer of the two. He kept the conversation as intelligent as possible: which isn't saying much.

'So you're a game-keeper! Oh, you're quite right! That sort of game is worth a man's while, eh, what? The test of a woman is when you pinch her bottom. You can tell just by the feel of her bottom if she's going to come up all right. Ha-ha! I envy you, my boy. How old are you?'

'Thirty-nine.'

The knight lifted his eyebrows.

'As much as that! Well, you've another good twenty years, by the look of you. Oh, game-keeper or not, you're a good cock. I can see that with one eye shut. Not like that blasted Clifford! A lily-livered hound with never a fuck in him, never had. I like you, my boy, I'll bet you've a good cod on you; oh, you're a bantam, I can see that. You're a fighter. Game-keeper! Ha-ha, by crikey, I wouldn't trust my game to you! But look here, seriously, what are we going to do about it? The world's full of blasted old women.'

Seriously, they didn't do anything about it, except establish the old free-masonry of male sensuality between them.

'And look here, my boy, if ever I can do anything for you, you can rely on me. Game-keeper! Christ, **but it's rich**[2]! I like it! Oh,

[1]大笑起来。 [2](口语)真有趣!

I like it! Shows the girl's got spunk. What? After all, you know, she has her own income, moderate, moderate, but above starvation. And I'll leave her what I've got. By God, I will. She deserves it for showing spunk, in a world of old women. I've been struggling to get myself clear of the skirts of old women for seventy years, and haven't managed it yet. But you're the man, I can see that.'

'I'm glad you think so. They usually tell me, in a sideways fashion, that I'm the monkey.'

'Oh, they would! My dear fellow, what could you be but a monkey, to all the old women?'

They parted most genially, and Mellors laughed inwardly all the time for the rest of the day.

The following day he had lunch with Connie and Hilda, at some discreet place.

'It's a very great pity it's such an ugly situation all round,' said Hilda.

'I had a lot o' fun out of it,' said he.

'I think you might have avoided putting children into the world until you were both free to marry and have children.'

'The Lord blew a bit too soon on the spark,' said he.

'I think the Lord had nothing to do with it. Of course, Connie has enough money to keep you both, but the situation is unbearable.'

'But then you don't have to bear more than a small corner of it, do you?' said he.

'If you'd been in her own class.'

'Or if I'd been in a cage at the Zoo.'

There was silence.

'I think,' said Hilda, 'it will be best if she names quite another man as co-respondent and you stay out of it altogether.'

'But I thought I'd put my foot right in.'

'I mean in the divorce proceedings.'

He gazed at her in wonder. Connie had not dared mention the Duncan scheme to him.

'I don't follow,' he said.

'We have a friend who would probably agree to be named as co-respondent, so that your name need not appear,' said Hilda.

'You mean a man?'

'Of course!'

'But she's got no other?'

He looked in wonder at Connie.

'No, no!' she said hastily. 'Only that old friendship, quite simple, no love.'

'Then why should the fellow take the blame? If he's had nothing out of you?'

'Some men are chivalrous and don't only count what they get out of a woman,' said Hilda.

'One for me, eh? But who's the **johnny**[1]?'

'A friend whom we've known since we were children in Scotland, an artist.'

'Duncan Forbes!' he said at once, for Connie had talked to him. 'And how would you shift the blame on to him?'

'They could stay together in some hotel, or she could even stay in his apartment.'

'Seems to me like a lot of fuss for nothing,' he said.

'What else do you suggest?' said Hilda. 'If your name appears, you will get no divorce from your wife, who is apparently quite an impossible person to be mixed up with.'

'All that!' he said grimly.

There was a long silence.

'We could go right away,' he said.

'There is no right away for Connie,' said Hilda. 'Clifford is too well known.'

Again the silence of pure frustration.

'The world is what it is. If you want to live together without being persecuted, you will have to marry. To marry, you both have to be divorced. So how are you both going about it?'

He was silent for a long time.

'How are you going about it for us?' he said.

'We will see if Duncan will consent to figure as co-respondent: then we must get Clifford to divorce Connie: and you must go on with your divorce, and you must both keep apart till you are free.'

'Sounds like a lunatic asylum.'

[1] 家伙,汉子。

'Possibly! And the world would look on you as lunatics: or worse.;

'What is worse?'

'Criminals, I suppose.'

'Hope I can plunge in the dagger a few more times yet,' he said, grinning. Then he was silent, and angry.

'Well!' he said at last. 'I agree to anything. The world is a raving idiot, and no man can kill it: though I'll do my best. But you re right. We must rescue ourselves as best we can.'

He looked in humiliation, anger, weariness and misery at Connie.

'Ma lass!' he said. 'The world's goin' to put salt on thy tail.'

'Not if we don't let it,' she said.

She minded this conniving against the world less than he did.

Duncan, when approached, also insisted on seeing the delinquent game-keeper, so there was a dinner, this time in his flat: the four of them. Duncan was a rather short, broad, dark-skinned, **taciturn Hamlet of a fellow**[1] with straight black hair and a weird Celtic conceit of himself. His art was all tubes and valves and spirals and strange colours, ultra-modern, yet with a certain power, even a certain purity of form and tone: only Mellors thought it cruel and repellent. He did not venture to say so, for Duncan was almost insane on the point of his art: it was a personal cult, a personal religion with him.

They were looking at the pictures in the studio, and Duncan kept his smallish brown eyes on the other man. He wanted to hear what the game-keeper would say. He knew already Connie's and Hilda's opinions.

'It is like a pure bit of murder,' said Mellors at last; a speech Duncan by no means expected from a game-keeper.

'And who is murdered?' asked Hilda, rather coldly and sneeringly.

'Me! It murders all the bowels of compassion in a man.'

A wave of pure hate came out of the artist. He heard the note of dislike in the other man's voice, and the note of contempt. And he himself loathed the mention of bowels of compassion. Sickly sentiment!

Mellors stood rather tall and thin, worn-looking, gazing with flickering detachment that was something like the dancing of a moth on the wing, at the pictures.

---

[1] 一个哈姆雷特式沉默寡言的人。

'Perhaps stupidity is murdered; sentimental stupidity,' sneered the artist.

'Do you think so? I think all these tubes and corrugated vibrations are stupid enough for anything, and pretty sentimental. They show a lot of self-pity and an awful lot of nervous self-opinion, seems to me.'

In another wave of hate the artist's face looked yellow. But with a sort of silent **hauteur**[1] he turned the pictures to the wall.

'I think we may go to the dining-room,' he said. And they trailed off, dismally.

After coffee, Duncan said:

'I don't at all mind posing as the father of Connie's child. But only on the condition that she'll come and pose as a model for me. I've wanted her for years, and she's always refused.' He uttered it with the dark finality of an inquisitor announcing an auto da fe.

'Ah!' said Mellors. 'You only do it on condition, then?'

'Quite! I only do it on that condition.' The artist tried to put the utmost contempt of the other person into his speech. He put a little too much.

'Better have me as a model at the same time,' said Mellors. 'Better do us in a group, **Vulcan**[2] and Venus under the net of art. I used to be a blacksmith, before I was a game-keeper.'

'Thank you,' said the artist. 'I don't think Vulcan has a figure that interests me.'

'Not even if it was tubified and titivated up?'

There was no answer. The artist was too haughty for further words.

It was a dismal party, in which the artist henceforth steadily ignored the presence of the other man, and talked only briefly, **as if the words were wrung out of the depths of his gloo-my portentousness**[3], to the women.

'You didn't like him, but he's better than that, really. He's really kind,' Connie explained as they left.

'He's a little black pup with a corrugated distemper,' said Mellors.

'No, he wasn't nice today.'

'And will you go and be a model to him?'

❶(法)倨傲。 ❷罗马神话中的火与锻冶之神,Venus的丈夫,容貌丑陋。 ❸好像他的话是从矜持,忧郁的内心深处挤出来的。

'Oh, I don't really mind any more. He won't touch me. And I don't mind anything, if it paves the way to a life together for you and me.'

'But he'll only shit on you on canvas.'

'I don't care. He'll only be painting his own feelings for me, and I don't mind if he does that. I wouldn't have him touch me, not for anything. But if he thinks he can do anything with his owlish arty staring, let him stare. He can make as many empty tubes and corrugations out of me as he likes. It's his funeral. He hated you for what you said: that his tubified art is sentimental and self-important. But of course it's true.'

CHAPTER 19

Dear Clifford, I am afraid what you foresaw has happened. I am really in love with another man, and do hope you will divorce me. I am staying at present with Duncan in his flat. I told you he was at Venice with us. I'm awfully unhappy for your sake: but do try to take it quietly. You don't really need me any more, and I can't bear to come back to Wragby. I'm awfully sorry. But do try to forgive me, and divorce me and find someone better. I'm not really the right person for you, I am too impatient and selfish, I suppose. But I can't ever come back to live with you again. And I feel so frightfully sorry about it all, for your sake. But if you don't let yourself get worked up, you'll see you won't mind so frightfully. You didn't really care about me personally. So do forgive me and get rid of me.

Clifford was not inwardly surprised to get this letter. Inwardly, he had known for a long time she was leaving him. But he had absolutely refused any outward admission of it. Therefore, outwardly, it came as the most terrible blow and shock to him, He had kept the surface of his confidence in her quite serene.

And that is how we are. By strength of will we cut of four inner intuitive knowledge from admitted consciousness. This causes a state of dread, or apprehension, which makes the blow ten times worse when it does fall.

Clifford was like a hysterical child. He gave Mrs Bolton a terrible shock, sitting up in bed ghastly and blank.

'Why, Sir Clifford, whatever's the matter?'

No answer! She was terrified lest he had had a stroke. She hurried and felt his face, took his pulse.

'Is there a pain? Do try and tell me where it hurts you. Do tell me!'

No answer!

'Oh dear, oh dear! Then I'll telephone to Sheffield for Dr Carrington, and Dr Lecky may as well run round straight away.'

She was moving to the door, when he said in a hollow tone:

'No!'

She stopped and gazed at him. His face was yellow, blank, and like the face of an idiot.

'Do you mean you'd rather I didn't fetch the doctor?'

'Yes! I don't want him,' came the sepulchral voice.

'Oh, but Sir Clifford, you're ill, and I daren't take the responsibility. I must send for the doctor, or I shall be blamed.'

A pause: then the hollow voice said:

'I'm not ill. My wife isn't coming back.' — It was as if an image spoke.

'Not coming back? you mean her ladyship?' Mrs Bolton moved a little nearer to the bed. 'Oh, don't you believe it. You can trust her ladyship to come back.'

The image in the bed did not change, but it pushed a letter over the counterpane.

'Read it!' said the sepulchral voice.

'Why, if it's a letter from her ladyship, I'm sure her ladyship wouldn't want me to read her letter to you, Sir Clifford. You can tell me what she says, if you wish.'

'Read it!' repeated the voice.

'Why, if I must, I do it to obey you, Sir Clifford,' she said. And she read the letter.

'Well, I am surprised at her ladyship,' she said. 'She promised so faithfully she'd come back!'

The face in the bed seemed to deepen its expression of wild, but motionless distraction. Mrs B olton looked at it and was worried. She knew what she was up against: male hysteria. **She had not nursed soldiers without learning something about that very unpleasant disease**[1].

She was a little impatient of Sir Clifford. Any man in his senses must have known his wife was in love with somebody else, and was going to leave him. Even, she was sure, Sir Clifford was inwardly absolutely aware of it, only he wouldn't admit it to himself. If he would have admitted it, and prepared himself for it: or if he would have admitted it, and actively struggled with his wife against it: that would have been acting like a man. But no! he knew it, and all the time tried to kid himself it wasn't so. He felt the devil twisting his tail, and pretended it was the angels smiling on him. This state of falsity had now brought on that crisis of falsity and dislocation, hysteria, which is a form of insanity. 'It comes', she thought to herself, hating him a little, 'because he always thinks of himself. He's so wrapped up in his own immortal self, that when he does get a shock he's like a mummy tangled in its own bandages. Look at him!'

But hysteria is dangerous: and she was a nurse, it was her duty to pull him out. Any attempt to rouse his manhood and his pride would only make him worse: for his manhood was dead, temporarily if not finally. He would only squirm softer and softer, like a worm, and become more dislocated.

The only thing was to release his self-pity. Like the lady in **Tennyson**[2], he must weep or he must die.

So Mrs Bolton began to weep first. She covered her face with her hand and burst into little wild sobs. 'I would never have believed it of her ladyship, I wouldn't!' she wept, suddenly summoning up all her old grief and sense of woe, and weeping the tears of her own bitter chagrin. Once she started, her weeping was genuine enough, for she had had something to weep for.

Clifford thought of the way he had been betrayed by the woman Connie, and in a contagion of grief, tears filled his eyes and began to run down his cheeks. He was weeping for himself. Mrs Bolton, as soon as she saw the tears running over his blank face, hastily wiped her own wet cheeks on her little handkerchief, and leaned towards him.

❶她以前看护士兵时就对这种讨厌的病有所了解。 ❷英国诗人(1809—1892)。他重视诗的形式完美,被封为桂冠诗人。

'Now, don't you fret, Sir Clifford!' she said, in a luxury of emotion. 'Now, don't you fret, don't, you'll only do yourself an injury!'

His body shivered suddenly in an indrawn breath of silent sobbing, and the tears ran quicker down his face. She laid her hand on his arm, and her own tears fell again. Again the shiver went through him, like a convulsion, and she laid her arm round his shoulder. 'There, there! There, there! Don't you fret, then, don't you! Don't you fret!' she moaned to him, while her own tears fell. And she drew him to her, and held her arms round his great shoulders, while he laid his face on her bosom and sobbed, shaking and hulking his huge shoulders, whilst she softly stroked his dusky-blond hair and said: 'There! There! There! There then! There then! Never you mind! Never you mind, then!'

And he put his arms round her and clung to her like a child, wetting the bib of her starched white apron, and the bosom of her pale-blue cotton dress, with his tears. He had let himself go altogether, at last.

So at length she kissed him, and rocked him on her bosom, and in her heart she said to herself: 'Oh, Sir Clifford! Oh, high and mighty Chatterleys! Is this what you've come down to!' And finally he even went to sleep, like a child. And she felt worn out, and went to her own room, where she laughed and cried at once, with a hysteria of her own. It was so ridiculous! It was so awful! Such a come-down! So shameful! And it was so upsetting as well.

After this, Clifford became like a child with Mrs Bolton. He would hold her hand, and rest his head on her breast, and when she once lightly kissed him, he said! 'Yes! Do kiss me! Do kiss me!' And when she sponged his great blond body, he would say the same! 'Do kiss me!' and she would lightly kiss his body, anywhere, half in mockery.

And he lay with a queer, blank face like a child, with a bit of the wonderment of a child. And he would gaze on her with wide, childish eyes, in a relaxation of **madonna-worship**[1]. It was sheer relaxation on his part, letting go all his manhood, and sinking back to a childish position that was really perverse. And then he would put his hand into her bosom and feel her breasts, and kiss them in exultation, the exultation of

[1] 圣母崇拜。

perversity, of being a child when he was a man.

Mrs Bolton was both thrilled and ashamed, she both loved and hated it. Yet she never rebuffed nor rebuked him. And they drew into a closer physical intimacy, an intimacy of perversity, when he was a child stricken with an apparent candour and an apparent wonderment, that looked almost like a religious exaltation: the perverse and literal rendering of: 'except ye become again as a little child'. — While she was **the Magna Mater**[1], full of power and potency, having the great blond child-man under her will and her stroke entirely.

The curious thing was that when this child-man, which Clifford was now and which he had been becoming for years, emerged into the world, it was much sharper and keener than the real man he used to be. This perverted child-man was now a real business-man; when it was a question of affairs, he was an absolute he-man, sharp as a needle, and impervious as a bit of steel. When he was out among men, seeking his own ends, and 'making good' his colliery workings, he had an almost uncanny shrewdness, hardness, and a straight sharp punch. It was as if his very passivity and prostitution to the Magna Mater gave him insight into material business affairs, and lent him a certain remarkable inhuman force. The wallowing in private emotion, the utter abasement of his manly self, seemed to lend him a second nature, cold, almost visionary, business-clever. In business he was quite inhuman.

And in this Mrs Bolton triumphed. 'How he's getting on!' she would say to herself in pride. 'And that's my doing! My word, he'd never have got on like this with Lady Chatterley. She was not the one to put a man forward. She wanted too much for herself.'

At the same time, in some corner of her weird female soul, how she despised him and hated him! He was to her the fallen beast, the squirming monster. And while she aided and abetted him all she could, away in the remotest corner of her ancient healthy womanhood she despised him with a savage contempt that knew no bounds. The merest tramp was better than he.

His behaviour with regard to Connie was curious. He insisted on seeing her again. He insisted, moreover, on her coming to Wragby. On this point he was finally and absolutely fixed. Connie had promised to

[1] (拉丁语)伟大的圣母玛利亚。

come back to Wragby, faithfully.

'But is it any use?' said Mrs Bolton. 'Can't you let her go, and be rid of her?'

'No! She said she was coming back, and she's got to come.'

Mrs Bolton opposed him no more. She knew what she was dealing with.

I needn't tell you what effect your letter has had on me [he wrote to Connie to London]. Perhaps you can imagine it if you try, though no doubt you won't trouble to use your imagination on my behalf.

I can only say one thing in answer: I must see you personally, here at Wragby, before I can do anything. You promised faithfully to come back to Wragby, and **I hold you to the promise**[1]. I don't believe anything nor understand anything until I see you personally, here under normal circumstances. I needn't tell you that nobody here suspects anything, so your return would be quite normal. Then if you feel, after we have talked things over, that you still remain in the same mind, no doubt we can come to terms.

Connie showed this letter to Mellors.

'He wants to begin his revenge on you,' he said, handing the letter back.

Connie was silent. She was somewhat surprised to find that she was afraid of Clifford. She was afraid to go near him. She was afraid of him as if he were evil and dangerous.

'What shall I do?' she said.

'Nothing, if you don't want to do anything.'

She replied, trying to put Clifford off. He answered:

If you don't come back to Wragby now, I shall consider that you are coming back one day, and act accordingly. I shall just go on the same, and wait for you here, if I wait for fifty years.

She was frightened. This was bullying of an insidious sort. She had no doubt he meant what he said. He would not divorce her, and the child would be his, unless she could find some means of establishing its illegitimacy.

After a time of worry and harassment, she decided to go to Wragby. Hilda would go with her. She wrote this to Clifford. He replied:

[1] 我要让你履行诺言。

I shall not welcome your sister, but I shall not deny her the door. I have no doubt she has connived at your desertion of your duties and responsibilities, so do not expect me to show pleasure in seeing her.

They went to Wragby. Clifford was away when they arrived. Mrs Bolton received them.

'Oh, your Ladyship, it isn't the happy home-coming we hoped for, is it!' she said.

'Isn't it?' said Connie.

So this woman knew! How much did the rest of the servants know or suspect?

She entered the house, which now she hated with every fibre in her body. The great, rambling mass of a place seemed evil to her, just a menace over her. She was no longer its mistress, she was its victim.

'I can't stay long here,' she whispered to Hilda, terrified.

And she suffered going into her own bedroom, re-entering into possession as if nothing had happened. She hated every minute inside the Wragby walls.

They did not meet Clifford till they went down to dinner. He was dressed, and with a black tie: rather reserved, and very much the superior gentleman. He behaved perfectly politely during the meal and kept a polite sort of conversation going: but it seemed all touched with insanity.

'How much do the servants know?' asked Connie, when the woman was out of the room.

'Of your intentions? Nothing whatsoever.'

'Mrs Bolton knows.'

He changed colour.

'Mrs Bolton is not exactly one of the servants,' he said.

'Oh, I don't mind.'

There was tension till after coffee, when Hilda said she would go up to her room.

Clifford and Connie sat in silence when she had gone. Neither would begin to speak. Connie was so glad that he wasn't taking the pathetic line, she kept him up to as much haughtiness as possible. She just sat silent and looked down at her hands.

'I suppose you don't at all mind having gone back on your word?' he said at last.

'I can't help it,' she murmured.

'But if you can't, who can?'

'I suppose nobody.'

He looked at her with curious cold rage. He was used to her. She was as it were embedded in his will. How dared she now go back on him, and destroy the fabric of his daily existence? How dared she try to cause this derangement of his personality?

'And for what do you want to go back on everything?' he insisted.

'Love!' she said. It was best to be hackneyed.

'Love of Duncan Forbes? But you didn't think that worth having, when you met me. Do you mean to say you now love him better than anything else in life?'

'One changes,' she said.

'Possibly! Possibly you may have whims. But you still have to convince me of the importance of the change. I merely don't believe in your love of Duncan Forbes.'

'But why should you believe in it? You have only to divorce me, not to believe in my feelings.'

'And why should I divorce you?'

'Because I don't want to live here any more. And you really don't want me.'

'Pardon me! I don't change. For my part, since you are my wife, I should prefer that you should stay under my roof in dignity and quiet. Leaving aside personal feelings, and I assure you, on my part it is leaving aside a great deal, it is bitter as death to me to have this order of life broken up, here in Wragby, and the decent round of daily life smashed, just for some whim of yours.'

After a time of silence she said:

'I can't help it. I've got to go. I expect I shall have a child.'

He too was silent for a time.

'And is it for the child's sake you must go?' he asked at length.

She nodded.

'And why? Is Duncan Forbes so keen on his spawn?'

'Surely keener than you would be,' she said.

'But really? I want my wife, and I see no reason for letting her go. If she likes to bear a child under my roof, she is welcome, and the child is welcome: provided that the decency and order of life is preserved. Do you mean to tell me that Duncan Forbes has a greater hold over you? I don't believe it.'

There was a pause.

'But don't you see,' said Connie. 'I must go away from you, and I must live with the man I love.'

'No, I don't see it! I don't give **tuppence**[1] for your love, nor for the man you love. I don't believe in that sort of cant.'

'But you see, I do.'

'Do you? My dear Madam, you are too intelligent, I assure you, to believe in your own love for Duncan Forbes. Believe me, even now you really care more for me. So why should I give in to such nonsense!'

She felt he was right there. And she felt she could keep silent no longer.

'Because it isn't Duncan that I do love,' she said, looking up at him.

'We only said it was Duncan, to spare your feelings.'

'To spare my feelings?'

'Yes! Because who I really love, and it'll make you hate me, is Mr Mellors, who was our game-keeper here.'

If he could have sprung out of his chair, he would have done so. His face went yellow, and his eyes bulged with disaster as he glared at her.

Then he dropped back in the chair, gasping and looking up at the ceiling.

At length he sat up.

'Do you mean to say you're telling me the truth?' he asked, looking gruesome.

'Yes! You know I am.'

'And when did you begin with him?'

'In the spring.'

He was silent like some beast in a trap.

'And it was you, then, in the bedroom at the cottage?'

So he had really inwardly known all the time.

'Yes!'

He still leaned forward in his chair, gazing at her like a cornered beast.

[1] tuppence=two pence.

'My God, you ought to be wiped off the face of the earth!'

'Why?' she ejaculated faintly.

But he seemed not to hear.

'That scum! That bumptious lout! That miserable cad! And carrying on with him all the time, while you were here and he was one of my servants! My God, my God, is there any end to the beastly lowness of women!'

He was beside himself with rage, as she knew he would be.

'And you mean to say you want to have a child to a cad like that?'

'Yes! I'm going to.'

'You're going to! You mean you're sure! How long have you been sure?'

'Since June.'

He was speechless, and the queer blank look of a child came over him again.

'You'd wonder,' he said at last, 'that such beings were ever allowed to be born.'

'What beings?' she asked.

He looked at her weirdly, without an answer. It was obvious, he couldn't even accept the fact of the existence of Mellors, in any connexion with his own life. It was sheer, unspeakable, impotent hate.

'And do you mean to say you'd marry him? — and bear his foul name?' he asked at length.

'Yes, that's what I want.'

He was again as if dumbfounded.

'Yes!' he said at last. 'That proves that what I've always thought about you is correct: you're not normal, you're not in your right senses. You're one of those half-insane, perverted women who must run after depravity, **the nostalgie de la boue**[1].'

Suddenly he had become almost wistfully moral, seeing himself the incarnation of good, and people like Mellors and Connie the incarnation of mud, of evil. He seemed to be growing vague, inside a nimbus.

'So don't you think you'd better divorce me and have done with it?' she said.

'No! You can go where you like, but I shan't divorce you,' he

[1] (法)对污秽之物念念不忘。

said idiotically.

'Why not?'

He was silent, in the silence of imbecile obstinacy.

'Would you even let the child be legally yours, and your heir?' she said.

'I care nothing about the child.'

'But if it's a boy it will be legally your son, and it will inherit your title, and have Wragby.'

'I care nothing about that,' he said.

'But you must! I shall prevent the child from being legally yours, if I can. I'd so much rather it were illegitimate, and mine: if it can't be Mellors'.'

'Do as you like about that.'

He was immovable.

'And won't you divorce me?' she said. 'You can use Duncan as a pretext! There'd be no need to bring in the real name. Duncan doesn't mind.'

'I shall never divorce you,' he said, as if a nail had been driven in.

'But why? Because I want you to?'

'Because I follow my own inclination, and I'm not inclined to.'

It was useless. She went upstairs and told Hilda the upshot.

'Better get away tomorrow,' said Hilda, 'and let him come to his senses.'

So Connie spent half the night packing her really private and personal effects. In the morning she had her trunks sent to the station, without telling Clifford. She decided to see him only to say good-bye, before lunch.

But she spoke to Mrs Bolton.

'I must say good-bye to you, Mrs Bolton, you know why. But I can trust you not to talk.'

'Oh, you can trust me, your Ladyship, though it's a sad blow for us here, indeed. But I hope you'll be happy with the other gentleman.'

'The other gentleman! It's Mr Mellors, and I care for him. Sir Clifford knobs. But don't say anything to anybody. And if one day you think Sir Clifford may be willing to divorce me, let me know, will you? I should like to be properly married to the man I care for.'

'I'm sure you would, my Lady. Oh, you can trust me. I'll be faithful to Sir Clifford, and I'll be faithful to you, for I can see you're both right in your own ways.'

'Thank you! And look! I want to give you this — may I?' So Connie left Wragby once more, and went on with Hilda to Scotland. Mellors went into the country and got work on a farm. The idea was, he should get his divorce, if possible, whether Connie got hers or not. And for six months he should work at farming, so that eventually he and Connie could have some small farm of their own, into which he could put his energy. For he would have to have some work, even hard work, to do, and he would have to make his own living, even if her capital started him.

So they would have to wait till spring was in, till the baby was born, till the early summer came round again.

The Grange Farm Old Heanor 29 September

I got on here with a bit of contriving, because I knew Richards, the company engineer, in the army. It is a farm belonging to Butler and Smitham Colliery Company, they use it for raising hay and oats for the pit-ponies; not a private concern. But they've got cows and pigs and all the rest of it, and I get thirty shillings a week as labourer. Rowley, the farmer, puts me on to as many jobs as he can, so that I can learn as much as possible between now and next Easter. I've not heard a thing about Bertha. I've no idea why she didn't show up at the divorce, nor where she is nor what she's up to. But if I keep quiet till March I suppose I shall be free. And don't you bother about Sir Clifford. He'll want to get rid of you one of these days. If he leaves you alone, it's a lot.

I've got lodging in a bit of an old cottage in Engine Row very decent. The man is engine-driver at High Park, tall, with a beard, and very chapel. The woman is a birdy bit of a thing who loves anything superior. **King's English**[1] and allow-me! all the time. But they lost their only son in the war, and it's sort of knocked a hole in them. There's a long gawky lass of a daughter training for a school-teacher, and I help her with her lessons sometimes, so we're quite the family. But they're very decent people, and only too kind to me. I expect I'm more

[1] 规范的英语。

coddled than you are.

I like farming all right. It's not inspiring, but then I don't ask to be inspired. I'm used to horses, and cows, though they are very female, have a soothing effect on me. When I sit with my head in her side, milking, I feel very solaced. They have six rather fine Herefords. Oat-harvest is just over and I enjoyed it, in spite of sore hands and a lot of rain. I don't take much notice of people, but get on with them all right. Most things one just ignores.

The pits are working badly; this is a colliery district like Tevershall. only prettier. I sometimes sit in the Wellington and talk to the men. They grumble a lot, but they're not going to alter anything. As everybody says, the Notts-Derby miners have got their hearts in the right place. But the rest of their anatomy must be in the wrong place, in a world that has no use for them. I like them, but they don't cheer me much: not enough of the old **fighting-cock**[1] in them. They talk a lot about nationalization, nationalization of royalties, nationalization of the whole industry. But you can't nationalize coal and leave all the other industries as they are. They talk about putting coal to new uses, like Sir Clifford is trying to do. It may work here and there, but not as a general thing. I doubt. Whatever you make you've got to sell it. The men are very apathetic. They feel the whole damned thing is doomed, and I believe it is. And they are doomed along with it. Some of the young ones spout about a Soviet, but there's not much conviction in them. There's no sort of conviction about anything, except that it's all a muddle and a hole. Even under a Soviet you've still got to sell coal: and that's the difficulty.

We've got this great industrial population, and they've got to be fed, so the damn show has to be kept going somehow. The women talk a lot more than the men, nowadays, and they are a sight more cock-sure. The men are limp, they feel a doom somewhere, and they go about as if there was nothing to be done. Anyhow, nobody knows what should be done in spite of all the talk, the young ones get mad because they've no money to spend. Their whole life depends on spending money, and now they've got none to spend. That's our civilization and our education: bring up the masses to depend entirely on spending money, and then the money gives out. The pits are working two days, two and a half days a

[1] 好斗的人。

week, and there's no sign of betterment even for the winter. It means a man bringing up a family on twenty-five and thirty shillings. The women are the maddest of all. But then they're the maddest for spending, nowadays.

If you could only tell them that living and spending isn't the same thing! But it's no good. If only they were educated to live instead of earn and spend, they could manage very happily on twenty-five shillings. If the men wore scarlet trousers as I said, they wouldn't think so much of money: if they could dance and hop and skip, and sing and swagger and be handsome, they could do with very little cash. And amuse the women themselves, and be amused by the women. They ought to learn to be naked and handsome, and to sing in a mass and dance the old group dances, and carve the stools they sit on, and embroider their own emblems. Then they wouldn't need money. And that's the only way to solve the industrial problem: train the people to be able to live and live in handsomeness, without needing to spend. But you can't do it. They're all one-track minds nowadays. Whereas the mass of people oughtn't even to try to think, because they can't. They should be alive and frisky, and acknowledge **the great god Pan**[1]. He's the only god for the masses, forever. The few can go in for higher cults if they like. But let the mass be forever pagan.

But the colliers aren't pagan, far from it. They're a sad lot, a deadened lot of men: dead to their women, dead to life. The young ones scoot about on motor-bikes with girls, and jazz when they get a chance, But they're very dead. And it needs money. Money poisons you when you've got it, and starves you when you haven't.

I'm sure you're sick of all this. But I don't want to harp on myself, and I've nothing happening to me. I don't like to think too much about you, in my head, that only makes a mess of us both. But, of course, what I live for now is for you and me to live together. I'm frightened, really. I feel the devil in the air, and he'll try to get us. Or not the devil, Mammon: which I think, after all, is only the mass-will of people, wanting money and hating life. Anyhow, I feel great grasping white hands in the air, wanting to get hold of the throat of anybody who tries to live, to live beyond money, and squeeze the life out. There's a bad

[1] 希腊神话中的畜牧神，人身羊足，头上有角。

time coming. There's a bad time coming, boys, there's a bad time coming! If things go on as they are, there's nothing lies in the future but death and destruction, for these industrial masses. I feel my inside turn to water sometimes, and there you are, going to have a child by me. But never mind. All the bad times that ever have been, haven't been able to blow the crocus out: not even the love of women. So they won't be able to blow out my wanting you, nor the little glow there is between you and me. We'll be together next year. And though I'm frightened, I believe in your being with me. A man has to fend and fettle for the best, and then trust in something beyond himself. You can't insure against the future, except by really believing in the best bit of you, and in the power beyond it. So I believe in the little flame between us. For me now, it's the only thing in the world. I've got no friends, not inward friends. Only you. And now the little flame is all I care about in my life. There's the baby, but that is a side issue. It's my **Pentecost**[1], the forked flame between me and you. The old Pentecost isn't quite right. Me and God is a bit uppish, somehow. But the little forked flame between me and you: there you are! That's what I abide by, and will abide by, Cliffords and Berthas, colliery companies and governments and the money-mass of people all notwithstanding.

That's why I don't like to start thinking about you actually. It only tortures me, and does you no good. I don't want you to be away from me. But if I start fretting it wastes something. Patience, always patience. This is my fortieth winter. And I can't help all the winters that have been. But this winter I'll stick to my little Pentecost flame, and have some peace. And I won't let the breath of people blow it out. I believe in a higher mystery, that doesn't let even the crocus be blown out. And if you're in Scotland and I'm in the Midlands, and I can't put my arms round you, and wrap my legs round you, yet I've got something of you. My soul softly Naps in the little Pentecost flame with you, like the peace of fucking. We fucked a flame into being. Even the flowers are fucked into being between the sun and the earth. But it's a delicate thing, and takes patience and the long pause.

So I love chastity now, because it is the peace that comes of fucking. I love being chaste now. I love it as snowdrops love the snow. I love this chastity, which is the pause of peace of our fucking, between

[1] 圣灵降临(基督教重大节日之一,每年复活节后的第七个星期日,即第50日)。

us now like a snowdrop of forked white fire. And when the real spring comes, when the drawing together comes, then we can fuck the little flame brilliant and yellow, brilliant. But not now, not yet! Now is the time to be chaste, it is so good to be chaste, like a river of cool water in my soul. I love the chastity now that it flows between us. It is like fresh water and rain. How can men want wearisomely to philander. What a misery to be like **Don Juan**[1], and impotent ever to fuck oneself into peace, and the little flame alight, impotent and unable to be chaste in the cool between-whiles, as by a river.

Well, so many words, because I can't touch you. If I could sleep with my arms round you, the ink could stay in the bottle. We could be chaste together just as we can fuck together. But we have to be separate for a while, and I suppose it is really the wiser way. If only one were sure.

Never mind, never mind, we won't get worked up. We really trust in the little flame, and in the unnamed god that shields it from being blown out. There's so much of you here with me, really, that it's a pity you aren't all here.

Never mind about Sir Clifford. If you don't hear anything from him, never mind. He can't really do anything to you. Wait, he will want to get rid of you at last, to cast you out. And if he doesn't, we'll manage to keep clear of him. But he will. In the end he will want to spew you out as the abominable thing.

Now I can't even leave off writing to you.

But a great deal of us is together, and we can but abide by it, and steer our courses to meet soon. John Thomas says good-night to Lady Jane, a little droopingly, but with a hopeful heart.

[1] 唐璜，西班牙传奇中的一个浪荡子。